Acknowledgments

As in the first book of the Blue Ridge Legacy series, the story of Abigail Faith Porter and her family is fiction. But it is based in the reality of a group of people who were my ancestors.

A number of books helped to bring this reality home to me in what I believe and hope are historically correct ways: *Our Southern Highlanders* by Horace Kephart; *The Land of the Saddlebags* by James Watt Raine; *A History of Buncombe County, North Carolina* by F. A. Sondley; *Appalachia Inside Out: Culture and Custom*, edited by Robert Higgs, Ambrose Manning, and Jim Miller; *The Man Who Moved a Mountain* by Richard C. Davids; *Mountain Voices: A Legacy of the Blue Ridge and Great Smokies* by Warren Moore; and *Asheville: A Pictorial History* by Mitzi Tessier. These were the key resources that helped me know the history of the people of western North Carolina. Others, such as *National Geographic Eyewitness to the 20th Century*; *The Century* by Peter Jennings; *A People's History of the United States* by Howard Zinn; and *Hard Times* by Studs Terkel all grounded me in the basic facts of the twentieth century. I am grateful for the kinds of study these authors have accomplished. Their work makes my story come alive with truth. Any historical mistakes in this story are mine.

As always, my thanks go to editors David Horton and Luke Hinrichs who made sure the details in this story fit like details should. Their assistance always makes a story better.

Finally, I express gratitude to my wife who smoothes out my life in the bumpy places. Although I don't dedicate every book I write to her, I at least need to acknowledge her kind support of the work I do on these pages.

GARY E. PARKER is the author of numerous works of fiction, including *The Ephesus Fragment*, *The Last Gift*, and *Highland Hopes*. He also serves as senior pastor at the First Baptist Church of Decatur, Georgia. Gary, his wife, and two daughters make their home near Atlanta, Georgia.

PROLOGUE

"In bleak times a body's true character pushes out," said Granny Abby, her hands busy with her crocheting. "Kind of like new rocks that show up in the cornfield after a cold winter. Hard weather shoves them up where you can see them."

My fingers scribbling down every word my great-grandmother said, I tried to imagine life in the highlands of North Carolina during the 1930s—my ancestors scraping out a living, the long hours digging in a field on a rocky hillside. Money was scarce back then. "Things got bad in the Depression, didn't they?" I asked.

Granny Abby raised her left eyebrow, a gray wispy thing. She leaned forward in the wood rocking chair her pa had built a century ago. "It's hard for a homely man to grow much uglier," she declared. "But the Depression showed that it can happen. Folks who already knew poorness had to cinch up their britches another notch or two. Cash-payin' jobs just about disappeared altogether. If folks needed something, they had to make it themselves, make do, or do without."

Although an educated woman compared to most born in her time and place, Granny Abby still carried the mountain accent in her speech. I nodded encouragement for her to keep talking. Behind me I could hear the *whir* of the camcorder I'd set up on a tripod on Granny's front porch. The sun warmed my shoulders. A small flock of chipping sparrows flitted from a bush to the ground by the steps. I looked around, drew a deep breath. Somehow it felt right to be here with Granny.

Having started this project three days ago, I'd already learned more about my family's past than I ever thought possible. This morning I would hear another chapter in the story, a story that had started long before Abby's birth in 1900.

"The schools pretty much shut down in those days," Granny Abby continued. "The children went back to full-time laboring on their farms."

Abby stopped rocking and studied her hands. I knew not to press her to speak too fast. Over a hundred years old now, she needed little breaks from time to time. Her skin was pale and thin. Her white hair hung loose on her shoulders today, not pinned up like she usually kept it. She wore a pleated brown skirt that reached to just above her black shoes and a white blouse that buttoned to her neck.

Abigail Faith, Granny Abby to her family, had already told me about the first thirty years of her life growing up near Blue Springs, North Carolina, a shanty of a highlands town twenty-seven miles northwest of Asheville. Mostly toil and tough times was how she'd described those years. Years when she emerged from girlhood and blossomed into a woman, when she took a husband, birthed two boys, and left the remote mountains of her forebears. Now I wanted to know what happened next.

Granny Abby glanced up. Her copper eyes sparkled as she started to rock again. "Prices for everything that might fetch a few dollars—hogs, apples, eggs, quilts, you name it—fell right through the porch floor. About the only cash crop a body could count on came from corn and burned your throat like a live coal as you drank it."

"You mean moonshine?"

Granny grunted. "We called it the doublings."

I nodded and made a note with my pen. She'd already told me how most of the men—and women too, for that matter—"took the drink" on a regular basis.

"Most everybody made at least a little whiskey," she continued. "In spite of Prohibition coming in nineteen and nineteen. Usually for medicinal reasons or to, you know, warm a body when the snow fell real deep.

But a few . . . well, some men made enough doublings to fill their pockets plumb full of illegal dollars."

"None of our folks, though," I said, assuming this to be the case.

Granny smiled. "Well, Lisa, that's yet to be told."

I sat up straighter. I had so much more to learn about my kin. "Tell me, Granny, how did the Depression affect our family? You and Stephen and your boys? Daniel and Deidre, their kids? What happened to them? And Luke too, after your pa, Solomon, died in 1929?"

Granny Abby reached toward the floor. Her fingers curled around the top edge of a round basket. She pulled out a piece of yellow cloth and laid it across her lap. Granny loved making things. Everybody in the family owned something warm and pretty that Granny had made.

She closed her eyes as if searching inside her head for the answer to my question. She was twenty-nine when her pa died and the stock market crashed. Married to a lawyer in Boone, she had two boys—Beaufort James, Jimmy for short, and Stephen Jones Junior or Stevie. Seems like she had all a woman could ever desire. But hard times had come in 1929. Surely that upset all that and changed everything for Abby and her family.

I wondered how I would have coped with the struggles Granny Abby had faced. If my recent troubles gave any indication, I wouldn't have managed too well.

One of the sparrows flapped its wings and flew out of sight. I realized I had no more clue about where I was headed than I did that bird. My fingers gripped my pen. Formerly a reporter with a Washington newspaper, I had recently resigned. I had few close friends and no special man in my life. Never married and no prospects for it.

I didn't have any faith either, least not the kind Granny Abby had talked to me about in the last couple of days. The truth was, I didn't believe in much of anything, at least not anything that made a difference. Though I didn't like to admit it, not even to myself, I had come to a dead end. Something had to change. That's what had brought me here to Blue Springs, I knew that now. A feeling that I had to come, had to come or . . .

Forces I couldn't explain had brought me back here after spending many years away, forces that grabbed me by the scruff of the neck and pulled me to this interview with my great-grandmother. My brother Todd had called me a month ago to remind me of the annual family reunion to celebrate Granny Abby's birthday. I immediately said I wouldn't attend. I never went to such things. Why should I start now? So what if I hadn't seen any of my family in almost two years. I thought that was the end of it.

But I was wrong. In the days that followed Todd's call, my mood sank lower and lower. I couldn't get Granny out of my head. I'd heard my whole life how much I looked like her when she was young. And, in years past, when I did spend time with her, she treated me like a queen. How could I skip such an important birthday?

A few days after Todd's call I found myself in my closet doing some cleaning. Under some old clothes, I uncovered a stack of family pictures. Digging through them, I found a black-and-white of Granny Abby. For a few seconds I studied the picture. Then I put it away, shut the closet, and tried to forget the picture. But I couldn't.

I'd always admired Granny Abby, her ability to accept the hardships of her life without complaint or bitterness. She had a peace about her that made me envious. Within a week of finding the photograph, I found myself at my lowest point in a long time. Drinking coffee in front of my kitchen window early one morning I finally admitted how alone I was. I knew a lot of people but called few of them a friend. I'd achieved a fair measure of success yet still felt a void in my spirit.

In that instant I made a decision to go to Blue Springs for Granny's birthday. The idea to record her life story dawned on me almost at the same time. I had always wanted to do it. Why not now?

I quickly got things ready, gathering together notebooks, a camcorder and tapes, even books on how to research and write a family history. Busy with my plans, I told myself it was just a project, something to keep me occupied during the reunion. But deep down I knew this was a lie. Deep down I needed to get something out of Granny's story. Just what that *something* was, I didn't quite know yet. But I somehow felt that my future depended on a return to my past, to the roots of my family tree, to the soil that had nourished those roots. Granny Abby had held that soil in her hands, had walked over it with her bare feet. That soil had grounded her and made her strong. Maybe if I walked on that soil with her, it would do the same for me.

Granny Abby tightened her fingers on the rocker's arms. "You sure you want to hear the rest of this story?" she asked, staring me right in the eyes. "Not all the memories are such as to make you smile."

My stomach knotted up, but I pushed away my concerns. "Yes," I answered. "I want to hear the story, every word. Don't leave anything out."

Granny Abby rested her hands in her lap. I clicked my pen. She said, "I already told you what happened in my first twenty-nine years."

I nodded. I had it all on videotape and in my notebooks. Abby's mama, Rose, had died giving birth to Abby. Her pa—a closemouthed mountain man—had held Abby at arm's length, almost to the day he died. Only in the last hours of his battle with cancer had the two of them finally faced their love for each other.

"After we got through Pa's death, I thought times might have turned for the good," Granny Abby said. "Daniel now had the money to purchase back our land."

Again I remembered the first part of the story. Abby's brothers, Daniel and Luke, had saved enough money to re-claim the family homestead—nearly a thousand acres of rough country in the mountains and meadows above Blue Springs.

"Then the Depression rushed down on us. Gnarled up our lives quicker than moonshine can make a sweet man mean."

A cut of fear ran through me. "What happened to the land?" I asked.

Granny Abby rubbed the top of one hand with the other. "I hate to even speak it," she said. "What it did to Daniel especially. Makes it seem so real again."

"I want to hear it," I said.

"Remember that I heard a lot of this from others. After it all happened. But it's a true tale all the same."

"I remember."

She rocked forward. A spring breeze touched through her hair. She spoke softly. "The blight killed off the chestnut trees in nineteen and twenty-nine. Trees that had stood longer than anybody's memory just turned black, as if a fire had licked 'em over. We should have figured that as a portent of things to come."

I wrote as fast as my fingers allowed. This tale is what Granny Abby told me. It is the story of her kin. It is the story of mine as well.

SECTION I

1929–1931

CHAPTER ONE

Sometimes life can treat a man worse than a hungry dog chewing a bone. Least that's the way it seemed to Daniel Porter in the years following his pa's death. It all started with the run on the bank down in Asheville. Not the big bank all the history books talk about, Central Bank and Trust, which closed its doors for good the following year on November twentieth. No, the bank where Daniel kept his money was none other than the small one operated by Mr. Woodrow B. Shaller, the pa of Daniel's wife, Deidre.

The run on the Buncombe County Bank began about noon on a Thursday. Nobody knew exactly what set it off. Some said a man from Raleigh rode in on the train and then went around town telling how in the past week up in New York the stock market had fallen faster than a shot deer. Although most folks in Asheville didn't know what a stock market was, the news that it had crashed still shook them up worse than anything since the French Broad River had washed over the town's banks back in the big flood of 1916. Soon word had spread to every home in the mountains that hard days were coming, and anybody who had any money in the bank had better get their hands on it real fast and hide it in a can somewhere. Folks said the banks wouldn't have enough dollars to go around anymore, and if a man didn't get his money from them right away, he and his kin might not eat too well for maybe a long time.

The people waiting in front of the bank started out single file, no more than five or six folks standing in the November sunshine. At first, they spoke politely with each other. After all, no matter how bad things got, highlander people still kept their manners. But within an hour, the line stretched out longer than a fence around a crop of corn. People became louder as the line grew, and before anybody knew it, the street sounded like a crowd at a political meeting. As the crowd got more vocal, some forgot their manners. One man yelled out right rough at another, and the one being yelled at hollered back just as mean, and then it seemed everybody took a hint from those two and the noise swelled until it made everybody's ears hurt.

More minutes passed. The crowd pressed in closer and closer, one man's face against the back of another man's head, one man's backside to another man's belly. That made everybody real uneasy. Highlander men liked their space more than anything. After a while, a man tried to bully his way to the front, and the crowd yelled at him and forced him to return to the back. A few moments later a bear-sized man shoved somebody and a scuffle broke out. Two men jumped on the big man and punched him in the face. The man hit the ground, his nose bleeding between his fingers. The people stepped over him, pushing toward the double doors of the Buncombe County Bank.

Those who managed to get inside the bank came out again just a few minutes later, some with sheepish grins on their faces as if ashamed of their good fortune, others with a fistful of dollars held up like a boxing champion after winning a big fight. As the people with their money walked away, the folks still waiting outside muttered to themselves about their bad luck in showing up too late to get their dollars.

Almost three hours after the bank run started, the president of the bank, Mr. Woodrow B. Shaller, came out and raised his hands and asked everybody to quiet down. His white shirt had wet patches the size of pie plates under the arms, and his hair was all mussed. His round face looked as white as flour. The crowd settled down to listen to what he had to say. Some of the men took off their floppy hats and combed through their beards with their fingers.

"You all know me," Mr. Shaller called out. The crowd nodded in unison, and Shaller seemed to draw courage from their response. "You can trust me." The banker looked down at his shoes for a second, then back up at the somber faces. "We've had ourselves a rough day," he said. "I won't lie to you about that. But if we stay calm, I promise you, we can make our way through this."

Many nodded at this. Mr. Shaller made sense. They could trust a man who admitted his struggles, even if the admission made them feel a touch uneasy. A couple of folks looked at each other, then turned as if to go home.

"You got my money!" The shout erupted from the big man who had gotten knocked down earlier. He had a piece of rag stuck up the left nostril of his busted nose.

The crowd stood at renewed attention.

"Yes, we have money," Shaller said, "but not enough for everybody to take out all their dollars all at once."

"I don't give a mule's bottom about nobody else!" yelled the man pushing toward Mr. Shaller. "I just want mine. And I want it right now, all of it!"

"Me too!" a man called from the back. "Every last cent."

Everybody surged forward then, a wave of scared folks as bent on moving ahead as a river full of heavy rain. Shaller threw up his arms and demanded they all stay calm, but he never had a chance against the flood of folks pressing in. By the time the sun set that day, they'd rushed through the Buncombe County Bank and left nothing behind—not a dollar, not a dime.

Daniel Porter didn't find out about the run on the bank until he returned from Blue Springs later on that evening. But once he heard about what happened, his whole life turned upside down.

Mr. Shaller met Daniel and Deidre and their kids, Marla, Edsel, and Raymond, on the front steps of Daniel's house as he pulled into the front yard in his black 1922 Model T Ford. Daniel saw right off that something was out of sorts. Mr. Shaller's eyes looked like somebody had loosed them from their sockets, and his shirt and wool trousers were so wrinkled Daniel guessed he hadn't changed them in a while. Daniel wondered why Mrs. Shaller, a much-refined woman, had let him out like this. Shaller wore no coat. What was he doing here, Daniel wondered, and why was he looking all frazzled?

"It's gone," Shaller said to both Daniel and Deidre. "All gone . . . smoke from a chimney."

"What's gone?" asked Daniel, moving to open the front door.

Shaller didn't answer right then, so Deidre and the kids followed Daniel inside the house, the kids running upstairs as soon as they entered, their feet clomping across the wood floor. With his eyes down, Shaller trailed Deidre. Daniel could see the man carried something heavy on his mind. Still, he didn't probe Mr. Shaller to speak out his troubles. Like all decent highlanders, Daniel refused to be nosy, figuring a man with a bad bite in his gut needed to spit out such things in his own good time.

"Let me get you a blanket," Daniel said to Shaller. "You got to be cold."

"I'll make some fresh coffee," said Deidre.

Shaller stared at his daughter with blank eyes.

Daniel propped his walking stick in the corner, hung his floppy black hat on a peg on the wall, and went to the bedroom for the blanket. A few seconds later he walked to the kitchen where Deidre had taken her pa. Mr. Shaller sat in a chair at the table. Daniel threw the blanket around Shaller's shoulders, patted him on the back and said, "Deidre's coffee will warm your bones and put the color back in your face."

He glanced up at Daniel, then lowered his head to his hands.

Daniel moved to the fireplace, on the wall opposite the table, and arranged paper and kindling to get a fire going. He found a match in his denim overalls, struck it on the hearth, and lit the paper. A minute or two later he began adding small logs to the blaze. Although curious about Shaller, Daniel stayed patient. Let Shaller have a chance to gather his wits. Daniel threw a larger log onto the fire and returned to the kitchen table.

Shaller sat dead still, his elbows propped on the table, his face buried in his hands.

"Here's your coffee, Pa," Deidre said. "Nice and hot the way you like it." She carefully set the cup in front of him and then poured one for Daniel and herself and joined them at the table.

Daniel smiled at Deidre. She had always been a frugal woman, despite her upbringing as a banker's daughter. She wore a long navy skirt, a brown high-neck blouse with an ivory brooch pinned to it, and black shoes with buttons on the front. Her hair, a brownish color, came to her shoulders. More good fortune than he deserved had come to him when he married up with Deidre Shaller. She was as slender as a maple sapling, with long fingers and a nose that sat up real cute on her face.

Mr. Shaller held his coffee cup, his lips pressed tightly. Daniel cleared his throat. Even a highlander man had a limit to how long he could wait for another to say out loud what was eating at him. If Mr. Shaller had something to say, he ought to just come right out and say it. Deidre caught Daniel's eye and raised her eyebrows.

"It's all right, Pa," Deidre said. "You can tell us. You said before that it's gone. What did you mean?"

Shaller waved his hand as if dismissing the silliest thing he'd ever heard. "Everything is gone," he said.

Daniel slid to his chair's edge. Shaller held some bad news in his gut, he just knew it.

"Down at the bank," said Shaller.

Daniel looked at Deidre, then back at Shaller. "What happened at the bank?" Daniel asked.

Shaller licked his lips. "All any of us ever had. It's gone, I already said it."

"You talkin' crazy," Daniel said, a hard lump slowly rising in his chest. "Unless you been robbed. You ain't been robbed, have you, Mr. Shaller?"

Shaller grunted but said nothing else for several seconds. Daniel waited, still unsure what all this was about. A bank didn't lose its money except when somebody took it with a pistol. But if someone had robbed the bank, why didn't Shaller just come out plain and tell them so?

Daniel's mind raced back to when Mr. Shaller had talked him into putting his bricklaying wages in the bank, how he met Deidre the day he walked into the bank for the first time. The only woman working there, Daniel took a liking to her from the very start, though he didn't get to know her till later, after he went off to war and wrote her a letter. To his surprise, she wrote back. Then, when the war had ended, he returned home and started courting her right away. Ten years had gone by since then, years full of more ups and downs than a man's backside in a bumpy wagon. He had fought in a war and lost a brother in those years, married Deidre and sired three children. He'd scrimped and saved his earnings and done without so he could save enough to throw in with his brother Luke and buy back his family's old place a few miles up from Blue

Springs. In just a couple of days he would finish off that deal and make good on a mighty big promise he'd made.

Daniel laid a hand on Mr. Shaller's back. Mr. Shaller raised his eyes. Daniel saw sorrow lying deep in them and he shivered. A premonition of something bad ran through him. He recalled when he was a boy, the time a crow had flapped its wings through the front door of his family's cabin, just three days before his aunt Francis died. Daniel didn't have the highland superstition in him like some of his neighbors and kin, but he knew enough not to make light of such feelings. A man didn't have to see a crow to know something dark rode the wind.

"You don't know, do you?" said Shaller, glancing from Daniel to Deidre, then back to Daniel.

Daniel shook his head.

"Your money, my money, everybody's money. Cleaned out."

Daniel felt his breath catch, and a fear as tight as anything he'd suffered while fighting the Germans suddenly grabbed hold of his throat. His thoughts rushed back to his last words with his pa, to the promise he had made him to get back the thousand acres his family had owned since the late 1800s. That promise had comforted Solomon as he lay dying.

Buncombe County Bank held the money for that purchase in its thick steel vault.

Daniel's hands dug into the legs of his overalls as he fought off his fears. "What are you sayin' about my dollars?"

Shaller's face twisted into a grin. He looked as if he'd lost his mind. "You don't have any more dollars," he said. "Nobody does, least nobody who kept anything at Buncombe County Bank. Folks came at us all day, all of them, wanting their money. Never saw anything like it. All of the people pushing and shoving and pulling out every last cent."

Daniel's face flushed. He wanted to jerk Mr. Shaller up by the collar and tell him to stop his crazy talk!

"But why?" Deidre asked. "What happened?"

Shaller looked at his daughter. Softness came to his face, and he took her hands. "It's hitting everybody," he said. "All over the country." He told them of the calamity in New York.

"But we ain't in New York!" exclaimed Daniel, not educated in such matters. "We're down here in North Carolina. What's all that got to do with us?"

Shaller reached for his coffee, a semblance of steadiness returning to him as he focused on Daniel's question.

"It's real complicated," he said. "What happened in New York, what they're calling the Crash, has made people skittish everywhere. They don't trust that their money is in the banks. So they want it in their hands. But no bank has enough money to give it all back at one time."

Daniel started to ask why not, but then it dawned on him that banks didn't hold on to every dollar folks put in their vaults. They used it for loans and such. And if one day their customers showed up all at once to ask for all their dollars to be given back, the bank just wouldn't have enough to cover what people wanted.

As the meaning of it all sunk in, Daniel's heart shrank. If what Shaller said was true, then everything he'd labored for since coming home from the war had come to nothing. Was that what Mr. Shaller was saying, that all of it, everything he owned had disappeared like a fog getting burned off by the sun? He couldn't believe it, wouldn't let himself believe it.

A sudden hope rushed through Daniel. He and Deidre and the kids were part of Mr. Shaller's family. Since Shaller was in charge of the bank, hadn't he saved some money for his own kin? Daniel knew the thought was selfish, but a highlander man needed to make provision for his family, didn't he? Was it wrong to hope Shaller had stuck away some dollars to take care of his blood relatives?

"Let me make sure of what you're tellin'," said Daniel. "The dollars I gave your bank to keep, mine and Luke's. All that money ain't there no more . . . and I can never get it back?"

Shaller buried his head in his hands again. Heavy sobs wracked his body. Deidre reached to her pa to console him.

Without thinking, Daniel rose and stood over Shaller. His hands seemed to move of their own accord, and he grasped Shaller by the biceps and yanked him to his feet. Shaller stared blankly at Daniel. Daniel squeezed Shaller's arms, and the worst anger he'd ever felt gripped him. He heard Deidre crying and he wanted to cry too, but highlander men don't do such things, so the tears that might have washed away some of his fury turned into fuel instead, a fuel that stoked his anger till it burned in him like a coal stove at full heat.

"You lost my money!" Daniel roared. "Years ago you talked me into putting it in your bank, told me I could make interest from it. I ought to—"

His fury overcame him then, and he drew back his hand before he could stop himself. He wanted to hit Shaller, to make him pay for what had happened. Now the promise to his pa and his brother Laban would be broken! Shaller had made him a liar!

Daniel's whole body heaved as he fought against the desire to smack Shaller in the face. In the highlands, a man didn't mess with another man's money. Yet Mr. Shaller had talked him into trusting his money to the bank. That money was now gone because Shaller hadn't taken good care of it. Such doings made Shaller a low-down man, as sorry as a man who didn't watch out for another man's dogs when they're put into his care.

A low-down man needed a good beating, something to remind him never to do such sorry things again. Daniel's fist shook.

"Daniel! Daniel!"

Daniel blinked when he heard Deidre's voice. "Daniel!" Deidre touched his elbow. Daniel moved away from the edge of his anger. He dropped his fist, and his shoulders slumped. His head cleared some and then it came to him that Mr. Shaller hadn't done any of this on purpose. What happened at his bank had hit him as hard as anybody else. Sometimes a man couldn't control what went on. Daniel remembered how Laban had died, how he couldn't do anything to stop it.

Daniel let go of Mr. Shaller and faced Deidre. He opened his arms, and she moved in and hugged him.

"I was saving our dollars," he whispered to her, "in your pa's bank . . . all these years."

"I know," she said. "I took your first deposit, remember?"

"I planned on buyin' back my pa's land."

"I figured something like that. It was your money, yours to do with as you wanted. You labored so hard for it, you and your brother."

"But now it's all gone," he said, still not quite believing the words.

"We'll do okay. You're a good provider. I knew that the first day you walked into the bank—the day I saw the calluses on your hands, the tan on your neck and face. Nobody toils as hard as you, or saves as much."

Daniel hugged her as tight as he could. God had blessed him with such a faithful woman. She ought to hate him right now for losing their money, hate him for not letting her spend more dollars on things she wanted over the years, hate him for a lot of reasons.

"My money's gone too," Mr. Shaller mumbled. "All of it."

Deidre raised her chin, and Daniel kissed her on the forehead and let her go to her pa. She knelt beside him and took his hands in hers. They stayed that way for what seemed a long while, all of them stuck in place by the sudden doom that had rolled into their lives.

Daniel thought of some words his pa used to say: *"God can bring good results from everything that comes to us, hard or easy, good or bad. You'll see the good things if you just keep your eyes open."*

He looked at Shaller and Deidre. The man looked like a sad hound dog. He saw fear in Deidre's face, mixed with questions about what all this meant. But he had no answers for her.

Daniel stooped closer to Shaller. "Look at me, Mr. Shaller," he said. Shaller slowly faced him. "You sure it's all gone?" Daniel asked, deciding to make double certain.

"I got a hundred and fifteen dollars out," Shaller said. "But I didn't feel right . . . didn't think I ought to keep more than that . . . what with everybody else losing all they owned. I got that money for you and Deidre, your kids. Thought I should do at least that much."

Shaller reached into his pocket, pulled out a wad of bills, and handed it to Daniel. A wave of guilt hit Daniel. Shaller had saved some money for him and his family. But he had almost hit him.

Daniel took the money and walked over to the window and stared out. A bunch of questions ran through his head. Did the bank closing mean hard times were around the bend for everybody? Would his building work dry up? He didn't know if he could stand that. So long as he had something to keep his hands busy, he could make do. Growing up in the highlands had taught him that, no matter what, a laboring man who kept his lips off the liquor jug could keep a roof over his family's head, clothes on his kids' backs, food on the table.

He studied the scene past the back porch. The house where he and Deidre lived stood no more than a hundred yards out behind a fine brick one that Shaller had built about eleven years ago. That's when Daniel first met Mr. Shaller, when he laid the brick for the large ten-room house. The two houses sat on three hundred acres of land that extended up to a ridge. A stream ran through about fifty yards from the bigger house, along with a grove of apple trees that edged up close to the creek.

Daniel eyed the ridge. Oaks and hickories and maples and pines and dogwoods covered it all the way up. Yes sir, a prime spot of land. At least they still had all this. Or did they? Daniel gritted his teeth as he considered the possibility that maybe they didn't even have a place to live anymore. What would he do then? How would he care for his family?

Holding his breath, Daniel stepped back to Shaller. "Is this property paid up?" he asked. "Your house and ours?"

For a second, Shaller said nothing. By the look on Deidre's face, Daniel could tell she had figured out what he was asking.

"Tell me," said Daniel. "Do you own the land where our houses sit?"

"Not completely," Shaller finally said. "I borrowed money back in '17 to build my place, been paying on it ever since. Most of the loan is paid up."

Fear sank deep into Daniel's stomach again. The fact that Shaller had paid most of what he owed gave him little comfort. If Shaller missed even one payment, somebody might call for the rest of the dollars. What would happen then? Could Shaller come up with enough money to pay them? Or would they all have to pack up and leave?

Daniel clenched his teeth. He'd been thrown out of a house once before, and the notion of facing that shame again made him want to pick up his gun and go shoot somebody. But, since he didn't know who to shoot, he quickly pushed that notion away.

Another notion suddenly rose up in Daniel's head. He wanted a drink. For a second he stood still and weighed the idea.

Maybe he ought to go and find some liquor. Go to a moonshiner and lay down three dollars to buy a jug. Then yank the cork out of it, hold his head back, and take a good long swallow. The liquor would warm up his belly, he knew, because he'd tried it a few times back in his younger years. Every mountain man had. If he swigged down enough of the liquor, it would make him forget all his troubles.

Most men he knew drank the doublings. It seemed to help them, made them less anxious about the nettlesome things that sprung up in life. Washed them away with a liquid so warm it felt like hot molasses sliding down the throat.

Daniel rubbed his beard. Curious that he would desire a drink in this hard moment. Like his pa before him, he had not taken to liquor in spite of his earlier flirtations with it. He didn't like what it did to a man, how it made him lose his head and all, do things no self-respectin' Christian man ought to do. Besides, drinking the doublings only showed what a coward a man was, that he couldn't face his troubles without the crutch of a drink.

He thought of his family. Deidre and the children needed him to show courage right now, not run off and get drunk. No, he wouldn't yield to the temptation to buy a jug. But it was strange how the idea had come on him all of a sudden. He wondered if this was how his brother Laban had felt when he took out after the doublings.

Turning from the window, Daniel faced Deidre again. Overhead he heard a bump. One of the kids must have knocked something over. The idea of getting drunk left Daniel as he caught Deidre's eye. He thought back to the day he first saw her in the bank. Although most folks said a woman's place was in the home, Deidre got away with working at the bank because she was the boss's daughter. She had more spunk than any woman he'd ever known, except maybe for his sister, Abby. Of course, Deidre had stopped work after their first baby, Marla, had arrived. Took quickly to her chores as a mama. Kept the house clean, cooked real good, and guided the children with a firm but loving hand. Now she not only tended to the family, but also collected the dollars people owed him for his work.

Daniel moved to Deidre, and they hugged again. Maybe he could work his way through this. Hard labor had always gotten him past low times. No reason he couldn't do the same now.

His mind made up, Daniel let go of Deidre, took the hundred and fifteen dollars and approached Shaller.

"Here," he said to Shaller, handing him back the wad of bills. "You keep it. You and your missus need it more than us."

Mr. Shaller started to protest, but Daniel pressed the money into his hands and then turned back to Deidre. Although her eyes were moist, she smiled at him and returned to his open arms. As the two of them stood in the middle of the kitchen, Daniel's mind started figuring on two things: first, he had to find a way to make enough money so his family could stay in their house. Then, second, he had to make a plan to one day start saving again to get back his pa's land. Only when he had done those two chores could he ever rest easy again.

CHAPTER TWO

Abby left the doctor at just after three-thirty. The sun wore a weak face. Dark shadows reached out from every building and tree. A brisk wind pushed Abby's shoulder-length auburn hair off her face, and she pulled her tan shawl tighter around her shoulders and wished she'd worn a heavier blouse than the navy one she had on with her gray wool skirt. Her eyes fixed on the next step, she moved by the Boone City Hall without glancing up. Her cheeks flushed red in the cold air. Several people strode by her, but she paid them no attention.

After walking past the Methodist church, she started to cross the street but then heard a horn blaring and stopped dead in her tracks. She saw a logging truck bearing down on her. Abby jumped back. The truck skidded as the driver hit his brakes. Abby's eyes widened, and she jerked back another step. The truck swerved so that the fresh cut timber piled on the back zipped by her face by a distance of no more than two feet. The logs smelled sticky and sweet. The driver stuck his head out the window and shook his fist before disappearing around the corner.

Her breath coming in short gasps, Abby stood frozen and told herself to bear up. But so much had happened in the last few days. After a long bout with cancer, her father Solomon had died. The two of them had spent his last hours sorting out a lot of hard things they had ignored for years. Even though in the end they forgave each other and he had died at peace, the whole episode had shaken Abby, made her sad and guilty that she'd waited so long to make things right with her pa.

After the funeral, she had returned to Boone not feeling well. Fact was, she hadn't felt well for over a month. Body weakness kept hitting her at odd times, and her stomach suffered from a recurring queasiness. In addition to that, her joints felt as though she had too much bone for the skin around them—all puffy and achy, especially in the mornings.

At first Abby figured she had a touch of a cold. Or maybe some body aches from the change in the seasons. She knew people who felt all out of sorts as one time of the year moved into another. But then, when the ailments didn't let loose after she returned home from Blue Springs, she started to consider all manner of diseases, cancer mostly. Her family had a history with it. Before her pa, the cancer had eaten up her aunt Francis, the woman who had been a mama to her in her early years. Did cancer have a hook in her now? Did it work that way? Move from one member of a family to another?

But she was just twenty-nine years old. People her age didn't get the cancer, did they?

Abby felt silly for worrying over such a thing. Her sickness hadn't taken that serious a turn. Yet, given what had just happened to her pa, she couldn't help but ponder on cancer as a possibility.

Abby squared her shoulders. The doctor had just told her plain out what her problem was and it wasn't cancer. But it still had lots of complications. She started walking again. It only took her a few minutes to reach her house—a white, six-room place a quarter of a mile off the town square but still on the main road. The house had a front porch, parlor, kitchen, three bedrooms, and bathroom. Standing on her porch, she looked back down the street. A row of houses lined both sides of the street, most of them with trim fences surrounding the yards and some with autos parked out front.

Abby sighed. Born in the upper reaches of North Carolina, she'd never taken well to city ways, autos included. She had lived in Boone a full decade yet still felt out of place sometimes. She was a woman no longer bound to the old ways of the highlands but one not completely at ease in the city either. Since most of her kin were too poor to own an auto, a highlander woman walked most of the time, even in 1929. Abby saw herself as nothing more than that—a simple highlander woman who had gotten some education.

A chilly breeze blew. Abby studied the trees that grew along the street—mostly oak, maple, and hickory. They had dropped almost all their leaves. She shivered, feeling the way the trees looked. Helpless against the cold days soon to arrive. She knew she ought to have a stouter outlook on things. After all, she and her pa had exchanged some healing words before he passed on to see Jesus, words that had lifted her heart and given her hope for the future. But now, after her visit with the doctor, she had matters on her mind that made her last hours with her pa fade into the background.

Abby heard a dog bark and the sound pushed her back to the present. She opened her house door and hung her shawl on a wall peg. The house felt cold, and she knew the fire in the stove had died down. She called out, but Mrs. Lollard, an older lady friend who often watched her boys for her when she ran errands, didn't answer.

Abby went to the kitchen but saw no one. Were the boys playing outside? She left the kitchen to check her bedroom. To her surprise, she found her husband, Stephen, there. He was lying on the bed with a half-empty bottle of liquor in his left hand, a cigar in his right. A curl of thick smoke rose up from the cigar and hung in the room.

Abby knew immediately something bad had happened. Although she had known for a long time that Stephen partook of the spirits now and again, he'd always respected her wishes that he not bring liquor into the house. She started to fuss at him about it but something told her to hold back.

Stephen took a swig from the bottle. Abby wondered where he had bought the illegal drink. She waved a hand to break up the smoke.

"You're home early," she said, keeping her voice as calm as she could.

"I always . . . always said you were a shhmmart woman," he said, his words mushy from the drink.

Abby noted the sarcasm but decided not to let it bother her. When she and Stephen fought, which seemed a frequent happening over the last couple of years, it usually started when she took offense at his mean remarks. She moved to her dresser and sat down in a chair in front of the mirror.

"Is everything okay?" she asked, looking at him through the mirror.

Stephen grunted. "Shurr. Why would . . . wouldn't everything be just peachy?"

"You don't usually smoke at home," she said.

"Been smok . . . smoking for years." He rolled onto his side and eyed her as if she was a stranger. Red streaks cut through the whites of his eyes, and his face looked like he had a fire roaring beneath his cheeks. His white shirt, usually well pressed, was full of wrinkles and his black wool pants were twisted to the side. "Why not at home?"

Abby decided to ignore the issue. "You seem off your feed some," she said cautiously. "You feelin' all right?"

"Well, shurr. Don't I look like I'm doing all right?"

Abby picked up a brush. "You usually keep your clothes real smart," she said, still watching him.

Stephen grinned but it had no joy in it. "Maybe I'm weary of looking so respectable. Maybe I got more on my mind than whether or not my britches are pressed."

"And what might you have on your mind?" She ran the brush through her hair, then turned and faced him. Maybe he'd tell her why he had come home drunk in the middle of the day if she made him see she meant business.

Stephen rolled up to a sitting position on the edge of the bed. For a second he seemed ready to admit what was bothering him. But then he stubbed out the cigar on his shoe and shook his head. "It's a man's business," he said. "Nothing for a woman to worry her pretty head about."

Abby faced the mirror again, calmly picked up a hand cloth and wiped her face. Inside she wasn't calm at all. She knew what drink could do to a man. Had seen how it turned even good-hearted men like her older brother Laban into its slave, how it made them do hurtful things to themselves and those around them.

"Where are the boys?" she asked, still trying to avoid a fight.

"I run them out! Mrs. Lollard too. They're with her and her brats! I wanted some peace and quiet. Is it too much to ask for a man to come home to rest his head without a couple of kids banging around and bothering him so much he can't think?"

A rush of anger ran through Abby as she thought of Jimmy, now four, and Stevie, two and a half. Boys ought not see such things as this, she figured. A self-respecting pa would want to give his sons a good example.

Before she could stop herself, she pointed at the liquor bottle and asked, "They see that?"

Stephen held up the bottle and waved it at her. "You mean this little bottle?"

Abby bit her tongue. Some things she could abide from Stephen because he provided so well. He'd kept a good roof over their heads and plenty of food on the table ever since she married him back in 1924. She appreciated him for that. She came from a place where cash was scarce, where most lived their whole lives in the house where they first drew breath, where few ever saw a doctor or took any education past the sixth grade. So, she'd left the hollers of the Blue Ridge many years ago, met and married Stephen Jones Waterbury, a lawyer in Boone where she was attending school to become a teacher. Stephen's parents lived in Raleigh, a fine upstanding couple whom Abby hardly ever saw. But they were fine folks regardless of how seldom they visited, even to see their grandchildren.

Tears edged into Abby's eyes as sadness suddenly overwhelmed her anger, a sorrow that her boys had to deal with a pa who drank. When she married Stephen, she believed he would provide everything she ever wanted, and she hadn't just been thinking of a solid house and ample food and clothing. No, she meant all those other things a woman expected from her husband—a comforting shoulder when she needed to cry, a ready supply of kindness, and enough kisses and hugs to keep away any loneliness that might visit from time to time. But Stephen had failed at a lot of that.

He drank in spite of her bitterly disliking it, and he sometimes stayed out late into the night. Twice he had even raised a hand as if to strike her. While he had never done so, she often wondered when he might, and the thought scared her to her core. Not that she couldn't recover from a licking or even protect herself from it. She wasn't some weak city woman, after all. As a young girl she had dug and planted and hoed in the family cornfield, had cut and hauled in wood for the fire, had learned to shoot a gun and stitch a wound with a sewing needle and thread. She had a good portion of steel in her spine and brass in her bones. But the notion of taking a blow from her husband made her shake in her shoes, because she didn't know what she would do if that ever happened. Would she protect herself? A man had tried to have his way with her once years ago and she felt afterward that she ought to just take a gun and go shoot him. She could never do that to her husband, of course. So what could she do? Leave him? But a good Christian woman would never walk away from her husband.

Pushing away such questions, she focused on Stephen once more. This time she didn't act shy or timid with him. "I think maybe you've had enough of that bottle," she said.

Stephen laughed and lifted the bottle to his lips.

Abby stood, walked over to him, and held out her hand. "Stephen, give me that."

He glared at her and then drew his arm back and flung the bottle against the wall. It shattered and the amber liquid slid down the wall to the floor.

Abby froze. Stephen's eyes looked crazy. She realized then that something awful must have happened. But what? Her feelings softened. Men had to deal with problems she couldn't even imagine. Stephen was not a bad man, but something had scared him so much he needed to strike out at it. She knew that. She could never have loved a bad man. And she did love him.

Her hands clenched, Abby took a seat on the bed beside him. He had a lot of faults, but he wouldn't act like this without a reason. He did love her and the boys, she knew that as surely as she understood he had little or no power over the bottle.

She took one of his hands. It trembled in her fingers. "You can tell me," she soothed. "Please, tell me."

Stephen buried his face in her shoulder as great sobs swept over him. She rubbed the back of his neck.

"I'm bankrupt!" he cried. "All our cash money is gone!"

Abby's hands stilled. "What?"

"The crash! It's affected all of us, everybody in town! No money, none . . . nowhere!"

Abby shook her head. A couple of things suddenly made sense. In the last couple of days she'd noticed an unusual quiet on the streets, had seen glum faces at the general store. People had taken to whispering too, whispering about troubles on the way, what with banks running out of dollars and stores closing their doors because they'd run out of goods.

Abby hadn't thought too much about it. Dollars had been hard to come by in other times as well, but people had moved on and made do until things picked up. Now she realized something much worse had happened. A sickness had come to Boone, and it wasn't something like the measles. No, this sickness had infected folks' pocketbooks and nobody was immune, not even her family.

For several minutes she held Stephen close, hoping if she stayed strong it would give him courage. But Stephen continued to weep, one moan followed by another, his tears soaking her blouse.

A wave of nausea suddenly rolled through Abby, and she swallowed back the bile that rose in her throat. Sweat broke out on her face, but she gritted her teeth and held still. Stephen needed her, so she wouldn't leave him till he gathered his strength.

She wondered how much money they had left. Would they have to leave their house? But where would they go? To Raleigh to live with Stephen's folks? She'd never even visited there. Would they take in her and the boys, let them live with them? They seemed so aloof.

Though frightened, Abby held off asking Stephen anything. He might hear her questions as accusations, as blame for his failure to manage his law practice better.

Abby stared out the window to her right, saw the sun dropping lower. A sense of loneliness fell on her. She needed Stephen to comfort her, to give her strength. But he seemed incapable of such a thing. As the darkness deepened, Abby held her husband and admitted for the first time what she'd long known but refused to accept. She had married a weak man. The liquor proved that. When a hard time raised its ugly head, Stephen turned immediately to the bottle. A stronger man wouldn't do that.

A strong man took hard times head on, saw the dilemma as an opponent to fight with fist and knife, tooth and claw—an enemy to wrestle, a dare to overcome or die trying. But Stephen Waterbury wasn't such a man.

Abby closed her eyes. Times were turning hard. And she wasn't a man, but she knew about fighting terrible times. Truth was, she'd fought them all her life, so much so she had come to expect difficulties to cross her way. And when they did, she had always refused to back away.

How could she do anything else? She was a Jesus woman. She believed God would stand by her in her darkest hours. Besides that, she'd married Stephen for better or for worse, and she wasn't the kind to go back on a sacred vow, no matter what kinds of problems she and Stephen faced.

Another wave of nausea came over her and she remembered she had another reason to fight. The doctor had confirmed only hours before what she'd already come to suspect. She had another baby growing in her womb. From what the doctor could tell, she was about two months along.

Tears came to Abby's eyes. At first, she'd hoped the doctor had it wrong. Yes, she wanted more children, a little girl for sure, somebody she could dress up in pretty dresses and black shoes with buckles. She already had a name picked out—Rose Francis—after her mama whom she'd never seen, and the aunt who had raised her. But for reasons she couldn't figure, she felt uneasy about having another baby.

She also suspected that Stephen might not want another child. They hadn't actually discussed it, yet he spent so little time with the two boys they had, why would he want another?

Stephen coughed, and Abby focused back on the moment. Troubles had come her way again and she had to fight them, not only for her boys, but also for the new baby now growing inside her. She closed her eyes and breathed a quiet prayer. With the good Lord's help, she could do what she had always done. She could stand up and fight for what she loved.

CHAPTER THREE

For the first few weeks after Abby found Stephen drunk at home, he seemed to have repented of his bad behavior and decided to stop. He left the house each morning as if to go to work only to trudge home at night to declare few people had need of a lawyer these days, at least not enough to spend their precious dollars for one.

He came home every day in the late afternoon, took his supper with Abby and the boys, and then spent the evening by the fireplace listening to the radio. The news was almost all bad. Prices for eggs and hogs and cattle had dropped. People everywhere had lost their jobs. Food lines had grown longer and longer in the bigger cities. And thousands of folks had left their homes to try to find work. Hoboes rode the rails by the score, some of them becoming traveling bandits with quick fists and knives. Abby could see that the news depressed Stephen. Sometimes after listening to it, he sat still in his chair for hours, his head down as if asleep, his hands gripping the chair's arms. She tried to talk to him when he was this way, but he just shooed her away so she learned to keep her distance.

"Nobody can afford to hire me," he moaned on a regular basis. "Just about everybody is as broke as we are."

Abby tried to encourage him. A man needed a woman to stand by him in days like these, she figured, a wife who would help him to feel strong and capable.

Abby kept wondering whether or not they'd lose their house. Did Stephen have enough dollars set aside to pay for it? She realized she knew almost nothing about their finances, or about finance in general. Her husband had always handled that kind of thing. Now, sensing Stephen might need her help in this area, she found herself wanting to learn about money matters. So, without saying anything to anybody, she visited the library at the teachers college and picked up some books on economics.

The days passed slowly, each one seeming grayer and more somber than the last. Then the weather turned frigid and stayed that way as if in agreement with the grief that had come over their town. A quiet settled on everybody too, and there was very little laughing.

Week after week Stephen's appearance became gradually worse. As Abby's unborn child grew, her husband seemed to be going the opposite direction, shrinking right before her eyes. He failed to polish his shoes, barely combed his hair anymore, and wore the same pants day after day without asking her to press them. Some mornings she even had to remind him to put on a fresh shirt. Abby found herself holding her breath as she sat with him each night. Would he go over the edge, resort to whiskey again?

On the second day of December Stephen didn't show up for supper. Abby tried to stay calm. Maybe a new client with urgent business required him to stay late. She liked that notion and forced her thoughts toward it. But still she wondered. More than once she went to ring him on the telephone but then remembered they'd had their phone taken out to save a few dollars. She considered walking to his office but knew Stephen would figure she was checking on him and wouldn't like it. So Abby waited, her worry mounting with each passing hour.

She finally heard him on the front porch at about one in the morning. Jumping from the bed where she'd been lying awake, she quickly threw on her robe and rushed to the living room. She could smell the whiskey when she entered the room. Again something bad must have happened, she told herself. Stephen had tried hard the previous weeks to do right by her and their sons. She needed to give him a chance to explain.

Without speaking, Stephen staggered to the fireplace and collapsed into his chair. Abby helped him take off his coat and boots. After hanging up the coat, she cautiously moved back to him. His chin hung on his chest; his eyes were closed. Abby wanted to ask him what had happened but knew from past experience she would have to wait. She put a couple of logs over the embers in the fireplace, stirred them with the poker, then sat down across from Stephen.

"They took my office," Stephen said, his eyes still closed.

Abby nodded, for the news didn't surprise her. She had expected ill tidings.

Stephen looked up at her with wild eyes. "Did you hear what I just said?" he shouted. "The bank took my office! Just barged in, showed me some papers, and told me I hadn't made my payments. Said I had to hand the place over to them and move out right away!"

Abby kept herself from crying. Since Stephen was so frail, she needed to stay firm. If she broke down too, where would that leave their boys? She reached to comfort him, but he pulled away and folded his arms across his chest.

"I'm finished in this town," he said. "There's nothing left for me here."

Abby's heart sank. Was he saying they'd have to move? But she couldn't just take their children and leave Boone. Where would they go? Raleigh? Where Stephen's ma and pa lived? Was that his notion? But she barely knew Mr. and Mrs. Waterbury. They had kept their distance all these years. She suspected they looked down on her, saw her as beneath their son. She couldn't move to Raleigh to live with them! Whatever she had to do to prevent that, she would do it.

"You can move your office here to the house," she said, a quick plan forming in her head. "It's mostly just law books. You can put the telephone back in, and people can call you here. We'll cut expenses. I've been reading a little about business. We can make it, you'll see. And I can maybe take in some students to teach. I can—"

Stephen bolted upright and cut her off. "No! It won't work! A man can't do his work from his house. What kind of appearance does that present, for a lawyer especially? A lawyer needs a place that inspires confidence, shows his mastery of the law. I can't very well do that with the boys running in and out, now can I?" He now stood over Abby, his whole body a challenge to her suggestion.

"I don't know about all that," she said, not willing yet to give up her idea. "But if you've lost your office, what else can you do?"

Stephen's eyes narrowed. He shoved his hands into his pockets and walked to the window to the right of the fireplace. A burning log shifted and sent up sparks. Abby followed him to the window, and he pivoted around and faced her.

"I'm just tryin' to help," she said. "If you've got a better idea, I'm ready to hear it."

Stephen hung his head. Several seconds slipped by. Then he looked her in the eyes but said nothing.

Abby touched him on the shoulder and recalled the man she'd married—a proud, educated man of refined tastes and respectable background, a man with a bright mind and a future of unlimited possibility. What had happened to that man? Had he all but disappeared, or had she only imagined him in the first place? Imagined him out of her own need to find such a suitor? Her need to be with someone completely opposite of the boys back in Blue Springs, mountain boys with hardly any education, who rarely wore shoes, who never read a book. Was that what had drawn her to Stephen Jones Waterbury? Her desire to find somebody to take her out of Blue Springs? Was that what had made her blind to his weaknesses?

"All right, I'll bring the office to the house," said Stephen, his shoulders slumped in resignation. "I'll put the telephone back in here. You can work for me."

"What?" Abby's heart sank. She didn't want to work for Stephen. She wanted to teach, had wanted it for as long as she could remember. She had attended the teachers college to educate herself so she could help boys and girls learn to read and write, do their numbers, better themselves. Though she ended up marrying Stephen and not quite finishing her degree, she still felt the good Lord wanted her to teach someday.

"You don't need to do any teaching," Stephen continued. "If you work for me, I won't have to pay an assistant."

"Do you even need a helper?" asked Abby. "As little as you've had to do lately. Can't you do everything yourself?"

Stephen grinned. "You don't want to work for your loving husband?"

"No, that's not it. You know that a lot of kids have stopped going to school full time. But their families still want them to learn their letters. I can do that for them cheaper than any other teacher. And everybody knows me, trusts me. I won't make much, but anything, even a little will help. If I work for you, I'll be costing us money, that's all. Why not bring some in instead?"

Stephen sat in the chair by the fireplace. "I told you a long time ago that no wife of mine would take a paying job," he said. "That hasn't changed. So long as I keep body and soul together, that's the way it will be."

"But it would be better if I were teaching," Abby said through clenched teeth. "I'm good at it, and I can earn us some money."

Stephen threw another log on the fire, then wiped his hands and faced her again. "I don't have much of anything left," he said. "Not money, not much of a law practice, and no office. But so long as I got breath, my wife won't take a job. It's a matter of pride. You got to leave me that or I got nothing, nothing at all."

Abby started to argue some more but then abruptly stopped, knowing it wouldn't help any. Stephen had made up his mind, and he seldom backed down from an argument with her. Heartbroken, Abby stalked back to their room and fell on their bed crying. She'd married a man who seemed to have no pride about the right things and far too much about the wrong.

Her heart heavy, Abby traveled with Stephen and their boys up the mountain past Blue Springs to visit her pa's widow, Elsa, and the rest of her family for Christmas of 1929. On Christmas Day, she sat at the table in the cabin where she'd witnessed her pa's death only two months before and looked at her kin, wondering what would become of them now that the bad times had hit. What would happen to Elsa and Solomon Jr., her late pa's widow and son? What about her brother Daniel and his wife, Deidre, and their three kids? Or her other brother Luke, the brother who made his living playing the guitar, traveling and singing in different churches?

Elsa sat at the head of the table, her hair turning grayer by the day as she edged closer to fifty and faced her first Christmas without Solomon. While many had wondered about Elsa when she and Solomon first married, she had proven herself a woman of character. Born fifteen years after her husband, Elsa had originally resisted moving to the high mountains. Too rough for her, she had said to anyone who would listen.

Time and circumstances showed she'd been wrong about that. If anything, she turned out to possess more grit than anybody could've thought possible. She had suffered three miscarriages and buried a son and a husband, yet she had done most of her grieving in private. Solomon would have appreciated that. No use putting on a show by wailing out everywhere. Elsa now had some wrinkles clinging around her eyes and she carried a few extra pounds around her waistline, but she still struck a fine figure. Abby knew a lot of men would no doubt come calling on her before too long.

Solomon Jr., who everybody called Sol now that he'd grown to be a man, sat between his mama and his wife, Jewel. He wore a shiny badge on his brown shirt and a holstered pistol at his hip. Almost twenty-five years old, Sol had served as the county sheriff since Sheriff Rucker had quit back in the summer. Almost six feet in height, Sol had black hair like his mama in her earlier days and eyes as brown as Abby's.

Watching Sol, Abby saw her pa in him, the way his eyes lay deep in his head, his squared-off shoulders. She wished she knew him and Jewel better.

Daniel and Deidre and their kids filled up the left side of the table—Marla who was nine, Laban Edsel, seven, who everybody called Ed, and Raymond going on two. They ate as though they might not see another morsel of food for a long time.

Daniel's eyes looked overly tired to Abby. She wondered what made him so weary. Had his building business slowed so much as to cause him a fright? But nothing frightened Daniel. Not the war he'd fought over in France, not a hard day's work in the blazing sun, not bullies like Hal Clack and his boys.

He forked a bite of beans into his mouth. Abby smiled. If Sol had a few similarities with her pa, Daniel practically carried the spitting image. Same brown beard, only more trimmed, same floppy black hat, same dark eyes and tightly muscled frame. He'd been living in Asheville for years now, yet the city hadn't done anything to take the mountain out of him. He still talked as simple as he always had, slept with the bedroom window open even in the middle of winter, and smoked a pipe using tobacco from a patch he grew in his own backyard.

With no more formal education than any other highlander boy, Daniel had nonetheless become fairly good at reading and figuring numbers. Using his smarts together with a lot of hard labor had made for a powerful combination. Daniel had done well in the world. Despite his needing to use Solomon's old walking stick because of a war injury where he took a bullet to the hip, he had become the head of a building crew and made a heap of dollars back before the Depression.

Abby saw Daniel's cane leaning in the cabin's corner. Solomon had handed the stick to Daniel just a few hours before he died. Cut and carved by her pa, the staff was about six feet high and over five inches around. Solomon had cut different images into the cane: Moses' stone tablet, the temple of Jerusalem—which he'd seen a picture of in the back of a Bible—the cross, a serpent, a kingly crown. Solomon had added new carvings as he got older, like the face of Blue Springs Mountain, his family cabin, and his favorite dog, Sandy, now gone.

Abby studied Deidre next. A woman of slight stature with a round face and eyes that appeared to be spaced a touch wider than most, Deidre had a finishing school education and experience far beyond Abby's. Unlike her own situation with Stephen, Deidre's folks seemed to appreciate Daniel and how he had provided for their daughter and grandkids.

Abby shifted her attention to Luke, the brother with the lazy left eye and a stutter in his speech. While slow in learning, Luke had made out just fine because of his gift for music. A guitar at his side most of the time, Luke's nimble fingers strummed and picked the strings with great skill. He and his group, the Jubilees for Jesus Band, had been playing and singing in churches, county fairs, and at special events around the area for years and made a decent living from it.

Abby wondered if the hard times would cause folks to stop inviting Luke's band to come and play. Would the church offerings come back empty after they finished their singing? What would Luke do for a living then?

Looking around the table, Abby realized that nearly all her kin were here together, a small circle of folks actually, tied together by their common ancestors—the Solomon and Rose Porter people. Her kin had originally come over from Ireland to scratch out a living in a spot where they could walk half a day and never see a neighbor.

Taking a bite of corn bread, she thought about how she'd lived in Blue Springs two-thirds of her life. Her family had once owned almost a thousand acres in some of the highest reaches of the Blue Ridge, land her pa's family had settled on together over the last hundred years since his grandma and grandpa first came to the southern highlands from Pennsylvania. She knew only a little about her ancestors, that they were Scotch folks who had traveled to the New World from Ireland in hopes of gaining freedom from government meddling, to make something of themselves among the high mountain slopes.

Abby's eyes grew moist. She loved this land, loved the laurel and rhododendron, dogwood and maple, the oak and chestnut and pine that covered it. She loved the streams that spilled over the mossy rocks, the wildlife that filled the forests, the birds that nested in the branches.

Wiping her eyes, she inwardly scolded herself. The truth was, she hated the land as much as she loved it. It was a hard land for people, yielded up a living like it had a grudge against those who struggled to make something out of it.

Like her pa used to say, some made it, some did not. Her ma and pa had made it. They had added to the land their folks had staked out and settled. Bought up bits and pieces whenever any money came to hand. Scraped and scrimped and did without so they could have something to hand down to their offspring.

But then their offspring had lost the land. And no one, no matter how hard they tried, had figured out a way to get it back. She wondered if they ever would, or if it would even matter. Had the loss of the land condemned them all to the scattered lives they now lived—one in Asheville, one in Boone, one in Blue Springs, one traveling around from place to place? Would getting the land back change any of that? Would it bring them back home, glue them all together in one place? Would it tie them into a family again, like a string holding sticks together? Abby suspected not. Too much had happened.

Abby heard a thump and looked back at Elsa. Elsa tapped her spoon on the table, and the talking stopped as everybody gave her their attention. Laying down the spoon, she placed her palms on the table. "I have an announcement," she said. "I'm going to move to my mama's old house in Blue Springs."

Surprised by the news, Abby's mind flew back to when, as a young girl, she'd lived in that house with Elsa and Amelia, Elsa's mama. Lots of memories—both good and bad—hung around the walls of the place. But why would Elsa want to go back there now?

"What'll happen to this place?" asked Sol. "You and Pa did so much work on it. A shame to just let all that go to waste."

Abby silently agreed. Their uncle Pierce had provided this patch of ground as a place for her family to live, after the trouble with Hal Clack way back in 1907. While she and Elsa and her boys stayed with Amelia in Blue Springs, the men had slaved like crazy to build this cabin and harvest a garden before the winter hit. The next year Elsa had left Blue Springs and moved her boys and herself in with Solomon. Those days had made for some hard living, but they bucked up their spines and overcame everything that threatened to push them down. As the years went by, Solomon had paid Uncle Pierce for the land and added on to the cabin. Now it had six rooms, glass on the windows, two fireplaces, and smooth plank floors and walls. A barn big enough for a pair of cows and a mule, chickens and dogs, had been built out back. To the left of the barn was a garden that produced more food than most families could eat in a year. All of it was a testament to the labors of Solomon and Elsa.

"What happens to this place is another announcement," said Elsa, unexpectedly turning to Daniel. "Why don't you make known that news?" All eyes were on Daniel now.

He rubbed down his beard a couple of times, then said, "Me and Deidre and our brood are movin' in here. Deidre's pa needs our house. He gave it to us a long time ago, but now that he's lost his place, I thought it only fittin' we offer it back to him."

"He lost his house?" said Abby, finding her voice.

Daniel hung his head. "He ain't the only one. Lots of folks in Asheville are sufferin' mighty bad. A couple of men done gone out and put themselves down."

Abby nodded. She and Daniel had talked earlier in the day as they hauled in wood. The Depression had hit Asheville real hard. Daniel had lost his money when the bank went under and his building work had dried up quicker than a mountain stream in a July drought. Many other workers had been dealt a similar fate. Not all of them could take it. Tough times did indeed show a man's character, one way or the other. The weakest ones didn't make it. Abby glanced at Stephen but then pushed the fear away.

"Why don't you take another place in Asheville?" Stephen asked Daniel, glancing up from his plate long enough to ask the embarrassing question.

Daniel rubbed his beard again. "Fact is, not much there I can afford to rent. Business is real bad."

Abby bit her tongue. Stephen sometimes made her so mad. Anybody with any sense at all would know not to raise that issue at such a time as this. Making a man admit in front of others that he didn't have the wherewithal to provide shelter for his family showed poor form on Stephen's part.

"Can't imagine leaving the city to move back up here," Stephen added.

Daniel grunted. "That ain't a problem for me. City livin' ain't never been my choice. Too much noise. And the houses are all shut up so a man can hardly breathe. But I done it for the wages . . . that and Deidre here likes it, she grew up there." He took his wife's hand. She smiled at him and then looked down at her plate.

"What about your garden, Ma?" Sol asked, shifting the conversation back to Elsa. "You take your food from it."

"There's almost a hundred acres around the house in Blue Springs," she answered. "More than enough space to put in a good crop."

"Sounds like it's all settled, then," said Sol, a hint of uncertainty in his tone.

"It is," Elsa said. "Thing is I need a few more folks around me than I got up here. When I found out that Daniel and Deidre needed a place, then the idea came to me. At first I thought we could all just live here together, but then I remembered that Solomon got back my mama's old house for me just before he died."

"You don't think your pa will mind?" Sol asked.

Abby's face showed her concern. Elsa's pa, Hal Clack—the most cantankerous man around—had crooked teeth, hair as dark as coal, and a nose like a hawk's beak. Hal and his boys, all of them grown now, spent most of their time on the other side of the ridge, up past Blue Springs. The Back of Beyond some folks called it, a land still wild regardless of the law coming to the mountains in recent years.

In the Back of Beyond, men still fought with knives and pistols and took no sass from anybody, not even a government man if and when they ran across one. Most of the Clacks were bootleggers, men who made and sold corn liquor for the highest price they could get. Hal Clack's oldest boy, Topper, had been tried once for killing a revenuer with a Winchester rifle, but the jury let him off when they determined it was self-defense. Everybody in the highlands knew better, though. Topper had bushwhacked the man, shot him in the chest as he rounded a curve in the creek bed that led to the hideaway where the Clacks kept their biggest still. The government man never had a chance.

The Clack men made all mountain folk look bad. When they weren't working their stills, they were causing all manner of trouble—drinking past all reason, picking fights with others, stirring up a fracas at every turn. They seldom bathed, were hard on their women, ruled their kids with an iron hand, and generally served as a pestilence on the land.

Abby had no patience with such fellows and barely managed to hide her disgust for them, despite the fact that Elsa and Sol had Clack blood in their veins. Sometimes she wished the law would just come in with a hundred gunmen and clean out the Clacks, like farmers sometimes had to clean out the rats in their barns.

Elsa cleared her throat, and Abby snapped back to attention. "I'm not concerned about whether or not my pa likes what I do," Elsa said. "As you know, he and I parted ways a long time ago."

Abby's heart hurt. She knew well the sad feelings that rose up when a daughter and her pa didn't live in harmony. It had to hurt Elsa that she and her pa kept such distance from each other.

"My pa has no more say over the house," Elsa continued. "It's mine again, just like it should have been all along."

In Abby's mind, what Elsa said made perfect sense. Even though Elsa had lived for over twenty years up in the highlands, many of the town ways still clung to her skirts. And a smart, social woman like Elsa ought to live in a less isolated place than the holler where she'd been staying for so long. She ought to have stores around that she could walk to in less than half a day, a house with electricity, maybe even a telephone. As it was, she didn't have even an indoor privy, and anybody wanting to visit her had to park their auto on the dirt road a good mile down the holler and walk uphill the rest of the way to the cabin.

"When do you plan to move?" Sol asked.

Elsa picked up her fork. "Soon as the weather turns good enough to load my things and make the trip down the mountain. March or April probably."

Sol took a biscuit from his plate. Everyone else started eating again too. Yet, even as Abby took a bite of green beans, she had a feeling that Elsa's move back to Blue Springs might not go as Elsa hoped. From her own history with the Hal Clack clan, she knew events hardly ever came about smoothly where they had any say in it. If Elsa's pa got wind that his daughter planned to move into his old place, helped a Porter in any way at all, he would turn fractious real fast. And when Hal Clack turned fractious, folks tended to get hurt.

A few hours after the Christmas feed, Daniel stepped out onto the porch with Sol to take in some fresh air before turning in for the night. To his surprise, he saw Stephen sitting on the steps of the porch, his coat pulled up tight around his neck. The light from the windows showed Stephen's breath in the cold night air.

Daniel pulled a pipe from his overalls, stuffed it with tobacco, and handed the pouch of tobacco to Sol, who followed suit. Stephen glimpsed back at them but said nothing. Daniel noted that Stephen held a flask. A flare of upset rushed through him. Liquor wasn't allowed in the home of Solomon Porter. But, clenching his hands, he decided to hold his tongue. Sol handed Daniel back the pouch.

Though still mad, Daniel lit his pipe and leaned over the porch railing. He puffed on it until it burned good. Balancing his elbows on the railing, he peered into the yard. Sol moved to his side. Daniel stared at the stars and thought on how much difference a year could make. Just last Christmas they'd all found out about his pa's cancer. Just last year he had enough work on hand to keep four men busy all week and Saturdays too. Just last year he lived in a fine house with his family down in Asheville. Except for his pa's sickness, things had looked a lot rosier last year.

Behind him, Stephen swigged from the flask. Sol poked Daniel in the ribs and tilted his head toward Stephen. Daniel tried to figure out how to tell Stephen to stop his drinking without causing a ruckus. The man was Abby's husband, after all, and he didn't want to cause his sister embarrassment. So he spoke out into the dark, hoping to keep his tone steady.

"You got somethin' to warm a body in that flask?" Daniel asked Stephen.

Stephen held up the bottle. "Quicker than a hot poker," he said. "And not as heavy to lug around." He smiled at his humor.

Daniel swallowed back his distaste for the man. How could Abby have married him? Women sure did mystify a body, that's the truth.

"You boys want a taste?" Stephen offered. Sol stiffened and stood up from the rail. Daniel put a hand on his arm.

"Reckon not," Daniel said. "We don't take much to illegal spirits in this house."

Stephen grunted, then said, "You boys think you're pretty high and mighty, don't you? Good churchgoing men, think you're more righteous than everybody else."

Daniel wanted to teach him a lesson with a smack in the face but again held back for Abby's sake. "That ain't it at all," he replied. "I've had a taste of the jug. Still want it sometimes. But we were brought up different, that's all. Don't mean we're better or worse than anybody else."

Stephen took another drink. "You're right about not being better," he said. "Just listen to your speech. I've never heard anything more crude. And you got—"

"Where did ya get your liquor?" interrupted Sol, apparently fed up with Stephen's rudeness.

Stephen faced them once more as he patted the flask. "A man can get whiskey in these parts if he wants it."

"You stop in Blue Springs on the way up here?"

"Indeed I did. Met some fine people too. Man by the name of Topper Clack for one. He was very neighborly."

Daniel gritted his teeth.

"Don't be forgettin' I'm the sheriff 'round here," Sol said. "Whiskey's illegal, in case it has slipped your mind."

Daniel felt the hair go up on his neck. Sol took his job real serious. Like his pa afore him, he was a straight arrow. If Stephen crossed him too much, he might end up sitting a day or two in jail, Abby's husband or not.

Stephen laughed and lowered the flask as if to hide it. "I'm just fooling you boys," he said. "It's just water I got in here, don't you know that?"

Quiet fell for a while, the three men looking out into the night. Daniel thought the danger maybe had passed. But then Sol turned, stood before Stephen and asked, "Where did you scoop up that *water*? My guess is you got it from Topper Clack."

With Sol acting the lawman now, Daniel hoped Stephen would have enough sense to keep his mouth shut.

"Can't recollect at the moment," said Stephen, his eyes on the porch floor. "My mind is a touch foggy tonight."

"Well, give your mind a second to clear up," Sol told him, crossing his arms. "Maybe somethin' will come to you."

Stephen put a hand to his chin as if pondering the matter. "No, I'm sorry but nothing occurs to me."

Sol started to move, but Daniel stepped off the porch and grabbed him by the arm. Sol pulled his arm away and returned to Stephen, his hand outstretched. "Let me have a taste of it," he said. "Maybe I can recognize the creek it come from."

"Sure," said Stephen. "A taste of Christmas cheer to buck up the spirits will do you good. Lord knows we could all use it." He stood and handed Sol the flask. Sol touched it to his lips. His mouth wrinkled, and he quickly wiped his lips on the back of his hand. "Don't taste like no water to me."

"So you found me out," Stephen said with a grin. "But what you just tasted is a lot more refreshing than water, wouldn't you say?"

Sol ignored the remark. "You didn't get this liquor in Boone, that's for sure. This stuff is pure highlander whiskey; it'll take the paint right off a barn."

Stephen reached to get his flask back. Sol gave it to him. Then Stephen swung around and held it out for Daniel. "Take a taste," he encouraged. "It'll put grit in your gizzard."

Daniel puffed on his pipe and tried to stay calm. He didn't like Stephen Waterbury swiggin' the doublings on the porch of his pa's cabin. Felt like a foulin' of the grave somehow, like Stephen had spit right down on the dirt over where Solomon lay. What kind of son would stand by while another man did that? Daniel thought of Abby again and once more decided against fighting with her husband on Christmas night, no matter how grievous the transgression.

"I reckon I'll pass on the drink," Daniel replied. "I don't much cotton to whiskey. My pa didn't either." Daniel hoped Stephen would take the hint. But he didn't have the sense, or maybe the drink had already addled his brain to the point he didn't hear it.

"Suit yourself," said Stephen. "It seems to me, though, that only a foolish man would turn down such fine-tasting water."

Daniel clenched his fists. Didn't Stephen know better than to call a highlander man foolish? He might as well curse a man to his face as to call him a fool.

"You sayin' my brother is a fool?" Sol interjected. "My dead pa too?"

Stephen's grin disappeared as he apparently heard the anger in Sol's voice. Daniel eased a half step closer to Sol, ready to spring between the two men. If anybody took a swing at Stephen, he wanted it to be him. Let Abby get mad at him, he figured. For the pleasure of hitting Stephen

Waterbury in the mouth, it might be worth the trouble.

Stephen slowly screwed the cap back on the flask, slid it in his coat pocket, and looked up at Sol. "I'm not calling anybody a fool," he said. "Just saying this is mighty good drink."

Sol took a breath. Daniel could see his little brother didn't know what to do next, one part wanting to crack Stephen in the teeth, another part wanting to leave him alone for Abby's sake.

Sticking out a hand, Sol said, "Maybe you oughta give me that flask. I'll keep it for you till you head back to Boone."

Stephen hesitated, and Daniel wondered if he'd refuse. A highlander man would. No way would a mountain man give over his whiskey. Easier to get him to hand over his firstborn son than to yield up his jug. But Stephen wasn't a highlander man. Fact was, he was right weak in the spine. Daniel had figured it out years ago, just after he met him. He'd seen men like Stephen in the war, men all blustery when on the boat on the way over to the fighting, when making ready to head to the trenches. But once the shooting started, a lot of them curled up on themselves like babies and pressed their hands against their faces and cried. No, not much backbone in Stephen Waterbury.

Stephen glanced from Sol to Daniel. "I see there's two of you," he said, "and both of the same mind. Not good odds for me, I suppose."

"I'm the law here," said Sol. "Reckon I'm enough to take that flask from you if I want it."

Daniel watched as Stephen inspected Sol head to toe, obviously trying to figure his chances of beating him in a fight. Was the man crazy? Or was he just too drunk to see that Sol would no doubt whip him inside of two minutes and leave him busted and bleeding in the snow?

His teeth clenched, Stephen reached into his pocket and pulled out the bottle. Sol took it from him and stuck it in his back pocket. Then, without a word, Stephen turned and stalked off into the yard.

Daniel took a big breath and looked at Sol. "I reckon he's probably got another bottle hid somewhere."

"Maybe so," said Sol. "But he better not bring it near the house. He's an ornery one. Hope he's treating Abby right."

"If he ain't, I better not ever find out about it," Daniel said.

Sol grinned. "You reckon you could best him, brother?"

"Him and you both. At the same time too, mind you."

Sol patted the flask in his pocket. "Sounds like you been swiggin' on this here bottle," he teased.

"I've been tempted once or twice," Daniel admitted. "But so far my lips are clean."

Sol grinned again. "Well, mine ain't," he said. "That is some stiff drink, I got to tell you."

Daniel cupped his pipe in his hand. "It taste like local product?"

Sol nodded. "Hal Clack's makings, I reckon."

Daniel stared out into the yard. Hal Clack again. The man and his sons had lived in the coves and hollers around Blue Springs as long as his family had. But where the Solomon Porter kin had tried to live right and do good, the Hal Clack brood had seemed bent on causing trouble almost from the first. Whenever there was a scrape in the area, a person could just about expect a Clack to be at the bottom of it. Whenever a man got drunk and mad, it was a sure bet that a Clack had made and sold the man the liquor that made him so riled. If Daniel didn't know better, he would say God had made a big mistake when He created the Clack boys, a mistake as big as Blue Springs Mountain from what he could see.

Every now and again Daniel wondered why God had seen fit to let a man like Hal Clack live while he let Solomon die. The ways of the Lord were a mystifying thing, that was for certain.

"You staying busy lookin' for Clack's stills?" asked Daniel.

"Always," Sol said. "That's part of my job. So long as whiskey makin' is against the law and I know the Clacks are cookin' up the doublings, I'm searching for his stills."

Daniel knocked the ashes from his pipe on the porch railing. "Best you go careful," he said. "We got more law up here than ever before, but Hal Clack still ain't bashful when it comes to gunplay."

Sol fingered the pistol on his hip. "I ain't afraid of no Hal Clack."

"I don't reckon you are. Keep your eyes peeled is all I'm sayin'. Clacks don't fight fair, you know that."

Sol nodded. Daniel placed a hand on his shoulder. Although nobody in his family had ever locked into a shooting match with the Clacks, they'd come real close more than once. Others hadn't turned out so fortunate. And, though pistol shooting in the highlands had slowed some over the last few years, the possibility for gunfire still remained.

The two men stared up at the dark sky. Even on Christmas night, they both knew to stay careful when it came to Hal Clack and his boys.

CHAPTER FOUR

In April of 1930, on a day full of bluster and bright sunshine, Daniel moved his family up to the holler above Blue Springs. The trees danced in the breeze, their new leaves going this way and that. His hat pulled down tight on his head, Daniel felt no sentiment to join the trees in their dancing. His heart felt like a brick in his chest. It wasn't that he didn't like the notion of moving out of the city and back to his home mountain. That pleased him just fine. What he didn't like was that a lack of work in Asheville had forced him to do it. He had always wanted to return to Blue Springs Mountain but only after he'd made enough dollars to get back the family land and build a new cabin for his family. But that hadn't worked out, and now he was hauling his brood back with a touch of shame pressing down on his shoulders. A man ought not to come home all broken like this, he figured. But sometimes life didn't hand him no choice.

Shame wasn't the only feeling eating at Daniel the day he moved. He held some sadness too, because he had left Deidre's parents in his family's former place back in Asheville. Mr. and Mrs. Shaller had taken the loss of the bank real hard, and nobody seemed sure how to help them. The bank that owned their property had forced them to sell their fine brick house and all their land except twenty acres.

Daniel's sadness gripped even harder when he walked into Elsa and Solomon's former bedroom and laid a sack of shirts on the floor. His pa had died in this room only a short time ago. A tug of grief hit him, and he stood still for several seconds and let it have its way. Then Deidre entered the room, her arms full of sacks. She put them down and moved to Daniel.

"A man's miseries come at peculiar times," he said. His eyes searched the room, taking in each corner.

"You built this place with your pa and brothers," said Deidre. "No wonder it means so much to you."

"With our own hands," he said. "The year after Laban lost the land. It rained about every day that spring and summer. But we just kept on working. Cut and hauled the logs, laid up the walls, chinked them with moss and mud. The rains fell and soaked us to the bone, but Pa wouldn't let us quit. We had us a place before we knew it, rough for sure. But somehow we made it a home."

"Elsa joined you with Sol and Walter later on that year, is that right?" Deidre asked.

"That's right," he said, thinking for a moment of Elsa's boy Walter who had died of the flu at age twelve. "But Elsa was used to finer things. Balked for a while at the notion of livin' in such a rough place."

"She grew to love it," Deidre said.

Daniel took off his hat. "The Lord took a gentle hand to her, nursed her along until she finally saw the beauty of the place."

"She loved your pa too. Love for a man will lead a woman to do things she might not normally do."

Daniel put a hand on her waist and said, "This is sure to go hard on you. You've lived in the city all your life."

Deidre covered his hand with hers and looked him in the eyes. "Love for a man will lead a woman to do things she might not normally do," she repeated.

Daniel's eyes grew moist and he felt silly. Highlander men didn't do much in the way of crying. "Reckon I'm going soft," he said.

Deidre smiled. "Yes, you are."

Daniel touched her chin, eased her head to his shoulder. "I will make this home for you," he whispered.

"We will make it home for each other."

"I'm a blessed man, for certain."

"And don't you forget it," she said.

They held each other for several moments in silence. But then Marla ran into the room and asked Deidre where to put a handful of kitchen things. Deidre pulled away from him and went to help Marla. After she left, Daniel set his hat back on and ran a hand over the bedroom's back wall to check the chinking. To his relief, he saw the logs had held up good. He pushed up the back window. It had glass now instead of the wood shutters he and his pa had put on long ago. The breeze hit him full in the face. He looked out at the barn, then past it to the ridge above. The graves of his kin were out there.

As if smacked in the face with an iron skillet, a truth suddenly hit Daniel. He loved this place! Had missed it far more than he'd ever realized. Asheville had done good by him, he couldn't argue with that. He had found his wife in Asheville, had fathered three fine kids there. Yet here and now he knew without a doubt that he belonged here in the highlands, in the hollers where paved roads hadn't yet come, where the trout still ran plentiful in the creeks. He belonged on the steep hillsides, making a living from the dirt, hunting for his meat instead of buying it, looking up at night and seeing the moon and stars and planets, and nothing else.

His heart pounding, Daniel snatched his walking staff from the corner, left the room, and headed out of the house. Deidre stood in the kitchen, her attention focused on a shelf she was filling with canned goods.

"Back in a few minutes," he told her, moving out of the kitchen. She waved him on.

Outside, he walked past the barn in the direction of the ridge. The wind pulled at him, yet didn't slow him any. Within a short time he reached the spot he wanted to see—a high, cleared-out space overlooking the cabin and creek below. The space contained two graves with rough wood crosses for markers, each about waist high. The crosses had names cut into them: Solomon Randall Porter and Walter Earl Porter.

Daniel took off his hat. One of Solomon's old dogs—a mixed hound named Whip that Elsa said she couldn't take with her to Blue Springs—came from around an oak tree and over to Daniel. Daniel scratched the dog's head and saw that he had lost his left ear in a fight. Apparently satisfied with the attention, Whip lay down by Solomon's grave.

The wind played with Daniel's beard. He set his cane across his shoulders so it was parallel to the ground, his forearms resting near each end, and stared down at the graves. A bumblebee buzzed near Solomon's marker. Whip licked his lips. Daniel squatted down, laid the cane on the dirt, and rubbed a hand over the ground where his pa was buried. Whip lifted his head to watch.

Daniel thought of another grave dug into a hillside, on the land they'd once owned, a grave marked with the cross for his ma, Rose Sharon Porter. He remembered the morning he and his family had moved off that land. He'd found Solomon standing by his ma's grave just as the sun peeked out, saying his last respects to his wife before leaving. Though only a boy at the time, Daniel made a solemn promise to his pa that day, a promise that he'd get back the land so they could all visit his ma's grave again. But Daniel hadn't been able to keep the promise.

"I ain't done so good, Pa," Daniel said to Solomon's grave.

Whip tossed his head from side to side as if to say he didn't agree.

"It ain't that I ain't tried," Daniel continued. "I tried hard, I hope you know that."

The bee buzzed by Daniel's face, but he ignored it.

"Seems like the Lord done decided to take a dislikin' to me," Daniel said. "I don't rightly know why. I toil as hard as any man. Do good by my wife and children. Don't touch the doublings, though they be mighty temptin' sometimes."

Whip stood and walked over to Walter's marker, lay down by it.

Daniel glanced at Walter's grave, then back to Solomon's. He needed to admit one other thing to his pa, the one thing he had hoped never to have to say. But how could he avoid it? It was the thing that caused him the most heartache.

Resigned to what he had to do, he sat down beside the grave, his face toward the cross. "I failed on the promise I made you," he confessed. "The one about the land. I want you to hear it from my own lips. I don't know that I see it as my fault entirely, but I took my money and Luke's and put it in Mr. Shaller's bank. Reckon that was my mistake right there, trustin' something I didn't rightly understand. But, anyway, I did it. I told you that, just before your passin'. I had it all right there in my hand—all the land ours again, just waitin' for me to pay it off. I thought it was all done. Wouldn't have told you I had the property if I didn't think I did. You need to know I didn't lie deliberate or anything. All I had to do was pull the dollars out of the bank and take 'em to the man in Asheville. But then this depression thing up and hit us, and the money was gone, just like that. Like somebody had tossed it all in a fire and burned it to ashes."

Whip yawned real big. Daniel looked over at the hound. The old dog had spent many hours with Solomon, many of them hunting, many more on the front porch by Solomon's rocker. The dog's presence made Daniel feel his pa was close by.

Daniel focused on the grave again. "I ain't much of a son, I reckon," he said. "Not one you can trust anyway." He touched the rough wood of Solomon's cross. "I'm here to tell you this, though. I won't leave this land again. I'll be livin' here the rest of my days. I'm finished with all those city things, with that business everybody calls progress. Puttin' my money in the bank was my mistake. I know that now. But I won't make such a one as that again. I'm a highlander man like you, and I aim to stay one from now on."

The bee flew around his head. Daniel used his hat to swat at it and then faced Solomon's marker one more time. Whip moved closer to Daniel as if to hear better. He reached out and scratched the dog.

"I already failed you on one big promise," Daniel said to Solomon. "But I ain't gone fail this one. I'm here to stay. Born here, plan to die here. Just like you."

Whip nudged his head against Daniel's leg, and Daniel patted the old dog. After a long time gone, he had come home again. This time he would stay.

CHAPTER FIVE

On the third of May, Abby woke up with a bad backache. But with two boys to take care of and a husband who liked mornings about as much as he liked having a tooth pulled, she set her jaw and crawled out of bed. Sweat beaded up on her forehead as she made breakfast, and twice she felt so sick to her stomach she had to grab hold of the counter to stay on her feet. She thought of rousing Stephen to tell him she was sick and needed to go back to bed but then remembered the day not long after Christmas when she told him she had another baby on the way. That hadn't gone well.

She had broken the news to him on a Sunday afternoon following church. Feeling sick, she stretched out in the bedroom. After a while, Stephen stepped in and asked what was ailing her. She hesitated to say. Something made her suspect he wouldn't take well to the news. These days he didn't take well to much of anything she said, trivial or important. She started to blame her sickness on something she ate, but then she realized hiding her condition couldn't last much longer. Her middle had already begun pushing against her apron.

"I'm expecting another baby," she had told him, her tone as neutral as she could say it.

Stephen took a step back. "What?"

Abby sat up. "I'm about three months or so along with another child."

Stephen took a seat on the edge of the bed, and Abby took it as a sign of concern.

"Are you sure about the baby?" he asked.

"The doctor said so."

Stephen bit on a thumbnail. "We can't afford it," he said as though referring to a fancy radio. "We barely got enough money to feed and clothe the two we already have."

"Well, this baby's coming whether we can afford it or not," said Abby.

Stephen bit his nail again. Abby could see he had an idea he was afraid to speak out.

"People can do things about this," he said. "Things like—"

"I'm having this child!" Abby insisted, filled with horror at the suggestion. "And I'll not hear of what *things* people can do. How dare you even ponder such a notion!"

Stephen shrugged. "I'm a practical man," he said. "I know what it takes to bring up a child, and we just don't have the money right now. That's all I'm saying. No reason to go into an uproar."

Abby relaxed but only a little. Stephen returned to his thumbnail.

A moment of silence passed, then he asked, "You say you're three months along already?"

"That's right. The baby will be born around the end of May, maybe early June."

Stephen stood and moved to his dresser. He slid open a drawer and pulled out a small bottle. Abby felt her stomach lurch. She'd asked him over and over again not to bring liquor into the house. He twisted open the bottle and took a long pull from it.

"You want some?" he asked mockingly.

Abby did all she could to keep herself from lighting into him. How could he flaunt his drinking like this, disregard her wishes and act so spiteful of her feelings? She stood and started to speak, but he kept his eyes glued on her and she saw he wanted to engage in a fight. But why? Why did he want trouble at such a rough time for both of them? Did he find some kind of pleasure in the arguing, or did he need her to call him back into line? A mama to scold him and make him feel guilty. But would that change him? She'd scolded him lots of times before, yet he never paid much attention to what she said. Within a few weeks after the scolding he always drifted back to his old ways.

A wave of nausea hit Abby again and she lay back down, too sick to pursue the quarrel. Stephen took another drink of liquor, tipped the bottle at her as if making a toast, and promptly left the room.

Now, going on months later on a rainy and chilly morning, Abby knew she had come to the end of her strength. This baby had given her far more trouble than her first two, more sickness at the beginning and more weakness as the months moved off the calendar. Every now and again Abby recalled what had happened to her mama, how birthing a child had killed her. Did something like that pass down from a mama to a daughter, some built-in weakness of the body that meant a woman could deliver only a certain number of babies before she was in danger of losing her own life in the process? But how many could she birth? Her mama had had three boys, then her. And birthing her was what took her mama's life. Was it Abby's time now? Would she bleed out like her mama? Deliver this child and then pass on to glory?

With no way to know, Abby prayed extra hard every morning and left the questions to the good Lord. Thank goodness she only had a few more weeks before the delivery was due.

Feeling sick yet again, Abby leaned against the wall and knew she couldn't go on like this. She needed help. She made her way to the bedroom and woke Stephen and told him she didn't feel well.

While grumbling at her for waking him so early, he lifted his head and brushed back his hair.

"I don't believe I can walk the boys to Mrs. Lollard's house," Abby said. "I need you to take them over there. They're going to play with her boys this morning."

For a second she thought he might refuse, but then he licked his lips, climbed out of bed, and stumbled to the bathroom to get ready. About forty minutes later, after she had served him and the boys their breakfast, Stephen loaded Stevie and Jimmy into his auto and left.

Still queasy, Abby managed to finish cleaning up the kitchen, then headed toward the bedroom to lie down. Halfway there she felt a twinge in her lower body and sagged back against the hallway wall. Wetness drenched her dress at her knees, and she knew it was time.

She waited there, her face flushed, hoping to gather her energy and figure what to do. Stephen hadn't said whether or not he would come straight home after delivering the kids. Sometimes when he took them he stopped by Wister's General Store to have a cup of coffee with some buddies from town. She prayed that today he'd skip the coffee.

Mustering her strength, Abby pushed away from the wall and staggered to the living room. She pulled the telephone receiver off the wall cradle. Her mind reeled from her aching back as she rang the operator. She shut her eyes and tried to concentrate.

The operator answered as Abby put the receiver to her ear.

"Hello," said Abby. "P-please connect me to the Lollard home."

The operator made the connection.

"Yes," she sputtered when Mrs. Lollard answered. "This is Abby. Stephen is bringing Jimmy and Stevie. Has he come yet?"

"Yes, he's already come and left. The boys are here."

Abby leaned against the wall. The wetness on her dress felt heavier and had turned warm. It was trickling down toward her ankles now. She lifted the dress and looked, and the color ran out of her cheeks. A streak of red covered the inside of her right ankle.

Her heart began to race and she sank to the floor. She heard Mrs. Lollard talking through the phone, but her voice sounded a long way off. Spots appeared before Abby's eyes then, and her friend's voice faded. She tried to fight the spots, to shake her head and make them go away. She glanced down and saw that the wetness on her legs had formed a circle around her feet. Water mixed with blood seeped out from her and stained the wood floor. She turned over onto her hands and knees and tried to stand up to go for help, but she had no strength and couldn't raise herself.

Way off in the distance she heard Mrs. Lollard calling her name. She tried to answer, but her mouth refused to work. Fear gripped Abby, a fear greater even than what she'd felt as a child when her aunt Francis had died. The fear raised its bony finger and beckoned to her, and she understood why the fear of death topped all others.

With amazement, however, Abby realized it wasn't her own death she feared. No, the fear she felt was for the child within her. If she died, her child would perish too. If she gave up, then death would come to her baby.

Abby ground her teeth and resolved she wasn't going to let that happen, not without a fight anyway. She understood now what her mama must have felt, the feeling of not caring whether she forfeited her life for the sake of her baby.

Groaning against the pain, she took a deep breath and lifted herself halfway up before collapsing again. Her head banged against the wall, and the spots returned.

But she wouldn't give up. Again she tried, this time using a chair for support. With a shriek, she jerked to her feet and dragged herself toward the front door. *If I can just make it to the neighbor's,* she thought.

Finally at the door, she pushed it open and staggered out onto the porch. The rain felt cool on her face and revived her some. She grabbed the railing and started down the steps. One step, two steps, only three more to go. She put a foot on the third step. The rain came harder now, and thunder rumbled not far away. Her foot slipped. She stumbled on the wet steps, and her right ankle twisted under her body. She heard a pop like a twig breaking. The fall knocked her forward, and her chin hit the railing and she bit her tongue. The taste of blood filled her mouth.

Grabbing the handrail once more, Abby tried to pull back up. But the injured ankle refused to hold her weight. Not able to stand, she crawled down the steps. *Crawl,* she told herself. *If I can't walk, I'll crawl.* She reached the yard.

The rain drenched her. Her dress clung to her legs. She questioned whether she could drag her weight across the yard to the house next door. She heard thunder, saw lightning flashes. Something cracked loudly, and she wondered if lightning had struck a tree close by.

Her thoughts rushed back to her mama. She had gone into labor in a heavy rainstorm too. Abby closed her eyes and heard roaring. The sound reminded her of the waterfall at the base of Slick Rock Creek, the stream that ran near the cabin where her mama had died during her labor. In a strange way, the roaring comforted Abby, and she lay her head on the grass to rest a minute, to catch her breath before attempting to crawl again.

The roaring grew louder. Abby's mind spun off toward the waterfall. So peaceful there, so beautiful. Her eyes still closed, her body relaxed as the rain continued to splatter down. The rainwater mixed with the wetness her body had produced in its effort to birth her baby. The twin streams ran down and into the grass at the bottom of the steps where Abby now lay motionless. But she no longer noticed because the roaring in her ears had faded away and now she heard nothing.

When Stephen pulled up to his house almost two hours later, it surprised him to see another vehicle on the street in front of the gate. Unsure of why they had a visitor, he suddenly got a bad feeling and grabbed a bottle from under the front seat and took a good shot of whiskey. Capping the bottle, he shoved it into his coat pocket, hopped out of the car, and sprinted through the rain to the front door. When he entered the house, he heard the voice of Dr. Jonas Sills, a thin man with a bushy mustache and pointed nose.

Stephen thought of his sons. Had something happened to one of them? His jaw set, he hurried down the hall. Sills's voice came from the main bedroom. Abby? Was something wrong with her? She had mentioned earlier that she didn't feel well, and her face had looked flushed as she fixed breakfast. He paused at the bedroom door to take another quick drink. The flask back in his pocket, he wiped his mouth and opened the door. He saw Sills and Mrs. Lollard sitting by Abby, who was stretched out on the bed under a thick stack of quilts. The doctor looked at Stephen and held an index finger to his lips. Stephen searched Abby's sleeping face. Her cheeks looked hollow and pale, her eyes with dark circles around them. The color in her skin had mostly disappeared.

For several seconds Stephen stood frozen. How and when had Abby turned so sick? He knew the baby had caused her some trouble, but Abby never let on that things were this bad. Had she been suffering all along without telling him? Or had she tried to tell him but he hadn't listened? Was he so tied up in his own problems that his wife went through a whole pregnancy without his support? What a poor husband he was! What a sorry man!

But Abby could have told him if she was really hurting. If he had known the seriousness of her condition, surely he'd have taken better care of her. No one could blame him for not doing more if he didn't know. He had no reason to feel guilty. Stephen chewed his thumbnail, his mind working. What if Abby didn't get better? How bad was she anyway? No matter if he had done all he could to help her, people might still blame him for her sickness. He didn't know if he could deal with that. As if given a revelation, Stephen suddenly made a decision. If Abby lived, he would make sure this kind of thing never happened again, that they had no more children to put Abby through such danger. They already had two fine boys. Stevie and Jim were enough.

Sills stood and motioned him to the bed.

"What happened to her?" Stephen asked, taking a spot on the side of the bed.

"The baby came early," Sills replied. "Your wife started bleeding, heavily. Apparently she tried to go for help and fell on the steps. She broke her right ankle, it looks like."

"How did you get here?"

"Mrs. Lollard called me. Said your wife had called her and was looking for you. But then she dropped the telephone. Mrs. Lollard could hear her breathing at first, but then nothing. Mrs. Lollard got worried and called me right away. She found Abby out in the yard, soaked to the bone and just about past saving. I got here a few minutes later, and we carried her inside. We were so busy getting her stable, we didn't have time to track you down."

Stephen hung his head. "I was down at Wister's," he said. "Trying to scare up some business. You know how it is."

"Nobody's blaming you," said Sills. "A woman's time for delivery can't be figured with any true accuracy."

Stephen touched Abby's cheek. "Is she going to be all right?"

"Yes, I think so. I got her in here and staunched the bleeding right away. She's been resting ever since."

"She's a strong woman," said Mrs. Lollard. "She'll do fine."

Stephen turned to her and nodded his thanks. Mrs. Lollard smiled, and dimples the size of dimes became visible in her heavy cheeks. "Jimmy and Stevie are still at my house with my boys," she said. "Figured to let them play on for a while."

Mrs. Lollard had red hair pinned back in a bun. She and her husband, Thomas, and their four kids attended church with Abby and his boys. Although she had to be close to forty, she had kids from twenty to six. Stephen wondered why he didn't know the woman better. He and Abby had lived here for years. Was Mrs. Lollard a close friend of Abby's? Did the two of them sit on the porch and talk and watch their kids play when he left to go to town? How strange that he knew so little about what his wife did all day.

He faced Abby again, his heart thumping as he pondered his next question. Where was the baby? Sills had said nothing about the baby except that it came early. Stephen knew he wasn't sure he wanted the baby and that he'd sunk real low to think this way. But they had so little money, they couldn't afford any more children. Yet what kind of a man measures a new addition to his family by how much it would cost him? A sorry kind, that's for sure. He thought of the bottle in his pocket and wished he could steal another drink or two. But he didn't want the doctor and Mrs. Lollard to think poorly of him.

He looked at Sills, his hands at his side. "What about the baby?"

The doctor shook his head. "I'm sorry, but nothing could be done for the baby. The umbilical cord was looped tight around the neck. And the labor came early."

Stephen's skin turned clammy. He had a hard time breathing. "What . . . what was it?" he asked.

"A girl," said Mrs. Lollard. "You want to see her? I got her wrapped and lying in the bassinet in the other room."

Not knowing what to say, Stephen sat still for a moment. How should he answer such a question?

"Does Abby know?" he asked finally.

Sills nodded and said, "I couldn't lie to her."

"How did she take it?"

The doctor tilted his head. "How do you think she took it? I gave her something to make her sleep. She's been out since then."

"Did she see the baby?"

Sills nodded again. "She insisted. She held her for a couple of minutes."

Stephen bit at a thumbnail and wondered what the baby looked like. Like Abby? He didn't think he could take it if he saw her. He turned to Mrs. Lollard. "I don't reckon I'll see the baby," he said. "Least not now."

"I understand," said Mrs. Lollard.

Stephen turned to the doctor. He had one more question yet wasn't sure if it was proper to bring up the matter. He swallowed hard. "Can Abby, can she have . . ." His words trailed off.

"Can she have any more children? Is that what you're asking?"

"Yes."

"Don't know for sure," said Sills. "Probably dangerous for her if she does, perhaps for the baby too. She'll need a doctor from Asheville to do some tests on her before you'll know for certain how she'd do with carrying another child."

Stephen sighed with relief. What the doctor said helped his case about their having no more kids. "Thank you for all you've done today," he said. "You saved my wife's life."

Dr. Sills handed Stephen a piece of paper and told him, "She'll need to stay off her feet for a good while. I wrote down a couple of things you'll need to do for her. And here"—he pulled two bottles from a black bag—"this is medicine for her to take every six hours. I wrote it all down."

"I'll help any way I can," Mrs. Lollard said. "I'll get some other ladies to help too, from the church. We'll stay with her night and day. Take care of your meals and such."

Stephen took the paper and bottles. Everyone seemed so willing to help—the doctor, Mrs. Lollard. He knew so few of Abby's friends, hardly ever attended Sunday services with Abby and the boys. What kind of husband was he? What kind of father?

Mrs. Lollard followed the doctor out of the bedroom. Stephen placed the bottles and paper on the dresser and met them on the porch. The rain had stopped but gray clouds still hung low in the sky.

"I'll be back in an hour or so," said Mrs. Lollard. "I need to do some things at home and then I'll come right back and stay with Abby."

Stephen thanked them both again and watched as they drove away. When safely alone, he pulled the flask from his coat pocket, took three swallows and drained it. That bottle empty, he strode to his car, got another from under the seat and headed back inside the house. After taking another drink, he pocketed it and returned to Abby's side. For a long while he watched her breathe as the whiskey began to take effect.

What else bad can happen to me? he wondered. His law practice had about dried up. The economic collapse had cost him his office. Now this. A sick wife, an infant daughter lying lifeless in the other room.

He hung his head in defeat. He had nowhere to turn, no one to bail him out. Who would take care of his boys while he tried to make a living?

Abby stirred and he stared at her. She opened her eyes. He laid a hand on her side. Her eyes focused, and she licked her lips. Even though the liquor had clouded his head a bit, Stephen still knew enough to fetch a glass of water from the kitchen. The glass in hand, he gently raised Abby's head and touched the glass to her lips. She drank some of it and then shook her head. He quickly moved the glass away and set it on the dresser. Abby lay back on her pillow.

"You're okay," said Stephen, his words soft from the liquor. "Dr. Sills says you're going to mend just fine."

A pair of tears traced down from Abby's eyes. "I . . . I lost the baby," she cried.

Stephen took her hands. "I know. But you survived. That's what we have to think of right now. You're okay." He needed her, he realized, needed her badly. She and the boys were all he had left.

Abby gripped his hand, the tears coming heavy now. She tried to speak but her words got choked off and she couldn't make herself clear. Stephen tried to shush her, to calm her down. The last thing he needed was a wife falling apart. Yes, she had lost a child, but that happened to women all the time. How could he make a go of his law practice if he had a wife who couldn't function and he had to stay home and take care of her and the boys all the time?

As Abby continued to weep, Stephen found his patience growing thin. He wanted another shot of the whiskey, though he knew he couldn't drink in front of her in such a time as this. So he stayed quiet and let her cry it out. When she'd finally wrung her body empty of tears, she wiped her face, adjusted her pillow behind her back and sat up a little.

"I'm so sorry," she said.

"You're not to blame," insisted Stephen. "You did all you could." There, he sounded real kind. He was a good man, a good husband.

"But I lost my girl. Rose Francis, that's what I wanted to call her." A couple more tears rolled down.

"A fine name," he said. "I know she would have been a fine girl."

Abby squeezed his hand, obviously grateful for what he'd said. To comfort her, Stephen almost started to tell her they could maybe have another girl, but since he didn't know for sure that was possible and didn't want another child even if it was, he decided to remain quiet. He picked up the water glass and took a drink for himself. As he did, a thought hit him, one that made great sense. He and Abby shouldn't have any more children, and not just because they didn't have enough money. If she got pregnant again, she might die. Also, if another child came along and Abby didn't make it, he would have two boys to tend to all by himself. That wouldn't be good for his sons. If he had to take care of them, his law practice would fail for sure, which would cause them to suffer even more.

In that instant, Stephen Jones Waterbury decided he would take real care about sleeping with his wife. Maybe he ought not have relations with her too often anymore. To protect her, of course, protect her from having another baby that might kill her during the delivery. To protect his boys too, boys who needed their mother around to care for them as they grew up. That's what he would do. For her sake and that of the boys, he would make this sacrifice. Maybe he wasn't such a bad husband and father after all.

CHAPTER SIX

The summer of 1930 moved quickly off the calendar, and Abby's family prayed extra hard for her and Stephen as the fall rolled in and turned to winter. When Christmas arrived and the family gathered for dinner in Blue Springs, Stephen and Abby failed to appear but everybody understood. Her health remained frail, and with the bad roads and all between Blue Springs and Boone, nobody expected them to come. January passed and February too, the days snowy and short.

In Blue Springs, Sol and Jewel Porter kept watch over Elsa, Sol's mama. Sol visited Elsa at least a couple of times a week, cutting and hauling firewood, making repairs around the house, and bringing in food when the snow fell real deep. Elsa complained some that he treated her like an old woman, but Sol just laughed and continued with his attentions.

Toward the end of March in 1931, just as the last of the snow melted, Sol, Jewel, and their one-year-old son, Nathan, joined Elsa on a clear Saturday afternoon at Elsa's kitchen table for a bite of supper. The smell of biscuits and chicken and potatoes and gravy made Sol's mouth water. It didn't take him long to load up his plate. A biscuit in one hand, a spoonful of potatoes and gravy in the other, he faced Elsa.

"Mama, you'd never know from your table that people are bad off these days," said Sol.

"You know I grow most all of this," Elsa said. "And Jewel brought one of your chickens."

Sol munched his biscuit. "I don't know how you don't weigh at least two hundred pounds eatin' this good."

Elsa smiled, obviously pleased that Sol was enjoying himself.

"She eats a whole lot less than you," said Jewel. "Wants to stay slim for the widow men, hoping she'll catch one someday."

Elsa shook her head. "I don't need a new man. Solomon Porter was enough man to do me a lifetime."

Sol picked up a chicken leg. A year and a half had gone by since his pa moved on to glory. Yet he never seemed too far away. People told Sol he looked more like his pa every day. And even though he'd shaved off his beard, he had to admit the truth of what they said. He certainly had Solomon's structure—all bones and angles, with just enough meat on him to remind people he could lift a baby calf off the ground with no trouble at all. Not that he lifted many calves. A sheriff didn't do much of that kind of thing.

Elsa poured everybody a cup of coffee, and Sol watched her with admiration. In spite of her arguments to the contrary, he suspected she might take another man one day. Probably ought to, though not for a while yet. Maybe Solomon wouldn't do her for a lifetime, but it would take more than a couple of years to get over his passing.

Sol drank some coffee, then set the cup down as he glanced at his wife. A most capable woman, and pretty too. Jewel came from a good family over near Hickory. Had gray eyes and hair so blond it looked like hay. Like most mountain women, she had a slim waist. She didn't say much, but since he didn't either, they had lots of time for comfortable silence between them. Jewel liked to cook and prepared a table as good as any woman on the mountain. In addition, she played a mean mandolin and could dance a clog that left a man gasping for breath. Of course, in his family they didn't do much dancing, clog or any other kind. But Jewel's family did, and Sol enjoyed watching them and clapping along.

Sol grinned to himself. All the Porter men seemed to reach farther than their arms could stretch when it came to their women. As Solomon used to say about Elsa: *"The fact that I married her gives me positive proof that God is still in the miracle-workin' business. No way I could have gotten her on my own."* Sol felt the same about Jewel.

He took another sip of coffee. Funny how his pa's words kept popping up in his head. Did all sons have their pas' words in the back of their minds, forever lying in wait to speak out at the right time? Sol didn't know for sure. All he knew was that folks often said that Solomon Porter had come to life again in his boy. The way he carried himself, puffed his pipe while pondering weighty matters, and the plain, straightforward manner in which he spoke to others.

For the most part, Sol liked it when people said these things. It made him feel good. But at other times, it felt like too much to live up to, and he didn't know if he could muster the strength to pull it off. Carrying Solomon Porter's legacy around could put a stoop in a man's shoulders in a hurry if he wasn't careful.

A knock sounded on the back door. Sol looked over at his mama and asked, "You expectin' more company?"

Elsa shook her head and stood. "I'll go check. Probably just somebody looking for a little something to eat."

Sol nodded and then felt guilty about the food still on his plate. Though Blue Springs had never been that prosperous and didn't feel the burden from the hard times as much as the bigger towns did, the place still had some men down on their luck and needing a meal now and again. Elsa's house had become known as a spot where a body could find such a meal. With a good garden and a son who made a few dollars from sheriffing, she had more on her table than most and a heart kind enough to share.

A minute later his mama stepped back into the kitchen. Sol saw right off that something had happened. Her face had flushed. "What's the matter?" he asked.

"My pa is dead."

Sol pushed back his chair and went to her. She hadn't spoken to Hal Clack in years. Even so, the man was her pa. Sol opened his arms to her, but she shook her head and he stopped in his tracks.

"He turned me away when I was twenty years old," she said. "The day I told him I planned to marry Solomon. We had no relationship from that day on. I don't plan on pretending no grief at this late date."

Sol studied his boots. He knew the story. His grandpa Hal had disowned Elsa because of his pa. The Clacks and the Porters had long battled with each other. One family was known for honesty and hard work, the other for making moonshine whiskey and using their guns and knives to keep a whole town under their thumbs. Since being sworn in as the sheriff, Sol had started some efforts toward breaking up the control the Clacks held over Blue Springs.

Jewel stood now and stepped to Elsa. "But he was your pa," she said.

Elsa simply nodded, then moved back to the table and sat down. Sol and Jewel stood by, not moving, Sol wondering whether she really cared so little that her pa had died.

"Topper is at the door," Elsa said, pointing toward the back of the house. "Said he needs to see you." She looked at Sol.

Sol patted Elsa on the back.

"Pa fell off Edgar's Knob," she said, her tone neutral. "Topper said maybe he got pushed."

"What makes him think that?"

Elsa shrugged. "Best you ask him that question."

"Stay with her," Sol said to Jewel. "Let me see what this is about."

After kissing his mama on the head, Sol left the room. He found Topper Clack on the back stoop, his floppy hat in his hands, his face covered with a scraggly beard. For a family with heaps of money from their whiskey making, the Clacks dressed and smelled like the hoboes that passed through Blue Springs on the train.

Clack tipped his head at Sol but offered no greeting. Sol said, "I hear your pa has died."

"That's right," said Topper. "Yesterday sometime. We found him this morning at the bottom of Edgar's Knob."

"I'm sorry to hear it."

Topper grunted. "I would think that Hal Clack's passin' might cause a Porter to dance a jig."

Sol studied Clack for a second. A scar cut down the right side of his face just above his beard. Some gray hair poked out over his ears, and his eyes looked all clouded.

"I know your pa and mine had their share of troubles," Sol said. "But your pa was my grandpa. Even though he never acted like one to me."

Topper's fingers tightened on his hat.

Sol tried to take the edge off his last words. "And you're my uncle."

"A Clack and a lawman ain't no kin," Topper said with a chuckle. "No matter how thick the blood."

Sol shrugged. "Suit yourself. But my mama is your sister. At least you can claim that."

Topper rolled his hat in his hands. "She *is* my sister. That's why I come to her house. I thought she ought to know. Then she told me you were here. Figured I might as well report it to you too, you bein' the law and all."

"You got any notion what happened?"

"Maybe he fell. Maybe not."

"What you mean?"

Topper stared at him. "You know—my pa had some enemies."

Sol held back from laughing. Hal Clack had more enemies than anyone else in their parts. "You sayin' you think maybe somebody pushed your pa off Edgar's Knob?"

Topper scowled. "That's a possible."

"But he was known for taking a drink now and again," said Sol, stating the obvious. "Maybe he had one too many swigs of the doublings and then stumbled off the ledge."

Topper raised an eyebrow, and Sol could see he'd spoken too directly. To suggest that Hal might've been so foolish as to get drunk and do harm to himself wasn't polite. To Sol's relief, Topper ignored the offense.

"It's possible you're right."

"You got anything showing to the contrary? Because I'd be glad to take a look if you do."

Topper considered the question. "Pa had a fallin' out with some man a couple weeks ago. Business disagreement, you know?"

"Your pa's business?"

Topper inspected the brim of his hat. "I don't talk much about my pa's business. Not to no lawman, anyway."

"Well, you got any idea about this man's name?" Sol asked, changing the subject. "Where he comes from?"

"Maybe I'll ask around, see what I can find out."

Sol propped his right hand over the gun in his holster. He knew not to press too much here. As the eldest man in the family, Topper had to protect the family now, had to take responsibility for keeping the stills open, the whiskey flowing. With Prohibition pushing prices up, Sol knew that a man could make up to a thousand dollars a month making and selling liquor. Given that hardly anybody else around Blue Springs saw much cash at all, that kind of dollars made a man real dangerous if he thought somebody threatened it.

"I ain't asking you to show me your stills," Sol said. "Or a list of your workers neither. But if you want me to check on the possibility of foul play with your pa's dyin', I might have to ask a few questions here and there. If you don't want to answer, that's fine, I can do without the headaches. I'll just write this down as accidental and that'll be the end of it. But if you want me to do any real sheriffing, you got to offer me some kind of starting place."

Topper tightened his grip on his hat again. Sol could see his mind was weighing the matter. Which would be better, for folks to think his pa had gotten so drunk that he fell off Edgar's Knob and smashed his head, or for them to hear something had gone wrong with a whiskey deal and an enemy had shoved him off and killed him? Sol guessed that Topper would see more honor in his pa dying at the hand of an enemy than in falling stupidly to his own death.

"We gotta put Pa in the ground," said Topper. "Take a few days to do that. But then you and me and Ben will go up to Edgar's Knob for a visit to where we found Pa's body. We'll take a look around, see if maybe we can find anything. That's your job, ain't it? Finding lawbreakers and throwin' 'em in jail?"

"I do some of that."

"Then we'll plan a trip up to Edgar's Knob. See what we can see."

Sol nodded.

Topper put his hat back on. "We'll go after we lay Pa to rest. I'll show you the spot." He walked away then, and Sol headed back inside and found Elsa still sitting at the table with Jewel beside her. Nathan was sitting on the floor gnawing on a spoon.

"Reckon there'll be a funeral," said Sol. Elsa looked at him but said nothing.

"Lots of people will come," he said, trying again.

"Liquor people," Elsa said with a look of disgust on her face.

"I expect so. But he *was* your pa, my grandpa."

For the first time, Elsa seemed to recognize the truth of what he was saying. She reached out and took Sol's hand. "We will pay our respects," she said. "But that's far more than he ever did for anybody else."

Sol knelt by his mama and patted her hand. Elsa and her pa had long ago buried the natural love a daughter and pa ought to have for each other. He could see that was hurtful to her. Still, she'd somehow made her peace with it. He, however, felt different. Maybe it was because he knew so little about the Clacks, had never spent any time with them. To him they were bad people, sure. Yet they were also his kin. And in the highlands, love didn't usually matter near so much as blood did. Sol figured a person was what his blood made him, love or no. As far as he was concerned, if it was true that somebody pushed Hal Clack off that mountain, Sol would see to it he faced his just rewards. A lawman had no other choice. But even if he wasn't a lawman, he figured he would feel the same way. A grandson had no choice either, no matter how mean his grandpa had been.

CHAPTER SEVEN

Almost a year had passed since Abby lost her baby, yet she still felt weak most days, her body weary and her heart sad. She knew a lot of it wasn't just physical anymore, that some of her tiredness came from the grieving. Still, she pushed on and kept up the house, provided for her sons, and taught a Bible lesson every Sunday at Gospel Spirit, all the while doing all she could to keep Stephen happy.

When word came that Hal Clack had died, Abby decided immediately to travel to Blue Springs. It wasn't that she cared at all about Hal Clack, the Lord knew she didn't. But she did love Elsa, and no matter the strained relationship between Elsa and her pa, his sudden death was sure to shake her up some. And, just as important, Abby knew that Elsa, as the only surviving daughter, would be expected to play hostess to those showing up at the Clack house to pay their respects. She would need help with this, and Abby saw it as her duty to make sure she got it.

Leaving the boys in Mrs. Lollard's care, Abby took the train to Blue Springs, hopped off at about four in the afternoon with her one bag, and walked straight for the largest house in town—a two-story place of red brick, with eleven rooms, an indoor privy on both floors, and electrical lights in every room—all paid for with liquor money. That liquor money not only made Hal Clack the richest man around but also guaranteed him a big crowd for his going away. As mean as he was, people wouldn't come for any other reason. But now his boys had his dollars, and if folks didn't show their faces at Clack's laying out, one of his boys might take offense and as a result make their lives real miserable, and for a right long spell too.

As expected, Abby saw a lot of cars in front of the house when she arrived. There were only three horse-drawn buggies in sight. How much things had changed in just a few short years. She thought of Daniel's house farther up the mountain. He still had no paved road up there, no way for a vehicle to make the last mile or so. Though the world had changed all around him, Daniel and his family stayed pretty much the same.

Inside the Clack house Abby quickly made her way past the men sitting in the living room, some holding plates filled with food, and others standing with coffee in their hands or smoking their pipes. She wasn't surprised to find Elsa sitting at the head of the kitchen table and a number of other women scurrying around the kitchen keeping plates filled. Elsa's hair was pinned neatly on top of her head, and her navy blue dress was cinched at the waist and buttoned high on the neck. Abby hugged her, and the two of them held each other for a long time. Abby remembered the day Solomon died, recalled how Elsa had held up in spite of her sorrow.

"You all right?" she asked Elsa.

"I haven't talked to my pa for many a year," Elsa said. "It's not like we were close."

Abby started to respond but then held her tongue. She decided to let Elsa deal with this in her own way. Looking around the room, Abby noted, "The house looks real fine."

Elsa chuckled. "You should have seen it yesterday. With my pa and brothers caring for it, the place looked like a bunch of pigs had lived here. I cleaned all night."

Abby nodded, then asked, "Where's he laid out?"

Indicating the parlor across the hall, Elsa said, "The room's full of people right now. We decided to close the box. He's pretty beat up from the fall."

"Of course."

The Clack family held to the custom of laying out the deceased person in his own house for everybody to come and see. Someone would typically stay with the departed every hour of the night and day until the burial. They called it the Sitting Up Time, the time for folks to wait in the room with the dead and talk about the weather and the crops and eat fried chicken and potato salad as if it were a Fourth of July picnic. Children would dart in and out of the room, and the adults would shush them and eventually run them out. The women would knit and nurse their babies, all in full view of the dead. They would ask about each other's kin and who was marrying whom and when. The men would spend less time in the room than the women, coming in only now and again from the porch and the yard. When they did come to sit by the coffin, the men would smoke their pipes and pull their pistols from the waists of their britches to show to each other.

Every once in a while, somebody would walk over and gaze at the body for a moment and say how good the dead person looked, how peaceful and all. Some of the sitters would pray too, their voices usually loud enough for others to hear, as they wailed out what the deceased had meant to them.

Abby was glad the Clacks had chosen to close the coffin. The notion of staring into his rough face and not feeling sad—which she didn't think the Lord would approve of—made her squeamish.

"You want to go to the parlor now?" asked Elsa.

Abby sighed. She'd rather not go in there but felt she should. To not approach the coffin and say a short prayer would show disrespect to Elsa, and everybody would be sure to notice it. So, taking a deep breath, she said, "Let's go. I'm right beside you."

Elsa gripped her hand, and together they stepped across the hall. The coffin was set up in the center of the room. All the wood chairs arranged around the room were occupied. The smell of smoke from burning cigarettes and pipes caused Abby to feel faint. She backed up against the wall to brace herself and catch her breath. Elsa took her by the elbow.

"Come on," Elsa whispered. "It won't take but a minute."

Abby's eyes cleared, and she squared her shoulders and moved with Elsa to the dark-stained coffin. She recalled how Hal Clack had caused her family so much heartache, how every time she turned around it seemed he'd bested her pa one way or another. He had run them off their land, burned down their cabin. At the time, she thought he'd destroyed their lives forever. Through a strange turn of events, she had ended up living with Hal's wife, a good woman named Amelia. Then one day Hal came home drunk and mean and nearly killed her and Abby. If Amelia and Elsa hadn't faced him down and run him out . . . she pushed away the thought. Abby's heart warmed as she shifted to thinking of how Mrs. Clack had stood up for her. But then, some time later, on another terrible day, Hal Clack and his boys threw her out of Amelia's house, out into the street.

Standing by the coffin, Abby tried to think of something good about Hal Clack but nothing came to mind. She couldn't help wondering why God had allowed a man like him to live as long as he had. She heard someone move up behind her and figured it was Elsa. But then she felt hot, foul breath touch her neck.

"It's been a long time since I laid eyes on you," a man said.

Abby's stomach lurched when she recognized the voice. The blood drained from her face. She spun around and there stood Ben Clack, so close she could see the brown and yellow stains on his teeth. Her stomach roiled again and she felt sick. She looked for Elsa, but she'd wandered away to speak to somebody and hadn't noticed Ben sidling up to her.

With nowhere to run, Abby turned back and stared at Ben Clack, the younger of Hal's two surviving sons. He had a crooked nose and a patchy beard. Abby and Ben had some history together, a history that terrified her even now. She wanted to slap him and run from the parlor, except her legs refused to move. Anyway, how could she rush out without making a scene?

"You get prettier every time I see you," said Ben. "Dressin' real fancy too." He inspected her from head to toe, like a man eyeing a horse he wanted to buy. "That fancy green dress, pretty buttons and all, shiny black shoes. That citified husband makin' you happy buying you these fine clothes?"

Abby felt like she might throw up. How dare he talk to her like that? But the Clacks had no manners at all, not even the least shred of decency. She gritted her teeth and turned to leave, but Ben grabbed her by the arm. Abby quickly looked around; no one seemed to have noticed his behavior. She tried to pull away but it was no use. Ben held her tight.

"You and me messed up our first chance for romance," he whispered. "Maybe you been wantin' another one?"

Abby grew more frantic. Her shoulders knotted, and her knees wobbled. Somebody put a hand against her back. She recoiled against it, afraid that Topper Clack had come to join his brother in harassing her. She prayed for a way out of the situation.

"Sorry about your loss, Ben," said a voice from behind her, a voice she once knew well but hadn't heard in years. "I'm sure you are all broken up from it."

Ben Clack let go of her arm and stepped back a pace. Abby's heart raced. He'd rescued her again, just as he had so many years ago. She pivoted to see Thaddeus Holston standing behind her, the only man other than Stephen whom she had ever kissed.

"I'm surprised to see you here," said Ben to Thaddeus.

Thaddeus shrugged. "I was in town for a couple of days to see my sister. I heard about Elsa's pa and thought I ought to pay my respects to her."

"Well, I'm sure we all appreciate your thoughtfulness."

"I'm sure you do. But let me say that my coming here has nothing to do with you or your pa. I'm here for Elsa's sake, that's all."

Ben's fists balled up tight. Abby thought he would swing at Thaddeus. But Thaddeus seemed unmoved by the threat. As if dismissing a child from the room, he turned away from Ben and faced Abby.

Ben grabbed Thaddeus and swung him around, and the two men locked eyes. Abby wondered if Clack would actually start a fight right here at his pa's laying out.

"You finished visiting with Mrs. Waterbury here?" Thaddeus asked politely.

Ben hesitated, glanced around the room. "I reckon I am for now."

"Good," said Thaddeus, slowly removing Clack's hand from his arm and dropping it. "Seeing as how I'd like to talk with her alone, if I might. That all right with you, Mrs. Waterbury?"

She nodded, too shocked to argue. Not that she would have anyway. She wanted to talk to Thaddeus as much as he wanted to speak with her, probably more.

"You can be sure we'll be seeing each other again," Ben said to Abby. He walked away with her glare on his back.

"Shall we walk outside?" said Thaddeus.

Still feeling stunned, Abby took his offered arm and they left the room. So far as she could tell, nobody noticed what had just taken place between her and Ben and Thaddeus.

Abby pulled her sweater tight around her shoulders as she and Thaddeus stepped outside. She couldn't tell if she was feeling a chill in the air or if it was the fright from Ben Clack that caused her to begin shivering. Her throat felt tight too, as if someone had twisted a rope around it and squeezed. For several minutes they walked together without saying anything. Abby gazed at the sky. The moon shone down on them as if it had a personal interest in seeing which of them would speak first. They walked along Main Street and out past the school where she and Thaddeus had attended classes together so long ago. His pa had taught in the school, and his sister had once been Abby's closest friend.

As they strolled, Abby kept throwing glances his way. He hadn't changed much since the last time she saw him, the night before he left for the war, the night he proposed marriage to her. His blond hair still fell into his eyes. He stood maybe six feet and weighed real solid but not round anywhere. His eyes reminded her of the sky on a cloudy day. He wore a gray pinstriped suit and blue-and-gray tie. If she hadn't known better, she could have sworn he was a lawyer or businessman, somebody with a good eye for fashion. Of course, he did have an education—his schoolteacher pa had seen to that. So he ought to know how to dress properly. She wondered what he did for a living, hoped he might speak soon and tell her.

Abby smiled. She and Thaddeus had aggravated each other all through their childhood, never admitting they liked each other. Contrary to her desire to move away and see the world, he always said he loved Blue Springs better than anywhere else. He swore on his mama's grave that he would stay in Blue Springs forever, making a fortune as a lumberman.

"I'll fish the streams and shoot deer for food and mount the antlers on the wall of a cabin I'll build myself," Thaddeus used to brag. "The biggest cabin anybody in Blue Springs ever saw."

Well, he hadn't held to his oath to stay in Blue Springs, and Abby suspected she carried most of the blame for his breaking it.

They reached the Jesus Holiness Church. Thaddeus stopped and stared at the old building. "They put some new paint on the place," he said.

"They're taking care of the church pretty well. Got a new preacher too."

"He as good as Preacher Bruster?"

"Not quite as loud, but everybody seems to like him fine."

Thaddeus pointed to the front steps. "Care to rest a minute?"

Abby said yes, and the two of them sat down on the wood steps. "Be sure not to catch any splinters," he warned.

Abby smiled. Thaddeus always liked to make jokes. That had been one of the things she admired most about him. He'd always made her laugh, even when she had little cause for merriment. She wanted to hug him, friend to friend, to let him know she still cared for him. But she knew she couldn't do such a thing, for he might take it the wrong way.

They sat there silently on the steps, with Thaddeus fixing his eyes on the woods out past the church, his hands on his knees. The spring wind blew through Abby's hair. Thaddeus cleared his throat, looked at the sky.

She stared again at his face. A good face, smooth and even. She'd known that face a long time ago. But when did it grow up so? Had she changed as much as he had since they last saw each other? People changed, she knew that, on the outside at least. She wondered about Thaddeus's heart. Had that changed too?

From what she could see, some people stayed the same in their heart their entire lives. Those that started out mean just stayed that way as the years went by. Same with those kind and sweet; they stayed kind and sweet. But others got transformed somewhere along the way. Sometimes the ornery ones changed to become gentle and mannerly, and the sweet ones took on horns, their ways going from kindness to contrariness as quick as a caterpillar changes to a butterfly.

Had Thaddeus undergone any altering in his heart . . . in how he felt toward her? Did he still love her like he once had? Part of her hoped so. But another part, the wiser one, knew she shouldn't wish such a thing. Nothing could come of any love he might still hold, so it would be better for them both if he'd long since let it go.

"I guess it shocked you to see me back in town," he said, finally breaking the silence.

"That's a true statement if I ever heard one," she replied. "But it was a good shock, coming when it did and all."

"You want to know why I'm here?"

"I'm some curious. Lindy didn't tell me anything about it."

"Why would she?" he said, sounding slightly offended.

Abby studied her shoes. Since her move to Boone, she and Lindy hadn't stayed close. Both Lindy and Thaddeus had a right to some anger.

She remembered what had happened like it was yesterday. She had left Blue Springs while Thaddeus was abroad fighting in the war. Before he could return, she had disappeared from his life, started courting another man and eventually married him.

"I came to see Lindy to talk about some plans I have, maybe to leave here for good," said Thaddeus. "A coincidence you showed up at the same time."

Abby quickly faced him, her heart in her throat. The thought of him moving away permanently scared her more than it should have. But she couldn't help herself; she didn't want him to leave again. She wanted him to stay, to stay so . . .

She pressed her lips tightly together and told herself to stop dreaming. She had nothing to do with his life anymore. He could do as he pleased.

"I'm thinking hard about maybe moving to another country, to work with children who don't have much. Maybe in a place without a school, where I can teach kids how to read and write. Like my pa did."

Abby remembered Mr. Holston. He'd always thought well of her. Said she had a brain too big for her head. He told her she should get a college education, make something of herself. Mr. Holston was now in a nursing home near Knoxville. And Thaddeus was about to move for good as well. She figured she had driven him away.

"Where you think you're going?"

"Not sure just yet. Somewhere to teach, I reckon, work with children. That's what I've done the last few years."

They grew quiet again. A dog barked down the street.

Thaddeus stood and picked up a rock. "I knew you were in town." He threw the rock into the woods. "Lindy told me you came to help Elsa. I went to the Clack place hoping I'd run into you. Didn't know you'd have Ben Clack so close by, though."

"You saved me from a bad plight with him," Abby said, trying to keep her thoughts from the fact that Thaddeus was leaving and she felt sadder than a married woman ought to feel about it. "I was going to have to slap Ben if you hadn't come along."

He bent down and scooped up another rock. "I believe you would've done just that. From what I recall, you take care of yourself pretty well."

"I don't know about that. But I won't let Ben Clack treat me with such disrespect."

Thaddeus tossed the rock, then shoved his hands into his pockets and faced her. Abby wondered if he was wanting to say something but the words had gotten stuck in his throat. She sighed. Highlander men could be so backward when it came to speaking out loud what they wanted to say. Why did the men in her world keep so much tied up inside them?

"That Ben Clack can't leave you alone."

Abby rubbed her hand on the step. The wood was rough. "Nothing I can't handle," she said.

Thaddeus smiled. "You seem able to handle most anything."

She looked in the direction of the woods. "I'm not sure that is true. Least it feels different from that to me."

More silence. Thaddeus eased back down onto the steps. Abby wondered what would happen if someone walked by and saw her sitting so close to a man who wasn't her husband. She inched as far away from him as the steps would allow.

"Lindy told me in a letter all about your losing your baby girl last May," said Thaddeus.

Abby's breath caught at the memory. The hurt still stuck like a knife in her stomach when she thought of her little daughter, how beautiful she was lying in her arms. Abby hadn't had the strength to attend the gravesite when they lowered the tiny coffin into the ground, and she'd always felt guilty about that.

"I want you to know how sorry I am that she died. I wanted to come visit you, but then I thought maybe I shouldn't."

"It would have pleased me to see you," said Abby. "It was a mighty hard time."

Thaddeus stared into the sky. Abby wanted to say much more but knew she couldn't. How could she tell him that sometimes she wondered if she'd made a big mistake in leaving Blue Springs, not waiting for him? That maybe she shouldn't have married the man who was her husband? That it appeared circumstances had led her down a path she now regretted? How could she even admit this to herself? And what did this say about the Lord's will? Didn't the Lord want her to marry Stephen? Didn't she trust Him to make sure she stayed on the right path? But what about Stephen's drinking and the pain this caused her and the children? Surely the Lord didn't will that.

Abby pondered the matter for another minute. Maybe the Lord allowed folks to make choices for themselves. Maybe He kept on working with people even when they did things that weren't exactly in the square of His will. Even if someone had messed up at some point, the Lord still allowed some measure of happiness in that person's life. At least that's what Abby hoped. Stephen hadn't acted like a husband to her in a long time. How many months would this go on? How much longer could she share his house but not share intimacies with him?

Abby listened to Thaddeus's steady breathing. What should she do? How could she change Stephen? Or did she need to change something in herself—maybe make herself more beautiful or try to be more supportive of his needs?

She sighed. More than once over the last few years she'd wondered what would have happened if she had never left the mountain to go to school, if she had taken Thaddeus up on his offer of marriage. Would they have been happy together? Or would she have regretted giving up her dream of an education and blamed Thaddeus for keeping her on the mountain?

"I heard you almost got married," she said, leaving her questions unanswered.

Thaddeus shrugged. "I broke it off two weeks before the nuptials. Daughter of a house painter over in Valdese."

"I reckon you broke the woman's heart."

"She recovered okay. She already married another man. Had a baby too, a little boy." He sounded almost regretful.

"You think you missed your chance?" Abby asked the question before stopping to think what it might mean to him.

"No. I missed my chance when I lost you."

Abby rested her head on her knees. Some moments later she said, "I expect you and I would have had a hard time of it. You wanted to stay in Blue Springs, and I wanted to leave as soon as I could get a horse to carry me out."

"We could have found a way. Love always does, you know."

Abby's eyes glistened. Thaddeus seemed to know a lot about love—what it was and wasn't. At times she felt as if she had no idea. She cared for Thaddeus—she knew that. But had she ever loved him? Yes, in a certain way. But had she loved him the way a woman ought to love a man so as to marry him?

She stood and walked away from the steps, toward the woods, still thinking of Stephen. He had seemed so sophisticated when she met him. He had an education, plenty of dollars, a handsome face. He spoke well and took her to nice places. He had pretty much swept her off her feet with his city ways and high manners. But was that love? Or had it just made her feel as though she'd bettered herself with a man very different from her own origins?

A gust of wind blew through her hair. What was love, anyway? A rush of fire in the stomach, a thrill running through the body? Or was it a quiet trust, a sureness that a man would treat her well and stay loyal the rest of his life? Was it the security of knowing he'd talk to her on the porch as she rocked on hot summer nights, kiss her softly and hold her with his strong arms when the hard times came and tears ran down her cheeks?

Folding her arms, Abby faced Thaddeus again. Even if Stephen no longer acted much like it, she was still a married woman, and Thaddeus was going to move a long way off, maybe forever. What good did it do to wonder about love? She and Thaddeus would walk away from each other tonight and years might pass before they saw each other again, if ever. Could she let him do that? Leave that way? But she had no choice. A married woman had no right to ask a single man to do anything, much less stay close by so she could see him from time to time.

Determined to put away her silly notions, Abby walked back to the steps and laid a hand on Thaddeus's forearm. "I'll always think fondly of you," she said, gazing into his eyes. "And I'll pray for you as you go on your journey."

He put his hand on hers, and their eyes locked. Then, before she could stop him, Thaddeus leaned closer. His hands cupped her face. She knew she ought to pull away but her body wouldn't cooperate. He ran his fingers over her lips. Abby's breath came in quick gasps. She felt as if she were dreaming, powerless to stop what was happening. Her stomach fluttered, and she told herself she needed to back away. But she and Stephen had so many troubles, and he hadn't touched her at all in a long time. Was this love? What she felt now for Thaddeus? Or was it just her loneliness and grief over what had happened to her and her husband and their baby daughter?

Though she knew it was wrong, Abby wanted to let herself go, to see what it felt like to touch her lips to his once more, just once, like they'd done so long ago. She leaned closer to him—closer and closer—but then she stopped. How could she do this? She'd taken sacred vows with Stephen!

Breaking from her trance, she pulled away and covered her face with her hands. "I'm a married woman," she said, guilt rushing through her. "God forgive me . . . I'm sorry. . . ."

Her eyes tearing, Abby ran away from Thaddeus, not daring to look back to see if he might dare to follow her.

CHAPTER EIGHT

Sol met Topper and Ben Clack two days after the funeral to take a look at the spot on Edgar's Knob where their pa had fallen to his death. He'd hoped to make the trip the day after he first learned of Hal's death, but Topper had insisted he wait till they could go with him. Sol had a good suspicion as to why. If he went by himself, what was to keep him from looking around for their stills? Sol had no doubt that a still was set up somewhere close to where Hal Clack fell. Why else would a sane man spend any time up on Edgar's Knob?

The three men met at the general store. Sol noticed that Topper had on better clothes than he normally wore—clean black boots, gray wool pants, and a blue shirt with white buttons. In addition, he had kept his face shaved since the funeral, and his hair was combed with a neat part on the left side. Though he wanted to ask about the newly found attention to appearances, he knew he didn't dare. Highland men didn't talk of such things.

After exchanging howdies with one another, the three of them climbed into the county truck Sol was driving and drove the six miles or so to where the road ran out. At that point they got out and prepared to walk up the mountain. Edgar's Knob, a round chunk of rock on the back side of a group of hills at least thirty-five-hundred feet high, stood about three miles off the road. The angle of the mountain was steep, the path little more than a rocky ribbon curving up through the trees. Climbing to Edgar's Knob would not go easy.

Buttoning up his jacket, Sol hooked a canteen to his belt, adjusted his gun holster, and tossed his sheriff's hat onto the truck seat. The sun peeked out from behind a bank of clouds, warming him some in spite of the stiff breeze blowing around his ears. He looked at the Clacks. As usual, Ben wore a floppy black hat, muddy brogans, britches hitched high on his waist, and a flannel shirt. Apparently Topper's new style hadn't rubbed off on his brother. Each man carried a rifle.

Sol touched his pistol to assure himself the weapon was still there. "You boys ready?" he asked.

Ben pulled a flask from his britches and opened it. "I ain't never ready to walk up Edgar's Knob."

Topper laughed. "Don't be such a dandy man. A little walk up a hill never hurt nobody."

Sol started to object to the whiskey but then thought better of it. This wasn't the time to go off on the illegality of drinking spirits, not so long as the two Clacks had rifles matched up against his pistol.

Now, if it came to shutting down a still, that was a different matter. Let the Clacks drink themselves into an early grave, what did he care? But he'd do all he could to stop them from making whiskey and selling it to others. If they happened to come upon a still on the trip to Edgar's Knob, he would apply his hand to tearing it up, two rifles against one pistol or not.

Ben swigged from his bottle, and the men left the road and pushed into the underbrush. It didn't take long for the last piece of civilization to disappear. The only sounds now came from the woods, a scratching here and there as some animal hid from them as they passed, the whip of the wind as it pushed a tree branch from side to side.

His head down, Sol kept his thoughts to himself for the first couple of miles. The Clacks stayed silent too. Sol wondered what kind of men were underneath all the meanness. What were their families like? While they were his uncles, he knew almost nothing about them other than they were both married to plump mountain women who hardly ever spoke when in public, and they each had a few kids. Ben had three teenage boys and

Topper two girls, early teens maybe, and one son. None of the kids had married yet. From what he'd heard, Topper maybe had one or two more children with a woman not his wife.

From time to time Sol saw the Clack kids down in Blue Springs, although they stayed higher up in the mountains most of the time. He wondered about that too. Since the Clacks owned the fine brick house in town, why didn't the women stay there with their kids? Best he could figure, the Clacks wanted their women close by, which meant they all had to live in the rough cabins the Clacks kept up in the hollers. Not an easy life for the wives, but Sol concluded that any woman who took a Clack as her husband most likely knew the lay of the land before the nuptials.

Sol studied on the kids. Besides the fact they all had the dark hair and eyes of their pas and almost never attended school, he knew little else. The boys dressed in overalls, flannel shirts, and brown brogans, the girls in simple cloth dresses and boots only slightly fancier. They were pretty much a mystery to him and everybody else, strangers of a sort even in a town as small as Blue Springs.

Sol tried to figure how such a thing could happen—how a man could live so close to his kin and know almost nothing about them. True, the Clacks didn't mix much with townsfolk. But kin, no matter what had gone on between them, ought to know one another, he thought. Who were these men who had bedeviled his pa's family for so long? He knew they'd both lost brothers, both to the war and the flu epidemic that came not long after the war ended. Did they grieve over those losses? What did they fear? What did they think about before they nodded off to sleep at night? Surely the death of their pa had to have made a dent in their rough hides.

They had showed up drunk at their pa's funeral. And during the service at Jesus Holiness, Ben hadn't even sat in the front row with the family. Standing against the back wall, he'd watched the whole event with a flask in hand and a pistol in the waist of his britches.

"A bunch of hogwash," he had said of having the funeral in the church. "Pa never set foot in this place after he moved off from his folks. No reason for him to show up here now."

To some degree, Sol agreed with Ben. Why say Jesus words over a man when he died if the man hadn't cared anything about Jesus when he lived? Seemed a touch backwards to Sol, like trying to bring a pig indoors and put a nice shirt and pair of pants on him. The way he figured it, no words could preach a dead man into the bosom of the Lord. Once a body had breathed his last, his chances to get right with the Almighty had passed. Sol smiled to himself at the unintended rhyme.

About an hour after they started, Sol, Topper, and Ben reached a clear spot about two-thirds up the mountain where Ben threw up his hand for a break. In spite of the chill wind, sweat dripped from his face, and his breath came in short gasps. He doubled over at the waist. "Let's . . . let's rest a spell," he said.

Topper chuckled at his brother. "You're worser than an old woman," he said, wiping his face with a handkerchief. Ben waved him off and sat down on a rock, his body still bent over as he struggled to get some air.

Topper turned to Sol. "You weary too?"

Sol shrugged. "I can use a rest," he said. "Or go on, either way's fine by me."

Topper pointed to a rock beside Ben. "We might as well sit a spell. Ben here won't want to move again for at least fifteen minutes."

Sol eased to the rock and unhooked his canteen. He drank from it and then glanced at Topper. Without thinking, he held out the canteen. "Climbing can make a man thirsty," he said.

Topper laughed as he pulled a bottle from his britches. "A Clack don't like but one drink. And it ain't water." He tipped the bottle to his lips, took a drink, and offered it to Sol.

Sol shook his head. "I ain't a drinkin' man."

"I reckon you're not."

"I ought to arrest you for having them doublings."

Topper took another drink, then said, "No judge in these parts would convict me, you know that. Half of 'em buy liquor from me, the other half are kin."

Sol stared at the ground, realizing what Topper said was probably true. A Clack just about had freedom from the law in these parts. Between their money, their kin, and their guns, they ruled the area and he could do little to stop it. He considered again the fact that he had Clack blood in him. How did he feel about that? Nothing, he decided. He felt nothing. The Porter folks had always been his people, not the Clacks. The Clacks were nothing but sorry blockaders and crooks. The Porters, on the other hand, were God-fearing and hardworking. The two didn't mix, simple as that. He raised his canteen to his lips again and decided to change the talk to another direction. "I see your daughters down in Blue

Springs sometimes. Two of them, I think."

Topper nodded.

"They growin' up fast, looks like," said Sol.

"It seems so, happens to all of 'em."

"They are pretty girls from what I see."

Topper spat on the ground. "I reckon they are. Real trouble sometimes, though."

Sol thought of his little boy, Nathan, wondered what he would be when he grew up. "Ain't they all?"

Topper grinned, and for a second, a feeling of good will seemed to pass between the two men. But then Topper grunted and stood up. Sol could see the talk made him uncomfortable. He capped his canteen and stood too.

"Maybe we ought to head on up," Sol said.

"Reckon so."

Although Ben kept griping, they resumed their walk up to Edgar's Knob. Sol kept his head down, his thoughts turning again to the strife between the Porters and the Clacks. Why did men have to dislike each other just because they carried certain names? He knew most of the tale behind the feud between the two families. His pa and Hal Clack had both loved the same girl, Rose. Hal Clack's pa and Rose's pa had already reached an agreement about her marriage to Hal. Such things were done like that in the highlands in those days. But then Solomon Porter stepped into the picture, and Solomon and Rose fell in love.

After a good bit of discussion and deal making, Solomon talked Rose's pa into breaking off the agreement with the Clacks and letting her marry him. Hal Clack never forgave Solomon for taking his woman, started causing him trouble every chance he got. The bad feelings had lasted nearly fifty years now. Sol wondered if that would change now that both Solomon and Hal had died. Or would the rough feelings pass down to the next generation? So far it seemed so.

The trail got even steeper. Almost an hour went by, and they were still climbing. Sol glanced at Ben and Topper from time to time. Ben labored with his breathing. Topper seemed as well rested as if he were sitting in a rocker on his porch. The men fought their way through thick undergrowth, and Sol wondered how bootleggers got their makings to such hard-to-reach places. Had to have some serious motivation to do labor like that, he thought.

They came to a small creek and crossed over. Sol's legs ached. Ben cursed as he tripped on a tree root and almost fell. Topper laughed and Sol joined him. Ben glared at them both. Sol looked over at Topper and he appeared almost friendly, far easier in temper than Ben.

A few minutes later, the three of them rounded a curve and stepped onto a plateau that overlooked the back side of Blue Springs Valley. Sol took a deep breath. They'd finally reached Edgar's Knob. The huge rock jutted out from the mountain like a round knot poking out from a tree trunk. Though he'd never been here, Sol knew that Edgar's Knob was the only bare spot on the mountain for miles in every direction. It offered men like the Clacks a gathering place to build a fire, drink their whiskey, and gamble.

With Sol close behind, Topper slowly walked to the edge of the rock and stared down into the valley. Trees stretched out as far as the eye could see.

"Pa died right there," said Topper. He pointed to the rocks below Edgar's Knob.

Sol looked down and saw a ravine full of sharp boulders several hundred feet below. "How did you get him out?" he asked.

"We made our way down over there," said Ben, pointing to a slippery-looking path to his right, "and curved around them trees there." He indicated a stand of pines near the path. "Then we come up from the side. Had to use a rope to pull him out."

Sol studied the scene for a while. Nothing unusual jumped out at him. He scanned the valley but saw nothing strange, no smoke rising from anywhere to signal a working still. He turned and walked over to a hollowed-out spot in the rock. A couple of pieces of half-burned firewood lay nearby. Although he saw no ashes, Sol knew this was the spot for the fire. He wondered what had happened to the remains of the last fire here but then remembered it had rained hard for several days prior to Hal's death. The wind and rain must have washed the area clean.

Sol examined the space around the fire hole. A man's old boot sat by the firewood. Sol picked up the boot, looked it over, and put it back down. To his right he saw a metal can, upside down and wedged between a cluster of small rocks. A label advertising Dean's Beans was peeled halfway off the can's side, and Sol recognized it as a can of pinto beans sold at the general store. He picked up the can. It was empty. Underneath it, however, he found two cigar butts, each with a paper band wrapped at its tip. A couple of empty whiskey bottles lay next to the can.

Not sure why, Sol scooped up the trash and dropped it into the bean can. He then stood up and, with the can in hand, surveyed the area once more but saw nothing of any significance. "You got any notion whether your pa was up here alone?" he asked.

Topper and Ben shook their heads.

"You mentioned a business partner of your pa's," he said to Topper.

Topper shrugged. "I could've been wrong about that," he said. "No reason to cast no suspicions on anybody."

Sol gritted his teeth when he realized Topper didn't plan to give him a name. "I need your help if I'm goin' to do any real investigating here. I already told you once."

Topper took out his bottle and had a drink. Deciding to give him a minute to think, Sol moved to the edge of the rock and looked down into the valley.

Ben pointed a finger off to the left. "That's where your pa used to live," he said, a touch of satisfaction in his tone. "Back afore we took his land and burned down his place."

Sol's face turned red as he studied the area where Ben pointed. His pa had labored hard on that land almost his whole life to make it hospitable for his family. While he couldn't remember much about it, Sol and his brother, now dead, had once lived in the cabin Ben was so happy about destroying. But then Laban, his pa's eldest son, had lost it for all of them—the cabin and the land.

Although he knew he should keep quiet, Sol couldn't make himself do it. "A man can have all the land he wants," he said. "But if he don't have no honor, it don't matter how many acres he holds."

Ben took a step toward him, and Topper's hand tightened on his rifle. "Who are you to talk about honor?" said Ben. "You ain't a Clack or a Porter. You just a half-breed."

Sol squeezed the bean can. "I ought to throw you both in jail. The way you been drinkin' on the way up here. And I bet if I looked real close, I could find a still within a mile or so. You wanna dispute me on that?"

Ben laughed and raised his rifle. "Well, I ought to just go on and shoot you," he said. "Shoot you and push you down on them rocks where we found Pa."

Sol slowly set the can on the ground and moved his right hand to his pistol. Topper and Ben came a pace closer. Sol quickly weighed his options. Maybe he could shoot one Clack before the other one got him. But which one? Topper. Ben had been drinking more than Topper. Maybe Ben wouldn't be steady enough to aim straight.

His heart beating faster, Sol thought of Jewel and Nathan. What would happen to them if he died up here on Edgar's Knob? How long would it take for somebody to find him? Would the Clacks hide him after they killed him? Put him somewhere that would never be discovered?

Sol decided to ease the tension. He slowly raised his hands. "Let's just hold on here a second," he said. "No reason to lose our heads."

Topper lowered his rifle a little.

Ben glared at his brother. "You backin' down from this?"

"You show no more smarts than a possum," Topper said. "This man's the sheriff. A heap of people seen us head out with him. You think when we show back up and he ain't with us, nobody'll ask no questions?"

"But ain't nobody in Blue Springs can bother us," said Ben.

"He's the sheriff!" Topper repeated. "We shoot him and people beyond Blue Springs get involved. Not even we have the money to get ourselves out of that."

Although shaking his head in disgust, Ben finally got the picture and lowered his rifle. "I'll get my chance with you," he said to Sol.

"It'll give me pleasure to see that day come," Sol told him.

Ben glared once more at his brother and then stalked away.

Topper faced Sol. "Take another look around if you want," he said. "Before he drinks some more and forgets everything I just said."

Calmer now, Sol walked around the knob one more time but saw nothing. A couple of minutes later, Ben showed back up, and Topper gave him a sign. Sol picked up the bean can, and the three men began the trip back down the mountain, Sol with one hand on his pistol just in case Ben Clack wanted to start something again.

CHAPTER NINE

For most of the first year after he moved back to the mountain above Blue Springs, Daniel felt like he'd taken a hard slide backward. His spirits beat up, he walked slowly as he made his way up and down the steps of the cabin, his body weighing heavy on the staff his pa had given him. As if waking from a long sleep, his hip, injured in the war, started acting up badly, and he took to limping again, one foot dragging behind the other.

His old dream set back in on him, too. The one where his brother Laban walked up to him, dressed in his Army uniform, with his hands outstretched as if expecting Daniel to hand him something. From time to time, Solomon showed up in the dream and joined Laban, pa and son standing side by side, their hands open and ready for Daniel to lay something in them.

Daniel wasn't exactly sure what Laban and his pa wanted from him. Sometimes he thought they just wanted the land he'd promised to get back. In other moments, though, he sensed they expected something else. In his lowest moments, Daniel came to believe he had caused Laban's death. Maybe Laban wanted Daniel to give him back his life. And what about Solomon? Daniel carried his cane now yet felt he wasn't worthy of it anymore. Maybe Solomon wanted him to return it.

Usually he woke up when the dreams troubled him, sat straight up in bed in such a sweat that it streaked down his back and soaked his nightshirt. But he was cold instead of hot. So he shivered in the sweat and thought of pouring a shot of whiskey down his throat to warm himself up. The temptation for liquor made him shiver even more, because it had been coming on him with more regularity these days, and he didn't know why. In fact, his desire for a drink scared him more than the dreams. He knew what the doublings could do to a man, how they could take his head away, make him mean like the Clacks or reckless like Laban or lazy like so many other highlander men. Sometimes Daniel shook so much that he had to hug Deidre real close to make the shaking stop.

Not knowing how to treat his troubles, Daniel kept on doing the only thing he knew to do. He put his shoulder to laboring. It was what his pa had done when hard times sat down on him. Day after day he gave the sun some company as it rose, stayed with the sun all day long, and then witnessed its settling down for the night. Chores were plentiful, and Daniel seemed bent on making them less so. Plant the garden, dig out the weeds, cut and stack firewood for winter, fix the loose roof shingles and the fence around the hogpen, dam up a part of the creek for a swimming hole for the children. Daniel did what needed doing and then some.

While it was true the place had been in fairly good shape from the work Solomon and Elsa had done on it over the years, Daniel and Deidre improved it even more, as much as their few dollars would allow. By the time their first year in the place had come and gone, the cabin, barn, fences, and garden were as good as most any on the mountain.

September of 1931 rolled around, and Daniel decided to put Marla and Ed in school even though no one knew how long the school would be able to stay open, what with the money from the state drying up fast because of the times. That first morning, he walked them about a mile and a half down the dirt trail that led to the paved road that led to Blue Springs. From there they'd catch a ride with some neighbors a half mile away who had a truck and a brother old enough to drive it.

"You'll go to school so long as the door's open," Daniel told them that morning. "And your brother Raymond too, just as soon as he's old enough. Schoolin' will make you smart so you can make a good livin' someday."

Marla and Ed, their lunch buckets held tightly, nodded and hopped on the truck for the ride to school.

The days passed by as Daniel and Deidre kept hard at work to scrape out a living. They knew many who hadn't made it, who found themselves having to turn to the government for aid. But the government had only so much to give, and Daniel had promised himself he wouldn't go with his hand out and ask for help from anybody. He didn't have much pride left, but what he still had, he intended to keep.

For someone who grew up in the city, Deidre took quickly to tending the cabin and farm, her wiry body hoeing, hauling, cooking and cleaning. This freed Daniel to take on some odd jobs now and again—a little building here and there, repairing cabins and barns, and digging out wells. He even started fixing autos. Daniel's neighbors learned fast that they could call on him when they were in a pinch and he could figure a way to do almost any job they had. A few of them actually paid him for his toils. Others made promises of payment but later were unable to give him any money.

Daniel didn't fuss with them either way. When he finished a task, he took the promised wages if they were offered but said nothing when they weren't. It would all even out in the end, he figured. If he needed somebody's help one day and had no dollars to pay for it, maybe they'd return the favor.

So he kept to the sweat of his labors all through that fall, and the bad dreams seemed to come a little less often. He began to feel a sense of resignation about what had happened to his pa's land. True, he hadn't kept the promise he'd made to his pa and brother. But he had done all he could, had bent his shoulders toward working and saving every dollar. Even so, it hadn't fallen to him to own the land again.

At times he wondered if maybe God had foiled his chance at the land. Maybe the Almighty had another plan for him that he didn't yet understand. Maybe it was to test his faith, to see if Daniel would haul off and leave Him if what he wanted didn't come his way. Maybe he needed to bow his head and bend his knees and accept the will of the Almighty.

Determined to let go of his resentments, Daniel's heart gradually took on a feeling of quiet. Except on his worst days, he gritted his teeth and did his chores in thankfulness to sweet Jesus that he at least had a home, a family and some friends he could trust. Lots of men didn't have nearly as much.

Daniel also figured that maybe he could try for the land again someday, after the country got back on its feet and there was more paying work to go around. Just stay patient, he thought, let things settle down some. Bad times can't last forever. Who knew what the next year might bring?

One day, as September was approaching its end, Daniel washed up at the well outside his back porch, ate supper with Deidre and the kids, then strolled out onto the porch to light up his pipe. His stomach full of green beans, potatoes, corn bread and coffee, he felt more contented than he had for a long time.

He lit his pipe and stared out at the ridge beyond his cabin. The trees were fully clothed in their fall colors. The breeze picked up. He glanced at the sky and saw that a group of thunderheads had rolled in from the distance but not so close as to cause him concern. Looked like they might get a storm later that night. His dog Whip stepped onto the porch from the yard and nuzzled his knee.

"You want to go for a walk, boy?" said Daniel as he patted the dog. Whip yawned and lay down, resting his head on his paws. "Reckon not."

Daniel stepped back inside the house, grabbed his walking cane, told Deidre he wanted to walk a spell, and moved back outside. Off the porch now, he headed up the hill behind the house. As he often did about this time of day, he went up to his pa's grave and sat down beside it. Laying his cane down, he took off his hat, placed it in his lap and bowed his head. The wind picked up some more, and Daniel's hair blew across his forehead. He brushed it back and checked the sky. The clouds had gathered a little closer. Might rain sooner than he'd first thought. But still not for a little while yet.

He turned to his prayers again. He felt near to Jesus here under the oak tree with Solomon and Walter close by. It wasn't that he didn't go to church. He did, every time it met. But the preachers at Jesus Holiness came and went real often these days, and he found it hard to feel close to a man who showed up to shout and stomp for only a year or so before moving off. He missed Preacher Bruster from his boyhood days.

Daniel prayed for Abby, who had lost her baby over a year ago and almost died in the process. And, though he didn't know this for sure, he suspected she had some troubles with her husband, a snobbish man he didn't much like.

He prayed for Sol, too. He took his sheriffing job real serious. So much so that he spent a lot of time looking for stills, a dangerous way to make a living in the highlands. A man playing with a rattlesnake had a better chance of not getting hurt than a man bent on bringing blockaders to justice. Not only did the one looking for the still have to stay out of rifle shot of the still's owner, but others who had no direct link to the operation might also fire a bullet his way simply because highlanders took no shine to somebody interfering with the making of whiskey in their parts. And it didn't matter that Sol had pure mountain blood running in his veins. From what Daniel could tell, the threat of gunplay didn't slow Sol one bit.

He prayed for Elsa next. She'd dealt with Solomon's death about as well as anybody could expect, jumping in to all the activities in Blue Springs just about as soon as she moved back there. Close to seven hundred people now lived in the eight-mile-long by three-mile-wide stretch known as Blue Springs Valley. A group of ladies from Jesus Holiness met at Elsa's house at least twice every month. Men called on Elsa as well. Three widowers had made trips to her porch in the last four months. She'd spoken politely to each, but then refused their offers to go walking or sit beside them in church.

"Solomon Porter is a hard man to come after," she said when someone asked her about her new suitors. "After living with Solomon for so long, these new gentlemen seem too citified."

Daniel smiled. Nobody but Solomon had seen much good in her when they first married. Everybody said she had too much fight in her bones for a woman, too uppity to live in peace with a mountain man. Who knew then what a good woman she would become? That a woman with Clack blood in her could be so kindhearted.

Daniel's prayers moved from Elsa to his wife and three kids. The Lord had truly blessed him with them. Sure, he and Deidre had wanted one or two more maybe, but like a lot of mountain women, she had lost a couple of babies before they made it to the light of day. Part of the nature of things, women not finishing with all their children. The Lord's way of keeping balance, Daniel figured. Too many kids and a man couldn't feed them all.

Deidre had taken her losses with a steady heart, without complaining. She never said anything harsh about having to give up her life in Asheville to move here with him. If God ever made a true saint, Deidre had all the necessary qualities. He loved her—that was a pure fact.

Daniel heard a loud crack, and the ground shuddered under him. It sounded like somebody had pushed over a maple tree with one shove. He opened his eyes and saw that the sky had turned almost black. A shot of lightning suddenly cut through it, lighting up the whole sky. The hair on the back of his neck stood up. Then the wind started howling. Daniel grabbed his hat, shoved it on, and jumped to his feet. Another bolt of lightning struck a tree not more than a hundred yards away. He smelled burnt wood. The rain started then, a few spatters at first, then a sheet of solid water before he could even pick up his cane.

He took off running toward the cabin, his hip hurting him with every stride. Lightning flashed at shorter intervals now, and he recalled how it felt back in the war when the bombs exploded, a feeling that one of the bombs had his spot all marked out and no matter what he did, he wasn't long for this world. He thought of dropping down and hugging the ground for all he was worth, but he knew that, whether a bomb or bolt of lightning, it wouldn't make any difference. If either had him in its sights, then it would be all over—hugging the ground or not.

Soaked to the bone, Daniel broke into the clear from the woods and pushed faster for his cabin, about fifty yards away, his hip burning. Not more than thirty yards from the cabin, the hip locked up and he fell, his chin digging into the ground and his cane flying from his hands. The rain poured down on his head as he scrambled up. He'd just laid his hands on the cane again when another bolt of lightning shot out of the sky, a cut of silver so sharp it looked like a knife blade thrown from God's own hand to the earth. Daniel threw a hand up to shield his eyes.

The lightning smacked the cabin a little past the chimney on the front side, leaving a charred crack where it hit. The building seemed to quiver for a second. Instantly the roof caught fire.

Moving as fast as his hip allowed, Daniel reached the cabin and threw his body up the back steps. Deidre and the kids rushed out the door and met him on the stoop, their eyes wide. The wind continued to howl.

"Get the kids to the cellar!" Daniel shouted, pointing to a spot ten feet away where his pa had dug out a hole to store food during the winter. "Then we got to stop the fire!"

Deidre hurried off with the children. Daniel dropped his cane, rushed to the back porch and grabbed two buckets. In the yard again, he ran to the well and hauled up a bucket of water. Deidre showed up a few seconds later carrying a ladder.

"I'll bring the water!" she shouted.

Daniel took the ladder and headed toward the burning roof. He knew it was crazy. If the rain couldn't put out the fire, what good would the few buckets of water he threw on it do? But he couldn't just stand by and do nothing while it burned.

Seconds later he climbed up the ladder, a bucket of water in hand, with Deidre on the ground and holding the other. The wind tugged on the ladder, and Daniel thought the force of it might push him and the ladder away from the building. So he leaned forward, pressing his body against the ladder to keep it steady.

Between thunderclaps he heard a whining sound that suddenly broke into a bark.

Whip!

"Where's Whip?" he yelled down at Deidre.

"I don't know!"

Another bark sounded, and Daniel's heart sank. The dog was still inside!

Quickly Daniel tried to figure what to do. Let the dog die and try to save the cabin? Or go after the dog while it burned? It took just an instant to make the decision. He scrambled down the ladder. Deidre shouted at him to stop, but he refused to listen.

Headed to the cabin door, he took off his shirt and wrapped it around his mouth and nose.

"No!" yelled Deidre. "That dog's not worth risking your life!"

But Daniel didn't hesitate. No matter that Whip was only a dog. He was a loyal animal, had been for him and for his pa before him.

At the door, Daniel held his breath and pushed inside. Flames licked at him from the right, and a wave of black smoke billowed out of the house as he moved into the front room. He had a hard time seeing; his eyes burned from the smoke and his nose refused to take in air. He ducked lower, bent at the waist.

"Whip!" he called. "Whip!"

He heard a bark to his left, from the front room. "Here boy!" he shouted. He heard movement, then something nudged him on the knee. It was Whip. He grabbed the dog and hauled him to the front porch. Daniel set Whip down, and the dog immediately took off toward the woods.

The rain continued to pour. Daniel dropped his shirt to the ground, took a huge breath, and ran back to the side of the cabin. He saw Deidre on the ladder and called for her to come down. She started down, her hair drenched, her clothes sticking to her body. Daniel helped her off the ladder, then took her place after her feet hit the ground.

For the next fifteen minutes, he and Deidre fought the fire, the water in the buckets joining that from the sky in an effort to keep the cabin from burning to the ground. Bucket after bucket, Deidre ran between the well and the ladder, with Daniel hauling the buckets up and throwing the water at the flames. Before long, his arms ached from the lifting and his hip seemed to burn as hot as the roof. He could see that Deidre ached as much as he did, but she didn't complain as they fought together to save as much of the cabin as possible. Gradually, in spite of the rain and the bucketfuls of water they threw on it, the fire continued to spread. Daniel's body felt about ready to give up, yet he forced himself to keep pushing—up and down the ladder, one bucket after another. Tears mixed in with the rain streaming down his face, and his face burned—not only because of his closeness to the flames, but also because of his shame, shame that he'd once again failed to stop a bad thing from happening to him and his kin.

As the flames spread and he saw that he could do nothing to stop them, Daniel's shame turned to another feeling—pure rage—hot anger against the power that had sent the lightning from heaven above. Without realizing it, he started to groan in a deep-throated roar, a protest against everything God had thrown against him. Soon the groan turned into shouting, loud and mournful, questioning why such terrible things seemed to befall him at every turn.

Rearing back on the ladder, Daniel pitched his water bucket up toward the sky, a puny effort to smack God in the face. The bucket hung in the air for a second as the wind caught it, but then quickly dropped back down, aiming straight for his head. He moved to avoid the bucket and watched it hit the muddy ground beside Deidre's feet. She looked up at him with black smudges on her face. Daniel stared at her for several seconds and then at the bucket and then for some strange reason he started to laugh.

It wasn't a laugh of joy, though. It was more the laugh of a man right near to craziness, one who knew that no matter what he did or did not do, Almighty God had conspired against him to make his life as miserable as possible.

It didn't matter, Daniel decided as he laughed. Virtue or none, a man received what God wanted to give him. Bootlegger or Jesus man—none of that counted. The rain and the fire could fall on both the same. All a man could do was face up to what he received and make the most of it, life or death, prosperity or hunger.

Giving up on putting out the fire, Daniel climbed down the ladder, dropped to the ground and opened his arms to Deidre. She stepped into them, and he hugged her as tight as he could. The rain ran down his face and into his beard, the wind still blowing hard. But Daniel barely noticed. In that instant, Deidre was the only thing real to him, the only thing between him and the addled life of a crazy man, the only thing separating him from the sudden desire to get his hands on a jug and forget everything, including God.

Deidre looked up, and he gazed into her eyes like a lost man searching for a light to show him the way home. Overhead the rain fell even more fierce, even as the wind up and died away.

He kissed Deidre, a tender brush of the lips that said no matter what happened, they'd get through it together. Deidre hugged him tight. Daniel closed his eyes, knowing that so long as he had her and the kids, he could deal with most anything God put in his path. He broke off the kiss but still held her close.

Moments later, the rain began to let up some.

"Look, Daniel," Deidre said, directing his attention back to their cabin.

He glanced over his shoulder. To his surprise he saw that the fire had almost stopped. The rain had finally drenched the roof to the point it could burn no more.

Whip emerged from the nearby woods. Daniel whistled, and the dog sprinted toward him, his spirits apparently as light as if nothing had happened. Daniel patted the dog on the head.

"You had no business going after this fool dog," said Deidre.

"But he's part of the family," said Daniel. "Aren't you, boy?" Whip wagged his tail.

With nothing more to say on the subject, Deidre just shook her head. Daniel gave her his full attention again, hugging her close. The two stood still and watched as the fire flickered once or twice more as if to flare up again but then died completely. Ed and Marla suddenly appeared from the cellar, Raymond on Ed's hip. The kids huddled close, their faces wet and frightened.

The rain ceased completely now, leaving only the sound of dripping water, the hiss of the doused fire, and the occasional distant rumble of thunder.

"It ain't all burnt," Marla said, pointing to the cabin.

"Mostly just the one side," added Ed.

Daniel stared at his kids. Marla now eleven, Ed nine, Raymond three. They were growing up fast. Marla was much like him, with her dark hair and eyes. Ed took after his ma in his round face, high cheekbones. Raymond was a cross between the two.

Realizing he needed to stay strong for them and Deidre, Daniel gathered the kids close and walked them to the cabin to inspect it. The roof had a jagged black hole not far from the chimney, with the side nearest the chimney having caved in some. But the rest of the place still looked solid. Daniel told the kids to wait in the yard while he and Deidre took a look inside.

They crossed the front porch and stuck their heads through the doorway. The smell of burnt wood filled their nostrils, but at least it appeared safe enough for everybody to go back in.

Daniel stepped back onto the porch. "Come on," he called, motioning to the kids. "It ain't as bad as it could have been."

"Not as good either," said Deidre.

Daniel nodded. The five of them went inside, with Whip staying on the porch. Water dripped in on the left side from the open hole in the roof, and smoke had turned the walls a sooty black. It took Daniel a while to size up all the damage. The kitchen had suffered the most, the biggest of the three rooms they used for sleeping the least. For sure, the roof over the kitchen would need to be completely rebuilt.

"It'll be like cooking outside," said Deidre.

Daniel checked the chimney next and, to his relief, saw that it was undamaged. "I'll set to working on the kitchen roof first," he said. "Then the sleeping rooms."

"Some hard labor ahead of us," said Ed.

"Seems like there always is," said Deidre.

"Maybe that's the way the good Lord wants it," said Daniel.

"I wish the good Lord would let us rest a little every now and again," said Deidre.

"We'll rest plenty when we pass on to glory," said Daniel.

"Reckon so," said Deidre.

"You and the kids go on back to our room, see if you can make it passable for sleeping tonight. I'll start pickin' up the mess in the kitchen."

As Deidre and the kids left, Daniel picked up a piece of wood that had fallen from the roof and opened the back door to toss it out. Whip came along and pushed his nose against his knee. Daniel threw the wood into the yard, then stooped to pet the dog. The strength he'd showed for his family's sake suddenly disappeared, and he almost toppled over. But then, looking out, he spotted his walking stick lying flat in the mud. For a couple of seconds he stayed still and stared at it. What sense did the carvings on the cane make at a time like this? None, that's what. No sense at all.

Daniel tried to look away but then he thought of Moses and his staff, how God had used the staff to give Moses courage when he was afraid, how God turned it into a serpent in front of Pharaoh.

Well, he wasn't Moses, that was for sure. His cane wasn't able to come alive either, wasn't able to come alive and scare nobody and nothing. It was just an old stick—left behind by an honorable man, sure. But still an old stick and nothing else. For a second he considered leaving the cane where it lay. What good had it done him to follow the Lord its carvings pointed to? But then he knew he couldn't leave it in the yard.

Despite the fact that the cane had no power to make his life different, it still comforted him somehow, reminded him of his pa, the way Solomon Sr. used to protect him. Well, he didn't have a pa to do that anymore. He was on his own. All the responsibility for his life and his family rested on his shoulders. But he still loved that old stick.

Daniel stood and limped down the steps and over to the cane. Again he stared at it. The sun came from behind a cloud and landed directly on the cane, and the water on it glistened. It seemed strangely bright all of a sudden, almost glowing, almost as if it had fire inside. Daniel thought of Moses at the burning bush, stepped back a pace, then jumped as he felt something touch his leg. He laughed as he heard Whip whine for his attention. Nothing alive here but him and his dog.

Daniel bent down and picked up the cane. The wood felt cold, and mud caked it. Daniel chuckled again. Spooked by a soggy old stick. What a superstitious man he'd become. Like the witchy woman who lived way up past Edgar's Knob, the woman who made soup with spider webs, turtle necks, and rabbit innards.

Laying the cane across his shoulders and neck—one end pointing east, the other west—Daniel stared into the yard. His shadow stretched out over the wet ground, and he felt as empty as the shadow, as dead as if shot through with a rifle's bullet.

"I reckon it ain't meant for me to make no progress," he said to the sky. "No matter what I do, I keep bangin' my head against a wall that I ain't had no hand in building."

Whip pushed against Daniel's leg. Daniel yearned for a way to escape all this, to put all the hurts and struggles behind him. The desire for a bottle of whiskey rose up in his throat. He licked his lips. He hadn't tasted liquor since his seventeenth year, back when he was young and eager to try everything, even the doublings. In spite of the fact that he'd never developed a craving for whiskey, he now suddenly felt a need for it.

"I don't know how much more I can take," Daniel said to Whip. The dog whined as if he understood.

Daniel took the cane from his shoulders and squeezed it in his hands. He wondered if his bad dreams would come back again and he would have to start staying awake to avoid them. If that happened, he knew his strength would run low. His hip would hurt more and more, and he'd find it hard to labor all day long to rebuild the cabin. Daniel looked down at his dog. "You ever wish you could just run off somewhere?" he said.

Whip tilted his head as if to ponder the question.

"You know, just leave everything behind?" Daniel patted the dog on the head. He'd gone plumb crazy, he figured, first spooked by a cane and now talking to a dog. But he had to talk to somebody. He felt trapped, boxed in on all sides by forces he couldn't control, promises he'd made that he couldn't keep, no matter how hard he tried. He wished he could scream out at everything, throw up his hands, and get out of the trap that had snapped on him. Yet he realized that wasn't possible. He had a family to watch over. So long as he thought he could help them, he wouldn't leave them alone.

Wiping his eyes, Daniel squared up his shoulders and told himself it didn't matter if his dreams returned. Dreams or no dreams, sleep or no sleep, a man couldn't just sit down in the road and quit. He had to keep plugging along, taking one step and then another, pushing on till glory came and he received his just rewards.

Daniel patted Whip and then trudged back toward the cabin to get to work. Whatever God had in store, he had to deal with it. No escaping hard times for a highlander man who had any pride about him, no escaping at all.

CHAPTER TEN

Sol met Topper and Ben Clack at the general store almost six months after going up to Edgar's Knob with them to see the spot where their pa had died. Entering through the front door, he saw them standing by a table near the back. As usual, Ben looked like a hog that had rooted all night in the mud. But Topper seemed to have made the turn toward a more respectable appearance, that Sol had noticed the last time he saw him, a permanent thing. He wore black pants with a good crease, a brown shirt with little or no wrinkles, and a black hat with a band around it. Only a small amount of dirt covered his boots.

Curious, thought Sol. Maybe his new position as head of the Clack family business had made Topper tend to his untidiness. If so, did that mean he planned to straighten out in other ways, too? Or was the new look just a fancy way to cover the same old manner of doing things?

Sol moved toward the Clacks, the floors creaking under his shoes. The store smelled like old wood and coal smoke, and the shelves were nearly empty. Sol knew that goods like flour, beans, and sugar had gotten scarce since the bad times had come. If something didn't change soon, people might start to get truly fearful.

"Hey, boys," Sol said. "You two doin' all right today?"

"What do you care?" asked Ben.

"Just trying to be neighborly."

"Well, don't," said Ben. "We all know this ain't no social call."

"That's true," Sol agreed, laboring to maintain an even tone. "I've been nosing around some regarding your pa's demise."

Ben grunted but Topper pointed to the chairs around the table. "Reckon we oughta sit," he said.

Sol took a seat and Topper joined him. Ben remained standing, his rifle no more than a quick reach away by the wall. Sol glanced at Topper as if to tell him to keep his brother under control, but Topper only shrugged and Sol knew that Ben did what Ben wanted, older brother or not. His tensions rose some.

Topper lifted a coffeepot and offered him some. Sol saw a cup on the table and picked it up. Topper poured coffee into it. "You find out anything?" he asked as he poured some coffee into his own cup and set the pot down.

"Maybe," Sol said. "Still got some more checking to do, though."

"You've had six months," snarled Ben. "If I didn't know better I would think you didn't want to find who killed my pa."

Sol clenched his teeth and reminded himself to stay focused. Despite Ben's meanness, the Clack boys had every right to stay on him if they thought something fishy was connected with their pa's death. And if Hal Clack had died at another man's hands, then Sol had a duty to make sure the killer met up with justice. He pushed aside his dislike for Ben and pulled a paper sack from his pocket and opened it. "You recall I found these up at Edgar's Knob," he said.

Ben jerked the bag from his hand. "What you got there?" He opened the sack and dumped the contents on the table. Two items fell out.

Ben threw the sack onto the table. Sol scooped up the two items. "You saw me pick these up that day we visited the knob," he continued. "This here's about a third of a cigar." The word came out *see-gar*. "I found two of these, if you recollect. Well, this is the band that went around it."

Topper reached over and took the cigar stub from him. "So somebody was smoking a cigar. Who cares about that?" He threw the cigar on the table and leaned forward as though challenging Sol to come up with something more substantial.

"It ain't just the cigar that matters," said Sol. "It's the band too. You ever seen one like it?" He handed the band to Topper.

Topper held it, rolled it in his fingers. "Not from around here, is it?"

"My point exactly. That band says it's a Monarch cigar. You don't buy them in Blue Springs."

Ben took the cigar off the table. "Pa didn't smoke these that I ever saw," he said.

"So they ain't your pa's?"

Ben shrugged. "Could be he smoked one with some feller. Or the feller smoked them both with Pa. But they ain't both Pa's, I'd swear to that."

"Pa did business with lots of folks from out of town," Topper said. "The fact that you find a cigar from somewhere other than Blue Springs don't mean nothin'."

Sol nodded. "That is a truth, for sure. But this cigar was still pretty dry and fresh when I found it. Hadn't been up there too long. And if you remember, it rained the day before your pa died. If that cigar had been up there then, it would've been wet when I found it. So whoever smoked it did it on the night your pa died."

"But it was under a can," said Ben.

"Yeah, but that don't matter," Sol answered. "The rain would've still made a puddle under the can, made everything wet, maybe even washed it away."

Topper said, "You thinkin' whoever smoked this Monarch might've done harm to my pa?"

"Nah, I ain't sayin' that, least not yet. We found two of 'em. Maybe your pa and this fellow smoked together, celebratin' a deal of some kind."

"Or maybe," suggested Ben, "he and Pa smoked and then he went ahead and pushed Pa right off the ledge in the middle of the celebratin'."

Sol shrugged. "Either way, whoever smoked this cigar might know something about what happened. Probably a good idea to find him and ask him."

Topper glanced at Ben, and Sol thought he saw something pass between the brothers. He opened the paper sack and extended it to Topper, then Ben. They dropped the cigar butt and band back into the sack. Sol cleared his throat and weighed how to get at the question he needed to ask next. No fancy way came to him so he just said it out plain.

"You boys got any idea about who might smoke a fancy cigar like this?

Any help you could give will make it easier to know what happened up there."

Topper stared at the table, and Ben leaned back against the wall.

Sol thought maybe he needed to ask his question again but then Topper shook his head and said, "Nobody comes to mind right off. But, just so you know, whoever smoked this ain't from around here."

Sol tried another notion. "You got any idea where somebody would most likely buy these Monarch cigars?"

"Asheville maybe," said Ben.

Sol nodded. "I already made a call down to Asheville. A lawman down there checked a couple of the fancier stores. No Monarchs around that he could find. You know of any other places?"

"Reckon not," said Topper. "Maybe we can do some checkin'. With Pa gone, Ben and I have been doing the travelin' he used to do. Business an' such."

Sol rubbed the back of his neck. They all knew the kind of *business* Topper was talking about. And they all knew that if they actually did find the man who smoked the Monarch with Hal Clack, it was a sure bet the man had some dealings with illegal whiskey. Might even be the messenger between the Clacks and the folks who bought and distributed their makings. Catching him might lead to big problems for the Clacks.

What if they caught the man who killed their pa and they took him to the police and he told all about their moonshining and the location of the Clack stills? What if he made a deal with the law to turn in the folks who bought from him? Such a thing would do a lot of damage to the Clacks' livelihood.

But if that man had killed their pa, wouldn't the Clacks want him hauled in to pay for his crime? Wouldn't their desire for revenge weigh out heavier than their need to keep their whiskey trade going? Or would the Clacks take the law into their own hands so as to try and have it both ways?

Sol thought he might surprise them, see how they jumped. "Law down in Asheville said a man at one of the stores they called said about the only place he knew to buy a Monarch was up in Chicago. Your pa ever visit up there?"

Topper quickly looked at Ben again, and although not sure, Sol believed he'd shaken them up some. But then a grin broke out on Topper's face.

"You a smart man," he said to Sol. "'Course Pa always gave that to you Porters—being smart and all. You thinkin' you can spring something on us, get us to say something maybe we ought not to say."

Sol shrugged. Topper was obviously pretty smart himself. Best not to underestimate him. In a tight spot, such a thing could cause a lawman trouble.

Topper continued. "You think you got it all figured, don't you? We give you a name. You bring him into Blue Springs or maybe Asheville for some investigatin'. Law knocks him around some. Promises him they'll go easy if he helps them out. He blabs to you about our business, everything you need to know. Maybe he even lays some blame on the other side too, the boys in the big cities who make even more dollars than we do from our product. You come out a hero, maybe get your name in the paper, here and in Asheville too. That what you got figured?"

Sol rolled up the sack, placed it on the table. "But what if this man killed your pa? Don't you want me to ask him some questions?"

Topper put his hands on the table. A heavy breath escaped from his chest. He stared Sol straight in the eyes. "You listen here," he said. "If Pa was a-sittin' here today, he would say this. He would say that he was dead and the business was now in our hands, mine and Ben's. He would say we should not go to no law to square up our accounts for us. If somebody killed him and justice needs to get done, he would tell us to go on and do that justice. Then he would tell us to make sure the business keeps goin'. Pa cared more about the business than anything, you know that."

"So you're not going to give me a name?" asked Sol.

Ben grunted. "We're all done with you. You told us what we wanted to know. We can handle it from here."

Sol looked at Ben. It wouldn't surprise him at all if the two brothers tracked down the Monarch smoker, then stabbed him in the back. Or maybe they'd act like they didn't know a thing, invite the man back to Edgar's Knob for more business, and when they had the chance, push him off like maybe he did their pa.

Sol squared his shoulders. "You go takin' your revenge on somebody around here and I'll not hesitate to make you pay for it," he said. "You don't know for sure what happened, whether anybody had a part in causin' your pa to fall from that rock. So leave it to me to find the man if there even is one and get to the bottom of this."

Ben took up his rifle and stood up straight. "We're obliged for your help," he said. "Best you go now."

"If you won't tell me nothin' else, then I'm at a dead end with this whole mess," said Sol.

"Reckon that's so," said Topper. "Like Ben said, we'll take it from here."

"Just remember, you do anybody any harm in my jurisdiction and I'll slam my jail shut on you both and throw the key in the woods."

Ben chuckled. "You make a lot of threats. Too bad you ain't man enough to back 'em up."

Sol slowly stood. He'd just about had enough of Ben Clack.

Topper stepped between Sol and Ben. "I don't know who's worse," he said to Sol. "You or my brother."

Sol glared at Topper. "He's pushing too far."

"We're leaving," said Topper. "Just let us be."

Sol took a big breath and stepped back a pace. "Move on then," he said.

Topper gave Ben a push toward the store's front door.

Watching them go, Sol sat back down and took a drink of coffee. He would end up crossing with Ben Clack, he figured. No way to avoid it.

CHAPTER ELEVEN

As the evening of the last Saturday of October 1931 drew to a close, Abby well understood that her life had changed a good bit since losing her baby a year and a half ago. She and Stephen hadn't spent more than a handful of nights together as husband and wife since the day little Rose Francis had entered and exited their lives. Of course, Abby realized the reason for their separateness those first few months after that day. Stephen had explained it a few weeks following, his voice so sincere she wanted him to stop talking so she might kiss him.

"We have to go real careful," he had told her. "Doc Sills says we can't take any chances on you getting pregnant any time soon. And even after your body is all healed, he isn't sure whether you ought to have another baby."

Though she had cried at the thought of not sharing intimacy with her husband for a while, Abby accepted the decision for what it was—a precaution to make sure she didn't die delivering another child.

The first months after that passed slowly but not too unpleasantly. Stephen did a lot of the labor around the house in those early days, his attitude as kind as she had ever seen it. Still weak, Abby could do little more than lie in bed and watch.

Gradually her body started to heal. Her skin took on a fuller pink again, and her hair returned to its auburn color and thicker than ever. She started eating better and took to doing light chores. As she grew stronger, she noticed that Stephen began staying out longer during the day. She wondered about his law practice. Since his office was at home now, when did he do any work if he spent most of his time gone somewhere?

She thought of asking him about this but then remembered how well he had provided for her since losing the baby, and so she decided to keep her questions to herself. Christmas of that first year had arrived and everybody but her and Stephen traveled up to Blue Springs to see the rest of the family. Fact was, except for the brief visit when she attended Hal Clack's funeral, she hadn't seen any of her family for a very long time.

Now, standing in the kitchen, Abby moved to the sink and washed her hands. She'd just tucked Stevie and Jimmy into their beds, then decided she would return to the kitchen to make an apple pie. Stephen liked apple pies, and on the days when she figured he would stay home, she always tried to have one ready for him.

Abby pulled everything she needed from the cupboard and started making the crust. Her mind drifted back to the day after the Clack funeral when she and Daniel had visited on Elsa's porch for a few minutes.

"You past most of your weakness?" Daniel had asked, lighting his pipe.

"Pretty much so," answered Abby. Her rocker moved gently back and forth. "I hurt more from grief now than anything else. Not easy getting over what happened. Everybody in your house doing okay?" she asked.

Daniel shrugged. "Faring about as well as a body might expect what with the scarceness of dollars and all."

Rolling out the crust, Abby wondered how far Daniel had gotten on rebuilding his house. Building materials cost money. She hoped he had enough to make do before winter set in.

Sad, she thought, how every time she turned around, somebody in her family had a painful matter to overcome. Of course, not every day brought hard news. Her boys were growing up as sweet as she'd ever hoped. At six now, Jimmy had a mind as alert as a new puppy. He liked to help his mama around the house, his small hands often trying to grab the hoe from her as if to keep her from working so hard in the garden.

"Let me do it, Mama," he would say. "I'm strong."

Abby wondered if Jimmy could sense the problems between her and Stephen. He seemed to take on her moods, happy when she found cause for joy, downcast when his parents weren't getting along and his mama's heart drooped. If not for her sons, she didn't know what she would do, how she would survive.

Abby took some apples from a basket by the sink and started washing them. Elsa was doing good too, and that was cause to be thankful. She seemed happy in Blue Springs.

She tended to forget that Elsa was Hal Clack's only daughter. Hard to believe a man as mean as him could have sired a woman as good as Elsa, or a grandson like Sol. But Amelia had mothered Elsa, and Elsa and Solomon had raised up Sol. Maybe that explained the way the two of them turned out.

Finished with the washing and peeling, Abby started cutting the apples into slices. Her thoughts turned to Luke. She hardly ever got to see him. He hadn't made it to Hal's funeral. That had always been his way, though, on the road most of the time, living near Hickory when he wasn't traveling. She and Daniel had talked about Luke on Elsa's porch.

"His singin' and playin' has slowed a lot lately," Daniel had told her. "Not many dollars in the church collection plates these days. But he keeps body and soul together. You know Luke. He seems protected by the good Lord, no matter what."

Abby nodded. What Daniel had said was true. Luke with his light hair, pale skin, and milky left eye. As a child, he had never caught on to things as quickly as other boys, never completed what little schooling was available. He had tried hard yet just didn't take to learning numbers or to reading. His classmates had teased him, though Luke didn't seem to mind too much. Instead, he just grinned at them and then picked up his guitar and started playing it, his fingers flying over the strings quicker than a bumblebee's wings.

Abby knew the gift for music made Luke special, made him as close to a celebrity as highlanders ever saw. He'd sung on the radio and in churches all over North Carolina, Tennessee, Kentucky and West Virginia. Scores of people knew Brother Luke Porter by name, because the Jubilees for Jesus Band had been to their place to pick and sing.

"Luke lost any weight?" Abby had asked Daniel.

Daniel grinned. Luke had put on some pounds over the last few years.

"Not any that I can tell," he said. "Guess the offerings are good enough to keep him in biscuits and buttermilk."

Abby laughed. "What about you? Your work coming back any?"

Daniel studied his brogans and shook his head. "Not much call for brickin' or buildin' these days. But I'm still scratchin' out a living for the family, helping out with Aunt Erline too."

Abby patted his hand, proud of the fact that her brother labored harder than five men put together. Took after his pa that way. Seemed to stretch a day further than its hours would allow. Depression or no, his kids need never worry about their pa's efforts to keep them in good care. Abby had dropped her head in shame that day as she realized she couldn't say the same about her own husband.

Done now with the slicing, Abby picked up a spoon to squash the pieces of apple. When she and Daniel had concluded their talk that day, she left him with the notion that everything was all right with her, that her strength had returned and she was feeling fine. But Abby hadn't told him everything.

Yes, her body had regained most of its health, but she felt ill at ease in her soul. Part of it was the grief over losing a baby. No woman carries a child for even a month without feeling like somebody cut out her heart when she loses it. But Abby sensed something else wrong, something she couldn't quite identify. It hung there in the night, just in front of her eyes, the feeling that something had changed forever and not just in her body. Something had changed forever between her and Stephen. She knew it as certain as she knew she'd almost died on those wet steps off her porch. She never asked Stephen to say it out plain, but it was obvious to her that he didn't plan on loving her as a true husband ever again.

After Hal Clack's funeral and her visit with Daniel, she had returned to Boone and put her shoulder back into the work of caring for her family. The days had turned into weeks, the weeks into months, and now it was the end of October, another winter on the way. A year and a half had gone by since they'd buried little Rose, yet Stephen still kept his distance. As time went on, this weighed heavily on her, and she started to doubt herself more and more.

For a while she figured Stephen must think she wasn't attractive anymore, although when she looked in the mirror she saw a woman who appeared much like she always had. Sure, she was a touch fuller in the face and figure. But not in any way that a man would see as heavy. And her hair still had plenty of shine in it with no gray showing up yet. Fact was, she still got a good many stares from the men when she walked down the street in Boone. Far as she could tell, Stephen had no reason to turn away from her.

Then why had he lost interest? Had he taken up with another woman? She wondered about this for a moment, then decided it didn't make sense. In a town as small as Boone, she would surely have heard if that had happened. Somebody would have seen him with another woman and spread the story back to her in a hurry. But if not a woman, then what could it be?

Abby realized she'd reached a crossing point, that she couldn't go on without facing the situation. Stephen did less and less work at home, and despite the fact that she hardly ever asked him for anything, he'd started complaining about any money she spent. To help make ends meet, she not only worked in the garden out behind the house but had also started helping the children of Sally and Suggs Tatum—the owners of the general store—with their studies. Tatum paid her a couple of dollars a week, which she used for flour and sugar and a piece of ham every now and again.

Except for her children, their home stayed real quiet, Stephen saying little when he came home, usually late at night. Abby decided not to confront him about this, for men dealt with hard times in different ways. She knew that from watching her own pa. She wanted Stephen to see her as a good wife. Therefore, she let him keep it all buried in his gut. Anyway, things had to turn for the better soon, didn't they?

Abby sighed with sad resignation. She'd come to the point where she had just enough strength to mind her household but little else. She had prayed every morning for months for her husband to change yet nothing happened. After that, she prayed for herself to change, that she might become a better wife, that she would say and do the right things and look the right way so Stephen would talk to her and hold her again, like he did when they first married. Still, no matter how hard she prayed, how hard she tried to please her husband, nothing seemed to help. She felt she'd about reached the end of her wits, and she had no idea what to do next.

She poured a touch of sugar over the apples and stirred it in. Then she put the apples in a pot, pushed a lid over them, and placed them on the stove. Suddenly tired, she decided to finish the pie the next morning.

After checking on the boys one more time, she quickly undressed, climbed into bed, and read from her Bible for a few minutes. Then she blew out the lamp, turned over and tried to rest. An hour passed. Sleep refused to come. She wondered when Stephen would make it home. It had to be close to ten o'clock. She lit the lamp again and read some more. Another hour passed. Then she heard a bump in the kitchen. Stephen had finally come home.

At first she thought she would wait on him, but when he didn't come to their bedroom, Abby slipped on a robe and padded to the kitchen. She saw him sitting at the table, both his hands around a whiskey flask. He looked up and grinned at her.

"You have a busy day?" she asked cautiously as she walked to the sink for a glass of water.

Stephen drank from his flask, and Abby's face flushed. She'd asked him over and over again to keep liquor out of their house. She started to fuss about it, but something about the way he sat told her he had something on his mind. She decided to try a different approach.

"You want some food? I can fix you something quick," she said.

He shook his head, tipped the flask again. His eyes looked glassy in the dim light. Abby drank from her glass, then sat down opposite him at the table. She reached for his hands. He pulled them away and placed them and the flask in his lap. She sighed, not sure what to do. Did hard times make all men act this way? Or did Stephen respond worse than others? Did he have some shortcoming in his character that made him weaker than other men, less able to meet life's challenges when they rose up on him?

Abby thought of Daniel. Sure he had his problems—headaches that hit him at odd times and a sadness that settled on his shoulders some days like a wagon rolling over his bones. But he still got up every day and looked for work. No matter what happened, Daniel Porter refused to escape his troubles by yielding to drink.

Stephen tipped the flask to his lips and held its bottom up toward the ceiling. When he had drained it, he set the empty container on the table. He stared at Abby now, and she sensed he had something to say. Her stomach knotted up.

"I'm going to move out of here," he said.

Abby's eyes narrowed. "What do you mean?"

Stephen wiped his hands on his trousers. "I got some business," he said. "New clients. But I got to move to take care of them."

"Okay," she said, more fearful than she sounded. "We can do that. Where are we moving?"

"Not *we*. I . . . I am the only one moving away."

Abby tried to stay calm. Maybe what Stephen said made some sense. He would move first, get settled, and send for her and the children later. She knew sometimes a man had to move around to keep his family fed, to keep them warm during the wintertime. Survival meant having to make hard choices like this one. "How long before you send for me and the boys?" Abby asked.

Stephen ran his fingers over the tip of the flask. "Not sure. Soon as I can make enough money to get us a proper place."

Abby took one of his hands. A man needed a wife's support at times like this. This time he didn't pull away.

"I'm glad you're taking this so well," he said. "I was afraid you'd react much worse."

Abby laid his hand on the table and stroked the top of it. "I'm your wife. I'll do what I need to do to help you through this hard time. Lots of folks are moving to follow work these days. No reason to panic. We'll just make our way through it, one day at a time. As a family—me, you, and the boys."

Stephen looked kindly at her and for a second she saw the good in him again, the drive and ambition that had made her want to marry him. Her heart warmed, and she bent over and kissed his hand. He smiled and her heart raced.

He raised her hand and kissed it. "You're a good wife," he said. "I can't argue with that."

Abby smiled. He did love her, she knew, and all at once she wanted to make their marriage what it once was, happy again. "Come," she said, standing. "Let's go to—"

Stephen jerked his hand away as if she had burned him. "I can't," he said. "You're . . . you're—"

"I'm what?" Abby said, her tone full of hurt. "Am I diseased or something? Flawed in some way that makes you never want me again? What is it, Stephen? Tell me!"

"You . . . well, you almost died," he whispered. "I . . . I can't take that chance again."

Moved by the thought that he was concerned about her health, Abby wrapped her arms around his neck.

"I'm okay now," she whispered. "All healed. It's been a long time . . ."

Stephen suddenly pushed up, his hands moving her arms from his neck. A second flask appeared from his coat pocket, and he took a long drink from it. Wiping his mouth, he faced Abby again. She saw a look in his eyes that she'd not seen before, wild and desperate, the look of an animal trying to escape a sprung trap. She wondered where such a crazed look came from, what had welled up so strong in his heart that it would show up now, like this.

"I . . . we can't!" he said loudly. "Not now. I don't know. . . ."

"Then when?" pleaded Abby. "It's not my health anymore! You know that, and so do I."

Stephen drank from the flask. He was unsteady on his feet. Abby realized then that he'd been trying to work up his courage to tell her something, probably for a long time. He needed the whiskey to bolster his confidence. Though she feared what he might say next, she wanted to hear the words spoken aloud, to get it all out in the open so she could stare it down. Regardless of what people said about her, she took life as it came, no turning away no matter how bad the news.

"Tell me!" she demanded, unwilling to let the uncertainty go on for another second. "When will we act as husband and wife again?"

"I don't know," repeated Stephen. "I'm afraid for you—for your health, I mean. What if you become with child again? The doctor says you might not survive it next time. I can't have that on my conscience."

"I'll take precautions. There are ways . . ."

Stephen's eyes turned even wilder, and Abby sensed he had more reasons than just her health to stay away from her. Something else gnawed at his insides, and it finally dawned on her what it might be. Stephen's next words confirmed her suspicions.

"I don't want any more kids!" he declared. "You need to know that. I can't afford them and . . . and I . . . well, I'm not a good father. You know that as well as I do. I . . . I can't take the chance."

Abby stared at the floor. What did this mean? What kind of marriage did she have if her husband had come to this decision? How could he love her and say this at the same time? Was it really a concern for her health, or a conclusion he'd reached about his own unfitness as a father?

"Are you saying this is forever?" she asked.

Stephen held up a hand. "I can't say anything about forever," he said. "That's far too long for me to consider."

"So you're saying we just continue as we have been. A marriage in appearance only."

"Maybe my moving will make all this easier," said Stephen. "Until we know."

Abby started to ask, Until we know what? but then she realized he was referring to the future. But no one could know that. If they did, they might not even try anymore; they might just give up. What if she'd known the future when she first met Stephen? She would surely not have married him, would she? But if she hadn't, then Stevie and Jimmy wouldn't exist and she certainly couldn't imagine life without her boys.

With nothing else to argue, Abby eased to the table and sagged down. For a couple of minutes, Stephen stood by the wall and watched her, as if he didn't know what to say or do next. But then, without another word, he stepped to her, kissed her on the forehead, and left the kitchen, gently closing the back door behind him as he walked out.

Still at the table, Abby's throat closed tight as tears rolled down her face. Here she thought she had everything she'd ever wanted. An educated husband, a man of taste from a good family. Two fine boys, a home in a nice town, the respect of the community, a good church, friends and neighbors who loved her, and enough food to make do. Yet now her husband had to move away to make a living.

Was it only the difficult economic times that had caused this? Could she blame all of Stephen's idleness on the lack of call for lawyers? She didn't know. Maybe some of the trouble arose from his own weaknesses. After all, a lawyer who drank too much whiskey and had a dislike for hard toil didn't inspire much confidence. Maybe Stephen had brought on some of his failure himself.

Abby buried her face in her hands. Now Stephen planned to leave, not even bothering to tell her where he was going. He no longer desired her as a wife. Tears coursed down her face for several minutes. Then another truth hit her. She didn't have a husband anymore, at least not a husband as most people used the word. But she did have two fine boys, and they both needed her. She wouldn't let them down, wouldn't let the troubles of her marriage destroy the hopes she had for their future. Maybe she and Stephen would never know true happiness. Yet, despite that, she would stay strong and be a good mother to her boys as long as God gave her breath.

Wiping her eyes, Abby squared her shoulders and sat up straight. Whatever tomorrow might bring, she would face it and handle it for the sake of her sons.

SECTION II

1932–1937

CHAPTER TWELVE

For a few years after Hal Clack died, things seemed to settle down some in Blue Springs. Daniel and Deidre managed to rebuild their cabin from the fire and scratch out a meager living for their family. Since the schools had mostly shut down because of a lack of funds, Marla, Ed and Raymond stayed home and toiled along with their ma and pa. Daniel wished they could get more of an education, but in those years, even when it was open, the school only met a few weeks at a time. Besides that, Daniel needed them to help out around the farm because he himself took to doing some traveling to find work, and he didn't like leaving Deidre alone. He wouldn't normally have taken these jobs—in Asheville, Knoxville, and Hendersonville mostly—but they did put a few much needed dollars in his pocket. Often he had to leave on a Sunday afternoon, struggle to find work all week, and return home again late Friday night. A family man to the core, he hated staying gone so much. With money so scarce, however, what else could he do? Except for the wintertime when the snow and ice stopped most of the jobs in their tracks and he didn't bother venturing from home, he bucked up and did his duty.

Nearly five years peeled off the calendar. Marla was becoming a young woman and had celebrated her sixteenth birthday. Ed was on his way to becoming a stout young man at age fourteen. Raymond had celebrated his ninth birthday, and Daniel and Deidre their forty-fourth. Deidre traveled to Asheville with the kids every fall after they'd gathered their crops to visit with her ma and pa. Other than that, she stayed put on the farm, never complaining, always toiling away and making Daniel proud.

Marla started seeing a boy from over past Valdese, but Daniel discouraged the courting. Because the boy had no real prospects on how to make a living, Daniel helped Marla see that maybe she should wait a while before becoming serious with the young man. Ed showed no inclination whatsoever toward girls. Daniel recognized the boy to be a lot like himself in his earlier days—shy and bashful. Whenever Ed could get his hands on a book, he loved to sit and read for hours on end. Every now and again he picked up a used newspaper at the general store and studied it front to back. Having read of Charles Lindbergh and his flight across the Atlantic in 1927, he talked a lot about the notion of flying and swore someday he'd go off and become a pilot. Daniel hoped he would get the chance.

Raymond, on the other hand, seemed most interested in sticking his hands in the dirt. So he stayed close to Daniel in the fields. Daniel worried some about the boy, because he hardly ever spoke. But he had a disposition as sweet as his uncle Luke's and had even started to sing as well. Daniel figured maybe Raymond had some musical gifts that made up for his being so quiet.

As time moved on, Daniel's hip started paining him more, especially when the winters fell cold on the mountain. He kept his pa's walking stick with him all the time now, to make his way around the farm or out on the road to search for jobs.

In the spring of '36, Uncle Pierce's heart finally wore out on him and he died in his rocker on his front porch. Since Daniel was away most of the time, Ed took up most of the care for Aunt Erline, making the trip out and back to her farm at least once a week to help her with the heaviest work.

Daniel saw Sol off and on a good bit in those years. Sol's wife, Jewel, birthed two more kids, a girl named Katy Ruth and a second son, Horace Earl. Daniel and Sol hunted some together and spent a lot of time out on one porch or the other, smoking their pipes and talking crops and guns and dogs. Since Luke didn't come around much, Sol became a real brother to Daniel, in spite of his being half a Clack.

Daniel didn't hear much from Abby during this time. She stayed to herself in Boone, coming up to Blue Springs only at Christmas and usually without Stephen. She had told Daniel about Stephen moving off to Knoxville to find work, about his plans to move them in with him as soon as he could afford it. So far though, the move hadn't happened. It made Daniel sad to think about his sister all alone with Jimmy and Stevie. He wanted to help them in some way yet didn't know how. When he brought it up to Deidre, she told him that everybody had their own cross to carry and his was heavy enough so he better not try to load up anybody else's, even if that somebody else was his sister. That didn't help Daniel feel any better.

Luke dropped in to see him every once in a while but never stayed long. He'd lost some weight due to the lean times, although he said he had enough dollars to get by all right. Not sure whether to believe this, Daniel quizzed him some but Luke wouldn't go much further with his answers.

"I'm f-f-fine," Luke had said over and over again. "P-p-people in the churches feed me regular."

Daniel knew when to let it go. He wanted to ask Luke why he'd never married, but then remembered that Luke had answered the question a long time ago: "I'm too s-s-slow for a w-w-wife," Luke had explained, half kidding. "And besides, I'm always t-t-travelin' around. So I'm not home enough to m-m-marry and be a f-family man."

Whenever Daniel saw Luke, he asked him to take up his guitar and sing for him and his family. Luke always obliged, his head tilted back and his eyes shut as he picked and strummed and sang out his praises to Jesus.

Daniel's jobs came in bits and spurts in those days, but he somehow earned enough to keep his family fed and clothed. Daniel knew he had little reason for complaining. True, the troubles from his past still cropped up on him when he least expected it, particularly during the nighttime, and his headaches were coming on more often. Other than that, Daniel was almost ready to believe that God had decided to let up on him some. But, knowing what he did about the unpredictable nature of God's doings, he didn't quite feel like going out and shooting his gun in the air in celebration.

When he was home and the church met, he hauled his family in his old Model T down to Jesus Holiness. A number of different preachers traipsed through in those years but that didn't matter so much anymore.

Whoever preached, he listened. He agreed with some more than others but found them all full of gumption and sincere of heart. Life had meaning, Daniel decided. Not that he could always figure out what that meaning was. But it did have a purpose, he felt sure. His pa had been right. Just stay true and the Lord will give a man what he needs to go through whatever comes his way.

On a Friday night in early August 1936, Daniel had just come back from a week away working a job and had bathed and taken a bite of supper when he heard a knock at the door. Not used to much company and too weary to deal with any, he glanced at Deidre. She caught his meaning, pushed back from the table, and headed to the front porch.

Then, grabbing his cane, Daniel decided to follow her. Deidre, Ed, and Raymond reached the door at the same time, and Ed, grinning as if he'd outraced a horse, swung open the door to reveal Sol standing on their porch. The boys stepped back to let their uncle in. Though worried about what had brought him out so far on a day with no holiday hooked to it, Daniel shook Sol's hand and asked him to have a seat.

"Glad you come by," said Daniel, taking a spot in a rocker across from Sol. "You hungry?" He motioned to Deidre who was already on her way to the kitchen. Sol took off his hat and rolled it in his hands. Daniel could see Sol had something on his mind, but he didn't want to act all nosy.

Deidre returned with corn bread and a glass of buttermilk and handed them to Sol. Sol swallowed down the buttermilk and took a bite of the bread. Deidre sat down by Ed on the fireplace hearth. A few minutes later, Marla appeared from the back room and joined them, sitting in a chair by the fireplace.

Finished with the bread and milk, Sol set the glass on the floor and brushed his hands on his pants. Then he stuck his hat on his knee and wiped his face.

"I got some hard news," Sol said.

Daniel gripped the arms of his rocker. An awful feeling ran through his bones. "Tell it out," he said.

Sol looked at Daniel, then Deidre. "Luke's been in an auto wreck."

Daniel's knuckles turned white on the chair.

"He ain't dead," added Sol. "But he's bad hurt."

"What happened?" Daniel asked, trying to stay steady.

"All I know is a truck hit him. Over near Greensboro. Had a rainstorm there last night. On top of that, the truck driver had some doublings in him. He come around a curve too fast, and the truck slid across the road. Slammed into Luke straight on."

"Luke in a hospital now?"

"Yep, in Greensboro."

"What are his chances?"

Sol fumbled with his hat. "I ain't no doctor," he said. "Not for me to say. But he's all busted up inside."

Daniel stood and went to the fireplace. He put a hand on the mantel and stared at the wall. A heavy sigh passed through his body. All the life seemed to seep out of him. What sense did it make for a man to try to make something of himself? No matter what he did, God could twist it around as quick as a man snapped his fingers. Luke had never done anybody any harm. He'd spent his life pickin' and singing to try to win people to Jesus. He had a simple heart that loved everybody and everything. Yet it looked like God hadn't added any of that up to his account; He'd done nothing to protect even a good man like Luke.

All of Daniel's notions about life having a meaning suddenly drained away. Nothing had meaning, he decided, not if this kind of thing could happen to someone like Luke. He figured he was a fool to have let God take him in again and cause him to believe otherwise.

Daniel turned and faced Sol. "I should've figured on something worrisome to come along," he said. "Right when a little of the load seems about to roll off, God drops another down on me."

Sol kept his quiet. Deidre touched Daniel's hand.

"I'm goin' to see Luke," Daniel said. "Just as soon as I can pack up a change of clothes."

"You can take my truck," Sol offered. "I'll drive you to Blue Springs, and you can go from there."

Daniel rubbed his beard. After several years of hard but decent living, a mean thing had fallen on his life again. He thought of his pa, his simple faith in the Almighty. Daniel had always believed like his pa had. He'd come to Jesus as a boy, let Preacher Bruster bend him back and soak his whole body through and through in the waters of Slick Rock Creek. Up until now, no matter all the bad that had come to him along the way, he'd still not thrown up many questions about the Lord's goodness. Like his pa, his faith had always stood strong. But what had just happened to Luke gave Daniel pause. His brother didn't deserve any of this. Himself, maybe so. He'd done some bad things in his life. But Luke had only done good. If anything, Luke ought to get some reward for his deeds, shouldn't he?

Deidre stood and put her arm around Daniel. "We need to pray for him," she said.

Looking down at the floor, Daniel said, "I don't feel much like prayin' right now."

Deidre's eyes filled with tears. Ed moved to her, Marla and Raymond too.

Daniel's heart fell, and he felt guilty he'd made his wife and children feel uneasy. So he pulled them all close and said, "It's just that the Lord seems a long ways off right now. Every time I turn around . . ."

"I know," said Deidre. "But we just got to have faith."

Daniel's anger rose up at this and he spoke before he could stop himself. "I been havin' faith all my life, and it ain't got me nowhere." His voice grew louder as he talked. "Laban gets killed in the war. The bank loses the money I slaved over to save. I lose the land and break my promise to Pa."

Stepping away from his family, he stared out the window. He spoke now through gritted teeth. "Lightning strikes my cabin, almost burns it to the ground. Now Luke. One of the best-hearted men ever to walk this earth, and a drunk man in a truck just up and hits him on the road, puts him in the hospital! Maybe Luke will die, we don't even know. Seems my faith makes no difference to anything, God least of all. Seems that God lets a man do all right for a spell, lets him get all comfortable and all, almost out of the woods. Then just when a man thinks things have taken a turn for the better, God smacks him down with something worser than the first thing, like He's been building it up, holdin' back for a big surprise."

Daniel turned back to Deidre. She had a hand over her mouth to hold back from crying. The kids were still, Raymond clutching his mama's free hand. Sol studied his hat, eyes down. Daniel took a deep breath. His anger suddenly cooled down. He'd spoken his piece. He felt bad, though, that the children had heard his hard words. But he knew nothing he could do about it. Just as well, he figured. They might as well understand now as opposed to later. No reason for them to think life dealt anything but sorry hands, no reason to put false hopes in them. He had said what he meant and meant what he said. They would just have to deal with it.

"Give me a few minutes," Daniel said to Sol. "I'll need to put some things in a sack."

"I'll pack you something to eat," whispered Deidre. "It's a long drive to Greensboro."

Moving back to his kids, Daniel thought for a second he might should try to take the edge off his harsh words about God. But truth was, he believed every word that had come out of his mouth, and he couldn't bring himself to lie and say otherwise. So, his heart heavy, he hugged his children one by one, then headed to his bedroom to pack.

It took Daniel most of the night to reach the Greensboro hospital. After parking Sol's truck, he braced his throbbing hip with his cane and limped straight inside and asked for Luke Porter. A few moments later, he followed a heavy nurse with a nametag *Jenkins* on her white uniform to a door at the end of the corridor of the two-story building. "He's real sleepy," Jenkins said, stopping outside the door. "We had to give him something to ease the pain."

Daniel nodded. "What are his chances?"

"You'll need to ask his doctor that," she said. "He should be coming by later this morning."

Daniel took off his hat and stepped into the room. Two beds, one of them empty, sat against the far wall. Luke lay on the bed by the window. White bandages wrapped around his head. A cast covered his left leg, which was hung in a sling, the toes exposed. A thin blanket lay over his upper body. His right hand, bandaged to the fingertips, stuck out from under the blanket. Luke's eyes were closed.

Hat in hand, Daniel moved to the head of the bed, leaned his cane against the wall. He stood there over his brother and for several minutes didn't say anything. His mind skipped back to when the two of them were boys, to when they used to play in the woods and creeks around the old place. He remembered how they'd split up when the war hit, Daniel shipping overseas to fight and Luke staying behind because of his bad eye and slow speech. Luke hadn't liked getting left out of the war, though he never seemed too mad about it. Truth was, Luke never got mad about anything.

Daniel looked out the window, gripping his hat tightly now.

Thinking back to '29, he recalled how Luke had chipped in to help him buy back their pa's land. But then they both lost all the money they'd saved. Luke hadn't gotten mad about that either. Daniel wished he had, wished Luke had cussed at him or slugged him in the face or stopped talking to him, something to punish him for losing his dollars. Instead, Luke had simply accepted the loss. It just wasn't in his nature to blame others. Daniel faced his brother again, brushed Luke's hair back from his face.

"I'm here, Luke," he whispered. "I won't go nowhere until you're better." Luke just lay there. Daniel took Luke's left hand and patted it. "I might ought to sing you a song. Maybe my squawkin' will wake you from your slumbers."

A fly buzzed by Daniel's head, and he swatted it away.

"I wish you'd wake up and sing me a song," said Daniel. "That would make all of us feel a lot better."

Luke's breathing came slowly. He groaned and tried to turn over, but the sling on his leg wouldn't allow it.

Daniel caught sight of his brother's sore foot. He reached over and gently touched the toes. The big one had turned purple and black. *Is this what happens when a body gets hit by a truck?* he wondered. *Your toes turn purple?*

Daniel pulled a chair to Luke's bed and studied his brother from head to toe. Luke groaned from time to time and struggled to move. His restraints kept him in place, however, and after a while he'd give up and go back to sleep.

The doctor stopped by at about two o'clock and the two men introduced themselves, but Daniel felt too nervous to ask him anything. The afternoon eased by. Daniel never left Luke's side. Early that evening, the doctor appeared again. Daniel watched carefully as he checked Luke over. The doctor had sparse hair and thick jowls. His eyes were wide and dark blue and seemed to see more than he wanted to let on. Though afraid of what the doctor might tell him, Daniel was determined not to let him leave again before he learned the truth about Luke's condition.

Daniel stepped closer to the bed as the doctor finished. "How's he doing, Dr. Shuler?"

Shuler raised a thin eyebrow. "Not good," he said. "He has internal injuries around the kidneys. Liver too."

"Can't you fix him?"

"I operated a few hours after he came in," explained Shuler. "Put him together as well as possible. Only time will show if your brother will be all right."

"Nothing else you can do?"

"Not unless we can put a new liver in him," answered the doctor.

"He can have mine!" offered Daniel without thinking. "If that's what it takes, he—"

Dr. Shuler held up a hand. "I was just talking. We don't have the ability to do that kind of operation. Maybe in the future."

Daniel's chin dropped. He would have done it, no questions asked. He'd give Luke whatever it took—kidneys or liver—no matter that Daniel couldn't live without them. He pondered the idea. Luke deserved to live more than he did. But, for some reason, God hadn't seen fit to let it happen that way. Why did one man suffer while another didn't? Then again, which one was the hardest suffering—to stand by all healthy and watch his brother all hurt and everything or to lie in bed all busted up himself?

Daniel's head hurt. He rubbed his temples and told himself nobody could answer his questions so he might as well let them drop.

"Your brother has suffered some bad injuries," said Shuler. "But he's strong. We'll just have to wait and see how it all goes."

Shuler left then, and Daniel again took his spot by Luke's bed. Nurse Jenkins showed up a little after eight that night and asked Daniel how Luke was doing. He just shook his head and mumbled, repeating Dr. Shuler's words.

He tried to rest some, yet sleep never came. At about midnight he rubbed his eyes, drank a swallow or two of water, and continued his watch. A couple of times he tried to pray. But his words sounded hollow in the quiet room, and he didn't get far before he stopped altogether.

As the moon passed outside the window, Daniel found himself strangely torn. He wanted to be there with Luke until he woke up but he also knew that might never happen. Yet, since he'd already seen one brother die, he didn't want to see another one do the same thing. He wanted to stay, but he also wanted to leave.

Minutes ticked away slowly. Not quite an hour later Luke groaned and Daniel knew instantly that it sounded different from the others. Jumping to his feet, he grasped Luke's good hand. Luke's eyes opened slightly.

"Luke, you awake?"

Luke licked his lips. Daniel picked up a cup of water from a nearby table, lifted Luke's head, and poured a small amount over his lips. Luke swallowed, then blinked and pulled away from the cup.

"How you feelin'?" Daniel asked.

Luke licked his lips again.

"Luke, I come soon as I heard. Drove all night to get here."

Luke nodded.

Daniel brushed back Luke's hair and set the cup down. "You been sleepin' all day. I've been right here."

"I am some . . . some hurtin'," whispered Luke. "My hand."

Daniel's eyes watered as he glanced at Luke's bandaged right hand. Then it hit him. The right hand was Luke's pickin' hand.

"You got a good doctor," said Daniel, hoping to reassure his brother.

"P-p-pray for me," said Luke.

Daniel's heart lurched in his chest but he said nothing.

Luke closed his eyes. "Pray for me," he repeated, his voice weak.

Daniel looked to the floor as he realized Luke wanted him to pray right then and there. "I best get the nurse," he said. "She should check on you."

"Don't n-n-need no nurse. Need you to pray for me."

Daniel hesitated, then decided he had to tell the truth, even if he knew Luke wouldn't like it. At a time like this, a man shouldn't start lying to his only living brother. "I ain't too sure about what good my prayers will do," he whispered.

"Don't g-g-go talkin' no nonsense," said Luke.

Daniel took a deep breath. "I know this ain't the time or place," he said. "But I got to ask you. Don't the hard things that have come to us make you wonder about the love of Jesus? Don't all of it make you want to shake a fist at the Almighty?"

Luke shut his eyes. Seconds passed. Luke seemed to gather his strength. Then he opened his eyes again and stared straight at Daniel.

"I'm just a s-s-simple man," Luke whispered. "What I d-d-don't know is far more than what I d-do know." Licking his lips, he pressed on. "My head ain't b-big enough to hold all the r-r-rest, all that the good Lord is and d-d-does. So I j-j-just lay a whole lot down at the feet of Jesus, all that I can't f-figure, all I can't understand."

Daniel squeezed Luke's left hand. "Well, I ain't as good as you. Life has done put a hard edge on me."

"Remember what J-J-Job said. 'Though he s-s-slay me, yet will I trust in him.' "

"I ain't got the faith of no Bible man."

"Don't need the f-faith of a Bible man. . . ." His voice trailed away as he lost strength. "Just the faith God c-can give you, that's all."

He closed his eyes once more, and Daniel could see that the talk had worn him out. He felt guilty about making Luke say so much. Luke's hand fell limp in his grasp. Daniel quickly checked his breathing; it was okay. Luke hadn't died. At least not yet.

Abby heard about Luke's accident the morning after Daniel did. Sol had put a call through to the law in Boone, and they in turn got word to Abby at her house. Since Stephen had their auto in Knoxville where he worked, she walked to Mrs. Lollard's house and asked to borrow her telephone so she could call Stephen.

At first he tried to argue with her that he didn't need to come home for this. But when she insisted he come right away, that they were talking about her brother and he was near to dead, Stephen backed down, saying he'd head home as soon as the day ended. After hanging up the phone, Abby put in a call to Elsa.

"Luke is hurt," she said when Elsa answered. "He was in an auto wreck not far from Greensboro. I need to go see him. Can you come and take care of the boys while I'm gone? I'd ask Mrs. Lollard, but I don't know how long it'll be before I make it back, and I can't ask her to keep the boys more than a day or so."

Elsa didn't hesitate. "I'll come as soon as I can find somebody to drive me," she said. "Maybe the new preacher. He's a widower, you know."

Abby wanted to ask more about the preacher but decided to hold it for another time. "Let me know if anything slows you down." She gave Elsa Mrs. Lollard's number, hung up the phone, and headed home. Within an hour she'd thrown her things together and told the boys she had to go away for a couple of days.

"You going to see Pa?" asked Jimmy.

"No," said Abby, her heart nearly breaking at the question. He was only eleven, yet Jimmy had grown up fast and seemed wise beyond his years. Having taught him at home the last few years, Abby knew he had a lot of smarts. "Your pa is goin' with me. He's coming home to pick me up and then we're going from here."

"Will Pa stay home a while this time?"

Abby studied her older boy. He favored the Porter side of the family—all skin and bones as a boy yet with the frame to become pretty stout once he took on manhood. His hair was as dark as her father's had been and stayed messed up most all the time. He asked more questions than Abby had answers, as curious as a young puppy with his brown eyes and big feet. Lately he'd sprung up almost as tall as her. Jimmy started taking on more responsibility too, watching out for his brother, doing lots of chores around the house and yard. Like his late grandpa Solomon, he did good with his hands and could fix about anything that broke. Abby had come to depend on him for a goodly measure of comfort and support.

"Pa won't be able to stay for long," Abby said. "He has to drive me to Greensboro."

"What's in Greensboro?" asked Stevie.

Abby hesitated. But then she realized that Jimmy and Stevie were old enough to hear some of what was going on. "Remember your uncle Luke? The one who plays the guitar and sings?"

"Yeah," said Stevie. "He brings us candy when he visits."

Abby patted his head. "Well, Uncle Luke has been in a bad auto wreck. So say your prayers for him, that he'll get better."

Jimmy's mouth turned solemn. "We'll do that," he said.

"I'm sure he'll appreciate it," said Abby. "Now go on outside, the both of you."

"I'd rather stay," said Jimmy. "Maybe you'll need me for something."

Abby smiled. Her son had fine manners. "No, I'm okay," she insisted. "If I need you, I'll call."

Nodding, Jimmy led Stevie outdoors while Abby went to the kitchen to make sure she had everything in order. Five hours later, Elsa arrived in a car driven by a middle-aged man with silver hair and straight teeth.

"This is the new preacher, Robert Tuttle," Elsa announced, stepping back to allow him to close the car's door. "He was kind enough to bring me down from Blue Springs."

Preacher Tuttle shook Abby's hand and said, "I'll be praying for your brother. Put him on the prayer list at the church as well."

"Thank you," Abby said. "Luke grew up attending Jesus Holiness, you know."

"Yes, I know," said Tuttle. "The Porter family is well known and loved by the congregation. The folks will grieve to hear of Luke's injuries."

Abby led the two of them inside. After drinking a glass of tea, Preacher Tuttle said he had to return to Blue Springs. "Call me when you're ready to come home," he said to Elsa, "and I'll come right away to pick you up."

Abby thanked him again and he drove off. Back inside the house, Abby showed Elsa where to find everything. Before too long, Stephen drove up, climbed out, and made his way to the house.

Rather than hugging Abby as any normal husband would have done, he immediately started complaining about having to come home. "I have a big deal brewing," he said. "I can't afford to come running home every time you need to go somewhere."

Trying hard to stay calm, Abby's insides boiled at his meanness. How could he even question whether he ought to help her poor brother? And with Elsa there too!

"We have no time to argue," she told him, her temper causing her to speak more forcefully than normal. "I want to go as soon as we can." Stephen grumbled but then shut up.

They headed out not more than an hour later. Jimmy, Stevie, and Elsa stood in the road and waved as they sped away.

They reached the hospital by nine o'clock that evening and quickly made their way to Luke's room. They found Daniel in a chair by the bed. He got up as they entered, hugged Abby, and shook Stephen's hand.

Abby moved past Daniel and stood over Luke. "How is he?" she asked.

"He's been sleeping almost the whole time since I got here. Woke up for a short while earlier tonight. Doctor says the sleep is what's best for him."

Abby touched Luke's forehead. It felt cold and clammy. Her heart sank. The bruises around his eyes looked rough. She turned back to Daniel. "I didn't get many facts," she said.

"A truck hit him . . . a drunk man behind the wheel. He's busted up on the inside. Smacked in the head too. Doctor says they've done all they know to do."

"I suppose it's in the Lord's hands now," said Abby.

"I wish that gave me some comfort," said Daniel. "But I'm a mite short on trustability right now."

Abby held her tongue. Stephen stepped to her and whispered something. She shrugged, and he turned and left the room.

"Stephen thinks maybe we need some time alone," she said by way of explanation.

"That's mighty nice of him," said Daniel, his tone marked with some sarcasm.

She let it pass. Daniel motioned her to a chair, then he sat down in another. Abby took a good look at her brother Daniel. Gray now streaked his beard. His hat had pressed down his hair. His eyes looked empty. She could see he'd come to the end of his tether. But she didn't know what to do or say that would help him hold on.

Strange, she thought, how kin as close as a brother and sister can drift off from each other so much. They grow up hoeing the same field, taking their suppers at the same table, swimming in the same creek. But then they head down different roads, and life carries them clean away from each other. Then one day they sit in a hospital room beside somebody they both love and they don't know what to say to each other.

She knew life had tossed Daniel around real hard and she wished she had a ready-made way to help him. But life had been hard for her too, and she didn't know how to help herself. What could she say to him?

"How are Deidre and the kids?" Abby asked.

Daniel rubbed his face. "They're okay," he said. "We're makin' do. You know how it is. If a man and a woman toil hard enough, they can pull a living from the ground. Won't get ahead none, least not these days. But we eat and keep clothes on our bodies and a roof over our heads."

"You labor hard," she said. "Got your cabin better than before the fire, I hear."

Daniel sighed. "That fire would have burned it all. Just like when we were kids."

Abby closed her eyes. She pushed away the memory of the fire and stared at Daniel again. He had his eyes on Luke.

"What about you?" he asked. "You getting on all right?"

"Passable. Stephen stays gone most of the time. I don't rightly know all he does. Just know it brings home little enough money, just enough to scrape by. I raise the kids, do some teachin' on the side. Spend a lot of time at the church. Doing as well as most, I suppose."

Daniel stood and walked to the window. "How you manage it?"

"What do you mean?"

He faced her again. "Oh, you know. No matter what life throws at you, it don't seem to rile you none." He shoved his hands in his overalls pockets.

Abby could tell that Daniel needed an answer that made sense. After studying on the question a second, she tried out an answer. "I'm not as calm as I seem, for one thing. I get in a dither just like everybody else. Just keep it more hidden maybe."

Daniel scowled. "But it don't sway you none. Not that I can see. Nothing shakes up your head, makes any difference in what you believe."

"I suppose that's true. Least not to this point. It's not that I don't have some questions, though. Just that my questions don't change what I trust."

Daniel's jaw worked. "But look at this," he said, pointing to Luke. "A sweet man, never spoke ill of no one, and gentler than a bunny rabbit. Yet the Lord did nothin' to protect him from a fool drunk."

"Well, he *is* still with us," said Abby. "Don't give up just yet."

"That's true. But even if he walks out of here, the doctor says he'll have trouble using his hand again, playin' his guitar. The one gift he had and now this might take it right away from him."

"Still, we got to remember what Pa always said."

"For a man who spoke so little, Pa sure seemed to say a lot."

Abby smiled. What Daniel said was true. Solomon didn't waste words. But when he spoke, he carried truth in his words. "He said God could do some good things even in the worst times. All we had to do was watch and we would surely see it."

Daniel shook his head, and Abby could tell she hadn't convinced him. Her eyes searched the room as if looking for something to help her know what to say next. She spotted Daniel's walking staff standing in the corner. She walked over and picked it up and faced Daniel again. "You use this cane every day?"

"I surely do," he said.

Abby turned it in her hands, taking in the images her pa had cut into it so many years before. Moses, the Ark of the Covenant, Jesus' return in glory, the mountain by their old place. She studied the carving of the mountain. "You recall the story Pa used to tell about the mountain by our cabin?"

"Never forget it," said Daniel. "He told how he was ten, out coon hunting with his pa and brothers. In the middle of the hunt, he chased a dog on a false scent. The dog split off from the rest of the pack, and before he knew it Pa found himself cut off from everybody. Then a rain started to fall, made it so he couldn't hear it if somebody fired a gun so that he could follow the sound and find the group.

"He found a cave and stayed there until morning. When the sun came up, he did what his pa had told him to do if ever he got lost in the woods. He walked to the top of the highest peak he could find, hauled up into a tree and climbed to the top branch. From there he looked off in every direction.

"He saw the bald off to the northwest—the open face of rock on the front of the mountain over his home. 'Find Blue Springs Mountain,' Pa would say. 'Find our mountain, and it will take you home.'

"So Pa hollered at his dog and set out toward the mountain. At the foot of it he found his cabin. As he walked into the yard, his pa got up from a porch rocker and waved. 'I told 'em not to worry,' Grandpa said to Pa. 'Told 'em you'd know how to get home.' "

"Pa found his way home by looking for the mountain," said Abby. The room fell quiet for a second.

"I'm feeling sort of lost right now," Daniel finally admitted. "And I'm wondering if anything, even a mountain, can show me the way home again."

"You have trusted Jesus your whole life. No reason to change that now."

Daniel smiled. "Slick Rock Creek was mighty cold the day Preacher Bruster pushed me under."

Abby smiled back.

"But God feels a long ways off right now," continued Daniel.

"A brother near to dying will make it seem so," said Abby. She handed Daniel the cane, pointed to the face of the mountain carved on it.

Daniel stared at the carving. "It looks like the real thing," he said. "That rock in the middle sticks out like a man's chin. When the sun hits it late in the day, it appears just like a face. Pa always said he could see God's face on the mountain."

"All over it," agreed Abby. "For those who will look close."

Daniel handed her back the cane. "I'm still lookin'," he said. "Just don't know how much more I can stand."

"A man can stand a lot if he's got Jesus at his side."

Daniel rubbed his beard. "I think I'll stretch my back a mite," he said.

"Been in this hospital a mighty long time."

Abby started to go back to her words about Jesus but then stopped. Daniel had heard enough for now. "I'll stay here with Luke," she said. "You go on and get some air."

Daniel bumped into Stephen in the hallway, his back against the wall, a flask in his hand.

"He any better?" asked Stephen.

"Not so I can tell it."

"Must be hard."

"Sure is. You don't have any brothers?"

"No sisters either."

"You're lucky in some ways."

Stephen nipped from the flask.

"You carry that around with you all the time?" asked Daniel, indicating the bottle.

Stephen shrugged. "It's not heavy."

"You like the taste that much?"

Stephen held up the flask. It had a silver cover that shone in the hallway light. "I don't know. It just eases things some, smoothes out the rough spots." He offered Daniel the flask.

Daniel grunted as he looked at it. Why not take a drink? What harm could one small drink do to him? He took the flask from Stephen, fingered its neck. He needed some rough spots smoothed out. His mouth watered. Highlander men had been sucking from liquor jugs for as long as anybody could recall. Some folks said that a boy who didn't go straight from his mother's breast milk to a whiskey jug might as well go on and wear a dress and tie bows in his hair. Nothing wrong with the drink, no matter what all those temperance folks shouted. And it was legal again, what with the repeal of Prohibition in '33. He glanced at Stephen, who shrugged as if to say, Go on, have a drink.

Daniel thought of his pa. If Solomon were alive, he would never approve of such a thing as this. He would've said something like, *A man so weak that he needs the doublings to see him through a rough time ain't much of a man.*

Daniel lowered the flask, took a heavy breath, and handed it back to Stephen. He had fallen a long way, but not that far. At least not yet.

CHAPTER THIRTEEN

The heat that fell on Blue Springs over the next few days slowed everybody down some. It seemed to rise out of the ground, a stifling mix of hot, wet air that left Elsa soaked with sweat almost from the minute she crawled out of bed until she dropped back down that night. Regardless of the heat, though, she kept her hands busy caring for Abby's boys while Abby cared for Luke in Greensboro.

Up at dawn every day, Elsa prepared breakfast for Jimmy and Stevie, made sure they had clean clothes to wear, kept them on track with their chores until they finished, then sent them out to play. Watching them run outside, their young energy bubbling over, Elsa wondered where all the years had gone. Seemed like only yesterday that she and Solomon had married and soon afterward she'd been the one raising two little boys.

Closing the screen door, Elsa returned to the kitchen. The boys would stay gone most of the day, running and playing with their buddies, coming home briefly for a bite of food only to head out again until suppertime. In the meantime, Elsa found plenty of housework to do. She also tended to Abby's small garden in the backyard and the flower beds in the front.

Abby called Mrs. Lollard's house the day after she arrived at the hospital and asked her to pass on the message that Luke hadn't improved much. Unable to do anything else for him, Elsa kept her prayers regular, asking for strength for them all. Mrs. Lollard stopped by each afternoon about two or so to make sure Elsa had everything she needed. Elsa thanked her and said that so far she was doing okay.

On the fourth morning of taking care of the boys, Elsa braved the wearisome heat and walked to the general store to buy flour and other goods. The morning had a dead feel to it, like somebody had sucked all the life from the air. Nothing stirred—not a bird sang, not a dog barked, not a bee buzzed. Even though she had on a light cotton skirt and a white short-sleeved blouse and no hat on her pinned-up hair, Elsa still felt almost knocked out by the scorching temperature. Without knowing why, she sensed an uneasiness in the morning, as though the day were holding its breath and waiting on something.

Pulling her purchases in a rusty wagon, she made her way back to Abby's place by midmorning. As she stepped into the yard, she saw a tall stringy man standing on the porch. The man wore a brown suit and shoes to match and held a scratched-up black briefcase under his right arm. Elsa knew instantly the man's presence meant bad news. She figured Luke had died.

"Morning," she said, pushing open the front gate of the white fence that bordered the yard and pulling the wagon through it. "May I help you with something?" Even when bad news came, a body had to stay polite.

"I'm looking for Mr. or Mrs. Stephen Waterbury," the man said. "You got any notion where I might locate them?"

Not wanting to reveal too much until she knew more, Elsa moved onto the porch past the man, opened the front door and invited him in. "Have a seat," she said as they reached the parlor. "Would you like a glass of water? Some lemonade perhaps, we have a pitcher in the kitchen."

"Water will do just fine," he replied. He kept the black case tight under his arm.

Elsa went to the kitchen and filled two glasses with water. Obviously the man hadn't come to tell her bad news about Luke, for he wouldn't ask for Stephen or Abby if it was about Luke since they were in Greensboro by Luke's side. So the man must want something else. But what? Something about Stephen's business maybe. Why, then, would he be asking for Stephen *or* Abby?

Not sure what to do, Elsa decided she'd better have a talk with Abby before saying anything to the man.

Back in the parlor, she handed him the glass of water and took a seat opposite him. He had placed his briefcase on the floor. Elsa eyed it as the man sipped from his glass.

"Lon Cain is my name," he began. "I'm from the bank. Down in Greenville, South Carolina. Some banks are still in business, you know. About half or more."

"I am Elsa Porter. I'm looking after Mr. and Mrs. Waterbury's boys for a few days."

"They traveling?" Mr. Cain asked the question in a way that indicated she ought to talk on about where exactly they were. But Elsa preferred to keep her answers short.

"You might say that," she replied.

"When you reckon they'll be coming home?"

Elsa took a drink of water. In some of the most isolated parts of the highlands, a man who asked questions this particular might get his nosy head shot off. At the very least the nosy man would get a harsh look and stony silence. "You got a reason for askin' so much about the Waterburys, do you?"

Mr. Cain wiped his glass across his perspiring forehead. He set the glass on the floor and stared at Elsa with a firm jaw. "You any kin to them?"

"You think you got a right to ask such a question?"

Cain licked his lips. "I see no harm in it. The bank can't make you pay their debts. Least not yet."

Elsa sipped again from her water. Mr. Lon Cain had spilled at least a few beans, she figured. He had come about some money Stephen and Abby owed to his bank. She decided to play along for a minute to see what else she could learn. "Mrs. Waterbury's pa was my husband," she said. "His first wife died."

"I take it you know how to reach them?"

"I expect I can if the need arises."

Cain pulled the briefcase from the floor, laid it primly in his lap, and clicked it open. A neat stack of papers rested in the center. "Like I said, I'm from the bank in Greenville." He removed the papers and held them up to show Elsa. "And I'm here to inform Mr. Waterbury that he's over eight months in arrears on what he owes the bank on this house."

Elsa's heart about stopped. She knew right away what this meant.

Handing her the papers, he continued, "You can read it right here." He pointed to the top line of the document. "It's all legal and sorted out. The owners of the bank here in Boone had to sell most of their assets, including the paper on this house, to keep their doors open. So the bank I represent down in South Carolina now owns this house, and Mr. Waterbury seems unable to meet his financial obligations to us."

Elsa took the papers and read the first few lines. Everything seemed in order. She lowered the papers to her lap and faced Cain. "I see you're telling me the truth," she said. "But what do you want me to do about it?"

Cain cleared his throat. "I'm asking that you let Mr. Waterbury know that the bank is giving him until the end of the month to make some arrangements to catch up on his debts, otherwise he'll have to vacate the premises. You suppose you can do that?"

Elsa's mind raced. The month ended in three weeks. How could Stephen do anything about this in such a short time? Dollars were hard to come by for most everybody. "How much does he owe?" she asked.

Cain nodded to the papers, and she gave them back. He placed them neatly in the case, clicked it shut, and squeezed it under his left arm. "More than he can pay, I expect."

"He's got two kids, you know."

Rising to his feet, Cain said, "I'm sure they are fine children. Unfortunately, that makes no difference to the bank. A debt is a debt; every man has to pay what he owes."

Elsa stood too. She had the feeling that Cain enjoyed his job.

"Thank you for the refreshment," he said.

"I'll tell Mr. Waterbury about your visit."

"You do that," said Cain. "And tell him soon. He'll know how to reach us to make arrangements, if there is any need."

For a long time after Cain left, Elsa stood on the porch and stared into the yard. The day stayed as still as ever. Elsa hoped a storm would brew up to wash out some of the heat. She sat down in the porch swing and pondered what to do. News like this scared everybody. She considered keeping it to herself until Stephen and Abby returned. But that made no sense. If they stayed gone for more than a few more days, they would have less time to do anything after they got back. Yet she hated to add this to Abby's troubles. One more load of bricks thrown on her in an already bad time.

She wondered what would happen if Stephen failed to come up with the required dollars. Would the bank actually force them out of their house? Probably so. Banks had little or no heart over such things these days. Where would Abby and her boys go then? Would Stephen finally take them to Knoxville with him? Was that possible? Maybe this situation would force Stephen to do what a good husband and pa would have done long ago.

Standing up from the swing, Elsa realized that one way or the other she had to tell Stephen. She would report what Mr. Cain had said and then leave the matter alone.

Later that day, a woman in the hospital office fetched Stephen from a bench on the front lawn and told him he had a telephone call. He took it in the office, his head turned away from the two people working there so he could talk in private. It surprised him when he heard Elsa's voice on the other end.

"How's Luke?" asked Elsa. Her voice sounded scratchy coming through the line.

"Not that good," said Stephen. "The doctor says infection has set in. Plus he has some swelling in his head."

Elsa paused, and Stephen wondered why she'd asked to talk to him. Why not Abby or Daniel? Something told him she wouldn't have asked for him unless something serious had happened back home, something that directly affected him. "You want to talk to Abby?" he asked, hoping to put off hearing whatever she had to say.

"No, I need to tell you something," Elsa said.

Stephen squeezed the phone and closed his eyes. Which of his schemes had finally caught up with him? He had many in the works, some on the edge of the law. He pulled out a handkerchief and wiped his face. A surge of resentment boiled up. All his efforts, good or bad, had been to provide for his family. But no one would give him credit for that if it all turned sour.

"A man from the bank stopped by the house," Elsa said. "A Mr. Lon Cain."

"And what did Mr. Cain want?"

"Well . . . he said you were behind on the payments on your house."

Stephen breathed a sigh of relief. This wasn't as bad as it could have been. "I'm certain the bank made a mistake," he said, his voice full of confidence. "Happens all the time these days. The banks are in chaos."

"I'm sure that's it," agreed Elsa. "But he asked me to contact you if I could. Said you had until the end of the month to make arrangements."

Stephen licked his lips. "What happens if I'm not back by then? I'm here helping my wife take care of her injured brother. Surely the bank will understand that."

Elsa paused again. "I'm . . . well, that's way past me. I'm just telling you what the man said. I'll leave the rest to you."

Stephen touched the pocket of his jacket, felt his flask. "Thank you for calling," he said. "I'll tell Abby."

"Tell her I'm praying," added Elsa.

"I'm certain she'll appreciate that." Stephen hung up the phone and pulled out the flask. Leaving the hospital, he walked onto the front steps and looked up at the sky. A few white clouds hovered overhead. He tipped the flask to his lips. *The day was bound to come,* he thought, *sooner or later.* Trouble was, he didn't have any notion what to do this time to fix what he suspected would soon be coming down on him.

For the next few days Daniel and Abby remained at the hospital with Luke. After their earlier talk, they didn't say much to each other. Just sat by Luke's bed and held his hand and wiped off his forehead and kept their thoughts to themselves. Stephen stayed away from the room most of the time, wandering in only occasionally. Abby didn't bother asking him to hang around.

On the fourth day of their vigil, Dr. Sills called them outside of Luke's room and told them the infection in Luke's body had spread farther than they thought it would and there wasn't anything they could do to stop it. The doctor said he was doing all he could, but sometimes the medicines couldn't hold back an infection spreading this fast. Then Dr. Sills said if they had anything they needed to get clear with Luke, they ought to do so just in case. Daniel clenched his fists, and Abby thought for a second he might take a swing at the doctor. Instead, he just dug his fingers into the palms of his hands until they turned white. Abby wanted to hug her brother and tell him to leave it all with the Lord. She could see, though, that he didn't want to hear such talk right then, so she let it drop. Sills walked away, and Abby and Daniel returned to Luke's room and took up their watch again.

Another two days passed. Luke's skin took on a yellowish color, all but the fingers on his right hand, which had turned a purplish black. Sills said they might need to take the hand off. Daniel asked him if taking the hand would guarantee Luke would live. The doctor shook his head at this, so Daniel said to leave the hand alone.

Luke did wake up from time to time, and they talked to him in low tones, Abby telling Luke she loved him and he smiling back weakly at her, saying that he loved her too. Daniel leaned in and whispered to him, but Abby couldn't make out what he said. About midnight of the eighth day after the accident, Luke opened his eyes and beckoned them both to come closer. Abby realized Luke's time had about run out.

"You want some water?" Abby asked.

Luke nodded, and she eased a cup to his lips. Daniel held up Luke's head so he could take in the water.

"You are lookin' some peaked," Daniel said, pretending to tease him. "But I got chores for you that needs doing so you just better get up from this bed real fast and get busy."

Luke gave a half smile and waved Daniel off. "I stopped takin' orders from you a long time ago," he whispered.

Abby noticed with surprise that Luke had lost his stutter.

Luke grabbed Daniel's forearm with his left hand. "You keep my guitar," he said.

"I ain't got the gift of playin' that thing," said Daniel. "Best keep it for yourself. You gone be pickin' and singin' again soon."

"I didn't know you as no lyin' man," said Luke. "Don't go trying to fool me now."

Daniel hung his head. Abby marveled at Luke's straightforward way of dealing with his brother. Because of his slowness with learning, he had always followed Daniel's lead. But now, for the first time Abby could remember, Luke seemed truly the eldest brother, the one taking care of the younger.

"I plan on gettin' me a new guitar," Luke whispered. "One made of gold maybe, with some silver strings." Luke licked his lips.

"Hard to haul around a gold guitar," said Daniel. "With a bum hand to boot."

"I reckon the good Lord will make me a new hand," said Luke. "One strong enough to pick the strings of my gold guitar." Silence came for a few seconds, then Luke said to Daniel, "You're right that you don't have no gift for music. But your boy Raymond takes to pickin' some. Give my old guitar to him."

"He'll like that," Daniel said.

"I ain't got much else," Luke went on, his voice weaker by the second. "A few dollars in a sack. Divide that up among your kids. My old Ford, but I reckon it ain't much count now that a truck smashed it." He closed his eyes. "A pocketknife, a couple pairs of britches, and a few shirts. You go through the rest of my things, keep what you want, throw out the rest."

He opened his eyes again. He pointed to the corner of the room. Abby turned and saw Daniel's cane there.

"Pa's cane . . ." said Luke.

Daniel grabbed it and brought it over to the bed.

"Pa gave it to you," said Luke. "Not me."

"I'm sorry," Daniel said. "You should have gotten it, you were the eldest after Laban."

Luke shook his head. "No, that's not what I mean. Pa did right. The cane was for you. Some reason, I don't know why."

"Well . . . I ain't done too good by it," said Daniel, laying the cane on the bed by Luke's side. "Not good at all."

Abby fought back tears. She wanted to tell Luke that he would get better, that the sickness in him would soon go away, that his injuries would heal, that he would play again and sing in his sweet tenor voice and everything would be all right. But she knew Luke didn't want her to lie—not now, not when they had so little time for the truth to be said.

She kissed him on the forehead. He smiled at her and closed his eyes. She stepped back, and Daniel sat down on the edge of the bed. Luke's lips moved again. Abby waited to hear what else he had to say, but he started singing instead. His soft voice filled the room.

"There's a land that is fairer than day, and by faith we can see it afar. . . ."

Luke's voice grew weaker as he sang. *"For the Father waits over the way, to prepare us a dwelling place there."*

His voice turned into a quiet, clear whisper.

"In the sweet by and by, we shall meet on that beautiful shore. In the sweet by and by. . . ."

As Luke sang, Abby looked at Daniel. Tears rolled down his face and disappeared into his beard. Luke's voice rose one more time. *"In the sweet by and by, we shall meet . . ."*

Daniel stretched out on the bed beside Luke. And so Luke passed on to Jesus, the whisper of his sweet voice the last sound Abby and Daniel ever heard from him.

CHAPTER FOURTEEN

Regardless of their not having the money for it, Abby and Daniel signed a piece of paper the next morning that said they would pay the undertaker a couple of dollars each month if he would take Luke back to Blue Springs in his black hearse. Then, after Daniel had gone through Luke's things from his wrecked vehicle and packed up his guitar and clothes, they headed back to Blue Springs.

With Stephen driving on ahead, Abby rode with Daniel in Sol's truck, her voice and Daniel's as still as if somebody had sewed their lips shut. What could they say? Death had struck their family yet again and taken a good and sweet brother from their midst, and it made no sense. No words they might offer would change any of that.

A slow rain fell as they drove on behind the hearse. The windshield wipers whipped back and forth. The rain seemed to drive Abby's sadness even deeper into her bones, to stain her with grief in ways she felt she could never wash out.

Abby watched Daniel real close as they headed toward home. His heart had been broken once again. His eyes had dark circles under them, and his beard sprung out all unruly. His hair, usually covered with a hat, was mussed up. The hat had disappeared.

Abby wrapped her arms around her waist. She knew Daniel's temper had frayed as bad as his appearance. He'd snapped at her a couple of times when she tried to comfort him. That grieved Abby. Most of the time Daniel had a kind spirit, even when circumstances went in directions he didn't like.

The rain continued right through the day. They reached Blue Springs a little before suppertime, and Elsa met them at her front door. Abby hustled to the porch and into Elsa's arms. While standing in the rain, Daniel told the undertaker where to find the funeral man. The undertaker said he'd stop by there for a while and then bring Luke back to Elsa's and set him up.

"People will start coming to visit tomorrow," Elsa said as she hugged Abby again. "After you called Mrs. Lollard's, I reached Preacher Tuttle. He told some folks about Luke, then drove down and brought me and the boys home. I've prepared things at least a little."

They all moved into the house. "Jimmy and Stevie are with the preacher," Elsa said. "He took them to the store for candy while I did some tidying up."

Abby glanced around the house. It had never looked cleaner.

"We can put him right here," Daniel said, walking toward the parlor's fireplace. "Right here in the center of the room."

"People will be coming from all over," said Abby. "Luke sang in lots of churches."

Daniel cleared his throat. "I need to go downtown now, make some arrangements."

Abby nodded and Daniel left. Abby followed Elsa into the kitchen. Food covered the table.

"People started bringing in food as soon as they heard the news," Elsa said.

Abby touched a bowl of green beans. "When somebody dies in Blue Springs, all the women take to cooking," she said.

Elsa rearranged a platter of biscuits. "I'm so grieved about Luke. He never hurt a soul."

Abby sighed. "It's a shock for sure," she said. "Those autos are a danger to man and beast."

Elsa pulled an apron from a hook by the sink.

"I'll take one of those too," said Abby. Elsa handed her an apron. The two women locked eyes. Tears streamed down Abby's cheeks.

"I know it's hard," said Elsa, wiping Abby's tears with the apron. "He was a good brother."

Abby shook her head. "I'm not crying so much for Luke. He's with Jesus now. He loved the Lord, spent his whole life singing and playing to the Lord's praises. I don't fear for him anymore. I'm afraid for Daniel. So much has buffeted him. He's a strong man, but how much can a body take before he . . . before he breaks down?"

Elsa eased her to the table to sit. Abby's tears came harder.

"What about you, Abby?" whispered Elsa. "You have faced as much as Daniel, maybe more. How much can you take?"

Abby hung her head and her body shook. For the first time she could remember, she had run out of fight. And it wasn't just Luke either, bad as that was. It was the loss of Rose Francis, her troubles with Stephen, the heartache over all of it tossed in together. Elsa was right, how much more could she take? How much longer could she keep up this show of courage when her insides hurt so much, feared so much?

Abby opened her arms, and Elsa leaned over and embraced her. The two women cried together there in the kitchen as the rain drummed on the roof outside. Abby let it all out, the grief held in for so long, grief that had made her weary, weak.

When the sobbing finally wore itself out, she took a big breath, hugged Elsa one more time and leaned back. The crying made her feel better. She heard someone enter the front room and realized Daniel had returned. Soon they would set up Luke's body. She wiped her eyes. "Folks will come from a long way," she said.

Elsa nodded. "Everybody loved Luke Porter."

Abby ran water from the sink and washed her face. Time to face reality. No more time for tears, at least not right now.

They buried Luke two days later, up the hill behind where Daniel and Deidre lived. After the undertaker and some boys hauled him up from Blue Springs, they placed him right beside the dirt that covered Solomon Sr. and his boy Walter. A big crowd gathered under the oak trees that gave shade to the place. The morning air hung stagnant as Preacher Tuttle read the Scripture from First Corinthians fifteen and the people waved fans to stir the warm air and keep the flies away.

" 'Now this I say, brethren,' " read Preacher Tuttle, " 'that flesh and blood cannot inherit the kingdom of God; neither doth corruption inherit incorruption. Behold, I show you a mystery; We shall not all sleep, but we shall all be changed.' "

The preacher's voice rose as he repeated the familiar passage. " 'In a moment, in the twinkling of an eye, at the last trump: for the trumpet shall sound, and the dead shall be raised incorruptible, and we shall be changed. For this . . .' "

Her heart as heavy as an iron kettle, Abby kept her eyes on Daniel. He leaned on his cane on the other side of the grave, his black hat in his hand and his best britches, shirt, and coat as crisp as a hot brick would press them. But it was obvious that, in spite of his good appearance, Daniel's spirits were in a shambles. He'd barely spoken to anybody in the last two days. Deidre had told Abby he hadn't slept or eaten. In fact, bad dreams and headaches had kept him up every night since Luke died.

Abby wondered if Daniel had recently partaken of some drink. She had reason to think this, because she'd seen him standing on the porch with Stephen on more than one occasion. Not only that, but Daniel wouldn't look her in the eyes when she spoke to him.

Preacher Tuttle moved from the Scripture reading to the preaching. "I got to tell you, I am mystified today," he announced, his pace slow as he got started. "I am mystified by the ways of the Almighty."

Abby's head nodded in agreement. God's ways sure were a mystery.

"But," Tuttle continued, "the Good Book says there in Isaiah, chapter fifty-five and verse nine, that the Lord's ways are higher than our ways, and His thoughts are higher than our thoughts."

True words, thought Abby.

The preacher picked up the pace now. "Yes, I got to tell you my beloved friends and neighbors, the Lord has ways and thoughts way up higher than anything our short arms could ever reach. I don't know why Mr. Luke had to go home to be with Jesus right now, no sir, I just don't know. Maybe He needed a guitar player in the heavenly band, or maybe a good tenor for the choir. We know how Mr. Luke could sing those gospel songs, how he could make music so sweet we thought we'd already died and soared into heaven. My friends, Mr. Luke could make even a heavenly choir sound better, and so maybe our Lord wanted to hear Luke's music face-to-face. I just don't know.

"Or maybe it was something meant not for heaven but for here on earth. Maybe the Lord wants to use Mr. Luke's passing to teach us something. Maybe He wants us to trust Him more, to remember the truth that this old earth is not our final stopping point, that we're just strangers passing through. The Lord wants us to keep our eyes always peeled to the heavens, to the day when we too will go home to live with Jesus. I can't say for sure what the Lord wants to say to us with Luke's far-too-early demise. But this I can tell you . . ."

Abby glanced at Daniel. A blank look covered his face; he seemed to have his eyes fixed on something beyond the coffin and beyond the preacher. She wondered what notions he had about all this.

Preacher Tuttle wound down his sermon. "I can't preach Mr. Luke into heaven today," he said. "His own life, his own trust in Jesus has already put him there. Yes sir, that's the truth, my friends. So we leave him there now, in the arms of the Lord, singing and picking his guitar forever and ever, amen and amen. Let us pray."

Abby closed her eyes. Preacher Tuttle prayed softly. A bird chirped, a squirrel chattered. Preacher Tuttle finished praying, then bent down, picked up a handful of dirt and threw it into the hole where Luke's coffin lay. The dirt thumped on the wood. Abby moved closer to the graveside, gathered up some dirt and dropped it into the hole. Daniel followed her, then Deidre and their kids, then Stephen and Jimmy and Stevie. Everybody else followed them, each person passing by and dropping a handful of dirt down on Luke.

Moving away from the crowd, Abby leaned up against a tree. Her face felt hot. She sensed movement behind her and turned around to see Daniel close by. With the burial service over, the folks around them started to disperse, some remaining in clusters and talking quietly to one another. Daniel stared at the ground. He had his cane in his hands.

"This is a sad day," said Abby.

Daniel's knuckles turned white on the staff. He took a step closer to her and held out the cane. "I want you to keep this," he said.

Abby blinked, not raising a hand to take the cane from him.

"I don't want it no more," Daniel explained. "Don't know that I trust what it stands for."

Abby touched his elbow. "You're just grieved right now. Nobody is faulting you for anything."

"It's more than that and you know it. I'm not sure of anything anymore. It ain't right for me to carry Pa's cane around like I still hold to the faith he had when he carved on it."

"Daniel, I won't take your cane. Pa gave it to you for a reason, just like Luke said at the hospital. I won't take what Pa meant for you to have for a purpose."

"He only gave it to me because I got hurt in the war and couldn't walk good. That's all. You either take it or I'll cut it up and burn it in the fireplace."

"You wouldn't do that!" said Abby.

Daniel gritted his teeth. "You don't want to test me on this, Abby. Now take the cane."

It was clear that Daniel had made up his mind. He was like their pa that way. Stubborn. Not knowing what else to do, she grabbed the cane. "I'll keep this for you," she said. "You'll want it back someday."

"I reckon that ain't true."

"It'll be there when you want it."

Daniel studied his boots but then looked strong at her. "You're the last good one of us now that Luke is gone."

"I'm not in agreement with that," she said. "You will see it too one day, I'm sure."

Daniel looked at the cane.

Abby started to hand it back to him. But he quickly held up his hand and said, "I can't. Not fit to carry it."

"You know I will be praying for you."

"Do as you like," he said. "I don't reckon it can hurt anything."

With that he turned and walked away. The cane in her hand, Abby watched him go and wondered what next could possibly happen to her family.

The last of the sun had just dipped behind Blue Springs Mountain when Daniel stepped out of his house and onto the front porch. He saw Stephen and a couple of other men from town leaning over the porch rail and talking. His dog Whip lay by Stephen's feet. One of the men was smoking a store-bought cigarette. The men all tipped their hats to Daniel as he took a seat in a rocker next to Stephen and pulled his pipe from his coat pocket. Whip moved over, licked his hand, and then settled back down at his feet.

"Mighty still out here," said the man with the cigarette. "Maybe a storm brewing off somewhere."

"We done got enough rain for a while," said another. "Don't need no more today."

Daniel filled the pipe and lit it. Stephen moved to the rocker by Daniel and eased into it. "A long day," said Stephen.

Daniel nodded. He'd never liked Stephen Waterbury and his high-handed ways, but today he felt different for some reason. What right did he have to look down on anybody?

"I'll like it just fine when all this is over," Daniel said. "Too many people saying too many useless things if you ask me."

Stephen grunted. "I agree completely. A lot of pie in the sky, heaven this and heaven that."

Daniel pulled on his pipe. "You don't believe in heaven?"

"I don't believe in much of anything I can't count," said Stephen.

Daniel smiled wryly. "I used to believe in banks," he said. "But a bank lost all my dollars."

Stephen took out a flask, nipped from it, then tapped it on the rocker's arm. "My point exactly. The banks put your money where you can't see it, can't touch it. How do you know for certain you can get at your money if you want it?"

"Don't reckon you can. Least I couldn't."

"That's right," said Stephen. "All this heaven talk is the same way. How do you know it even exists when you can't see it right before your eyes?"

Daniel rocked a couple of times, thinking on Stephen's words. "I used to believe it," said Daniel.

"If you want my opinion, it's good for the women and kids but not worth much for a grown man."

Daniel puffed his pipe. Stephen extended the flask to him, offering him a drink. Daniel studied it for a second. His mouth watered. The last time he took a drink he hadn't liked it much. But it did hold some appeal at the present moment, he had to admit that.

"Go ahead, you'll find it's pretty smooth," urged Stephen. "Just what a man needs to set his mind at ease."

Daniel thought of his pa. Solomon wouldn't like him taking to drinking. He rocked faster. But his pa had been dead a long time now. How long would he let his pa's ways tell him what he ought or ought not to do?

"Reckon it can't hurt anything," he said.

"Might even help some," added Stephen.

Daniel took the flask and held it for several seconds. He glanced around the porch as if to see if anyone would stop him. No one did. Stephen was staring into the yard, a cigar now in hand. Daniel touched the flask to his lips. Then he hesitated. Why do this? He didn't need it. Only a weak man turned to the jug when things were bad. But then he thought of Luke lying in the hospital bed, the way he'd prayed for Luke to live. God had ignored those prayers, hadn't answered them even though Daniel had prayed harder than ever in his life. Why not take a drink? What difference did it make one way or the other? Life did to a man what it wanted to do and whether or not he took a little of the doublings every now and again changed nothing.

Daniel closed his eyes and swigged the whiskey.

It burned his throat as it slid down. Almost instantly his stomach warmed, and he drew a long breath. Lowering the bottle, he started to hand it back to Stephen.

"Go on and finish that one off," Stephen told him. "I got another right here." He patted his coat pocket and grinned.

Daniel started to say no, that he didn't need any more. But the flask fit so nicely in his hand, and the drink he'd taken felt good as it ran through his system. "I appreciate it," he said as he took a second drink. "Got to admit it calms the nerves."

"I told you," said Stephen. "Calms the nerves right well."

CHAPTER FIFTEEN

For nearly two weeks after Preacher Tuttle drove her and Elsa and the boys back to Boone following Luke's burial, Abby did little else but climb out of bed every morning and back in late in the afternoon. When she didn't have to do something for the boys, she mostly slept. Even when awake, she was so weary she didn't know if she could expand her chest to take in another breath. Her arms and legs felt heavy and difficult to move. About the only thing that allowed her and the children to get by was the fact that Elsa came to Boone with them to take care of the duties Abby had no heart to do.

Abby knew her sorrow was directly tied to Luke's death, Daniel's low spirits, and her problems with Stephen. The day before they left Blue Springs, Daniel and Stephen had spent hours on the porch together. Normally she would've liked that. In other times, it might have signaled the two men had finally come to some liking of each other; might have said they were just talking the way men often talked after a family member died, about politics and such as that.

Sadly, Abby discovered they weren't discussing anything of the kind. Fact is, from what she could see, they didn't say much at all to each other.

Which meant they had found something else in common.

She'd smelled whiskey on Daniel's breath the night of Luke's burial, and she had no doubt that it was Stephen who had given it to him. She didn't know which hurt the most—her anger at Stephen for handing whiskey to Daniel or her fear for Daniel, that he'd taken a step that might lead him down a rough path. What she did know was that the mix of everything—Luke's death, Daniel's drinking, and Stephen's all-around weakness as a husband and father—had put her into a state lower than she ever imagined she could fall.

On the first day of September Elsa woke Abby about half past eight for her breakfast. Elsa had prepared a plate of eggs, which sat steaming on the kitchen table, along with coffee and fried apples. Abby sipped the coffee, then sagged down in her chair. Breathing still took much effort.

"The kids out playing?" Abby asked.

Elsa nodded. "Jimmy hauled in some wood, swept off the front porch. He then took Stevie and headed out to Mrs. Lollard's."

"They're both good boys."

"Jimmy is a big help. Stevie too with what he can do."

Abby ate a bite of eggs. "You seen Stephen this morning?"

"He left about seven or so. Said he needed to do a few things. I think he's getting ready to go back to Knoxville in a couple days."

Abby took another sip of coffee and stared out the window. Strange how the sun kept rising no matter who died. Today it drifted through the white drapes like it did every day the clouds didn't cover it.

"Stephen didn't come home until almost one this morning," Abby said to no one in particular. "He woke me when he came to bed."

Elsa poured more coffee into her cup. "Stephen doing all right these days?" she asked.

Abby shrugged. "What do you mean?"

Elsa wiped her hands on her apron and sat down across from Abby. "Oh, his business and all, over in Knoxville. I expect folks don't call on a lawyer so regular when dollars dry up as they have."

"He does okay," said Abby, studying Elsa. "As good as most others. Why do you ask?"

Avoiding Abby's eyes, Elsa wiped a spill off the table, stood and moved to the sink. Abby watched her. Even as tired as she was, she could see that Elsa was uneasy about something.

"I know times are hard for everybody," said Elsa. "That's all. Can't I ask about my friend's welfare?"

Elsa's tone made Abby even more suspicious. It wasn't like her to ask questions like this. "You know something I don't?"

Elsa washed out the sink, her back to Abby, her hands jumpy with the rag as she swiped the counter. Abby's tension rose even more. Elsa *did* know something. But what?

A knock sounded at the front door. Abby started to get up, but Elsa touched her shoulder and held her in place. "I'll help you," she said. "Whatever way I can."

"What do you mean?" said Abby, her heart beginning to race. "What's happening?"

Again, knocking at the door.

"Go ahead and answer it," said Elsa. "And remember I will help you, whatever it is you need."

Confused but unable to wait for Elsa to say anything else, Abby pulled her robe tighter, pushed back her hair, and trudged to the front of the house. She wouldn't like what met her there, she knew that from the expression on Elsa's face. Whoever was standing on the porch carried bad news, no doubt about it. But how much worse could things get?

Abby opened the door. A tall, slender man in a brown suit, holding a black case under his left arm, stood facing her, sweat rolling down his chin. "Mrs. Waterbury?" he said.

"Yes, I'm Abigail Waterbury. Can I help you?"

"My name is Mr. Lon Cain," the man said. "I'm from the bank. May I come in for a minute?"

Her mind not working well, Abby didn't respond at first to his request. Instead, she stood in the doorway and tried to figure out what this meant. She had no dealings with the bank. Had the undertaker phoned the Boone Bank to see if she had the money to make the payments for Luke's funeral expenses?

"May I come in for a minute?" Cain repeated, a little louder this time. The sound of his voice cut through Abby's trance. She stepped back and quietly led him into the living room. They sat down, Abby near the fireplace, Mr. Cain by the window.

"Would you like something to drink?" she asked, finding her manners.

He shook his head, saying, "I'm not here on a social call." Then he took the briefcase from under his arm and opened it. "As I've already said, I'm from the bank."

Abby heard Elsa approaching and motioned her to take a seat, but Elsa decided to stay near the entryway to the kitchen.

Cain pulled out a piece of paper and handed it to Abby. Abby studied the paper for a minute. It took only a few seconds for its meaning to register. She held her breath and her heart thumped as she finished reading it. Dropping the document to her lap, she laid her head in her hands and closed her eyes.

"It's a notice of eviction," Cain said as calmly as if announcing he liked ham for breakfast. "The bank now owns your house."

Abby tried to speak but no words came out.

"I assume your husband has told you about this. We've sent Mr. Waterbury no less than three notices and tried to reach him by telephone on numerous occasions. He first received word some weeks back that he had until the end of the month to make the necessary arrangements to hold on to the house. It's now September first, and I'm afraid he's failed to respond."

Abby pressed a fist to her mouth in an attempt to hold back the tears.

"You have two weeks," Cain said. "I am not a man without feelings. Two weeks—not to catch up on the payments, though. It's too late for that. But fourteen days to vacate the property. The bank has its troubles too. Obligations have to be met."

Abby hung her head. What else could happen, what else befall her? Where would she and her boys go now?

"Do you understand?" asked Mr. Cain, leaning toward her and talking slower like he might to a child. "You have . . . two . . . weeks."

Again Abby tried to speak, yet no words could be formed.

She felt Elsa moving to her side, and she reached out and took Elsa's hands. Elsa bent low and whispered, "We can go to the preacher, ask him to take up a collection. I can come up with a few dollars myself, Daniel too. We can go to the bank, talk it all over."

Abby's heart soared at Elsa's idea. Maybe they could gather together enough money to hold off the bank! She could keep the house!

But then her spine stiffened as she realized she couldn't ask folks to give from the few dollars they had saved. Her pa hadn't raised her as a charity case, somebody who would depend on the handouts of others. A Porter made it by hard work and by praying, not by taking what others might need for their own purposes. Besides, her family and neighbors had needs as great as hers. What right did she have to go asking for their help, to keep a house her husband hadn't been able to pay on?

Abby shook her head. When she spoke, her words sounded more courageous than she felt. "Elsa, I won't take others' money," she said, her voice loud enough for Cain to hear. "People have no dollars to spare. That goes for you and Daniel too."

She looked Mr. Cain in the eyes, her fighting spirit rising as she heard her own voice. She refused to give up! No, her pa hadn't raised her that way. "I will *not* take anybody's money!" Abby exclaimed. "Me and my boys will make it just fine. . . ."

Suddenly her thoughts became confused, and her courage ran completely out. Even as she spoke, she knew it was all a lie. She felt so weak, so worn down by life's blows that she wondered if she could go on. She shut her eyes. *Just let me rest,* she thought. *Rest for a long, long time.*

She felt Elsa wrap an arm around her shoulders and hold her tight. It felt so good to have another human being close by, someone who cared for her. She'd felt alone for so long now, what with Stephen working in Knoxville, what with . . . Abby rested her head against Elsa's side, and Elsa cradled her there.

"What will I do?" Abby whispered, looking up at Elsa. "Where will I go?" She thought of Knoxville. Surely Stephen would insist that she and the boys move in with him. Yet she didn't trust that he would. He had only a couple of rooms rented in a boardinghouse, too little room for three more.

Elsa stroked her head. Cain shifted as if to speak, but Elsa held up a hand and he backed off.

"It's simple—you and the boys will come live with me," Elsa said. "Until Stephen's work picks up again. These hard times can't last forever, you'll see. Stay with me for now, and then later Stephen will come for you, I'm sure."

Abby's heart lifted a little. At least she had a place to live. But how could she go back to Blue Springs after all these years? She'd promised herself she would never return to the isolated town with all its backward ways.

Closing her eyes again, she felt as though her world had ended. At the age of thirty-six she would return to the tiny town where she'd grown up. Go back a failure, a woman who had gone off with all kinds of wild notions about making something of herself, of gaining an education and becoming a teacher who would make a difference in other people's lives. But she'd never quite finished her education and so had never become a regular teacher in a schoolhouse. Truth was, she'd never accomplished any of the dreams that had carried her away from Blue Springs.

Abby thought of Jimmy and Stevie. What would moving to Blue Springs mean for them? How would they ever get a decent education? Knowing that the schools in Blue Springs stayed closed a lot these days since the money had dried up, she worried over her boys' future should they leave Boone.

Her head ached as she tried to figure it all out. Yet what choice did she have? Stephen lived in Knoxville and up to now had said nothing about moving them there. Yes, she would ask him about that, though she already knew what his answer would be. So it looked like she had no other option. Whether she wanted to or not, she would have to go and stay with Elsa in Blue Springs.

Abby faced Mr. Cain again and set her chin. Though her insides hurt something bad, she wouldn't let him see it. Her pa had taught her to bear up strong in front of others when troubles arose. "I will move out within the two weeks," she said. "You'll have your house."

Mr. Cain organized his papers, then placed them in the center of his briefcase and closed it. "I'm sorry to have to bring you this bad news," he said. "But I am only doing my job."

Abby looked at Elsa. "We all have to do our jobs," she said. "Nothing to be sorry about."

CHAPTER SIXTEEN

On the second Saturday of September—on a morning that began unusually cold—Abby, Elsa, Preacher Tuttle, and Jimmy and Stevie loaded up what possessions they could carry in the preacher's Chevy and hauled them up the mountain to Blue Springs. Abby didn't say much on the trip, just sat in the back of the car under a sack full of the boys' clothes with her head down.

Abby had called Stephen on the evening that Mr. Cain paid his visit. She'd decided right off not to make a scene. Given the circumstances of the day, she wasn't going to blame a man for failing to have enough dollars to hang on to his house. Everybody she knew had trouble making ends meet. Stephen was no different.

For some reason, she hadn't cried much during the day. Once she settled on what she had to do, she just squared her shoulders and made the choice to keep moving ahead.

Without mincing words, Abby laid it out for him. "A Mr. Cain stopped by from the bank today," she said, "and told me we no longer own our house and that we have two weeks to move out. He showed me the paper that proves it."

Stephen was silent.

Abby continued. "I need to know if the boys and I can move to Knoxville with you. If not, we will go to Blue Springs to live with Elsa."

Stephen replied, "You know I want you and the boys with me. But I have no room here, and no money to rent anything bigger."

Abby sighed. Just as she expected. She questioned whether he planned to live with her ever again. She'd deal with that some other time. Right now, she had more immediate problems.

"Then we'll go to Blue Springs," she said.

"That's the best thing, don't you think?"

Abby realized for the first time that she'd lost all respect for her husband. She'd tried so hard and had put up with so much, yet he seemed to have an empty heart, a hole in the center of his spirit.

She thought about how he had failed to support her in just about everything that had come along. Over and over again, she'd stood alone as the strong one in their marriage. She hated to think this of her husband and recognized it sounded a little proud. Still, it was the plain truth.

Abby also realized something else. Stephen had little or no faith to hold him up when hard times knocked him around. True, he said he'd trusted Jesus when a boy, and his family had some connection with a Methodist church in Raleigh, but only on rare occasions would he attend Jesus Holiness with her and the boys. In their day-to-day life, she didn't see much evidence of any true connection to the Lord. Fact is, she didn't see that he had much of a connection to anything at all, except maybe to the flask he kept in his pocket most of the time.

"Going to Blue Springs is all we can do for now," she told him. "It's the only path the Lord has cleared for me."

"I think you're right, Abby. You're going to have to move."

Now Abby sat in the backseat of Preacher Tuttle's auto and wondered how she would make it. With no way to haul much of anything up to Elsa's, she'd had to sell all of the furniture she and Stephen had collected over the years. The little bit of cash she carried in her purse, the sum of her assets, had come from the sale of the furniture.

She couldn't help thinking how strange it was that a family could simply pull up from one place and head off to another and in just a matter of hours. She was reminded of the time Hal Clack had forced her family out of their cabin when she was a young girl. She always figured that when she grew up, she'd get to choose when and where she moved, whether to a different house or town or both. She now saw that she'd been wrong about that. The truth was, sometimes everything around her could suddenly shift without warning, pull at her and carry her somewhere else, like a stream carrying a stick of wood. Which is exactly what she felt like—a stick being pushed and shoved by currents and eddies and swirls, far beyond anything she could control.

The car bounced along the road, bottoming out in one hole after another. Abby hardly noticed the ride. Except for speaking to Jimmy and Stevie every now and again, she didn't look up. The boys seemed okay even though they'd cried when she first told them they had to move. Jimmy wanted to know why they couldn't stay in their house anymore, and Abby had decided she might as well tell him the truth.

"Times are hard," she'd said. "Lots of people have lost their homes. Some even worse than that."

Jimmy looked at her with eyes wide. "I can get a job," he said, all grown up in his concern. "I'm old enough now."

Abby hugged him. "No, I need you to stay around home and help me. We'll be fine. We're going to move to Elsa's."

"Maybe I can find a job in Blue Springs," said Jimmy.

"Me too," said Stevie. "If Jim can work, so can I."

Abby smiled at her youngest. He had recently started trying to best Jimmy, compete with him even though Jimmy was bigger. Abby knew that was only natural. Boys did compete, even close brothers. "We'll see," she said. "Jobs are hard to come by right now."

"We already know a few folks up there," said Jimmy.

"That's right. So you see, it won't be so bad."

The talk seemed to make both Jimmy and Stevie feel better, and they took the notion of moving as well as two boys their age could be expected. Abby prayed for them almost constantly.

When the brown Chevy finally pulled up in front of Elsa's house, everybody went right to work, hauling their belongings inside. Her shawl wrapped tightly around her arms, Abby struggled to do her part. *A disgrace,* she thought as she worked. *Everybody in Blue Springs will see this as a disgrace.* She'd been so ambitious as a child, somebody who would go off and conquer the world. But now she'd landed right back where she started.

The boys put their clothes in the back bedroom they would share, while Elsa showed Abby to the bedroom just down the hall from them.

Abby knew the room well. She'd slept in the room as a child, under the care of Elsa's ma, Amelia, now dead for almost nineteen years. In a trancelike state, Abby put away her clothes.

That evening Elsa served them all some supper—green beans and fried apples with corn bread. Abby ate little, her appetite as diminished as her spirits. During the meal, the boys made a lot of racket and told how they'd thrown rocks at a deer they saw in the woods. Abby started to tell them to quiet down but then decided against it. *Let them be,* she thought.

Preacher Tuttle joined them at the table, casually enjoying the beans and apples and speaking as if he'd had a meal in the house several times before. After supper, the preacher thanked Elsa for the meal, said his good-byes and left. Abby helped Elsa clean up the dishes and then excused herself. After putting the boys to bed, she shuffled off to her old bedroom.

The days and weeks and months passed slowly but surely. Abby suffered but survived. Christmas arrived. Stephen made the trip up to Blue Springs to see everyone. Abby did her best to celebrate Jesus' birth, but since Stephen said he saw no feasible way to pull the family together again anytime soon, no joy welled up in her heart.

Being back in Blue Springs jarred loose lots of memories for Abby, and she found herself reflecting about the past, about the choices she'd made and the ones she'd left behind. Thaddeus came to mind often during these months, and she let herself linger on the thought every now and again. But not for too long. No reason to torment herself with what might have been, especially when she was having so much trouble dealing with what actually was.

She saw a lot of old friends in these months too, particularly her childhood friends Lindy and Jubal. She sang next to Lindy in the choir on Christmas Eve. But since Lindy had always wanted Abby to marry Thaddeus, Lindy remained a touch standoffish, which proved awkward for Abby. To Abby's grief, a distance remained between the two of them, and the visits didn't occur nearly as often as Abby hoped.

One time, a few days before New Year's, Abby saw Lindy at the general store and they walked home together after finishing their shopping. Abby asked about Thaddeus, where he was these days. Lindy shook her head and said that Thaddeus had asked her not to tell Abby where he was, nor to tell him if ever Abby inquired about him. If he thought Abby had any interest in him, it would drive him mad and he would want to return home to see her. But, since she was married, this was something he knew he could never do.

Sometimes Abby thought maybe she just imagined the distance between her and Lindy, that in fact Lindy was as sweet and kind as ever. The memory can play tricks, she knew that, and whether Lindy and Jubal were more or less friendly now than in previous years, she couldn't tell for sure. Every once in a while Abby got the impression that Lindy wanted to ask her why she chose to marry that weak man from Boone when her brother—one of the best men God ever created—wanted to marry her and make her happy? The possibility that maybe Lindy wanted to ask her the question didn't bother Abby nearly so much as the fact that she found herself asking it as well.

January of '37 rolled through cold and snowy. Abby walked the boys to school every morning they held classes. Sometimes she hung around and helped the teacher, but more times than not so few kids showed up that the teacher didn't need her and so she returned to Elsa's.

She was often idle at Elsa's. Elsa had things pretty well under control, and after the cooking and cleaning were taken care of, Abby had little to do except sit near the window and look out at the frozen ground, either that or sew or read.

Sometimes she fell asleep in her chair by the window, her head back against the rocker with a blanket wrapped around her arms. At other times, when sleep didn't come, tears pushed to her eyes as she rocked. She tried fighting back the tears, but it seemed the more she fought, the harder the tears came. Elsa would sometimes sit beside her when she cried, telling her not to worry but to keep trusting the Lord and things would someday turn for the better.

Abby wanted so much to believe her, yet she wasn't at all sure that everything would come out all right like Elsa said it would.

January turned into February, and Abby continued to sit by the window and watch as time slipped by. The future seemed to have shut down on her as certain as the dark shut down on the light every evening. She had no future so far as she could tell. Just the present, which consisted of taking care of her sons, helping out Elsa, going to Jesus Holiness on Sundays, and sitting by the window and staring at the snow.

When not sleeping or crying, Abby worried about Daniel. Luke's death had smacked him right in the heart. He seldom attended church. Deidre said she hardly ever saw him, that he stayed gone a lot during the week, out trying to scrounge work. From what Abby had heard from others, Daniel had taken a bad slide downhill.

Talk in town said he'd started drinking heavy, buying a bottle every time he could lay his hands on the money. The drink no doubt was his way of trying to blot out the hurt that gnawed away at his insides. Abby wanted so much to help him, but other than praying, she didn't know what to do. One thing she did know, though. Liquor didn't fix anything. She understood that from her years with Stephen.

Consumed by grief and worry, Abby lost weight that winter. Her eyes dulled some, and her frame seemed to sink inward. Elsa told her she had to eat more and sleep better or she would fall sick for sure. But that didn't matter to Abby. If not for her boys, she might even have preferred to fall sick.

Let it come, she figured. What difference did it make? So what if she got so sick she passed on to Jesus? Elsa could raise her boys just fine. They would miss their ma for sure, at least for a while. But they were strong boys, and Elsa had a large heart. Given her condition right now, Abby suspected Elsa already did better with them than she did.

It was halfway through another mid-February day, and as usual Abby sat gazing out the front window of Elsa's house. Snow fell lightly, adding to the several inches already on the ground. The gray sky pressed down like a steel lid. Elsa worked in the kitchen, while Jimmy and Stevie played at a friend's house.

Abby saw a man walking toward the house. As the man reached the porch, she recognized him. Rousing herself, Abby hollered to Elsa, "Sol is here!"

She heard Elsa shut off the water faucet, followed by her hurried footsteps moving from the kitchen into the living room. "Mighty cold for him to visit today," said Elsa, going over to the window to take a look. "Especially on foot."

Abby nodded. Sol, his wife, Jewel, and their kids usually ate Sunday dinner with them. He sometimes stopped by at other times during the week too, to check on his mama. But lately, with the snow too deep for driving, Sol hadn't been around in a while. Abby figured, then, he must have a good reason for a visit today. She felt her heart beating faster, for she'd learned that when folks showed up at unexpected times, hard news usually followed.

Elsa rushed to the door and opened it just as Sol was about to knock. Brushing the snow off his shoulders and hat, he stepped inside and immediately headed to the fireplace.

"I'll get you some coffee," said Elsa.

"That should warm me up," he said.

With Elsa busy in the kitchen, Abby faced Sol. Since moving back to Blue Springs, she'd found him to be a good man, gentle and kind to his mama and his wife. A lot like her pa had been, like her brother Daniel too, back before he started drinking. Sol was a dependable, trustworthy man.

"You sure are out on a disagreeable day," Abby said.

He took a rocker by the fireplace, set his hat on his knee. "You're right about that," he said. "Not a day fit for man nor beast."

Abby wanted to ask why he'd come but thought it better to wait for Elsa.

"I see the boys from time to time," said Sol. "They seem to like it here."

"I think so. Kids make friends real easy."

"You've raised them well, Abby. Jimmy is gettin' to be a young man now, Stevie not far behind."

Abby looked down at her hands. Without warning, Stephen's long absence hit her hard and she missed him. Surely the boys ached for him as well, needed his fatherly presence. She felt tears welling up. To her relief, Elsa returned then, a tray in her hands.

"Here's the coffee," Elsa said. "Some spice cake too."

Sol took the tray from her. "You'd hardly know that times are bad," he said. "Not from what Ma serves up when a body comes visitin'."

Elsa eased into a chair with her coffee. Sol passed a cup to Abby. Then, leaning back in the rocker, he sipped his coffee and took a bite of cake. The logs in the fireplace shifted. Sol glanced at Elsa as he ate and then at Abby. Suddenly Abby knew the news he'd brought affected her more than Elsa. But what? And who? Was it Daniel? Had something happened to him, or to somebody in his family? Or was this about Stephen? She wanted to stand up and demand that Sol stop eating his cake at once and tell her what had happened.

Finally Sol put his coffee cup back on the tray and wiped his mouth.

He turned toward Abby, his hat in his hands again. "I got to tell you something," he said. "I guess you already figured that."

Abby held her breath.

"It's your husband, Stephen. Seems the law over near Knoxville arrested him yesterday."

Abby let out her breath. "Arrested him. . . ?"

"Then locked him up in jail."

"But why?"

"They say he sold some land to some folks."

"So?"

"He didn't actually own the land he sold."

"What?"

Sol hung his head, embarrassed for Abby. "Looks like Stephen sold about four hundred acres, land that wasn't his to sell. He made up a phony title, took some folks in for over six hundred dollars. The law says they might have some other charges too."

Abby couldn't make sense of what she'd just heard. Stephen involved in breaking the law, selling something he didn't own, cheating innocent people! She felt ashamed. She'd married a dishonest man, a fraud. How could she have been so blind? What had she ever seen in him? Had he always been this way? Or had he been a good man, a man worthy of her love when she met him? Surely he had. To believe otherwise said things about herself she didn't want to face. That she'd married Stephen because of his position, looks and charm, for the money he flashed around. But he had been different back then, a man of character whom the hard times had squeezed into something else. Maybe he'd taken some wrong turns because of the pressure of trying to do well for his family.

Convinced she'd figured it out some, Abby looked at Sol once more. Strangely, she didn't sound real upset when she spoke. So much bad had happened to her she felt numb to it all. "Where do they have him?" she asked.

"He's bein' held in a little town called Lolleyville."

"Will he go to trial?"

Sol nodded. "Could be it's all just a mix-up," he said. "Crazy things can happen in times like this."

"That's true," added Elsa, obviously wanting to comfort Abby. "He might be innocent. Best wait before jumping to any conclusions."

Abby glanced at her. "I appreciate your suggestions, but you know as well as I that . . ." She paused, not able to speak out loud the truth of what she knew. Stephen had almost surely committed the crime. Sizing the dire situation up, she saw it clearly, saw how he had this kind of thing pretty much stamped in his bones. The bad times had just revealed his true character, shown him as a man unable to stand up to the tests of life. Part of her felt sorry for him; the other part, anger and shame.

Abby took a deep breath. The worst had happened. The limited amount of dollars that Stephen had been sending home every month would now dry up. She had no help but Elsa to keep her family from heading to the poorhouse.

She folded her hands in her lap and stared into the fire. What next? What could she do to keep life and limb together? Several seconds ticked by as Abby tried to keep from panicking.

She thought of Stephen again and her panic turned to anger. What a weak man! What a failure! But she wasn't going to fail too. From out of nowhere a surge of determination rose up from deep within her, something she thought she'd lost when she had to leave her house in Boone. With Stephen behind bars, her last feeling of depending on him disappeared. For her and the boys to survive, she realized she must find her own way, chart her own course. For some reason, that notion freed her up to take charge again, to step out of her melancholy ways.

Abby looked Sol in the eyes and said, "I don't want my Jimmy and Stevie to know anything about this, you understand?"

Sol and Elsa nodded in unison.

"I don't want them carryin' around the shame of their pa," she went on. "No reason for his mistakes or mine to sully their lives."

"Don't worry, I promise to keep this to myself," said Sol. "Nobody else needs to know right now."

Abby stood and moved to the window. This time when she looked out, she had a firm set to her features. "Sol, do you think you could take me to see him?"

"Sure, just as soon as the weather gets better."

Behind her, the logs in the fire shifted again. But Abby didn't notice. She had the future on her mind, and this time, she decided, she'd choose what that future would hold.

CHAPTER SEVENTEEN

The worst of the weather broke about two weeks later, and Sol drove up in his county truck, Abby climbed in, and they headed over to Lolleyville, a small town about twelve miles east of Knoxville. A heavy rain fell as they drove, and Sol's truck got stuck in the mud three separate times. The trip took longer than they had anticipated and kept them so busy they talked little.

Abby appreciated the quiet. Since learning of Stephen's arrest, she'd become more and more angry. How dare he do this thing and bring such disgrace to their family? What kind of man dropped so low as to set out to cheat others? She purposely didn't talk about it with Sol, for then she might not be able to hold back her feelings. Instead, Abby bit her tongue so as not to show disrespect for her husband.

Soaked and covered with mud, she and Sol reached the Lolleyville jail late in the afternoon, both of them hungry and tired. Sol parked the truck next to the curb. The rain had stopped.

"You want me to go in with you?" he asked.

Abby rolled down the truck window as she pondered the idea. The smell of soggy earth touched her nose, and she breathed slowly in and out. She knew she would eventually need to talk to Stephen alone. But right now, as mad as she was, she didn't know if she ought. Without somebody like Sol around, she didn't trust herself not to get into a bad fight with Stephen. Which would accomplish nothing. Yet he'd caused her and her boys so much hurt and shame. First with all the drinking, then his failure to keep a roof over their heads, and now this—his sorry ways had led him into lawbreaking.

"Maybe you should stay with me to start out," Abby said.

Sol took off his hat and looked at his muddy boots. "Whatever you say," he agreed. "You ready, then?"

Abby paused again. Actually she wanted to turn around and leave the place and never come back, run from the jail and from Stephen like a deer running from a forest fire. The notion of facing her husband made her feel sick, humiliated. A highlander man would never pretend to own something that wasn't his just so he could make a profit from it. Sure, a highlander might shoot another man for some petty offense, but that was a crime face-to-face. To pretend to own another's property and then sell it to somebody else, well, that bordered on the cowardly. Such a man made for a sorry husband and an even worse pa.

Abby's shoulders slumped. She had married a man like this. So in a way, she shared some of the blame for what had happened. If she ran from Stephen, she would also be running from herself.

"We best go on in," she finally said. "Get over the worst part soon as we can."

Sol put his hat back on. Swinging open the heavy truck door, Abby stepped out. Sol joined her on the sidewalk in front of the square brick building that served as the Lolleyville jail. He took her by the arm and together they entered the jailhouse, walking down a narrow corridor to an office on the right.

From the office's ceiling hung a fan that rotated slowly, and under the fan, a well-groomed man with a mustache, in a perfectly pressed brown uniform, sat in a wood chair behind a desk. Hillbilly music sounded from a radio sitting on a filing cabinet in the corner. A stack of papers, neatly squeezed into a rectangular box, was placed in the middle of the desk.

Abby hesitated outside the office. "I appreciate your bringing me here," she said to Sol. "You are a good man."

"I'm just doing what any brother would do."

Abby smiled, then Sol removed his hat and led her into the office.

The mustached man looked up at them. "You Sol Porter?" he asked, inspecting Sol's beige uniform.

"Sure am, from over in Blue Springs. You gave me a call a while back, said you had a Stephen Waterbury in custody. This is his wife, Abigail Waterbury." Sol pointed his hat at Abby.

"Name is Conroy," said the lawman. "Elbert Conroy." He stood and shook their hands. "Ma'am, your husband is in the back."

"We'd appreciate it if you would take us to see him," said Sol.

Conroy picked up a black ledger, scribbled in it for a second, then put the book back on the desk and eyed them again. "We ready to go on back now," he said. "Just wanted to note that you come by and when." He opened a drawer and pulled out a ring of keys.

Sol and Abby followed him out of the office and down a hallway. They passed two empty jail cells and then reached a third one on their right. The light dimmed as they approached the last cell. Conroy stopped and pointed to a man lying on a single cot in the cell. The man had his back to them, his face to the concrete wall. A gray blanket covered half his body.

"There he is," Conroy said, nodding toward the gray form on the cot. "Mr. Stephen Jones Waterbury."

Abby waited for Stephen to turn over. He stirred a little but didn't turn. Conroy inserted the key into the cell's thick lock, twisted it, and pushed open the barred door. Stephen rolled over then and rubbed his eyes. His hair sprigged out in all directions; he hadn't shaved in days. Dark circles surrounded his eyes. He wore a dirty gray prison shirt and black pants but no shoes. If she'd passed him on the street, she might not have recognized him.

"Abby. . . ?"

She froze. Stephen seemed very distant, a stranger, not the man she'd married years before. How odd that a man and woman who had started out with so many big dreams could come to this—two strangers who didn't know what to say to each other, one of them in jail.

"I . . . I came to see you," she said, too confused to say anything more.

Stephen put his stockinged feet on the floor. Abby glanced around the cell. A single chair sat in the corner. A light bulb dangled on a cord from the stained plaster ceiling. Next to the chair on the floor was an ashtray, a stub of a cigar resting in it. The place smelled of old smoke. The desire to run returned to Abby, and she wanted to flee from the awful smell, the awful place, the marriage she and Stephen had messed up so badly.

But she knew she couldn't do that. After all, she'd married Stephen for better or for worse, promised to stay by his side till the day one of them died. She'd made that pledge to the good Lord, had stood in front of her friends and family and said out plain that she would love him the rest of her life. No matter how far Stephen fell, she had to live up to her vows and do her best to make the marriage work.

"Go on in," said Conroy. "That's what you came for, ain't it?"

Abby looked at the lawman, then at Sol. Gathering her strength, she walked slowly into the cell.

"Just holler if you need me," said Conroy. "I'm not far."

Abby turned and watched him go.

Sol stayed put outside the cell, his gaze sweeping the jailhouse. His eyes rested here and there as he inspected the space. Then he said, "I'll wait out by Conroy's office; I'll check back in a few minutes." He gave her a half smile, turned and left.

Abby had no choice but to shift her attention back to Stephen. "You look thin," she said to him.

Stephen rubbed his chin. "I haven't been eating well. The food's horrible here."

Abby almost laughed. Stephen liked to eat in fine restaurants and looked down his nose at folks who took most of their meals at home. Now he ate jail food. A far drop for a man of his background.

"You're thinner too," he said.

Abby placed her hands around her waist. "I haven't been eating much either. But for different reasons."

The two fell silent for a moment. Stephen stood and stared up at the small window as if to see the sky outside. "I *am* sorry I have put you in such a way," he said. "I know I've been a big disappointment."

Caught off guard by his words, Abby didn't know what to say next. She felt her breath come in and out.

Stephen faced her and said, "I've had lots of time to do some thinking since they brought me here. I know I've messed up bad. I see that now. Abby, you ought to just leave this place and see about a divorcement. You'd be much better off without me." He paused and waited for a response. When she offered none, he continued, "I'm a sorry man, I know that now. You know it too."

Abby's heart swelled at the tone in his voice. It sounded unusual for him, as though he'd come to grips with his weaknesses. A surge of hope rushed through her. Had Stephen changed? Had he finally come to his senses and recognized the hurtfulness of his ways? Would he try to make amends to her and the boys?

She stepped close to him, looked him in the eyes. "You have so much good in you," she whispered. "I know it's there. I wouldn't have married you if I hadn't thought so. With God's help, together we can—"

"Don't you see, I'm not strong enough for you," Stephen said, cutting her off. "Never have been."

For a long while they stood still, no more than a foot apart. She ached to have him near her again, to have him at home with her and their sons. They still had a chance as husband and wife, could fight their way through the sad days and once again share their lives with each other.

Stephen dropped back down onto the cot.

Abby started to say something, but he interrupted her again.

"My drinking gets the best of me," he admitted. "It makes me do things I know I should refuse."

Abby sat on the edge of the chair. "Stephen, you can quit the drinking. I will help you, others will too. Down at the church, we'll pray for you."

He bent forward, his elbows on his knees and his head down, and ran a hand through his hair. "You know I'm not one for praying much," he said. "The Lord don't take to someone like me."

Abby leaned over and touched his forearm. "The Lord takes to all those who come to Him in faith. You know that as well as I." She could see he was weighing what she'd said.

After a few seconds, he stood, walked to the only window in the cell and stared out.

"We can get you out of here," Abby said, looking at his back. "You've never had any trouble with the law before this, so they'll not go hard on you. You can come home, start over again with everything, the Lord included."

Stephen stuck his hands in his pockets. "I wanted to make you proud of me," he said. "I was just trying to provide for you and our boys, give you everything you ever wanted. That's why I ended up in this mess."

"All I want is for us to be together as a family." She put her hand on his shoulder. "We'll get you out, and you can come to Blue Springs with me and Sol. You and I will figure the rest out later. We'll make it past all this, you'll see."

He pivoted around. "You know you would never have married me if I hadn't had prospects," he said.

Abby paused as she pondered his words. Had she married him because of his status, his wealth? No, she suddenly realized. She had loved him, she knew that for certain! "That's not true," she said. "I married you because I came to love you. Yes, I liked it that you had an education, that you came from a prosperous family. But all that wasn't enough for me to marry you."

Stephen took his hands from his pockets. "You're telling me that you would have married me if I'd been as poor as one of your Blue Springs boys? And as ignorant?"

Abby took his hand and kissed it. "It doesn't matter what I might have done," she said. "You were who you were and I married you. What we have to do now is figure out how to get you free. We can get by in Blue Springs until the bad times pass. Then we can go back to Boone if you like. Or Knoxville, wherever seems best."

Stephen shook his head. The softer tone he'd taken only a few moments ago disappeared. "You have no idea, do you?"

Abby frowned. "What do you mean?"

"I won't ever live in Blue Springs! I'd rather eat from a garbage can in Knoxville than spend even a day as a resident in that backwoods mountain town." He sat down on the cot.

"Fine, then we can live in Knoxville," said Abby, panic rising in her voice as she felt Stephen breaking away from her. "It doesn't matter where. I'll go with you, me and the boys."

"What you should do is go on and leave right now," Stephen said. "I don't think you can do much for me here."

Tears rushed to Abby's eyes. She didn't want to leave like this. "But we have to try," she said, touching his shoulder. "We can hire a lawyer, get you out."

"We have no money for a lawyer."

"So we just give up. . . ?"

Stephen looked at her hard. "Forget about me. I expect I'll be here for a long time. Just pretend I've died and move on with your life."

"What about Stevie and Jimmy?"

Stephen studied the floor. "I'm not much of a father," he said. "Tell the boys I had to move far away to make a living. They'll believe it if it's you who tells them."

Abby wiped her eyes. Stephen seemed so sure about what she ought to do. Was he right? Of course, she would never pursue a divorcement from him. A Jesus woman like her wouldn't even consider such a thing. But should she try to forget about him, lie to his sons regarding their pa's whereabouts? Unsure of what to think, she drew close to Stephen once more but he quickly turned away from her.

"Go on," he said. "Leave me here."

"But . . . Stephen . . ."

"It's okay. You know I'm right about this."

"Well, I won't ever divorce you. I don't believe in such a thing."

"Do what you want," Stephen said, still looking down. "I'll spend at least five years in jail. Least that's what I was told. I don't expect you to wait for me that long."

"But I'm your wife. And I'm a woman of the Lord. I won't go runnin' from you, no matter how heavy the cross or how long the wait."

Stephen glanced up. "I admire your faith," he said. "But I don't share it with you."

Abby moved to him one last time. She touched his back. "I will see you as often as I can."

"Come if you want . . . I'm not going anywhere."

"I will pray for you. I'm still your wife," she repeated.

He turned to face her then, and she saw that his eyes glistened. Maybe this was harder on him than he wanted to show. In that instant an insight came to Abby. Stephen wanted her to forget him for her and the boys' sake. He'd only taken this hard stance to free her from waiting for him, to free her from feeling guilty about his situation. In spite of all his weaknesses, all his failures, he did love her and Jimmy and Stevie.

"Don't tell the boys I'm in jail," he said quietly. "I ask only that from you. Let me keep my dignity with my sons."

"I promise not to tell them about any of this. I will do that for you."

"You're . . . a good woman, Abby," he said through tears. "I wish I'd been a better man for you. . . ."

Abby moved to him and he opened his arms. She fell into them, her tears falling hard. While holding her husband she prayed silently that someday Stephen might walk free from this jail, return to his sons, and become the kind of father and husband she'd always wanted him to be.

Sol and Conroy waited in Conroy's office, the hillbilly music a steady stream in the background.

"Want some coffee?" asked Conroy as Sol took a seat by his desk.

"Sure," said Sol.

Conroy poured them each a cup, then carefully placed the pot back on the stove and handed one of the steaming cups to Sol.

"How long you been a lawman?" Sol wanted to know.

"About seven years now," said Conroy. "My pa was one too. And you?"

"Over ten years. My pa was a farmer up in the mountains."

The two men sipped their coffee. "I reckon the moonshining has about played out," said Conroy. "What with Prohibition over and all."

Sol set his cup on the desk. "Oh, there's still makings," he said. "Nothing like the old days, of course. But highland folks don't like paying tax on their drink."

"Expect that's true."

"But I don't bother them much anymore," said Sol. "Not enough to matter."

They drank their coffee a second. Then Sol said, "About six years ago we had a man pushed off a cliff down our way. A spot called Edgar's Knob."

"You say he was pushed?"

"Well, I should say he might've been pushed. We're not sure exactly."

"Why you mentioning this now?"

Sol lowered his cup and nodded toward the hallway that led to the jail cells. "The only real sign I found around Edgar's Knob was a cigar stub, a band around it that said it was a Monarch. You ever see one of those?"

"Can't say that I have," replied Conroy. "Why you ask?"

"Because I noticed a cigar butt in the ashtray back there. In Waterbury's cell. The band around it said *Monarch*."

Conroy fingered his mustache. "You sure about that?"

"I looked pretty close."

"That's curious, then," said Conroy. "So you think Waterbury had something to do with that man maybe getting pushed off the cliff?"

"No, just noted that he smoked a Monarch, that's all. He bring them cigars with him? Or get them after you brought him here?"

Conroy thought a minute. "Don't think he had them on him when we brought him in. He did have a cloth bag, though. We checked it real careful; I went through it myself. And I didn't see no cigars. A Monarch's a good cigar, is it?"

"Don't know about good," said Sol. "But real expensive, that's for sure."

Conroy produced a handkerchief from his shirt pocket and wiped coffee from his mustache. Finished, he folded the handkerchief into a neat square and stuffed it away. Sol heard the rain start falling again.

A thought occurred to Sol. "Mr. Waterbury have any company since you locked him in your jail?"

"Yeah, as a matter of fact. One time, some days after we arrested him. A tall man showed up. Had a hook nose, dressed kind of fancy but in a way that didn't fit him, like he didn't know how to wear the clothes. For one thing, his tie wasn't done right. It was way too short, you know how some folks do that?"

Stephen nodded. "You make note of the man's name?"

Conroy reached for his ledger, opened it, touched his finger to a page. "Right here," he said. "Exactly four days after we arrested Waterbury, a Mr. Topper Clack visited here with him and stayed for close to an hour. Came in at 10:02 that night."

Sol placed his coffee cup on the floor. "Mind if I see that?" he asked.

Conroy handed him the book, his finger still marking the page. "Topper Clack," he repeated as if to let Sol know he hadn't made it up. "You know him?"

"He happens to be a son of the man who died."

"Curious," said Conroy. "Real curious."

Sol tried to figure how Topper Clack connected with Stephen. Certainly they knew each other from Blue Springs. Stephen had bought whiskey from the Clacks back during Prohibition. But did Stephen ever work for the Clacks, like do some lawyering for them maybe? But why would Topper come see Stephen now, when he's in jail for the land deal? Sol thought back over everything he remembered from the day he visited Edgar's Knob. He recalled the can, the two cigar butts, the—

It dawned on him then. He'd always figured that the same man had smoked both cigars. But what if two men had each smoked a cigar and left the butts behind? For a long time he thought that if this were the case, it meant Hal Clack and the other man had smoked the cigars. But what if Hal Clack hadn't smoked a cigar at all? What if two other men smoked the cigars? That meant at least three men had been up at Edgar's Knob!

Were Stephen Waterbury and Topper Clack those two men? But what was their relationship? And which one, if either, pushed Hal Clack over the side of the mountain?

Sol shook his head at the crazy notions. Nothing proved either man had done anything of the sort. The fact that one or even both of them might have smoked Monarch cigars gave no true evidence that either had anything to do with any foul play.

"Mind if I talk with Mr. Waterbury after his wife leaves?" Sol asked.

"Fine by me," said Conroy. "When she comes out, you can go talk to him all you want."

Sol lifted the cup off the floor, sipped his coffee again. The lawman part of him wanted to find a connection between Topper Clack and Stephen, something to show what happened to Hal Clack six years ago. But another part hoped that nothing came of it. If Stephen had some part in the death of Hal Clack, deliberate or not, that wouldn't bode well for Abby and her boys. Stephen would end up in jail for a long time if he had any hand in causing Hal Clack's death.

Sol gritted his teeth. Abby had been in a frail state since she moved back to Blue Springs. This kind of news might just break her. *Let this be a coincidence,* he thought. Abby surely couldn't stand much more hurt to come her way.

CHAPTER EIGHTEEN

As March of 1937 rolled in all wet and windy, Daniel tried to dig his heels in to stop the tumble he'd started the night Luke died. When sober, he saw clearly the bad path he was now treading. No man's ever done well by partaking too much of the drink, he knew that. Sure, some he knew could swig liquor on a regular basis and still keep themselves under a measure of control. Most, though, hadn't the power to do this. Whiskey didn't seem to cotton to such handling as that. Instead, it tended to catch a man in the throat like a hook in a fish, catch him and throw him around until he flopped onto the creek bank gasping for air and near to death. Drink did nobody any good, that was a fact. Then why couldn't he leave it alone?

Unable to answer that question, he would fight it one minute and yield to it the next, usually on the weekends. One thing Daniel had to give himself: he didn't do any drinking when he had any kind of a paying job to do. No good man would do that, he figured. No good man would let the drink hook him so bad that he didn't provide for his family. People could say what they wanted about his use of whiskey when Saturday night came or when he had no labor to do, but he wouldn't let his family starve, no sir, not so long as he had breath in his body.

Fortunately for him, he heard the first week of the month that the federal boys needed some strong laborers to help them build a road they said would one day snake all the way through the Blue Ridge Mountains. Daniel and Deidre talked it over, and although it meant Daniel had to stay gone every night of the week, they decided real fast he ought to take the job if he could get it. Money like the government paid didn't come along too often in their neck of the woods.

With his experience in building, the government boys snapped him up quick, and he took up the labor. He drove off every Sunday afternoon with a couple of men from Blue Springs who were hired on as well, and they worked all week cutting trees, shoveling gravel, and smoothing the way for the road. He and the other workers stayed in tents the federal men provided and ate food the government served in big black pots. Though the tents let in some water when it rained and at times the nights turned so cold he shivered, the conditions didn't bother Daniel too much.

Every Friday near dark the work shut down, and Daniel and the rest of the crew lit out for their homes scattered all over the mountains. While he only had a short while to spend with Deidre and the kids before having to turn around and head back to the work camp, Daniel felt good because now he was earning a steady wage. A lot of men didn't have that. Anyway, the situation wasn't much worse than what he'd been doing before, leaving home for days at a time in search of a job.

And the work had slowed his drinking some. A man couldn't very well do a decent day's labor with the doublings in his belly. The mixture of baking sun, backbreaking labor, and burning whiskey just didn't go together. Only a fool would try such a thing, and Daniel Porter was no fool.

On the third Friday of March a heavy rain started just after midnight, and everybody knew when morning broke that they wouldn't be doing much work that day. It wasn't possible to drive the trucks uphill through the ankle-deep mud. So just after sunrise, the crew boss told them all to go home.

Daniel packed up his few belongings and caught a ride back to Blue Springs with a friend. Deidre ran out into the rain as they drove up, and Daniel gave her a hug once he'd jumped down from his buddy's truck. Ed and Raymond joined them then, Ed slapping Daniel on the back and Raymond pulling at his shirt. Daniel bent over and kissed Raymond on the head. For the first time in a long time, Daniel felt right jaunty. The government job had given him a sense of doing something worthwhile and, at the same time, put a dollar or so in his pocket each week that he could save. He never felt better than when he could set a little money aside for whatever tomorrow might bring. Though he'd given up his dream of ever owning a good amount of land, he at least had the hope that he might someday pull his family up from dirt poor.

He ate dinner that night and only wanted a drink a couple of times—once when he sat on the porch with Deidre, after the kids had gone to bed, and then again when he and Deidre lay down to sleep.

"The crew boss says it might take years to finish the road," Daniel told Deidre just before they dozed off.

"I'm sure glad you got the work," she said, laying a hand over his. "But I do miss you all week. The kids do too, Raymond especially."

Daniel rolled over to face her, touched her chin. "Marla is seventeen now," he said. "Ed fifteen. Reckon they don't hardly need me much anymore."

Deidre smiled and said, "You're right, Marla is getting older. But she needs you more than ever now that so many boys are calling on her."

"She wants me on the road all the time," he kidded. "So she can sit on the porch and spark with her fellas."

"That's why *I* need you," said Deidre. "Need somebody with a gun handy to keep those boys away from her."

They looked each other in the eyes, grinning. Then Deidre turned serious again. "It's awful lonely when you're gone," she said.

"I know, but sometimes a man has no choice. I got to go where the work is."

"I'm not blaming you. Just wanted you to know we love you, that we all miss you. That's all I'm saying."

Daniel kissed her. "You make me strong," he said. "You and the kids. When . . . well, when I get down out there, get all blue and all, I put my head to thinkin' about you all, our farm here, what we can make of it. That's what sees me through the long days—you and Marla, Ed and Raymond. Without you . . . I just don't know . . ."

Deidre squeezed his hand. "You're never without us. Never, I promise you that."

"I know I've been doin' some drinking lately," he admitted, feeling the need to confess, even though Deidre already knew everything. "And I know that ain't right. Not what I ought to do for you or the kids."

She stroked his forehead. "Daniel, you've never hurt me or the kids. But I am worried about you. I see how much it grieved you to lose Luke. Sure, I wish you'd stop your drinking. But I've just let it be, kept my quiet, figured you'd find your way through it soon enough."

"I'm grateful for your patience. You should know, I aim to cease with the bottle, stop it right here and now."

"That pleases me," said Deidre.

His mind firm, Daniel closed his eyes to sleep. Tomorrow he would throw away the bottle he had stuck in the pocket of his coat. Then he would be free of the whiskey forever.

The next morning a soft breeze blew in on Blue Springs. Birds filled the trees and sang out their eager approval of the mild weather.

His uniform pressed neatly and his gun and holster freshly oiled, Sol stepped out of the sheriff's office at just past ten, a toothpick in his mouth and his hat perched on his head, and walked across the street to his truck. A muscle under his left cheek quivered, and his hands kept clenching and unclenching.

In the truck he started the engine and pulled away from the curb. A minute later he shifted gears and drove past the last building in Blue Springs. He mentally sorted through everything he had learned in the weeks since talking to Stephen Waterbury. At first he hadn't believed it. But then as he checked on the facts and looked through all the possibilities, what Stephen said started to make sense. Turned out Stephen had told him the truth and now it was up to him as the sheriff to do something about it. As much as he wanted to put it off, he knew he couldn't. Some things a man just had to do, no matter how troublesome.

As he drove up the mountain, Sol wished he could have brought a deputy along. But he had no full-time man, and figuring there was no one he might enlist who would have agreed to stand up to what he had to face, he'd made the decision to go it alone. Probably will be okay, Sol told himself. Not even the worst kind of person wanted to cross a lawman.

It took him just over a half hour to reach the turnoff that led up to where most of the Clack family lived, then another half hour to navigate the truck over the deeply rutted road that led from the main one to their place. Finally, a little after eleven, he drove past a loose, rusty gate and spotted the house—a two-story stone building, built in the middle of a tall stand of oak and hickory trees, a shed with a saggy roof to its right. A swaybacked cow stood motionless at a post by the shed.

A pack of mangy dogs ran out barking to meet Sol as he came to a stop. Not far behind the dogs two young boys appeared, each of them shoeless, each with dark hair and eyes. Sol guessed them close to twelve. The taller one held a pistol in his right hand, its barrel pointed at the ground. The boy's long hair fell over his eyes.

Sol eased open the door and stepped carefully to the ground. The dogs bared their teeth and growled but didn't advance any closer. "I'm Sol Porter," he called. "Sheriff of these parts. I'm here looking for Topper or Ben Clack."

"Pa ain't wanting to talk to the likes of you," yelled the boy, the pistol waving.

"You best stay careful with that pistol," said Sol. "You liable to hurt somebody."

"Hurt you!" the smaller boy said.

Sol took a step forward. The boy with the pistol pointed it at him. "I can hit a rabbit at fifty feet with this thing," he said. "You are some bigger than a rabbit."

Sol stopped and weighed his situation. The boy seemed intent on his duties as the protector of the place. Maybe he ought to just leave it be and go on back. Then he heard a door open and glanced up at the house. A girl slipped out, and Sol's eyes widened. The girl, maybe fifteen, moved onto the porch and down the steps. He thought he'd seen her before around town, but didn't know for sure.

"Give me that gun, Wilbur!" shouted the girl, her diction crisper than any highlander woman Sol knew except for Abby and his mama. "You know better than to point that thing at a lawman."

"Go away," Wilbur told her without turning around. "This ain't no business for no girl."

The girl hesitated, and Sol studied her, wondering who she was. She looked vaguely related to the Clacks, like the youngest of the daughters whom he'd seen every so often in town. Was this her? But how come he hadn't seen her for so long? And she sure sounded more educated than the others of Clack blood.

"Wilbur, put down the gun!" she said, striding up behind the pistol-waving boy.

"I told you to stay out of this," said Wilbur.

Before Wilbur could turn around, the girl grabbed a rock off the ground, threw it, and struck him between the shoulder blades. He fell to the ground, and the pistol flew from his hand. She ran over and picked it up while the boy yelled in pain.

"Topper and Ben are up the mountain," she said to Sol, "about a mile or so. Take that trail over there"—she pointed the gun to Sol's right—"past the shed. You'll most likely find them at the bottom of Gap Falls. They're out hunting today."

"You okay here?" Sol asked, nodding toward Wilbur.

The girl smiled, and Sol saw her straight white teeth, surprising for a highlander woman. She walked over to Wilbur and bent over him to check his back where she'd hit him with the rock. "Don't worry about him," she said. "He knows if he gives me trouble, I'll pound him straight into the ground."

Sol started to leave when it dawned on him that he might be kin to the girl, a cousin at least. So he faced her again and asked, "What's your name?"

"She's Queeny," said Wilbur, his face still wincing from the rock.

"Queeny. . . ?" Sol stared at her.

She shrugged. "They say I act like I'm a queen."

"Are you Topper Clack's daughter?"

Queeny looked at the ground, then muttered, "It doesn't matter."

Sol thought about pressing her for more information but then decided against it. Maybe the girl had good reason not to want to say anything more.

"Her ma says she's Topper's," said Wilbur in a mocking voice. "But Pa sometimes don't always seem to claim her."

"You either," Queeny laughed. "Now get up already! Looks like you won't die." She reached down and helped the boy to his feet. Sol wondered what kind of girl would hit a boy in the back with a rock one second, then tend to him the next.

"You lookin' after these boys?" Sol asked her.

"I look after whoever needs it," Queeny answered.

Sol chuckled. "Like a regular Florence Nightingale."

"Maybe someday."

Wilbur laughed and darted off toward the woods. "She's too mean for Florence Nightingale," he yelled as he ran. "Way too mean."

Queeny glared at him for a second, then faced Sol again. "You go on now," she said.

"You sure about that?"

She nodded, and Sol headed to the trail that meandered farther up the mountain. Before walking past the shed, he looked over his shoulder to catch another glimpse of the Clack house. He saw Queeny follow the other boy back to the front door, her shining black hair bobbing as she closed the door behind her. *Strange,* he thought, *a Clack girl with an education.*

It took Sol forty minutes to reach the waterfall Queeny had mentioned. At the bottom of it, he stopped to catch his breath and to swallow down some water from the canteen he carried on his hip. While resting, he felt a twinge of sorrow over what he'd come to do. After all, Topper and Ben were his uncles, which made Queeny his cousin. Despite the apparent troubles between Queeny and her pa, she was still his daughter. What Sol was about to do would no doubt hurt her too.

He capped the canteen and put it back on his hip. He heard a rustle in the woods to his left. He reached for his pistol and whirled around to see Topper Clack stepping out of the laurel, his rifle pointed straight at him. Ben followed close behind Topper, his rifle also on the ready. Sol eased his hand from his holster. They had the drop on him. He studied the two men carefully. Topper had on a suit jacket with mud on the sleeves, brown wool pants just a cut too long, and two-toned shoes of black and white. The white, round-collared shirt he wore needed starching and hung halfway in his pants and half out.

Ben stepped to Topper's side. "Sheriff, what's your business so far up on our property?" he asked.

"I ain't checking for no stills, if that's what you're thinkin'," said Sol. "Those days are long past."

"Then what?" said Topper. "You too far up for a stroll, even on a day as nice as this."

Sol indicated the rifles. "I'll talk much better if I'm not under the stare of a rifle barrel."

Topper lowered his gun just a notch but Ben stayed still. "You can sit," said Topper, pointing his gun to a big rock close by. "Say your piece, then start headin' back to town."

Considering the situation, Sol thought maybe he should just back away, keep quiet about what Stephen had told him until he could return later, next time bringing a deputy with him.

"You come up here for somethin'," said Ben, "and I wanna know what it is."

Sol glanced around, looking for a way to escape. Coming here had seemed a good idea when he started out. Now it seemed pretty foolish, the act of a man not thinking clearly. "Well . . . it's about your pa's death," he said, hoping to catch them off guard with his directness. "I come across something I need to check with you."

Topper's eyes froze on him as Ben's fingers twitched on his rifle.

"Sit," said Topper.

Sol obeyed and sat down on the rock, his eyes still searching for some way out of this. But Ben and Topper stood over him, both clutching their rifles.

"Now spit it out," Topper demanded. "What you think you know about our pa?"

Sol tried to keep calm. If he showed fear, it would only give the Clacks more of an edge. He stared straight into Topper's face. To make it off this mountain alive, he had to take advantage of the fact that he was a lawman, an authority who could cause the Clacks more trouble than they'd ever known if they harmed even one hair on his head.

"I drove over to Lolleyville and had a talk with Stephen Waterbury," said Sol. "About a month ago."

"So?" said Topper. "What do we care about that sorry man?"

Sol focused on Ben this time. He wondered if Ben even knew. An idea came to him. "Ben, the way Waterbury tells it, your brother here was the one pushed your pa off Edgar's Knob."

Ben glanced at Topper, then back to Sol. "Waterbury's an idiot!" growled Ben.

Sol shrugged. "Maybe so. But he seemed right convincin', leastways to me he was. What you think, Topper?" asked Sol, looking at him now. "Is Waterbury just foolin' me?"

Topper grinned but it seemed forced. "Waterbury is nothin' but a drunk," he said. "You oughta know better than to believe anything comes out of his mouth."

Sol nodded as if in agreement. "I reckon he is a drunk. But he tells it this way. Says he was up at Edgar's Knob with you and your pa. That he served as a connection between your pa and a man from Chicago who bought up most of your pa's makings back in the days of Prohibition. Any truth to that so far?"

Topper hesitated.

Sol watched him closely. He had checked out Stephen's story to the last detail. A man in the FBI in Chicago told him they had a Stephen Waterbury in their files and that he had indeed worked as a middleman between some bootleggers and big city saloons. If Topper lied here, it meant Stephen probably told the truth about the rest of it as well.

Apparently Topper figured that out. He laughed and scratched his nose. "Yeah, he's true in that," he said. "Waterbury worked some for Pa back in those days. We was always needin' somebody to travel for us, connect us with city folks in the whiskey business. That way we wouldn't have to go. Less dangerous, and Pa hated any kind of travelin' he couldn't do on foot or horseback."

Sol checked Ben. He seemed steady.

"Waterbury also said you and your pa had arguments from time to time," Sol continued. "Said you wanted to spend money to start moving the family out of bootleggin', that you wanted to buy up more land, lots of it, and maybe put some dollars into logging trucks. Said you told your pa that Prohibition wouldn't last forever, and that when it ended, the big dollars would soon dry up. Accordin' to Waterbury, you said something about wanting to get into some proper businesses so when that day came, you'd have income to fall back on. That all true?"

Topper grinned again. Sol figured Topper knew where he was headed with all this. Which made Topper all the more dangerous. He was determined not to underestimate the man. He'd shown more than once that he was the brainier of the Clack brothers, as smart as most folks and then some.

"Sure, me and Pa had our spats," Topper said. "Every boy and his pa does. Nothing unusual about that."

Sol stood slowly. Ben raised his gun. Sol said, "Waterbury told me your pa would have none of the changes you wanted, stopped you at every turn. He didn't care much about the money that came from bootleggin', just wanted the freedom it brought, the outdoors, the sense of being his own man, in spite of what the federal boys said or did."

"I ain't arguing with any of that," said Topper, his voice slow but menacing. "But that's as far as I'm goin'."

Sol's eyes darted from Topper to Ben. Ben was looking at Topper now, and Sol could tell he'd begun to figure out what he was saying. "Well, regardless, Waterbury said you and your pa got into it real bad that day up at Edgar's Knob, started yellin' and manhandling each other."

"It's a lie!" shouted Topper.

"He said your pa pushed you away, shoved you down on the rock."

"A drunk man's lie!"

"He said you jumped up and pushed him back. Your pa staggered, then you pushed him again."

"I'll kill Waterbury!"

"Your pa was killed," said Sol, his voice growing louder, "by your own hand! He fell off Edgar's Knob 'cause you shoved him. And then you swore Waterbury to secrecy, threatening his life if he said anything to anyone. That's what happened and you and I both know it!"

Sol faced Ben now. "That's the truth," he said. "Your brother killed your pa—not intentionally maybe, but he killed him all the same."

Ben looked at Topper. "He tellin' it right?"

"Why would I go to the law if I was the one who pushed Pa?" said Topper. "Why not just call it an accident and leave it be?"

"That's easy," said Sol. "You knew folks would ask questions. A highland man like your pa don't just fall off a mountain, no matter how drunk. You had to act like you wanted me to find a killer. What better way to throw suspicion off yourself and onto somebody else?"

Topper cackled. The hair on Sol's neck about stood up.

"I can prove what I'm saying," said Sol.

"What you mean?" asked Ben.

Sol reached for his front pants pocket. "I got it right here, all the proof you need. You wanna see it?"

Topper raised his rifle. "You've shown us enough for one day. You pull anything from your pocket and you won't live to see another one."

"You feel the same way?" Sol asked Ben. "You want me to leave without showin' you the proof of what I've said?"

Ben hesitated, and Sol knew he was weighing what to do—whether to send him away and never know what really happened to his pa, or let him show what he had and make a determination one way or the other. Ben suddenly turned on Topper and pointed his rifle at his chest. "I wanna see," he said, "see if it's true you pushed Pa off the knob."

Topper's hands twitched, but Ben had the drop on him. So Topper glanced at Sol and said, "Show it then. Show us what you got in your pocket."

Sol pulled out a small brown bag, opened it, and lifted out the cigar butt he'd taken from Stephen's jail cell in Lolleyville. "This is from Waterbury's cell. Your brother"—he nodded toward Topper—"visited Waterbury there a while back. Took him a cigar, a Monarch cigar."

Ben glared at his brother.

"Any number of folks smoke them Monarchs," Topper said.

"Not many from around here," said Sol. "Only two from what I could find out. You and Stephen Waterbury—when he can afford 'em."

Topper took a heavy breath. Sol watched Ben, and Ben's eyes stayed glued on Topper. Sol waited. He knew Ben would have to do something soon. Either he'd let his pa's death go as an accident he could do nothing about or he'd pull the trigger and shoot his brother for killing their pa and then lying to him about it afterward. If he chose the first thing, it wouldn't go well for him.

Not willing to stick around and find out which way Ben would decide, Sol moved quickly. He jumped to his left, ducking toward a boulder. Ben and Topper acted in the same instant, their rifles sounding within a split second after Sol took off. A sharp pain cut into the back of Sol's left arm, and he dropped to the ground. He immediately rolled to behind the boulder and took a quick breath.

Then, back on his feet, he plowed into a thicket of laurel bushes, listening all the while for Topper and Ben chasing him. He heard nothing. He kept running, his body pushing through the woods as fast as his feet could carry him. A couple of minutes later he stopped again to inspect his wound and listen once more for the Clacks. The woods were quiet. He touched the place where the bullet had struck him. Though it hurt bad, he could tell it wasn't serious. The bullet had grazed him at an angle, hadn't actually lodged in his arm. He pulled out his canteen and poured water over the wound, then took a long drink. At that moment it came to him what the Clacks would likely do next.

Quickly capping the canteen, he hustled down the mountain. Unless he missed his guess, the Clacks would head straight to Lolleyville. With Stephen Waterbury the only witness to his deed, Topper wouldn't want him around to tell anybody else what he'd already told Sol.

CHAPTER NINETEEN

Daniel spent most of the morning cleaning out the barn. Ed helped him, his brow glistening with sweat not long after they'd gotten started. From time to time Daniel glanced approvingly at his boy. A young man now, he filled out solid and strong, had a head of thick light brown hair. Like all Porter men, his eyes were as dark as mountain dirt. Typical of a highlander man, he had on brogans, overalls, and a long johns undershirt, topped off with a floppy hat on his head. Like his grandpa, Ed was skilled with his hands, able to put together fine chairs and tables, anything made of wood. Liked to carve too, and Daniel had no doubt that if he ever gave up his notion of piloting an airplane and stayed around Blue Springs, he'd someday turn out rockers maybe as good as old Solomon himself.

As they worked, Daniel thought again about the vow he'd made the night before. No more drink, no matter what. In spite of everything he'd lost, he still had much to be thankful for. Only a foolish man would take a chance on messing up what he had left, all because of a weakness for the doublings. Daniel thought of Marla, who had started courting a boy whose pa owned a nice piece of land just this side of the Tennessee border. She wasn't married yet but had plans for a wedding running in her head pretty strong. The boy had helped Daniel cut up a stack of wood the last time he visited, and Daniel could tell from the way he handled the ax that he was well acquainted with hard work. He'd told Marla that if the boy asked for her hand, she ought to say yes.

And Raymond? Well, he took after his ma's side of the family. Had a softer look than most of the Porters. Curly hair and not so full of muscle. He'd taken Luke's guitar and started playing it some about every night. It didn't sound like he was going to be a tenor, though. He had a deeper voice than most boys.

Daniel picked up a shovel and began working in one of the stalls. The hard work made his heart feel good. Yes sir, he had plenty of reason to keep his head about him and stay as far away from the doublings as a chicken from a fox.

The day went by quickly as he and Ed labored on. Finished in the barn, they stopped about noontime and joined the rest of the family for some biscuits and molasses Deidre had laid out on the table. After washing down the food with big swigs of well water, Daniel and Ed left the table to go work on the fence behind the barn. Many of the posts had come loose over the winter and so needed resetting.

Daniel kept his eyes on Ed as they toiled. The boy didn't say much, just dug and lifted and labored like a man with nothing more important to do in the whole world than the job right in front of him. Deidre said that Ed took his drive for work right from his pa. Daniel told her that's where he himself got it—straight from his pa. Porter men had always labored hard, handled hoe and shovel and hammer and wood as though they were born with calluses on their hands, ready to scrape out a living for their families from the thin soil under their feet.

Of course, they all had good women close beside them who toiled just as hard. Women like Deidre who saw every sunup from her kitchen as she fried up eggs and bacon in good times or prepared biscuits and pieces of fatback meat in leaner days. The women made and mended clothes, cooked, and canned most of their families' food. Usually they bore their babies with no help but from midwives. And the only time off they got came in the evening when they sat on the porch or by the fire and rocked a few minutes before heading to bed.

"Lazy folks in the highlands got as good a chance of livin' as a frog in a snake's mouth," Daniel often said. Watching Ed tamp the dirt around a post, Daniel felt glad that neither of his sons had shown any leanings toward shiftlessness.

Just before dinnertime Daniel and Ed finished with the last of the fence posts and started walking back to the barn to put away the tools. The sun hung almost directly behind them, its lessening warmth square on their backs. Daniel felt exhausted but content. A few feet from the barn, they heard a shout coming from the front yard.

"Daniel!"

He recognized the voice. "Over here at the barn, Sol," he called back. "We'll be there in a minute."

He and Ed stood their shovels behind the barn door and then hurried to meet Sol. Coming around the corner, Daniel saw Sol standing on the front steps, and it didn't take but one look to see that Sol had a bother about him, had something important to say.

"Let's all go inside," Daniel said, "where we can sit ourselves down."

Deidre greeted them as they walked in. "Have a seat," she said. "I'll get you boys some fresh water."

Sol pulled out a chair and sat on its edge but kept his hat on.

Daniel noticed a white bandage wrapped around Sol's left arm above the elbow. It had a dark red stain. "You come a long way on a Saturday," he said. "What happened there with your arm?"

Deidre handed them each a cup of cool water.

Ignoring the question, Sol went straight to the purpose of his visit. "Daniel, I need some help. Sheriffin' help."

Daniel swallowed his water and set the tin cup on the table. "You been shot?" he asked, nodding at the bandage.

Sol shrugged. "It ain't too bad."

"What's the trouble?"

"Clack trouble," said Sol.

Daniel and Ed sat up straighter, and Deidre froze where she stood. "We have no quarrel with the Clacks," she offered.

"You know I ain't askin' lightly," Sol said. "But I got to tell you that I'm in need. I'm afraid Topper and Ben Clack are goin' after Stephen Waterbury. He—"

"What part does Stephen have with the Clacks?" interrupted Daniel.

"It's complicatious, but I think Topper pushed his pa off Edgar's Knob some years back—you recall his death."

Deidre and Daniel nodded.

"Well, it looks like maybe Waterbury saw the whole thing, that he was there at the time. Now Topper needs to take care of him because he's a witness and he talked to me."

"You went after the Clacks by yourself?" asked Daniel.

Sol dropped his eyes. "Yeah, maybe it wasn't too smart but I didn't know where to go for help. Nobody around here, didn't want to put anybody in danger. The Clacks got the drop on me."

"But you got away."

"Yeah. But now I got to go after them."

A fly buzzed near Sol's wound. He brushed it away.

"You got no deputy?" asked Daniel.

"You know how things have been. Not much need for a second lawman since all the bootlegging slowed down. And with times like they are, the county saw no need to pay for one."

"So you're asking Daniel here to help you with your trouble with the Clacks?" Deidre asked.

"I got nowhere else to turn," said Sol.

"What about somebody down in Blue Springs?"

Sol shook his head. "Nobody wants to cross the Clacks."

Deidre opened her mouth to speak again, but Daniel held up a hand. He'd heard enough. "You ain't facin' them boys by yourself again," Daniel said. "Simple as that."

"I hate to ask," said Sol. "I can't say it won't carry some danger."

"Don't matter. If the Clacks got it in for Stephen, I can't stand by and let them shoot my brother-in-law."

Deidre wiped her hands on her apron, and Daniel knew he'd upset her. But what choice did he have? His kin had come to him for aid. A man couldn't just turn his back and walk away in such a circumstance as this. What if Sol took off alone after the Clacks and got himself killed? He'd never sleep through another night if that happened. Upset wife or no, a man had to face some things no matter how fearsome. Daniel turned to her. "I gotta do this," he said.

She took his hand in hers. "I know," she said. "I'm not askin' you to refuse."

"You are a saintly woman," Daniel said.

Her eyes glistened. "You take care of yourself, you hear."

"I will." Daniel got up and kissed her on the cheek, gave her a hug.

"I'll pack my pistol," he said to Sol. "And let me change this dirty shirt and these britches."

Sol nodded. Ed stood up as if to follow his pa. Deidre grabbed him by the arm. "You're going nowhere," she said, "except right back outside to bring in some more water."

Ed started to protest, but Daniel shook his head and the boy held his tongue.

"I am now declarin' that Daniel Porter is my lawful deputy," said Sol. "Put this on." He handed Daniel a tin badge.

"I'll put it on my fresh shirt," said Daniel. "Just give me a minute."

When Daniel had left the room, Deidre moved to Sol. "Now let me check that wound," she said.

"No time for that. I promise I'll see a doctor soon as this is over."

Deidre touched his forearm. "Please, don't let those Clacks kill my husband."

"I don't aim to let them kill anybody."

On their way to Lolleyville, Sol told Daniel all that had recently happened with Topper and Ben. Daniel listened for a while, then asked, "If the Clacks just leave Waterbury alone, won't they be all right? Who's gone convict them of anything around here?"

"Maybe nobody," said Sol. "But Edgar's Knob is in another county. The judge over there might see this whole mess different than us. Might put Topper up for manslaughter or something."

Daniel nodded. No Clack would ever take to prison. Easier to coax a bear into a cage than a highlander man like Topper into a jail cell. "You call the law in Lolleyville to give them warning the Clacks might be comin'?"

"Sure did, before I drove up your way. A man named Conroy is over there, said he would keep an eye out."

Daniel stared out the window. The trees sped by real fast. "How quick are we going?" he asked.

"Probably thirty or forty miles in an hour. Not exactly sure. Speed ain't always calculated real good in these trucks."

Daniel shook his head. "I ain't done a lot of drivin'. Still don't have a road all the way to my place."

"Might be a long time before one makes it up that far."

"Fine by me. Can stay that way the rest of my life for all I care."

The two men turned silent as they drove on, the road zipping by under the wheels. Daniel took a heavy breath, and a sense of gloom fell on him. He tried to push it away but it hung on, stubborn as the smell of a skunk. He recalled the two worst things he'd ever faced: the night he lost Luke, and before that the night he lost Laban in the war. Bad things had happened those nights. Daniel folded his arms. No reason to dwell on such sad things, he figured, no reason at all.

They reached Lolleyville around eleven that night, and Daniel knew as they stepped into the jailhouse that something was out of sorts. The place seemed too still. Daniel noticed Sol reaching for his pistol.

"Conroy kept hillbilly music playing," said Sol.

"Don't hear any music," said Daniel.

"Let's go easy," said Sol. "Till we know what's goin' on here."

Daniel pulled his pistol from his waist. They stepped slowly down the hallway toward Conroy's office, saw that the door was half open, the lights turned on. At the door, Sol backed up against the wall, nodded for Daniel to take the other side.

"When I go, you follow," Sol whispered. "Squat down to make a shorter target."

Daniel gritted his teeth. The command sounded like the orders he'd received back in the war, right before Laban was killed. His mind flashed back to that night on the front line, the night that started all the headaches, the nightmares. From then on he had wanted to drink, had wanted to swallow down the whiskey in every jug he could lay his hands on. He licked his lips and pushed the memory away.

"On three," said Sol. "One, two, three . . ." Sol rushed through the doorway, his pistol ready and his body bent low. Daniel ran in behind him. They spotted a man lying face up on the floor behind the desk. Sol ran to him and put a hand on his chest. "It's Conroy!" he said. "He's still alive." Sol checked Conroy's pockets, the desk drawers. "His cell keys are missing. The Clacks have been here for sure . . . better we check the jail cells."

A few seconds later, the two of them stood in front of the cell where Stephen had been held. The door hung open, the cell now empty.

"He was right here," said Sol.

"They already got him," Daniel said. He stuck his pistol back in the waist of his pants. "Wonder where they took him?"

Heavy footsteps suddenly sounded, and Daniel twisted around just as Topper and Ben Clack appeared from behind them, their rifles leveled at him and Sol. Stephen stood with them too, his hands tied behind his back.

"We got him right here," said Topper.

Daniel reached for his pistol, but Topper pointed his rifle at Stephen's head and Daniel froze.

"Just go easy," said Topper. "Unless you're lookin' for gunplay."

Daniel glanced at Sol. He seemed real calm, like a bobcat before it sprang.

"Why did you come back?" asked Sol. "Why not take Waterbury up to the mountains and shoot him where nobody would ever find him?"

" 'Cause I already told you too much," Stephen said. "They figured you'd show up here, thought it best just to wait and finish you off too."

"But nobody would believe me," said Sol. "Not against Topper and Ben."

Topper laughed. "You need a higher opinion of yourself. Truth is, folks in Blue Springs put a lot of stock in what you say. So we got to make a cleanup of everything. You, Waterbury, and"—he nodded to Daniel—"well, he's just a treat nobody expected. Ain't that right, Ben?"

Sol stared at Ben. "You still with your brother?" he asked. "Even after finding out he pushed your pa off the mountain?"

Daniel saw that Sol was hoping to create trouble between the brothers, maybe give them an opening to escape.

"He's my brother," Ben said. "Only one I got left. Besides, Pa is dead—nothin' I do now can change that fact."

"So you lettin' Topper get away with what he did?"

Ben grunted. "You talk like our pa was some kind of saint," he said. "We know better. He was as mean a man as ever lived. Didn't coddle us, I can tell you that. Not the sort of pa a son feels kindly to. Pa lived his life; time for me and Topper to live ours."

Daniel saw that Ben didn't plan on crossing his brother, no matter what Topper had done. Daniel glanced around for a way out. If he ducked left, he could jump into Stephen's cell, maybe reach the cot and roll under it, squeeze off a couple of pistol shots on the way. That would be dangerous, though. What about Stephen and Sol? The Clacks would shoot Stephen first, then Sol. Then what would he tell Abby and Jewel? That he saved his own hide but not theirs? No, he had gone home one other time after a brother was killed and he had lived. He didn't want to do that again.

"Hand over your firearms," said Ben, "nice and easy like."

Daniel hesitated, then noticed Sol nodding at him and knew he had no choice. He took out his pistol and gave it to Ben. Sol did the same. Ben laid the two guns on the floor and pushed them up against the wall with his boot.

Looking over at Sol, Daniel tried to think of what to do next. One of them had to figure something and quick.

"I am sorry I got you boys in this scrape," said Stephen. "It was not my intention."

Daniel glanced at Stephen. He seemed genuinely sorrowful. He started to say something in reply, but then Topper stepped up close to him, so close Daniel could smell the whiskey on the man's breath.

"Hold it right there!" The voice came from behind the Clacks. Daniel's heart soared. Conroy! The sheriff came staggering down the hall toward them, holding out a gun with a shaky hand. Topper and Ben spun around, and Sol and Daniel lunged at them, Daniel shoving Topper against the steel bars of the cell. Two shots rang out, and Daniel heard a man grunt but he couldn't tell who had been hit.

Daniel grabbed for Topper's rifle, but Topper jerked away, rolling to his knees as he raised the gun and pulled the trigger. A hot pain tore into Daniel's left hand. Blood ran through his fingers. Daniel dove at Topper's boots. Topper kicked him off, then brought the rifle back up and fired a second shot.

Hearing somebody cry out from behind him, Daniel twisted and saw Stephen hit the floor, his side bleeding. Topper stood grinning at Daniel, his rifle now pointing at Daniel's chest. Topper had him dead to rights.

He wondered what it would feel like to die. Time slowed to a crawl. He thought of Laban and hoped he'd see his brother again, his pa and ma too. Deidre's face passed through his head next, and he wished he could hold her and the kids one last time, to feel their skin and hear their voices. But he had no more chance for that, no more time.

Grinning even wider, Topper's finger twitched on his rifle trigger. Daniel saw someone move in his peripheral vision. Topper fired his rifle.

Stephen jumped into the path of the bullet, and the bullet buried itself in Stephen's chest.

Daniel skidded to the floor where Ben had kicked his pistol against the wall, grabbed it off the floor, turned onto his knees and fired at Topper, hitting him in the neck. He fell in a heap.

Scrambling to his feet, Daniel saw Ben going after Sol, who lay on the floor with blood oozing from his back, up close to his neck. But before Daniel could take aim at Ben, Ben had a pistol pointed at him.

"Drop your gun!" shouted Ben.

Daniel ground his teeth, knew he had no choice. The pistol clattered to the floor.

"It's just you and me now," said Ben.

Daniel looked down at Sol. He couldn't tell how bad off he was. Stephen lay facedown behind him. Farther away was Conroy, also facedown and bleeding.

Sweat dripped into Daniel's eyes. Except for his hand, he had escaped serious injury. He prayed that Stephen and Sol weren't dead. If he came out of this alive and they didn't, he would never forgive himself. Stephen had taken the bullet meant for him. He could hardly believe it. What a crazy thing he had done! Daniel scolded himself for not being able to save anybody but himself.

"You aim to shoot me down?" Daniel asked Ben, hoping for a second to figure things out.

"I reckon so," said Ben. "The law will figure you and my brother had it out. You shot him, he shot you."

"You can be sure they'll guess you had a part in this too, that you shot Conroy."

"I suppose so. But with nobody to say different, they have to take my word on it. I'll say you and Sol broke into the jail, shot Conroy, my brother. Then I got you, Sol too. Stephen died in all the confusion." A wicked leer came to his face. "After I kill you, maybe I'll visit that sister of yours, now that her sorry husband is dead." He glanced down at Stephen's crumpled form.

Daniel heard something move. Ben jumped at the sound, as Daniel sprung into action. Ben turned back with a surprised look and fired his pistol, missing Daniel and hitting the floor instead. Lunging at Ben, Daniel drove him into the wall. Ben's gun dropped from his hands. Daniel grabbed it and smacked Ben in the head with the butt. Ben's eyes blinked—once, twice—then closed and he sank to the floor.

Daniel rushed over to Sol, saw that he was breathing, then turned to Stephen to inspect his wounds—one in his chest, one in his lower side. He'd lost a lot of blood and was barely alive.

Daniel lifted Stephen's head. "You hold on now!" he said. "I'll get you and Sol some help." Stephen tried to speak. Daniel wiped the blood from Stephen's mouth. "Stephen, you saved my life. Two times you saved me."

"I . . . I . . ."

"Don't try to talk," said Daniel. "I'll call for a doctor."

Stephen grabbed him by the wrist. "Wait," he whispered. "No time for that."

Daniel cleared his eyes with the back of his hand. He'd seen the look on Stephen's face more than once. The look of a man who knew he wouldn't see another sun come up. "I'm here," he said, praying that Sol could hold on while he saw to Stephen. "Won't go nowhere."

Stephen licked his lips. "Tell Abby . . ." he started. "Tell her . . . my boys . . . tell them I'm sorry."

"I will," said Daniel. "I'll tell them you saved my life."

"Tell her . . . I did a lot of thinking . . . and changing . . . these days in jail."

Stephen's eyes rolled up in his head for a second but then steadied again. "Tell her I . . . love her and the boys," he said. "Tell . . . them . . ."

"I will," said Daniel.

Stephen squeezed his hand harder. "Tell Abby one more . . . more thing."

Daniel's tears made it hard to see him now.

"Tell her I do . . . I do believe," said Stephen, his voice stronger as he pushed out his last words, his final confession. "Tell her I just . . . got off . . . track, but that I do . . ."

His eyes rolled up again but didn't steady this time. For a couple of seconds, Daniel stayed still, his tears tracing down his face. Once again a member of his family had died in his arms. Once again he'd come through a fight while others died. Guilt covered him like a dark cloud. What would he tell Abby, or Deidre? He wanted a drink worse than ever.

Laying Stephen's head down, he went back to Sol and checked his breathing again. Sol's chest moved slowly up and down. Daniel stepped over to Topper Clack, saw that he was dead. Conroy too. Unable to do anything else, he hurried to Conroy's office and picked up the telephone.

After imploring the operator to send a doctor, Daniel hung up. Taking a moment to ponder the situation, he realized that a trial would surely come of this. If Sol didn't live, it would come down to his word against Ben Clack's, who at the moment lay unconscious on the jailhouse floor.

In that moment, though, Daniel didn't care about the outcome of any trial. Jail might do him good, he figured. Better to rot in jail than to live in a world where people kept dying just to save his sorry skin.

CHAPTER TWENTY

The trial started almost three months later in the circuit court near Lolleyville on a June day so hot it wore out a person's wrist just to keep a fan moving in front of her face. People from Blue Springs and Lolleyville packed the tiny courtroom. Relatives of the Clacks lined up on the left side, many leaning against the wall, with friends and relatives of the Porters on the right. Conroy's family, a buxom wife with a pair of dimples the size of dimes and three girls between nine and fifteen, took places in the second row on the right. Abby sat beside Deidre and Jewel in the front row right behind Daniel, who sat at a small table with his lawyer. In spite of the heat, all three women wore black from head to toe.

Abby found her eyes drawn over and over again to the Clacks. They made quite a sight. Topper's wife, Eugenia, sat in the center of the group. With Topper dead she was now the matriarch of the family, and a striking presence. Her eyes, face, and body were large and round, and she had a head full of dishwater-blond hair she kept pulled up in a bun. At times her eyes looked haunted, like she had seen something nobody ought ever to see. At other times, they seemed calm, like she was sitting by a river with a fishing pole on a hot summer day. She was wearing an outfit Abby figured to be new and store-bought—a tan dress with hook buttons from neck to waist and a flare bottom all the way to her ankles. Her shoes shined black and had buckles on top.

Though Abby had seen Eugenia from time to time over the years, she'd never really paid her much attention. But now she wanted to know everything about the woman. Mainly, what made her stand by a man like Topper? Was it his money? Had she loved him?

The preliminaries of the trial began and pulled Abby's attention off the Clacks. Judge Waldo Wilson—a skinny man with wire-edged glasses and dandruff that fell onto his black robe—went over the details of the charges against Mr. Daniel Porter: Murder, attempted assistance to flight for a prisoner, trespassing on county property, and various other crimes he calmly read out loud. Sol was charged too, but they'd decided to wait till his health improved before bringing him to trial.

A lawyer by the name of Lewis Ricks, whom Deidre had hired by signing a mortgage against her father's house in Asheville, said some words on Daniel's behalf. Then the prosecutor, a blocky bald man in a tan suit that failed to meet in the front when he tried to button it, spoke against those words. When he'd finished, Judge Wilson called the lawyers up to the bench, and they went immediately into some private conversation as they stood in front of him, the flag of Tennessee on one side of them, the flag of the United States on the other.

Abby sat through the proceedings in a state of numb disbelief. The last three months had felt that way as one shock after another rolled over her. She recalled how she had heard about the shootout at the Lolleyville jail.

Daniel had called Preacher Tuttle's house and asked him to fetch Abby to his place so he could talk to her. An hour later he called back and Abby answered. Daniel told her of Stephen's death and Sol's injuries.

At first she couldn't believe it. It made no sense. But Daniel kept insisting on its truth.

"Stephen saved my life," Daniel repeated over and over again, as if that made the unbelievable more believable.

Abby heard the words but Daniel's voice sounded unconnected to her, like a radio announcer telling about something that had happened in Raleigh or somewhere else far off. How was it possible that Stephen was dead and lying in an undertaker's parlor in a town called Lolleyville? She turned to Elsa who stood by her, but Elsa just shook her head and pointed her back to the telephone.

Daniel filled her in on the details of the gunfight. She gradually started to understand. When he had finished talking, she asked about Sol. Daniel said he was hurt bad.

"He was shot in the back," he'd said. "He's in a Knoxville hospital. Can't talk or walk right now. But the doctor says he'll probably live unless somethin' else happens."

"We'll be praying for him," she said, trying not to cry.

"He'd appreciate that."

After another couple of minutes, Abby hung up and returned home. Elsa and Tuttle stayed with her that day. She wondered how to tell the boys, then realized she had to say it straight out.

Her heart heavy, she gathered Jimmy and Stevie in the living room. They knew something bad had happened.

"It's Pa, ain't it?" asked Jimmy.

Abby nodded and told them the truth. Jimmy cried quietly for a few minutes, then wiped his eyes.

"When can we see Pa?" Stevie wanted to know, his eyes dry.

"Another day or so, I expect," said Abby.

"Where will they bury him?" Stevie asked.

Abby stared at him for a second. Stevie seemed a lot more grown up all of a sudden. It surprised her that he wasn't crying and that he instead of Jimmy was asking all the questions. "Grandma and Grandpa from Raleigh will have a spot, I'm sure," she answered.

That seemed to satisfy Stevie's questions for the moment. He said he wanted to go outside. Abby nodded and both boys left.

Daniel arrived the next day, and after Abby sent Elsa to the store with Stevie and Jimmy, he told her the full story. "The police in Lolleyville will probably arrest me pretty soon," he said. "Soon as they sort through a few more things. Right now they're not sure who to believe, me or Ben Clack."

Daniel had told the police about Hal Clack's fall off Edgar's Knob, how Stephen had witnessed Topper pushing his pa over the edge. But the police had argued that since Hal's death had occurred so long ago, they saw no reason to go back that far to come up with an explanation for the killings that had just happened in Lolleyville.

"They'll have to charge somebody, and I guess it'll be me. Their lawman, Conroy, is dead, remember? And besides, Ben has a lot more money than I do."

Abby nodded.

He told her again how Stephen had come to his rescue. She nodded with understanding. Though she and Stephen had gone through a lot of troubles, he had seemed different the last time she visited him, like he had wanted to mend his ways. True, he hadn't changed completely at the time, but she had seen some good signs. Yet now . . .

Her tears fell then, and a deep grief washed over her. "I . . . I failed him," she cried. "Maybe if I had—"

"Don't," said Daniel, taking her hand. "Abby, you did all you could. You know that. You were a good wife."

She looked at Daniel. "I did try . . . tried hard."

"You sure did. Stephen wanted you to know he loved you. Told me to tell you that, you and the boys. His last words were that he loved you all."

Abby wiped her eyes. "His last words?"

Daniel nodded. "Said he loved you and—"

"And what?"

Daniel studied the floor. "He said . . . he believed," he continued. "That he had got off track, but that he believed and wanted you to know it."

Abby cried some more, although now her grief was mixed with a measure of gratitude. In spite of Stephen's mistakes, the dishonor he'd brought his family, he had loved her and in the end saw the error of his ways. And she had loved him—at least as much as she knew of love at the time she married him. No doubt she should take some blame for his mistakes along the way, should feel some guilt that she couldn't have helped him more. At least he'd died a noble death.

"He said he believed?" she asked Daniel.

"That's right. The last thing he said."

Abby wiped her eyes. In the end, Stephen had returned to his faith. That gave her comfort.

The next day she finally managed to reach Stephen's folks by telephone. To her surprise they said they had no burial spot for him in Raleigh and no money to purchase one. Daniel stepped in and said he would proudly have Stephen's body buried in the family cemetery, on the ridge behind Solomon's cabin.

The funeral was five days after he died, on a warm, windless late March day. Stephen's mother and father arrived the day before the burial and left the day afterward. Abby spent almost no time with them, and she realized again she hardly knew them. Grieving this, for her sake and her sons, she told herself that after this ended she would go to Raleigh to see them, to make amends for the years they had let pass without any real connection.

Abby stood by Stephen's coffin after Preacher Tuttle had said his words and just before they lowered him into the ground. "I am sorry," she whispered. "I wish . . . I'd known how to make you happier." She laid both her hands on the coffin. Jimmy stood on one side, Stevie the other. "I loved your pa," she said to them, hoping they understood.

"We know," Jimmy said. "Even when it wasn't easy."

Abby hugged both boys. Loving Stephen Waterbury hadn't been easy, but she'd done the best she could. *Lord, forgive me for the times I failed him,* she silently prayed.

Then, with her boys at her side, she walked away.

As the sun descended, she and Jimmy and Stevie sat in the living room, alone for the first time all day. Jimmy glanced at Stevie and cleared his throat. Abby sensed he wanted to say something. She put down the knitting she had started.

Jimmy moved to the chair beside her and took her hands. "Mama?" he said.

"Yes."

"We . . . me and Stevie. We want you to call us Jim and Steve now."

It took a second for Abby to catch on. Jim and Steve. But why? Then it hit her: Jimmy and Stevie were names for boys, but now with their pa gone, her boys had become young men.

"Of course," she said, her eyes glistening. "Jim and Steve."

That night had passed, then another. The law came and arrested Daniel, saying Ben Clack had sworn to them that Daniel and Sol had tried to break their kin out of the Lolleyville jail and that he and Topper and Conroy had tried to stop them. Daniel put up no resistance.

"Need to get this over with," he'd said to Deidre as they were taking him away. "One way or the other."

On the first day of the trial Preacher Tuttle drove Abby and Deidre and Jewel to the outskirts of Knoxville to the boardinghouse where Stephen had lived. They'd decided they would stay there during the time of the proceedings in the small rooms he'd rented. With Tuttle stopping by to see them from time to time, the boys would stay back in Blue Springs.

Abby felt strange when she entered Stephen's place. Although Preacher Tuttle had been there earlier to clear out Stephen's belongings, she had not been there. She wondered how she and Stephen had drifted so far apart. Had the Depression done that to them? Or would their marriage have faltered even in the best of times? She didn't know.

As if in a daze she examined the two rooms, looking for some clue about Stephen's life there. The rooms were neat but sparse. A lamp sat on a table by a bed with a brown cover. The floors were wood, badly scratched, with some dust in the corners but otherwise clean. For some reason she couldn't explain, it pleased her that the owner hadn't been able to rent the place since Stephen's death. At least now she could go through the rooms, try to get a feel for his life there.

She and Jewel and Deidre had cleaned the dust from the corners and moved into the two rooms.

Now Abby sat in the Lolleyville courtroom where her brother Daniel stood trial for a crime he surely didn't commit.

The authorities had of course talked to Sol about the shootings, but he had no recollection of the events, none at all. The doctors in Knoxville said that the trauma of his injuries—the shot to the back so severe he couldn't walk—had caused him to black out his memory. They said he might regain his recollections in a week or so. Then again, he might never regain them.

With people from all over pressing for a conviction against somebody for all the killings—and most of the folks unrelated to the men involved didn't care as to who—the police acted as though they had to do something, even if what they did turned out later to be wrong. So they arrested Daniel and proceeded with the trial.

As she fanned herself, Abby glanced over at Deidre. This whole thing had just about crushed her. She looked pasty-faced and thin. Abby took Deidre's hand. She shared Deidre's worry about Daniel. This had hit him hard. In fact, about the only person in the courtroom who looked worse than Deidre was Daniel. His cheeks seemed to have sunk in on his face, and his eyes stared out but didn't appear to see anything. His overalls and work shirt hung on him loose and baggy.

Abby sighed. It seemed that it didn't matter to Daniel whether he got justice or not. So many sad things had happened to him. Now this. Given he already had some weakness for the drink, she knew the trial would only make him worse off that way. The couple of times she'd talked to him since his arrest he had voiced heavy guilt about Stephen's death and Sol's injuries.

She squeezed Deidre's hand.

"Why does the Lord do this to me?" Daniel had asked her both times she visited. "Why do I keep livin' while others close to me get killed? Laban, Luke, now Stephen. And Sol shot up real bad. Yet I'm still breathin' as strong as ever. . . . I'm not worthy of it."

"I don't pretend to know the Lord's ways," Abby replied. "All I can do is accept them."

Daniel limped to his cell's only window and stared at the small patch of sky. "I'm not sure I can say the same anymore," he said.

Abby hadn't argued. The Lord would have to work on Daniel, not her.

The judge rapped his gavel, which brought Abby's thoughts back to the courtroom. Soon they would know the verdict. Daniel Porter would either go free, spend the rest of his life in prison, or receive the death sentence. Tears ran down Deidre's cheeks. Abby wished with all her heart she could make all this go away. But of course she couldn't. Crimes had been committed, and somebody had to pay.

Over the next four days as the trial unfolded, Abby found she didn't need to be versed on the legal language to understand the crux of the arguments presented. Daniel's lawyer called on a lot of witnesses who said good things about Daniel, how he'd never caused anybody any trouble, how he labored hard to make something of himself and his family, how he'd served his country during the war against Germany.

The prosecutor countered with some folks who talked about how Daniel liked to drink, how he got angry sometimes when he drank, adding that in the past Daniel and Stephen would share liquor together sometimes. And because they were kin by marriage, it made sense that Daniel would want to break his kinfolk out of jail. Fact is, a couple of the witnesses said they admired a man who cared that much about his kin. They didn't go so far as to suggest a man ought to kill a lawman to bust out a relative, but kin was kin and so it made sense that Daniel would try to free Stephen.

Ricks raised the question of why the Clacks were at the jailhouse so late at night, and that caused a few folks to raise their eyebrows and ask themselves the same question. But then the prosecutor said the Clacks had hired Stephen Waterbury to do some lawyer work for them before he landed in jail, and he had papers to show their prior lawyer-client relationship. So what if they visited at night instead of in the daytime? Men like the Clacks kept irregular hours but that didn't make them murderers.

Turning the question around, he asked the same thing about Daniel and Sol. Why had they come to the jail so late? A lawman like Sol should know better than to try to visit a prisoner at eleven o'clock. Unless he came for a different reason, like to help the prisoner escape.

Then Ricks tried introducing some evidence about a previous death—the demise of one Hal Clack. But before he'd hardly gotten started in telling how Daniel and Sol had gone to Lolleyville to protect Stephen because they knew the Clacks wanted him dead to protect their secret about their pa's death, Judge Wilson interrupted and stopped him. "What you're saying has no bearing on this case!" he said in a way that indicated he'd brook no more exploring in that direction. "Now let's move on." Ricks hung his head, returned to his chair and sat down next to Daniel.

On the fourth day, near the end of the afternoon, Ben Clack took the stand. Abby couldn't believe her eyes. He wore a smart gray pinstriped suit, a light blue shirt and matching tie, and shiny black boots. He had shaved and slicked his hair back into a smooth wave. Abby's heart raced with disgust. The man had plagued her for a long time. Now he had dressed himself up to mislead the jury. She wanted to walk right up and slap him.

She glanced at Eugenia. Had she told Ben to dress up like this? Was she watching out for her brother-in-law, protecting the last of Hal Clack's sons? What kind of woman was she? A couple of times Abby had nodded her way when passing her in the courthouse, and each time Eugenia had averted her eyes and moved on.

Ben smiled at the jury and then told the court that he and his brother had gone to the jail in Lolleyville to end their business with Stephen.

"Why didn't you just call the jailkeeper and ask him to give Mr. Waterbury the news?" asked Ricks.

"We thought it would be better to say it face-to-face," replied Ben. "More businesslike."

Ricks tried to get more out of him, make him contradict himself. But Ben stuck to his story. After a while, the lawyer shrugged and took his seat again. The prosecutor stood and asked Ben to tell the court exactly what happened the night of the shootings. Ben sat up straight and smoothed down his well-pressed jacket.

"We come in the jail building around eleven o'clock," Ben said. "Found it real quiet. We walked back to where the cells are, saw Conroy already dead on the floor." He paused and eyed the judge as if asking for approval to go on. Judge Wilson nodded. Ben continued, "We surprised Sol and Daniel Porter. They had Waterbury out of his cell. Sol and Daniel drew down on us. We shot at them to protect ourselves. They shot back." Ben swiped at his eyes as if he'd teared up. "Daniel shot my brother, kilt him straight out dead!"

Abby took a good look at the members of the jury. They seemed to believe him.

"Sure, I maybe shot Sol Porter," said Ben. "I admit that. But I was tryin' to shoot him." He pointed at Daniel. "Because he kilt my brother. Conroy too, I reckon."

The prosecutor said, "So you're saying right here today, before Almighty God and this jury, that you interrupted a jailbreak and that Daniel and Sol Porter started shooting at you and so you shot back at them in self-defense. Is that what you're telling us?"

Ben cast a look at the jury, at the judge, and finally at Daniel. "As God is my witness that is the gospel truth," he said.

Abby gasped. Such blatant lies!

The prosecutor smiled at the jury and sat down. Ricks tried one more time to push him off his story, but Ben had it down too well and the lawyer soon gave up.

"We will recess until tomorrow morning," Judge Wilson announced. "Court adjourned for the day."

Abby's heart sank. The jury had all night to ponder Ben Clack's testimony. He had sounded so earnest. She had no doubt they would go to sleep believing the story he'd just told. Her head down, she followed Deidre and Jewel out of the courtroom. In the hall outside she stopped for a moment as Deidre spoke to Daniel's lawyer. She heard a man's voice behind her.

"You got a chance for a real man now, Mrs. Waterbury."

Abby's stomach rolled when she felt Ben Clack's hand on her arm. He squeezed her elbow in a way nobody would notice. She whirled around to face him and smelled whiskey on his breath. "You make me sick," she said.

"I like a feisty woman," he whispered. "Glad that drunk husband of yours didn't take that out of you."

Abby wished Daniel had shot Ben along with Topper. Rid the earth of such a scourge. "You won't get away with this," she said, her words sounding weaker than she'd hoped.

Clack grinned. "You reckon not? From what I saw the jury bought it pretty good."

Abby pulled her arm away and stepped back. Clack leaned close and whispered so only she could hear. "Judge Wilson is a cousin," he chortled. "Either way, I go free. I'll visit you soon, don't you fret about that."

Abby clenched her fists. If she had a gun and he came after her, she might just shoot him herself.

Something shuffled behind Abby, and she turned in time to see Eugenia Clack coming their way. At her side now, Eugenia asked Abby, "He botherin' you?"

Abby studied the woman. Lines crawled up and down the sides of her mouth. Her hands were thick. Why had Topper married her? Was she once beautiful?

"He's just mouthing off," Abby said.

Eugenia showed just a hint of a smile. Abby saw her teeth needed work. "Clack men are always mouthin' off," said Eugenia.

"You best watch yourself, woman," hissed Ben.

Eugenia moved past Abby to her brother-in-law. Her girth made him look like a boy. Abby felt strength in her. She figured it took a woman like Eugenia to survive with the Clacks.

"You don't scare me none," Eugenia told Ben. He backed off a half step, and Abby realized the two had no liking for each other. Obviously, they were now in a fight to see who would lead the Clack clan. Eugenia turned to Abby. "I don't know what all happened between our menfolk," she said, "but whatever it was, it's over now. They's both dead."

Abby nodded.

"My way is to let bygones go," Eugenia went on. "Move on with life."

"I want that too," said Abby, finding her voice.

"Just don't bother us and we won't bother you."

"I am fine with that."

Eugenia gave her a nod and started to move off, Ben with her.

"We got your husband," Ben said in a parting shot. "Your brother now too. Comin' for you next."

Abby clenched her fists. Hard days were surely ahead. Unless something turned up soon, Daniel could lose his life over the murders of Topper Clack and Sheriff Conroy. And Ben would keep his promise and come after her.

It took another two days to finish up the trial. Ricks called Daniel to the stand and he told the courtroom about Sol making him a deputy to help arrest Topper for murder. Daniel said he and Sol were trying to get to Stephen to protect him from the Clack brothers who had good reason for wanting him dead. The judge cautioned the jury there was no evidence to support any such claim that Topper Clack murdered anyone but that Daniel had a right to say what he said because it explained his motive for going to see Stephen Waterbury. Daniel also told about how he and Sol found Conroy on the floor of his office, how they then went to check Stephen's cell, and how the shooting happened soon after that.

After Daniel was through, Ricks got Deidre on the stand to verify Sol's coming by and asking Daniel to serve as his deputy. But the prosecutor told the jury they should expect a wife to back up her own husband's story.

Both lawyers gave their closing arguments, and by midafternoon the day after Daniel gave his testimony, the prosecution and defense rested. Judge Wilson declared a recess until the next morning when he said he'd give some instructions to the jury before sending them off to consider the charges and decide on a verdict. Wilson rapped his gavel and the court adjourned for the day.

Her heart heavy, Abby left the courtroom, climbed into the car along with Preacher Tuttle, Deidre and Jewel, and returned to the boardinghouse. They all pitched in and made up a bite of supper in the small kitchen but nobody ate much. Conversation was pretty slim too. Once or twice Preacher Tuttle tried to offer hopeful words. Nobody responded.

The only sound was Abby and Deidre scraping off the dishes. So Preacher Tuttle stood and said he'd see them all in the morning, took up his bedroll and disappeared to the back porch where he'd made it his habit to lie down for the night. A few minutes after that, Deidre and Jewel headed to the one bedroom in the place, while Abby pulled a sheet out of the closet to lay over the sofa where she'd been sleeping since the trial began.

Abby dropped to her knees as she tucked the sheet under the cushions. Her arms felt heavy, worn out. Suddenly feeling overcome by grief and anger, she stayed on her knees, unable to rise or even lift her arms. She missed her sons, hadn't seen them in days. She thought of how proud they were that Stephen had saved Daniel's life, how they had clung to that one word of good about their pa. Abby started to cry. She found herself mad at Stephen for making such a mess of things, for giving up on their marriage and leaving her alone with the boys. If he'd only stayed home with them, he would still be alive. She would still have a husband, and Jim and Steve would still have a pa. Daniel wouldn't be in jail. Sol wouldn't be in the hospital with his legs not working, part of his memory gone.

Still sobbing, Abby recognized something else, something she hadn't admitted since Stephen's death. The notion of it scared her, made her see that no matter how good she was, she had plenty of bad still sticking to her bones. Even with as much pain as Stephen's death had caused, it had brought a sense of relief too, the realization that she no longer had to carry her burden and his on her shoulders. She knew a good Christian woman ought not to feel this way. Yet there it was, the relief just as real as her grief, the feeling that now she could move on with her life, put all that had happened with Stephen, all the unhappiness, behind her.

Another thought slipped into her mind. Thaddeus. She couldn't help wondering where he was. Would he ever return to Blue Springs? What if he found out about Stephen? Abby became angry with herself. How callous! She had caused some of Stephen's problems, after all. Whether she knew it at the time or not, her ambitions had fed his and the two together had become more than Stephen could handle.

Abby propped her elbows on the sofa, folded her hands and bowed her head. She was angry with Ben Clack too, plenty angry. For all he and his brothers had done to her family through the years. Fact was, she hated the man. God had made a mistake with Ben, she decided, a horrible mistake in letting him draw even one breath. If she had her way, she'd strike Ben down like an avenging angel, take the sword of the Lord and smite him dead.

Abby dug her nails into the back of her hands. She wished Ben dead, dead so he could never breathe his foul breath on her neck again, never keep his vile threats against her.

Then, in a moment she would remember the rest of her life, the Lord whispered a warning into Abby's soul, a warning that if she hated Ben Clack so much she wanted him dead, then she'd fallen into a state of rebellion from the Lord's will. The warning startled Abby, and she ground her teeth against it but it kept returning with a burning in her heart.

I want Ben to know my grace too, the Lord seemed to whisper. *As much as you. Your hatred toward him is hardening your heart.*

Abby shook her head. The thought hung on. *I want peace,* He whispered, *between your kin and theirs. You are the one to make this happen.*

Abby trembled. She'd not felt the Lord so near since the day she first trusted Jesus.

Forgive them, and I will forgive you.

Tears streamed down Abby's face and onto the sofa. How could she forgive the Clacks? How could she bring peace between her family and theirs? Nobody wanted peace.

Forgive them, and I will forgive you.

But what would Daniel say to this? Or Sol and Elsa? How could she forgive such a man as Ben Clack? Weary from crying, she lay down on the floor by the sofa. But the tears kept coming.

She heard the whispering again. She couldn't ignore it. Though not a woman given to visions, she had no doubt that God was speaking to her, that He wanted her to make peace with the Clacks. But how? She squeezed her eyes shut.

Abby didn't know. But if the Lord wanted it, then He would surely give her the strength to do it. The thought came as if out of the air, as if breathed into her heart.

She lifted her hands toward the ceiling.

"I'm yours, Lord," she whispered. "Show me what I should do."

A sense of quiet settled on her. Yes, she would do what the Lord wanted. She had no husband now. Her sons were growing up. She would devote herself to the task of making peace between the Porters and the

Clacks. It was time for this feud to end. And if the Lord had chosen her as the instrument to make this happen, she would accept the assignment. She opened her eyes and stared up at the ceiling. Her tears dried.

As she rolled over to stand up, Abby spotted the corner of something attached to the bottom of the sofa. She looked closer and saw a white folder. Pieces of tape held it there. What in the world? Her hands shaking, she pulled off the tape, took the folder, eased onto the sofa and opened the folder. A single piece of paper lay inside, a document of some kind.

Abby's eyes widened when she saw Stephen's signature on the document. She started to read, her heart racing.

CHAPTER TWENTY-ONE

In the morning Abby and the others took the document she had found under the sofa to Judge Wilson's office. The judge read it over and then suspended the trial while he considered the potential new evidence. Daniel got word from Ricks about the new development about noon that day. While Ricks looked pretty thrilled by the turn of events, Daniel acted indifferent, a shrug of the shoulders his only response. What did it matter to him? Jail or free, as far as he was concerned, he had no hopes left. So what if Judge Wilson agreed that the paper Abby had found had some bearing on his case and decided to let him go? Sooner or later something else just as awful would come his way. Troubles shot at him with as true an aim as the best marksmen in North Carolina.

As a man who had given up on the Lord, Daniel tried to pass off all his hardship as nothing but ill fortune, the flip of the cards, the unknowable winds of fate. Yet, deep inside, he trusted chance no more than he trusted the Lord. Somehow he kept returning to the notion that the Lord had it in for him, a grudge that caused the Almighty to punish him over and over. As to why, he didn't know exactly.

Sure, he was aware he'd done some sinning along the way. But what had he done that separated him out as such a handy target? He had started out pretty fine—putting his trust in Jesus since his boyhood days. He took that faith over to the war, stayed away from the doublings the whole time, kept his distance from the women, the gambling, and the foul talk as well. But it seemed God hadn't seen fit to honor any of that. When the bullets started whizzing he got hit just like everybody else. He received no more concern from the Lord than the worst of the men. So what good had his faith done him? Then or any other time, bad things seemed to take their aim at him and his family.

Daniel pondered that question a lot in the lonely days after Abby went to the judge with the document, in the days that came after everyone returned to Blue Springs to see to their families. Truth was, Daniel preferred the time spent alone. What man wanted people he loved to see him in the squalor of jail, with its single cot, stained sink, and privy that smelled loudly. Daniel had no desire for good people to see him in such surroundings.

He slept much of the time, though on occasion nightmares interrupted his rest. If he had a choice between staying awake and reliving the stares of the folks who thought he'd shot and killed Conroy, or having a nightmare where his pa or Laban showed up, he would just as soon fall asleep. Because when awake, he couldn't stop thinking of Conroy's widow, the way she looked at him with her large gray eyes, figuring him as her husband's murderer. Conroy's kids were also there at the trial, and their eyes, colored like their mama's, haunted Daniel even more so. He knew he hadn't killed their pa, but he hadn't saved him either. Their pa was dead and they blamed Daniel, and maybe they should.

The days moved past, and Daniel's beard grew more and more scraggly. His appetite gone, he lost weight. The muscles in his arms and legs started shrinking, his skin sagging. He hoped he would die. He didn't remember when exactly that notion took hold of him. But one day, sitting in his cell, listening to a hard rain falling outside, it sprung up in his head like a weed in a corn patch. At first he tried to hoe it out, to rid himself of the idea. But it proved itself a weed with a deep root. The more he dug at it, the thicker it seemed to grow. After a while he stopped fighting and gave in to studying on it. Maybe he deserved to pass on from this life, he figured. Men a lot better than he had passed on—Pa, Laban, Luke, Conroy. Why not him?

The nightmares would disappear if he did. The eyes of the Conroy family would go away. True, Deidre and the kids would feel sad for a little while. But Marla and Ed were mostly grown anyway and Raymond not far behind them. Deidre could move back with her folks in Asheville till she took up with another husband. She was still pretty enough to find her a man with prospects, somebody who wouldn't shame her by ending up in jail for murder.

The more Daniel pondered his death, the more it appealed to him. It would settle a lot of things, he figured. Occasionally he did wonder about what might come after the grave, whether or not he would end up in heaven. The idea of hell scared him some. But then he remembered he'd tossed out any belief in the Lord, so any notion of an afterlife made no sense either way. Once a man was dead, that's it, like a rabbit shot with a rifle.

Another week passed and Daniel ate even less. His overalls hung on him all loose. When Ricks visited him, he mostly grunted and mumbled. The fifth week after Abby found the document Ricks came to escort Daniel back to the courthouse. He told Daniel that Judge Wilson had reached a decision. The judge might say the document had no bearing and then they'd move on with the case to the jury's deliberation. He might say the document lent new light on the case so that he'd allow it as evidence in the court. Or he might declare Daniel free, saying the document cleared him of all charges. Of course, Ricks didn't know which way it would go but he had high hopes.

Daniel slouched back into the courtroom in handcuffs. His hair was a tangled mess, his beard all shaggy, and his eyes bloodshot. But he had no care about his appearance, and whatever Judge Wilson did made no difference to him. He figured he was dead either way.

Similar to the first day of trial, people lined the walls of the courtroom as Judge Wilson entered. Daniel glanced over his shoulder but then dropped his eyes when he saw Deidre and Abby. He wished Deidre hadn't come and felt glad that he had strictly forbidden any visits from his kids.

The bailiff called everyone to order. Daniel and Ricks took their seats. Wilson hammered his gavel a couple of times, and the court became silent. Daniel wondered if Mrs. Conroy had come with her kids. He hoped not.

The judge indicated for Daniel to stand. Ricks motioned, and Daniel did as he was told.

Wilson adjusted his glasses, cleared his throat and said, "A little over a month ago this court heard closing arguments from the prosecutor here in Lolleyville and from the defense regarding Mr. Daniel Porter in the case accusing Mr. Porter of willfully shooting and killing Mr. Elbert Conroy and Mr. Topper Clack. The court was about to hand this case over to this fine jury"—he gestured to the twelve to his right—"to bring back a verdict. But on the morning this court would have done so, Mrs. Abigail Waterbury, sister of the accused, brought before this court by way of the defense a document she claimed she found in the former dwelling of Mr. Stephen Waterbury, her late husband and another of those killed in the Lolleyville jail shooting."

Wilson adjusted his glasses again. "Now, it seemed apparent to this court that Mrs. Waterbury, since she's a sister of the defendant and all, would have plenty of reason to produce a fake document in hopes of steering this court away from convicting her brother as the killer. That was my predisposition when she first approached this court with the document. I have therefore looked over the document with a skeptical eye."

He placed both hands on the bench and stared at Daniel over his glasses. Daniel studied him. Ricks had told him about Wilson being married to a woman who was a distant cousin to the Clacks, so Daniel saw no reason to believe the judge would do him any favors.

Judge Wilson continued. "I am convinced, however, that the document is valid."

Those sitting in the courtroom let out a collective gasp.

"This document, drawn up by Stephen Waterbury, a lawyer I should remind you, details Waterbury's account of the events of March 27, 1931, the day of Hal Clack's death over at Edgar's Knob in North Carolina. According to Mr. Waterbury, Topper Clack and his father, Hal Clack, did indeed come to blows at Edgar's Knob that day years ago where, again according to Waterbury who was present at the time, Topper Clack knocked his father off the cliff, which resulted in his death."

Wilson stopped and looked around the courtroom. "Of course, this fact proves nothing about what happened in the Lolleyville jail on the night Mr. Clack, Mr. Conroy, and Mr. Waterbury were killed. But it does lend support to Mr. Porter's claim that he traveled to Lolleyville with Sheriff Sol Porter in the attempt to protect Mr. Waterbury from the Clack brothers. In fact, Mr. Waterbury explains in his document that he drew up the statement precisely in case something happened to him. He wanted the authorities to know the Clacks had motive to do him harm."

Removing his glasses, the judge peered at the prosecutor. "So, given this new evidence, I'm hereby suspending the charges against Mr. Daniel Porter until such time as the prosecutor can show just cause why I should not accept Mr. Porter's word against that of Mr. Ben Clack. Until then, this case will remain open. Neither Mr. Porter nor Mr. Clack shall be held liable for these deaths at this time, and Mr. Porter will be released from custody. As to the future, I will examine any new facts if and when they become available." Then Wilson stood, rapped his gavel and announced, "Court dismissed."

Not sure what had just taken place, Daniel turned to Ricks, who was beaming at him. The lawyer grabbed Daniel's hand and shook it as if they'd just won a prize pig at the county fair.

"Is it over?" asked Daniel.

Deidre and Abby approached Daniel but he held up a hand as they neared him. He focused on Ricks. "Well, is it?" he asked again.

Ricks relaxed his smile and said, "The judge has suspended the case. That means you're not completely free—not yet anyway. But you can at least go home now. And, unless somebody brings more evidence against you than the court now has, you'll never again have to face the charges."

"You mean to say I'm not off the hook?"

"Not exactly, Daniel. But I doubt Judge Wilson will continue. There just isn't enough evidence against you either way."

Daniel glanced at the Conroy family; the kids had their eyes on him. He lowered his gaze. "So I'm not proved innocent," he said.

"No, but not proved guilty either."

Daniel smoothed down his beard. He didn't know which was worse—a jury pronouncing him guilty or this in-between situation that left him under a cloud of suspicion. "How long will this suspend thing last?"

"As long as Judge Wilson says it should," Ricks replied.

"What if the judge never finds any more facts?"

"That'd be good. If nothing else shows up, you won't be put on trial again."

"But then some folks will always see me as guilty of the killin'," said Daniel.

"Let me tell you something, my friend," Ricks said. "Even if a jury finds you innocent, there will always be someone who still believes you're guilty. That's true the other way around too—if a jury finds you guilty, there will be someone out there who believes you're innocent. That's the way the law works. Nothing's ever certain. But in the end it doesn't matter all that much."

"Matters to me," said Daniel. "Matters to them." He nodded toward the Conroys.

"I'm sure it does, but we can't change the way things are. You want some advice?"

Daniel shrugged.

"Go home, Daniel. Thank the good Lord you're not in jail anymore. Have yourself a good stiff drink, go love on your wife, hug your kids and put all this behind you. Don't let it eat at you."

Daniel knew Ricks had it right. Yet he didn't know that he could do as he advised. Too much had happened. Too many people had died or been hurt and he'd been too weak to stop it. Weak summed him up pretty well. No matter what happened, he had no control over it. His head down, he turned to Deidre and Abby and hugged them both.

They left the courthouse then, gathered his belongings from the jail, and got into Preacher Tuttle's auto for the trip back to Blue Springs. Daniel said little the entire time. When they finally arrived in town they stopped at Elsa's house to spend the night. Daniel ate a little supper and tried to celebrate with everybody but it felt empty to him, like he had an ax hanging over his head that might fall at any second. After a while, he said he needed to rest. They all embraced him one more time, and he headed to the back bedroom.

Deidre crawled in beside Daniel less than an hour later. He pretended to sleep. So far as he knew, Elsa and Deidre might figure him guilty too. Maybe not for killing Conroy but for failing to protect Sol. More than that, he saw himself as guilty.

He thought of Sol, still in the hospital in Knoxville. Although he was getting some better, the doctor said he might not ever walk again. He said there was an operation they could do on his back that could maybe help him, but no one had the money to pay for it. And if Sol never walked again, what kind of a life would that be? As for the fact that he couldn't remember the shooting? Well, maybe that was the only blessing out of all of this. At least one of them had forgotten it.

Daniel rolled over and stared out the window. He thought about getting up and opening the window to breathe in the fresh mountain air, then decided against it. Elsa had become citified again and complained when folks left the windows open, saying it let in too many bugs. Daniel figured bugs deserved a spot in the world too—why try to keep them out?

He wondered about dying. Would a body feel anything when slipping from this life to the next? Would it hurt much? And what lay after that? He turned back toward Deidre again. She was on her side facing him. She looked so peaceful. Would death do that? Provide a sweet relief like sleep after a hard day's labor? Would it bring a gentle, easy slide from the tribulations of this life into the blessedness of heaven?

Daniel gently touched Deidre's lips with his finger. What if a man didn't end up in the blessedness? What if he lived and died in such a way as to end up separate from the arms of Jesus?

He shifted back to the window. What if a man had believed in Jesus all his life, right up to near the end? What if he'd tried to live for Jesus all that time but then made some mistakes, wandered away? Did all those early years count, or did the mistakes of the last years wipe all the early ones away?

Unable to settle such mysteries, Daniel tried to sleep. But the faces of Laban and Luke and Sol kept rising up in the darkness, rising up and staring at him as if watching and wondering what he would do next.

SECTION III

1937–1945

CHAPTER TWENTY-TWO

Life settled down some again after Judge Wilson suspended the trial in Lolleyville. Abby went back to Blue Springs feeling confused about what she ought to do next. Although she and Stephen hadn't spent much time together over the last few years, she still experienced a sense of emptiness after having lost him. As long as Stephen had been alive, she had clung to the hope they might someday make their marriage happy again; that when the bad times ended, Stephen might return to her and the boys and they would be a family again. But that hope had ended forever, and now she felt anxious about the future—where she would go, what she would do. Would she stay with Elsa the rest of her life? Would her boys grow up, marry mountain girls, and settle down within a few miles of her?

As the fall progressed, she wondered now and again what she could've done to help Stephen. A heavy cloak of guilt lay on her for what she saw as her mistakes. If only she'd loved him better. If only she'd found a way to make some money so he wouldn't have had to carry the entire load. If only she hadn't lost her baby girl. Would that have kept Stephen home—a little girl in the house?

The days grew shorter as 1937 drew to an end. The trees had lost their leaves, and snow now blanketed the ground. The poorness the land had known since 1929 settled in even harder. Abby did as much as she could for Elsa. Sol still couldn't walk; he needed a wheelchair to move around. Jewel's duties with her children kept her more than busy so Elsa spent a lot of time nursing Sol. Thankfully, the county had paid many of the bills from the hospital where Sol had stayed for almost two months. They also gave Sol a small pension, because his disability occurred in the line of duty. At least he and his family wouldn't starve.

Before long, Christmas was upon them. Abby sat behind Daniel and Deidre and their kids—Marla with her beau at her side—at Jesus Holiness on Christmas Eve night. But she didn't get much of a chance to talk to any of them. Abby could see that Daniel still suffered badly. His eyes looked haunted, and his shoulders were hunched over.

With the preacher wrapping up his sermon, Abby touched her brother on the shoulder. He turned to her and nodded, and his face had a hollow look to it. Abby almost burst out crying. Daniel took too much on his soul. Blamed himself for all the troubles that had visited their family, thinking he should've somehow prevented them.

Leaving the church and stepping into a star-filled night, Abby kept her eye on Daniel, watched him walk quickly down the church steps and into the yard with his pipe in hand, his limp more noticeable now that he no longer used his cane. He seemed to have become an old man since the trial.

Abby saw Deidre talking to Preacher Tuttle and headed in their direction. She admired her sister-in-law's strength. If not for Deidre she had no doubt that Daniel would have long since done himself some kind of harm. Only her love and that of his kids had kept him going. Abby looped her left arm with Deidre's right as Pastor Tuttle moved away. "If you need anything, let me know," she said.

Deidre hugged her and whispered, "Pray for Daniel. I fear for him."

"We all need prayer, more than ever."

Deidre gave a weak smile. "He's carrying so much, you know."

"I know. The trial . . . losing his job."

Dropping her eyes, Deidre said, "The crew boss held his job for weeks. But too many men need work. He had to let Daniel go."

"It's not his fault. You keep telling him that."

"Thank you, Abby, I will. I just got to get him to believe it."

Abby left the church that night and fell into bed and then the next morning dawned. Winter set in hard on the land, and the snows fell deeper and the weeks settled into a routine. Abby did her chores around the house and tried to let the future take care of itself. She would live in Blue Springs the rest of her life if that's what the Lord wanted and she would find a way to feel contented. She'd educate Jim and Steve herself if need be, and then they'd make their own decisions about what they would do with their lives. Whether or not they stayed in the highlands, her blessing would be with them either way.

The months passed and spring arrived. A new logging company started buying some property surrounding Blue Springs and moving their trucks and equipment into town. The boss of the outfit, Isaac Cooledge, and his wife, Louise, and their four kids moved into a large house just off main street. Isaac put five men from Blue Springs to work, together with the three he had brought with him. One day in late March, Louise visited Abby and told her she'd heard good things about her as a teacher and asked if she could teach her kids until the school started back up again. Abby told her she would think about it but then right away decided she would. She could at least do somebody some good and maybe earn a few dollars at the same time.

"Let's try for three days a week," Abby told her. "In the afternoons from April to June and then from mid-September until the end of November."

"Sounds wonderful," said Mrs. Cooledge.

They agreed on a fee, and then Mrs. Cooledge picked up her purse and left the house.

The spring ended and summer began. Aunt Erline died in early June, her body worn out by too much labor and kidneys that didn't work as well as they once had. Everybody in the family and almost a hundred other folks attended the funeral. Abby saw Erline's four kids—all grown now—for the first time in years. She studied them during the service, four cousins she barely knew. They had all moved away from Blue Springs, one as far away as Colorado. She wondered how that would feel, to just up and move away from all she knew and never look back.

They buried Erline beside her husband on the hill behind their small house. Erline's children left around nightfall the day of the funeral, staying just long enough to share a meal with everybody at their departed mother's place. Watching them drive off, Abby felt her old yearning to leave Blue Springs, a desire to go with her cousins, climb into one of their autos and tear away from the small town and never return. But then she thought of her boys, remembered Elsa and Daniel and Deidre. She couldn't leave them, not today and maybe never. For better or worse, God had put her back here and she needed to find contentment.

June ended and July moved to the front. Humidity settled in on the mountain, turning everything hot and soggy. The days felt like long wet blankets, one after another, the heat boring down from dawn to dusk for the next two months. Abby labored long hours every day in the garden. The work calmed her worries. The smells and sounds of digging out the soil, the sweat running off her nose, the feel of the hoe in her hands—all touched her in ways she found comforting. Maybe this was what she most needed, she thought. The simple task of taking food from the earth, as basic a job as anyone had ever taken up.

As she worked she tried to keep her mind on worthy matters, causes for praise to the Lord. Jim, now thirteen, had gotten a job with the logging company. She worried about him as he handled the heavy equipment, but it didn't bother him any. Steve, smaller at eleven than the other boys his age, spent most of his time at the general store. He seemed to have a head for business, and in spite of his young years, did a good bit of bookwork for the storeowner. While he hardly ever received any dollars for his labors, the storeowner did pay Steve in canned goods, flour and sugar.

The goods Steve brought home made a difference. Even better, Jim's job paid a real wage, and he faithfully brought the dollars he earned each week home to Abby. After giving him a little spending money, she gave the rest to Elsa for the household needs. At first Elsa refused the money. "Your boy has earned it," she'd said to Abby. "You keep it for him, maybe for more education someday."

Abby shook her head. "We'll not worry about someday. You need this now. It wouldn't be right for us to live here without paying what we can."

Reluctantly Elsa accepted the dollars, though she spent only enough to make ends meet. Abby thought she knew the reason why. Elsa had started saving to pay for a doctor to do surgery on Sol's back. Even though Dr. Sills said he couldn't give any guarantees, he thought he could find a doctor to perform the surgery Sol needed to walk again.

On the last Friday of August Abby started out as usual in the garden right after breakfast, leaving Elsa in the kitchen to finish up with the dishes. At just past ten o'clock, Elsa stepped outside and offered Abby a glass of water. Abby wiped the sweat from her forehead and took the glass from Elsa. "You reckon it'll ever turn cool again?" she asked.

"Not before fall, I reckon," Elsa replied.

"You going to see Sol today?"

Elsa started to answer, but a voice calling from the side of the house interrupted her.

"Back here!" yelled Abby.

Some seconds later a squat man without much of a neck walked around the corner and made his way over to them. "You Elsa Porter?" the man asked Abby.

"I am," said Elsa.

Abby stood straighter. Unexpected visitors usually brought ill news. But what could it be this time? Had something worse happened to Sol?

"The name is Murray Maloy," he said, holding out his hand for Elsa. "I'm a lawyer from Charlotte."

Abby's fists clenched.

"You got a cooler place we might talk a minute?" Maloy asked. Sweat dripped from the man's round face.

"What's your business?" Elsa said suspiciously.

"I'd rather talk inside," said Maloy. "More private there."

Elsa glanced at Abby, and Abby shrugged. "I reckon we could go inside," said Elsa.

Abby thought of Daniel. Did Maloy have some word about his case, the trial that was suspended? But Ricks was Daniel's lawyer, and he lived near Knoxville. And why would Maloy ask for Elsa if he had news about Daniel? It had to be Sol. Maybe Maloy represented the hospital where Sol had stayed. Did the hospital want money from Elsa? Had the county failed to pay all the costs of treating Sol's injuries?

Holding her breath, Abby followed Elsa and Maloy into the parlor. Abby offered to get water for everyone. In the kitchen she again tried to figure what was happening, but no new ideas came. She placed three glasses and a pitcher of water on a wood tray and hurried back to the parlor. Maloy had taken a spot on Elsa's sofa, Elsa in a rocker across from him. Abby served the water. Maloy looked up at her, and Abby suddenly wondered if she ought to leave. But then Elsa pointed to the straight chair beside her and said, "Abby, you sit here with me. Nothing's secret between us." Abby sat down and set the tray on the floor.

Maloy slurped down his water, then wiped his mouth and faced Elsa. "I'm a lawyer," he said, "from down in Charlotte."

"As you already mentioned," Elsa said nodding.

"Yes, well, I'm here to bring you some news about your father . . . his estate."

"But my pa has been dead for many years now. I haven't heard anything about an estate. Did he owe debt or something?"

Maloy grinned. "No, ma'am. Nothing like that." He looked at the water tray. Abby got up and quickly refilled his glass. He gulped the water straight down and swiped his chin with the back of a plump hand. "Your pa, he had money," Maloy continued. "Quite a lot of it. He—"

"I wasn't close to my pa," Elsa said. "So what he did or didn't have is of no interest to me."

"Well, regardless of your relationship, your pa left you two thousand five hundred dollars and about a hundred acres of land up by Edgar's Knob."

Wide-eyed, Abby looked at Elsa. "Why am I just now hearing about this?" asked Elsa.

Maloy tugged at his collar. For the first time he seemed uncertain. "Uh . . . you see, your brother Topper had control of all the finances," he said. "He kept things with a tight rein."

"You saying my pa left this money to Topper, then to me if Topper died?"

"No. Your pa left it to you back a long time ago. But Topper, well, he wouldn't let me—"

"He wouldn't let you tell me about it," Elsa finished for him.

Maloy looked down at his shoes.

So that was it—Topper had kept Maloy from giving Elsa the money her pa had left her. And now that Topper had died, Maloy had come to do what the law demanded.

"My brother died more than a year ago," Elsa said. "What took you so long to get here?"

Maloy shrugged his shoulders. "I've been busy figuring. These matters can be complicated."

"You were worried about my brother Ben, weren't you?" Elsa said.

"Worried he might not want you telling me this news?"

The lawyer glanced at the water pitcher again. Abby poured him another glass, and he drank it straight down. "A man has to take care," he said to Elsa.

"But you finally decided to come anyway?"

"Something like that. It took me some time to make sure, but apparently Ben doesn't know about this particular portion of the estate. From what I can tell, Topper never told him. And I don't plan on saying what he has no need of hearing." He stared at Elsa as if hoping she would assure him she wouldn't tell Ben either.

Elsa rose and moved to the window by the fireplace and stared out at the sweltering day. Turning around, she said, "This takes me by surprise. I never figured Pa as the kind to leave a will."

Maloy grinned again. "Your pa was a lot of things, but stupid was not one of them. He paid close attention to his finances, more than anybody knew. Told me once he didn't want his boys to kill each other over the money he left them, that he wanted some say in how his property would be handled after he died. So he doled it out real carefully, this much to that one, this much to the other one."

"Me and Pa . . . well, as I said, we weren't close at all. I can figure no reason he would leave me money or property."

Maloy rubbed his large nose. "Who knows, maybe he wanted you to think better of him after he was gone. When people write out their wills they sometimes do surprising things. Guess it's the consideration of their dying that makes them do some heavy thinking about how they want people to feel about them after they've passed on."

"When did he write this will?"

"Long time ago, I believe in 1929 right before Christmas."

Elsa glanced at Abby. Solomon Porter had died in October 1929. Apparently Hal Clack still cared about her yet not enough to give her anything in his will while Solomon still lived.

"You mean what happened back in '29 didn't wipe out his money?" asked Elsa.

"Not at all. Your pa kept a lot of money in cash. Most men who made their living as he did . . . well, they didn't take very much to the banks."

Abby shook her head. Hal Clack had a lot of faults, but he had been shrewd when it came to his dollars.

"Where's the money now?" Elsa asked.

"Inside a vault in my office in Charlotte," he answered.

"You plannin' on bringing it to me . . . in cash, then?"

"Of course," said Maloy. "That is, for a small fee. Or if you prefer, you can come to Charlotte and get it. You could also leave it in the bank. Two thousand five hundred is a mighty lot of money for a woman to keep in her house."

Elsa wiped her hands on her apron. "Thank you, Mr. Maloy, for coming," she said. "Even if you are somewhat late. I will pay you your fee to deliver the money to me."

Maloy stood. "I apologize for my tardiness. But Topper Clack was a frightful man, and I wanted to keep on living. I'll make the arrangements for the delivery immediately."

"I know how he was," said Elsa, leading him to the door. "He was my brother."

After Maloy left, Elsa returned to the parlor, picked up her glass of water and sagged down in her rocker. Abby had taken a spot on the sofa. "It's a crazy world," Elsa said. "Why, after all those years when we never even talked, would Pa leave me anything?"

"Reckon he wanted to make sure you had something so you might remember him fondly," Abby said.

"Maybe he thought that when Solomon died, I would see the error of my ways and come crawling back to him."

"Could be. But maybe it's best to think the good of him rather than the bad."

"Wonder why he didn't change the will later, after Sol grew up and became a lawman. That had to disappoint him some."

Abby smiled at the irony. "Maybe he forgot what he'd done."

Elsa smiled, then giggled. "He drank so much he forgot a lot of things."

"Maybe he forgot he gave you two thousand five hundred dollars," laughed Abby, catching on to Elsa's suddenly light mood.

"And a hundred acres of good land," chuckled Elsa.

"You're a rich woman now," Abby went on, the mirth feeling good after so many months of grief.

"Almost makes me glad that Pa was a bootlegger," said Elsa. "His liquor money has made me a property owner."

"A regular baroness."

"A woman of high society."

Elsa and Abby doubled over in laughter. The inheritance money most likely made Elsa the richest woman in town. That and the hundred acres near Edgar's Knob, plus the ninety or so acres around the house where they sat and she had plenty. Used rightly, the money could do a lot.

The two women gradually sobered. Elsa stood and moved to the window. A sense of seriousness fell on the room. For a long time Elsa stayed by the window.

Abby studied her. She and Elsa had become close. If nothing else good had come from her move back to Blue Springs, at least that had happened. Although she'd never known a mama, Elsa had made a good substitute. She smiled as she wondered what Elsa would think of that. As pretty and young as she looked, she might not like it. Maybe an older sister, then.

Elsa faced Abby. "What am I going to do with this money?"

Abby raised her eyebrows. "Don't ask me."

"I won't just leave it to sit," she said. "Or put it in the bank. Does nobody any good there."

"I suppose you're right."

Elsa sat in her rocker.

"You could fix up your house," said Abby. "Put in a telephone maybe. Buy a radio."

Elsa rocked faster for a while. Then she stopped and said, "Remember, Ma gave me some money a long time ago?"

Abby remembered. Elsa's mother, Amelia Clack, had left Elsa just over eight hundred dollars upon her death. As Amelia explained it in a letter she left with her lawyer, she had slowly collected the cash over the years, taking it from her husband when he was passed out drunk.

"You gave me five hundred dollars of that money," Abby said. "Although I tried to keep you from doing it. That started me out in my schooling."

Elsa nodded. Abby felt grateful for how Elsa had treated her so kindly over the years.

"You never got to finish your education," Elsa said.

"After we married," recalled Abby, "Stephen didn't want me to complete my schooling. He said I wouldn't be needing it, that I should stay home and take care of the house. I was only a couple of classes short of my degree."

Elsa took her hand. "Now you can finish."

"Elsa, no, I can't accept any more money. Besides, I've got the boys to raise and Boone is a long way from here."

"But Jim and Steve are mostly grown now. Already got jobs, both of them. They can either go with you or stay here with me. My dollars can get you started again."

"What are you saying?"

Elsa reached over and squeezed Abby's hand. "I'm saying I want you to finish what you started so long ago. I want you to take half of this money and go back to Boone, complete your education. Then you'll have the chance to become a real teacher like you always wanted, maybe up in Raleigh or somewhere. Give you the chance to leave this place. I know you've wanted that since you were a girl, to spread your wings and fly. Abby, you're meant for more than Blue Springs, we've always known it. Me and your pa used to talk about it sometimes."

Abby swallowed hard as she considered the notion. Was this what the Lord wanted for her after all these years? Had this money fallen into Elsa's lap like it had years before so Abby might benefit from it? She could return to school and finish up her classes, then begin her life over. Her heart began to soar as she thought about the possibilities.

But then she hesitated. What sense did it make to even consider leaving? She was thirty-eight years old now, far too old for the classroom. Anyway, she wasn't the only one with dreams of a better life. What about Jim and Steve? They had taken well to Blue Springs. Would they want to go back to Boone, to return to a spot that held so many bad memories for them? And if they didn't, could she leave them behind as Elsa suggested? The answer was no. Their pa had left them for his own purposes and never returned for more than short periods of time. She wouldn't do the same thing to them that he had done.

Other than the fact that the teachers college was there, what did Boone offer her anymore? What other hold did the place have on her? With the exception of Mrs. Lollard, she had no family or friends there. Most of the friendships she and Stephen had made had quickly ended when their finances fell into such a sorry state.

All at once it hit Abby that she hadn't even considered Elsa's situation. What did Elsa want? Did she want to stay in Blue Springs? Or could she use this money to move down to Asheville where she'd once lived with her ma? Another notion rushed in on Abby, the only one that made sense. In her excitement she had forgotten all about Sol and his need for an operation. Elsa could use the money for that, so her only living child might get a chance to walk again. The county wouldn't pay for it, no matter how good a sheriff Sol had been.

"You should use the dollars for Sol," Abby insisted.

"I already thought of that," said Elsa. "I'll use half of it for Sol, half for you. And I'll sell the hundred acres at Edgar's Knob to the logging folks. The price has edged up some lately. If I do it right, I can help both you and Sol. Nothing would make me happier."

Abby weighed her choices. Maybe she should take Elsa up on her offer. Is this what the Lord wanted for her and her boys? Jim and Steve could go with her and attend school in Boone. Again she opened her mouth to say yes.

Then she pressed her lips together. She remembered her pledge to the Lord, after He spoke to her earlier, that she'd work toward ending the feud between her family and the Clacks. If she left Blue Springs, how could she keep her word? Was this offer just a temptation to prevent her from doing what she knew the Lord had called her to do?

She wondered what would have happened if she'd refused the money Elsa gave her years ago. What if she had never moved to Boone to go to school and had never met Stephen? Would she and Thaddeus have married instead? Is that what the Lord wanted for her then? Would she miss the Lord's will if she took the money now?

Her thoughts settled on Thaddeus. Where was he? What was he doing? Did he still have feelings for her? Maybe she could use some of the money to find him. She flushed as she realized she had no right to consider such a thing. Stephen hadn't been dead but a few months over a year. She pushed thoughts of Thaddeus away.

Abby rubbed her temples against the headache that had suddenly risen up behind her eyes. How did a person know what to do? How did the Lord reveal His will? How could she make sure not to make a mistake here?

Setting aside what she couldn't figure out, there was one thing she knew for sure. She went to Elsa. "I won't take your money," she said. "Not this time."

"But I want you to have it," insisted Elsa. "At least half of it. The good Lord knows my family put you through enough hurt that you deserve it."

Abby smiled at her. "You owe me nothing."

"But my own brother killed your husband," she said, her eyes pleading. "This money won't make up for that . . . but it will . . . will at least give you something . . . to start over, something to help."

"You have already done far more than you should have," said Abby. "You took me in, gave me and my boys a home, treated us like your own. Please, use the money for yourself, for Sol and Jewel and their kids. They need it far more than I do."

"But what about your schooling, your dream of leaving Blue Springs?"

Abby patted her hand. "Maybe it's time I let go of that dream. Replace it with something else, something more certain."

"Like what?"

"I got plenty to do right here. Things the Lord is wanting me to do, I believe."

Elsa nodded as if she understood.

"It seems the hardest things to see sometimes are the ones right in front of your nose," Abby continued. "Things the Lord desires from us."

"Maybe . . . maybe I can pay for that surgery for Sol," Elsa said, her eyes hopeful.

"I think that's best," said Abby. "Best for everybody."

Outside, the sun rose higher in the sky, the bees buzzed out and back among the flowers planted along the front gate, and the clouds drifted over the face of the sun. But inside Elsa Clack's house, two women who had become as close as mama and daughter sat and pondered what they would do next now that they had enough money to do just about anything they wanted.

CHAPTER TWENTY-THREE

Daniel loaded Sol's wheelchair into the back of a slick-tired truck the county law office had loaned him for the trip. It was the tenth of March, 1939, an overcast morning with clouds that looked eager to drop buckets of rain. Jewel and their three kids watched anxiously as Daniel grabbed Sol from off the porch, heaved him into his arms, and sat him on the passenger side of the truck.

"Here are some sandwiches," said Jewel, handing Daniel a brown sack as he took his place behind the wheel. "I'll come tomorrow with Preacher Tuttle and Elsa."

Daniel took the sack and thanked her.

"I'm the one should be thanking you," she said. "For all the times you've visited with my husband here, and now for takin' him to the hospital. We couldn't have made it these past months without your help."

Daniel cleared his throat. "We best get going," he said, obviously embarrassed.

Jewel stepped around the truck to Sol's side. "Tell the preacher to be careful," said Sol smiling. "He tends to drive with a heavy foot."

Jewel smiled back yet looked worried. "We'll all be prayin'."

"Sounds like a smart idea," Sol replied. "I'll see you tomorrow then." He gave Jewel a final kiss through the open window. Then Daniel started the truck and pulled out of the yard, pointing the truck toward Raleigh.

With neither man given much to talking, the trip went by quietly. Sol dozed some every now and again, while Daniel worked to keep the balky vehicle moving straight down the road. About two hours into the trip, a heavy rain started, a gray sheet of water pushed by a wind that buffeted them so hard it nearly forced the truck off the road. Daniel had to give even more attention to his task of driving. Two or three times he reached a spot in the road where the rain had flooded it real deep; he had to slow to a crawl and inch the bald tires through the calf-deep water. They stopped along the way to eat the sandwiches Jewel had made. The wind continued to rock the truck, the rain drumming on the roof as they munched their food. It took most of the afternoon to reach Raleigh. As they drove into the parking lot at the hospital the rain and wind suddenly eased off.

Weary to the bone, Daniel shut off the ignition and turned to Sol. "We made it," he said.

"Thought for a while there we might get blown right off the road," said Sol.

Daniel buttoned up his coat and climbed out of the truck. After unloading the wheelchair, he lifted Sol out of the seat, placed him gently in the chair, and wheeled him inside.

A large nurse met them at the door and took over behind the wheelchair to move Sol through the check-in station. Tagging along, Daniel felt out of place, a man without much education and with no liking for city life. All his experiences as a soldier, his years living in Asheville seemed to vanish. His hat in his hands, he trudged silently behind the nurse and Sol along the hospital's long corridors. After the necessary forms had been filled out, the nurse finally pushed Sol into his room and helped Daniel lift Sol onto the bed. The nurse told them they would be served some dinner about six o'clock, then disappeared.

Daniel looked around the room. It had two beds, one of them empty. A single window looked out over the parking lot. In one corner was a tiny bathroom with a sink and privy. The walls were beige and had no pictures on them. A chair sat beside each of the beds with a small table next to the chairs.

Daniel felt closed in. "How long they say you gone need to stay here?" he asked Sol.

"Not sure. A back operation can be real unpredictable."

"Wouldn't want to stay too long," said Daniel.

"I'll stay as long as it takes."

Daniel grunted. "Reckon that's true." He moved to the window and pushed it open. The rain had started up again but was much gentler now. He drew a deep breath. "The womenfolk are comin' tomorrow. The preacher too."

"I know," said Sol.

Clearing his throat, Daniel said, "Stayin' in this place all night don't rank up there real high on my list of fun things to do."

"You might as well sit," said Sol, pointing to a chair. "A while yet before supper, and a long night ahead."

Daniel thought of the truck. Maybe he ought to go take a nap in it after he ate something. But he had a couple of hours yet before supper arrived. Plus, he didn't feel right leaving Sol alone. So he tossed his hat on the table and sat down. For the next fifteen or so minutes the two men didn't speak. Daniel puffed on his pipe; Sol twisted a few times in the bed.

Daniel cleared his throat again and wished the women had already arrived. Then he could go sit in the truck and not have to talk to anybody. "Maybe your ma will marry Preacher Tuttle," he said out of the blue.

Sol grinned. "Preacher Tuttle would be a lucky man."

"No luckier than me and you."

"Can't disagree with that," said Sol. "Why you reckon that is, the Lord blessin' us with such fine women?"

Daniel spoke without thinking. "To make up for some other things that didn't fall our way." He wished he could take the words back. They sounded so peevish, not like a man at all. Everybody knew a true highlander didn't give in to griping about hard things. He just handled them, stayed quiet and kept his chin up no matter what happened.

"Thank you for bringing me here," said Sol, ignoring the remark.

Daniel waved him off with his pipe.

"No, I mean it. You have cared well for me since . . ."

Daniel hung his head. He and Sol hadn't yet spoken of what happened in Lolleyville that night. "You would have done the same for me," he said.

Sol straightened up some more. "Sorry I couldn't testify for you at the trial. I know all that went rough on you."

"It was beyond your means," said Daniel. "You did your part soon as you could."

"Don't know if it helped much."

Sol's memory of that night had come back only a few weeks ago. He had written up what had come to him, sent it off to Judge Wilson. The judge had added it to the record although he still refused to close the case. "A brother will back up another brother's story," Wilson had said.

"But he's a respected lawman," Ricks had argued.

"I'll give him that," agreed the judge. "But it's not final proof."

"He is Clack's half brother too, and he's not backing *his* story."

"Regardless, the case remains as it is," Wilson said, "open to hear further evidence."

Ricks had assured Daniel that the chances were slim he would ever have to deal with the matter again. Yet the whole thing still hung over his head.

"I'm sorry you lost your job," said Sol, apparently bent on saying some things heavy on his mind.

Daniel shrugged his shoulders.

"If I'd never asked you to go with me to Lolleyville, you wouldn't have ended up in jail and on trial."

"Suppose not," said Daniel. "But I'd rather have me on trial than you shot dead by them sorry Clack boys."

Sol stared past him to the window. "It's all my fault," he said. "The misfortune that has come to you."

"What about yourself? You're a lot worse off than me. Least I can still walk, do a job when I can manage to latch on to one."

Sol weighed the matter, then said, "I feel right blessed, if you want to know the truth of it."

Daniel raised his eyebrows. "You a more positive man than me, I suppose. I don't reckon I see much blessin' in what's happened to either of us. No good luck in sight."

Sol rolled over to an elbow to face Daniel. "I don't see luck as having any part of a Jesus man's days," he said. "It's all in the hands of the good Lord."

Daniel chewed on his pipe a moment, then replied, "I reckon I don't feel up to no religious talk. Am in some confusion about all that right now."

Sol smiled. "You afraid I might stumble on to something to call you back closer to the Lord?"

"You sayin' I ain't so close as I need to be? I still go to Jesus Holiness from time to time."

"Don't take no offense. You said yourself you had some confusion right now."

"That's true." Daniel relaxed again. "It's just that I don't take to that talk about it all being in the Lord's hands. Seems to me that if that's so, then the Lord's hands must have some hard calluses on them, that they've been busy doing some mighty harsh deeds."

"How you figure?"

Daniel studied Sol. He seemed eager to flap his gums—eyes all shiny, propped on his elbow. Daniel thought about just brushing off the question. He clicked his pipe on his teeth. Sol eyed him straight on. Daniel wondered how long it was until supper. Then he figured since Sol seemed set on talking Jesus, he might as well get it over with. Maybe if he spoke now, Sol wouldn't bring it up anymore.

"Look at all the dyin' folks," Daniel said. "Especially those who pass on so young. With the old, you expect that, the way of nature and all. But why my mama? Why Laban? Why Walter, your brother you never got to know? Why Stephen? You see what I mean?" He waited for Sol to respond and when he didn't, Daniel started in again. "And why does it seem that a good man suffers as much if not more than a bad man?" His voice rose as he warmed to his argument. "Look at you and Ben Clack. You as fine a Christian as I ever saw, taking care of the law and your wife and kids. But you end up in a wheelchair. And Ben? He's a skunk, everybody knows it. But he's doing just fine as you please. What sense does that make?"

Sol stayed quiet. Daniel thought he had him on thc run.

"And what about me? I know I ain't so good as you but I do see myself as some kinder than Ben Clack. Yet I had to sit in jail while Clack was free as the breeze. How you explain that?"

"I don't reckon I do," Sol finally said. "Still, what options have you got other than to believe it's all in the Lord's hands, that Jesus has some purpose in all this that we can't see?"

Daniel got up and walked to the window. He didn't like to say what he'd recently started to think. But it was there, right in front of his head. Might as well speak it out plain.

"Maybe there ain't no God," he said. "Some folks say that. Jesus was just a good man, a fine talker who loved everybody and everything. But that was all, a man and nothing more." He looked at Sol again, his chin set.

Sol turned over, grabbed one leg with his hands and pulled it over to the side of the bed. The leg dropped, the bare foot hovering above the floor. Some seconds later he swung the second foot beside the first. Sitting up now, he answered Daniel, "If there ain't no God, then how do you figure everything got here? The stars, the mountains and the trees that grow on them, the butterflies and the waterfalls, the fresh corn, and all the livin' creatures including us—where did all that come from? You think it all just appeared out of nowhere?"

"I ain't no preacher," said Daniel. "Don't claim to know the answers to those riddles."

"But it all had to come from somewhere."

Daniel refilled his pipe, then looked hard at Sol. "Some say we come from them monkeys."

"Well, you look a mite like one sometimes when you ain't trimmed your beard and it's a touch dark out," Sol said, grinning. "But where did the monkeys come from?"

"I admit to an ignorance on that point."

"What I'm sayin' is, somewhere back a long time ago, long before the mountains pushed up, long before the monkeys or anything else lived on this old earth, something, somebody, *God* in my way of thinkin', put together the makings of everything that is. It didn't just appear from thin air. Had to come from somewhere and God is the only answer to it all."

"But you still ain't answered my puzzlement over all the suffering except to say you can't figure it and so you'll leave it to the Lord."

Sol nodded. "I reckon that's the best I can do."

"You come out where Luke did then."

The two men fell quiet again. Daniel felt worn out from so much talking. Sol lay back and stared at the ceiling.

A few moments later the nurse that had led them through the hospital brought in two tin trays loaded with food. They ate in silence, the sounds of their forks and knives the only thing interrupting the stillness.

When they'd finished eating, the nurse took their trays away and

Daniel went outside to take in the fresh air. The rain had completely stopped. Leaning against the front of the hospital, Daniel lit his pipe. After a while, he went back up to the room, told Sol he would see him in the morning, and then returned to the truck to get some sleep.

The doctors operated on Sol in the afternoon of the next day. Jewel and Elsa arrived with Preacher Tuttle about an hour before the surgery. Their faces anxious and their voices soft, everybody met in Sol's room right before the nurses came to take him away. Preacher Tuttle said the time had come for them to bow their heads and pray together. All eyes turned to Daniel, and he knew what they expected. It was time to pray, and even though the preacher was there, they looked to the eldest man of the family to say the prayer. Daniel studied his shoes, not wanting to act the hypocrite and pray to a God he didn't exactly believe in anymore. But he couldn't say that out loud. Unsure what to do, Daniel glanced at Sol. Sol immediately seemed to understand the problem.

"Go on and start the prayin', Preacher," Sol said. "I expect they'll be comin' to cut on me pretty soon."

Tuttle caught Daniel's eye for just a second but then dropped to a knee and bowed his head. Everybody followed suit. Daniel took off his hat. His hip hurt as he knelt.

"Almighty God," Tuttle began, "we are your servants and we want your will to be done. . . ."

As he prayed, Daniel hoped God's will wasn't for Sol to stay crippled the rest of his life. If so, he didn't see much value in this kind of praying.

Tuttle prayed on for a spell but then eased off and Jewel took up the interceding, followed by Elsa. Before Elsa had finished, the large nurse pushed through the door and announced it was time to take Sol to the operating room. Elsa said a quick amen, and everybody stood and said their good-byes to Sol. The nurses then rolled him away on a gurncy. Tuttle and the women went to a nearby waiting room. Daniel stayed with them for a while, but then, feeling cramped, left them and headed for the open air.

Out in the parking lot he unlatched the back gate of his truck, pushed it down, and took a seat. After two days of steady rain, the sky had cleared to blue and now the sun boiled down on him. Daniel lay back in the truck and stared at the sky. He hated hospitals.

The desire for a drink suddenly came strong on him, and he wondered where he might find a place to buy a bottle. A robin landed in a pine tree to his right. Daniel watched the bird. He hadn't done much drinking since the trial in Lolleyville; the couple of times he had yielded to the temptation, he and Deidre had shared some sharp words. She didn't like it that he had broken his word to give up liquor and, for the first time, had lost patience with his lapses. He understood her complaints, even agreed with them. But sometimes a man felt out of control of certain things. Anxious to explain his failings, Daniel had given her his reasons—what she saw as excuses.

"The drink helps me sleep," he had told her. "You know sleep's been harder and harder for me. It stops my headaches too."

Deidre softened some when he said that. She saw firsthand that his nightmares visited him two or three times a week now, sometimes so bad they woke him up. Once awake, he hardly ever fell asleep again. And he almost always had a headache the morning after a nightmare, a grinding pain behind his eyes that felt like somebody had slugged him with a hammer. When she softened, Daniel usually eased up too. He knew she was right; he shouldn't drink whiskey anymore.

The robin chirped and dropped down a branch. It stared at him and Daniel wondered where the bird had its nest. He thought about what Sol had said. Who or what had made this red-breasted bird? Did it just show up one day? Or was God truly behind it all, the Creator of such things as robins and chickens and dogwood trees . . . and babies?

If not, then nothing made much sense. If no God existed, then no matter what a man did, it didn't matter. But if there was a God . . . then why did some of those babies God made sometimes die?

Daniel rubbed his eyes. A dull throb had started in his head. He felt weary from so much thinking but couldn't stop himself from considering something so important. Was there any option to the choices between the notion of "no God" and the notion of everything, even the bad things, being God's will?

The robin flew to the soggy ground, pecked around for a few seconds and pulled a small worm from the grass.

Was that God's will? wondered Daniel. That this robin would show up at this spot and eat that worm at this particular second?

Another notion popped into his head. What if God gave the robin some freedom? What if He created the bird to be free to make its own choices? The robin could find and eat that worm or it could hop on over to another spot and find and eat a different worm. Or if the bird didn't do its job well, it might not find a worm at all and go hungry. If it didn't find a worm in several days, it might even die.

If so, then maybe God did the same with people. With the whole world. Maybe the good Lord had made the world but built some freedom into it, freedom that folks could use as they saw fit. If that was the case, some people could choose bad things too, evil things that brought hurt and pain to those around them.

Daniel jumped out of the truck thinking he might walk a bit as he mulled over the matter. If God made it so folks had choices, then all the suffering didn't fall directly at the Lord's feet as far as Him causing it. Human beings took on some of the blame if that was the situation.

Pulling his pipe and tobacco from his pocket, Daniel turned the idea over in his head. Of course, the freedom God handed out didn't explain all the suffering that happened to folks. But it sure added up to a lot of it. He'd have to think some more on this.

CHAPTER TWENTY-FOUR

The day of Sol's surgery dawned clear and cool in Blue Springs, and Abby climbed out of bed just before sunup to prepare breakfast for everyone. A half hour later they all sat down to eat—Jim and Steve, Daniel's Ed and Raymond and Sol and Jewel's Nathan, Katy Ruth and Horace. Before starting in, Abby had them all bow their heads and she thanked the Lord for the food and asked Him to take care of Sol during the operation.

Everybody ate quickly so the older ones could get on with their work while Abby and the younger ones did their morning lessons. Jim and Steve kissed her on the cheek as they left and she realized again in a way that startled her pretty often these days that her boys were fast becoming young men. Jim, approaching age fourteen, stood at least six inches taller than her and had a deep voice and the beginnings of a dark brown beard. Steve, almost twelve, had lighter hair and didn't look like he would end up as tall as his brother. But he had a quick mind and a gritty spirit that made him real determined. When he and Jim argued—as all brothers sometimes do—Steve hardly ever gave in.

Abby stood on the porch and watched them disappear around the street corner. She folded her arms and rubbed the sleeves of her long-sleeved tan dress. The wind whipped up a little, and a squirrel ran down the side of one of the oaks to her left. A touch of sadness crept over Abby. She wouldn't have her boys with her much longer.

She wondered what would happen to her when they left. Would she stay here with Elsa? Would the two of them grow old together? Abby saw nothing wrong with that. She knew people did that all the time—led quiet lives where the days passed with a routine as regular as the sun and moon rising and falling. Could she do that? Take care of her family, tend her garden, read what books she could put her hands on, serve the Lord at Jesus Holiness Church, teach the children now and again, and live out her remaining days in contentment in Elsa's house in Blue Springs? She didn't know.

On one hand, it felt fine to do that. She'd seen enough in her life already, had lived beyond the small town and received more education than most. And what had all that gotten her? A marriage that had been far less than what she'd hoped. Nothing guaranteed that if she moved away again, she would find any greater peace of mind than she already had.

Abby leaned over the porch rail. In some ways, the choice might not rest in her hands. What if Elsa ended up marrying Preacher Tuttle? Elsa told her that he had proposed to her on Christmas Day.

"I couldn't give him an answer just yet," Elsa had told Abby the next day. "Not until I know what will happen with Sol."

"He's willing to wait until then?" Abby asked her.

"He says he will wait forever if that's what it takes. I promised him I would give him an answer soon after Sol's surgery."

"Don't wait too long," Abby teased. "Preacher Tuttle could pick just about any available woman on the mountain, young or old."

"He tells me I'm the prettiest woman in North Carolina," Elsa said. "Says if I don't marry him, he'll live the rest of his life a lonely single man."

Abby felt certain Elsa would eventually say yes to Tuttle. Why not?

The preacher knew how to make a woman feel special, and he obviously cared deeply for Elsa. Ten years had passed since Solomon's death, and Elsa was too fine a woman to stay alone the rest of her life. Plus, Elsa had come to love the preacher very much.

But where would Elsa and Tuttle live if they wed? Jesus Holiness owned the small parsonage where Tuttle lived now. Wouldn't they want to move to Elsa's much finer place after the wedding? Would the church members care if they did?

Abby watched the squirrel scamper back up the tree. Another squirrel appeared and the second one chased the first one back to the ground.

Church folks could sure act strange sometimes. Maybe they'd want their preacher to stay in the house the church owned. If so, Abby and her boys wouldn't have to move. But she couldn't do that, even if Elsa did move out. What right did she have to stay in a house not her own? Elsa would probably want to sell the place and use the money for other things.

Abby knew Elsa had spent most of the money her pa left her on Sol's operation, so dollars from the sale of the house would come in mighty handy. But where would that leave her and the boys? And after the boys moved away, where would she live?

The squirrels continued their play around the yard. Abby tried to push away the next thought that rushed into her head.

Thaddeus.

Abby shook her head as if she could cast out the name that way. But it stayed there. *Thaddeus.*

She stepped off the porch and headed toward the shed out back. Time to get started with the garden. Reaching the shed, she pushed open the creaky door and peered inside, pausing to allow her eyes to adjust to the darkness.

Thaddeus.

She pulled a hoe from the shed's corner and carried it outside.

Thaddeus.

Abby stopped and leaned back against the shed, her face tilted upward. The sun warmed her, the morning breeze played with her hair.

Thaddeus.

She couldn't ignore the thought any longer. Stephen had been dead for two years. Although she felt guilty because of it, she'd been thinking about Thaddeus almost since the week of Stephen's funeral. In the beginning she had passed the idea off as nothing more than the need to see an old friend during a grievous time. She and Thaddeus had grown up together. It was only natural to want to see him while she was facing a hard time. No reason for any guilt.

Abby closed her eyes. Her shoulders felt the rough wood of the shed through her dress.

The desire to see Thaddeus hadn't weakened as time passed. Not after she buried Stephen, not during Daniel's trial, not after she returned to Blue Springs and started to rebuild her life. If anything, she thought of him more than ever. Why shouldn't she? She was a widow now. But not so old that folks would think poorly of her if she married again. A highland woman didn't stay single, not if she could help it.

Opening her eyes again, she told herself to stop pondering such silly notions. Thaddeus had disappeared, and gardens do not tend themselves. She gripped the hoe and moved to the garden.

Abby thought of Sol, figured the doctors were now working on him. She prayed once more for him, then started her hoeing, determined to put thoughts of another husband out of her head. Anyway, if not for her affection for Thaddeus, she wouldn't even consider the idea. Nobody in Blue Springs appealed to her. And it wasn't that few of the available ones had any education. Her own pa never had any schooling either but he was one of the best men who ever lived. Daniel was the same way, Sol too.

No, it was more because the men in Blue Springs didn't care much for talking, much less to a woman. They just didn't say much, weren't apt to sit by a fire and hold a conversation that didn't center on the weather or the crops or the health of the animals in their barns. Silence seemed their best companion most of the time.

That trait left Abby cold. She wanted a man who could read a book and tell her what he thought about it, one who could listen to a politician give a fancy speech on the radio and make some argument about its merits or lack of such, who could look at the sky and talk about God, how he could see the fine order in all creation.

A man didn't necessarily have to have much education to do all this, but he did have to know his own mind on such things, and Abby knew of no eligible man in the county who qualified in this way. It wasn't that highland men lacked the smarts. Only that they hadn't had much opportunity to let their thoughts go in those directions. When a man has to store up food for the winter, dig a trench from the spring to the back door for water, and constantly tend to the animals when they've taken sick, he doesn't have time nor the tendency to think about much else.

Abby pressed the hoe to the ground, hoping to make some progress in the garden to get it ready for seeding. But her heart wasn't in her work.

Thaddeus.

But she shouldn't be thinking of him! He had moved away, was probably married by now. No reason to think otherwise. Even if he wasn't married, she had no right to go looking for him after all these years, upset the life he had made for himself.

And what about Stephen? Could she stop mourning him now? Was two years enough time that she could say she'd properly grieved him? Would Jim and Steve understand if she visited with Lindy and asked about her brother? Of course, she didn't have to tell the boys at first. If she found out from Lindy that Thaddeus was already married, her sons would never need to know that she had inquired about him.

But what if he wasn't married and Lindy contacted Thaddeus for her? Or what if she gave Abby his address and she wrote him a letter? What if he wrote her back and said he wanted to see her and showed up someday on her doorstep? What if they fell in love again? What would the boys say to all that? Would they accept another man in their lives?

Abby jabbed the hoe at the ground. Surely Thaddeus had married. Probably had kids too. Even if it turned out he was still a single man, why would he want to see her now? She had treated him so poorly, had gone off and married Stephen without even talking to him beforehand to give him the chance to prove his love, to see if she might still love him. But what made her think she could have a good marriage with Thaddeus? She'd failed with Stephen, and she couldn't blame all of it on him. Why would marriage to Thaddeus end up any different? A woman who failed once could fail again.

Abby threw down the hoe and sat on the moist ground. She covered her face with her hands. Her head hurt. She couldn't stop thinking about Thaddeus. She had to do something. One way or the other, she had to find out: Was Thaddeus married? What would he do if she contacted him?

She lifted a handful of the black dirt to her nose. It smelled so pure and simple. Why couldn't her life be that way? She rubbed the dirt between her fingers. Maybe she made life all tangled up by thinking too much. Maybe she just needed to do the simplest thing, the most obvious thing, the thing that would give her the answer she needed. Once she knew, one way or the other, she could move on with her life.

Abby brushed the soil from her fingers and stood. After returning the hoe to the shed, she washed up and changed clothes. Then she stepped out of her house and headed toward Main Street.

It took most of the day for the surgeons to finish their cutting and mending on Sol. Daniel waited as much as he could with Jewel and Elsa in the square room with the hard-backed chairs where they put families while the doctors did their duties. But the room had no windows and the air smelled stale, so he had to get up and leave the place every hour or so. As the sun passed over, Daniel skipped supper and moved out and back between the waiting area and the front of the hospital. He kept his pipe lit, the pull of the tobacco giving him about the only calm he could find throughout the day.

While the surgeons worked on Sol, Daniel kept a close watch on Jewel to see if he could do anything to help her. She stayed quiet most of the time, her head down, her movements slight and timid. Daniel had never seen her look so scared. A woman took days like this harder than men, he figured, harder maybe because they had a softer side to them, a side that poured out the tears as easy as if pouring milk into a tin cup. Not knowing what to say, Daniel made up for it by bringing her coffee. She thanked him with a smile, then dropped her eyes to her lap again.

Elsa hardly ever left Jewel's side. Daniel once more found himself admiring the woman his pa had married after his first wife passed. One thing he had to give old Solomon—he had an eye for a good woman. Daniel grinned to himself. His pa also had a way of attracting those women. Something about his strength, his steady ways. Not that his pa hadn't been a good-looking man, almost everybody said he was. What Daniel remembered most about his pa, though, was that nothing seemed to shake him. Folks said the mountains could crack wide open and swallow up everything around Solomon, and he'd just keep sitting on the porch in his rocker, smoking his pipe, and figuring a way for him and his kin to stay above ground.

Elsa must have seen that trait in his pa, Daniel decided. Seen it and compared it to what she saw in the men of her family and liked what Solomon had to offer better. She and Solomon had made a solid marriage, one that had seen its share of tests but made it right through them.

Daniel left the waiting room again and headed down the stairs. He left the hospital and meandered over to a wood bench under a tall tree. As he pressed tobacco into the bowl of his pipe and struck a match, his thoughts turned to Deidre. He feared he hadn't done as well by her as his pa had done by Elsa. His occasional drinking bothered her, and their arguments had become more regular lately, sometimes even when he hadn't drunk any liquor. She seemed more and more impatient with him.

Daniel fingered the wood of the bench and sat down.

"You mind a little company?"

He looked up and, surprised, saw Elsa headed his way. He quickly slid over on the bench.

"Jewel nodded off," she said as if anticipating the question he hadn't yet asked. "I needed a breath of air."

"I know what you mean," Daniel said. "Have yourself a seat."

Elsa eased down by him and smoothed her long black skirt. Daniel studied her for a second. She had on a simple white blouse and black shoes with pointed toes, and her hair was pinned back behind her ears. She wore no jewelry or makeup. Although nigh onto sixty years old, she remained a handsome woman.

"Preacher Tuttle ever gone marry you?" Daniel asked.

Elsa smiled. "We'll leave that to the Lord."

"The Lord won't be walkin' down that aisle. That'll be you and the preacher, if he ever works up the nerve."

"You and Deidre doing all right?" Elsa asked, patting him on the knee.

Daniel puffed from his pipe. "Depends on what you mean by all right. I got enough work to scare up a little money now and again. That plus the garden and what I can fish out or shoot keeps my family fed. That what you meant?"

Elsa shook her head. "I know all that. I see how hard you labor."

A sudden urge to talk to somebody pushed through Daniel. Elsa had been his mama once. Took over the duties the year he turned nine. Why not talk to her? She wouldn't judge him, would she? He cupped his pipe, stared out into the clear sky. "How did you and Pa do it?" he asked. "Things didn't go easy for you all the time."

Elsa smiled. "We had our ups and downs, let me tell you," she said.

"You were a spitfire," he said.

She laughed. "Your pa used to tell me I could make sparks just by batting my eyelashes."

"I reckon he liked that about you."

"I reckon he did."

Daniel saw that his pipe had died out. He pulled another match from his shirt pocket, struck it and relit the pipe.

"We got burned out of the cabin," said Elsa. "By my own pa of all people."

He remembered the awful day; he was sixteen at the time.

"I lost my ma," Elsa continued. "The war took Laban. I suffered miscarriages. Your pa died of the cancer. No easy road, I can tell you that."

Daniel nodded. "How did you put those things behind you? How did Pa do it? All the disappointments—the loss of his land, the death of his son. How does a man move on from all that, not give in to . . . to . . . ?" His words trailed off.

Elsa reached for his hand and gripped it. "You may not want to hear this," she said, "but I got to tell you it's the truth."

He felt his throat tighten up. His eyes filled with tears but he brushed them clear. "You gone tell me that Pa's faith in Jesus saw him through, ain't you?"

"You knew your pa," she said smiling. "He left it all in the hands of the Lord. Each day Solomon drew breath he saw as a gift from above."

"That's a mighty simple answer."

"Sometimes the simple answer is the right one," Elsa replied.

Daniel studied on the matter for a few minutes. Then he pulled his hand away and stood. "But life's too complicatious for what you say," he argued. "As thorny as a briar patch is what it is."

"I know it seems so," said Elsa. "A lot of it, though, is because we make it that way. Folks, I mean."

"Can't argue that." Daniel picked up a piece of a branch that had fallen from the tree overhead and rolled it in his hands. The wood, about a foot long and two inches around at its widest, felt rugged and stout. "Pa sure liked to carve," he said.

"You don't use his cane anymore, do you?"

"I gave it to Abby right after Luke died. Didn't seem right, me carryin' it around like I believed what it stood for."

"Your pa gave it to you for a purpose. He told me that. Said one day you'd need that old cane, he didn't know exactly when or why."

"Sounds like a witchy woman makin' predictions of the future."

Elsa chuckled and said, "Your pa was wise in a lot of ways."

"You reckon he knows?" asked Daniel, running his finger over the wood.

"Knows what?"

Daniel gazed out past the hospital. "About the land, how I lost it when the bank went under. You think the dead can know things like that?"

Elsa rubbed her forehead. "I never thought much about it. But I reckon not. Seems to me that if heaven is a place where you're happy all the time, then we can't know anything that would make us sad."

Daniel returned to his place on the bench. "I . . . I don't think I could stand it if I thought he knew," he said.

They both remained quiet for a long while. Then Elsa said, "I hear they've started some logging on the old place."

"What?" Daniel's shoulders stiffened.

Elsa shrugged. "Just what I heard. That the company that bought the land a while ago has moved in to start cutting for lumber."

Daniel's fingers pressed around the stick and it suddenly broke in his hand. He gripped the broken pieces so hard his knuckles turned white. He stood and faced Elsa, his face flushed. He started to speak, but the door of the hospital opened then and a nurse stepped out. "The surgery is all finished," she called.

Daniel threw the broken stick to the ground.

The nurse waved them over. "The surgeon said he'd like to talk to everybody together," she said.

Daniel led Elsa back into the hospital, his mind torn between worry about Sol and fury at the men now cutting timber on the land that still belonged, at least in his mind, to his family.

It took Abby longer than she expected to find Lindy. When she arrived at Lindy's house, she found Jubal pulling some rotten boards from the white fence that surrounded their property. He wore denim pants rolled up at the bottom, a white T-shirt, and scuffed-up shoes. Seeing her approach, he stopped his work, wiped his hands on a cloth rag he yanked from his back pocket, and offered her a cup of water. In spite of her hurry to find Lindy and ask about Thaddeus, Abby took the water and made idle chatter with him while she finished it. Handing back the tin cup, she asked where she might find Lindy.

Jubal cleared his throat. The notion that Jubal might press her for details as to why she wanted to speak with his wife passed through Abby's head. After all, she and Lindy hadn't talked much in a long time. Abby decided she wouldn't tell him if he asked. What if he started a gossip about her? It might get back to her sons.

"Lindy headed to the store," he said after what seemed a long time. "Lots of goods to buy when you got four kids."

Abby smiled. Lindy and Jubal had two boys in their teens, two girls just past ten years old. "She'll go to the post office after that," Jubal added. "A couple other places too, not sure where. Errands and things, you know how that is."

She nodded. Jubal looked long and hard at her. She figured he wouldn't ask her anything. Highland men hardly ever spoke right out if they wanted to know something; they just stared at a person as though they could squeeze out the information with their eyes.

"Thank you for the water," Abby said.

"Anytime," said Jubal, pocketing the rag. "Come see us again."

"I will. And real soon."

"Lindy would like that. Me too."

Abby left him and headed straight to the general store. Steve saw her as she entered, and she asked about Lindy. He told her Lindy had already left.

"You know where she went?" she asked.

"Nope, she didn't say."

Abby nodded.

"You need anything?" her son asked.

"Some salt and flour maybe. Bring it when you come home."

"You mind if I stay awhile after work? Mr. Spencer said I could listen to his radio." Steve loved hearing the news beyond Blue Springs, about politics in Washington in particular, about Roosevelt's plans to help the country out of the hard times.

"You will run for office someday," she told him. "Stay as long as you like."

Steve grinned but made no comment. She hugged him, left the store and made her way to the post office. Again she found that Lindy had come and gone. And, again, she had to stay a few minutes to catch up with the postmaster—a short, thick fellow who informed her Roosevelt had a handle on things and that better times were just around the corner.

By the time she got away from the post office, the morning was all but gone. She stopped at Elsa's to grab something to eat and to check with the telephone operator, to see if there had been any calls from Raleigh. The operator said nobody had called and that she'd get word to Abby as soon as anybody did. Abby thought maybe she should stay put till she knew what had happened with Sol but then remembered the doctor had said the operation would take many hours. Her mind made up, Abby headed back to town. Almost two hours later she finally caught sight of Lindy coming down the front steps of Jesus Holiness. Abby shook her head at not thinking of it. Lindy was part of a women's quartet that practiced every Tuesday afternoon. Abby hurried to her.

"Lindy!" she called.

Lindy looked her way.

Abby crossed the street. "You got a minute?" she asked as she reached her side.

Lindy's eyes clouded, and Abby felt the chill between them. "We've not talked in a long time," she said.

Abby wasn't sure how to start. "I need to ask you something," she said, deciding to forge straight ahead. "Can we go back inside the church?"

Lindy tilted her head but then nodded. A minute later they took seats on the back pew of the church.

Abby kept her eyes focused on her lap for a moment, then took a deep breath and turned to Lindy. "Look," she said, "I know you've had hard feelings about me for some time now."

Lindy didn't respond.

Abby continued. "I don't blame you for those feelings. Years ago, I—"

"You never owed me anything," Lindy interrupted. "Nothing back then, or now."

"No, that's not true. I should have talked to your brother, given him some warning, told . . ." She couldn't say his name.

"Thaddeus," said Lindy. "You should have warned Thaddeus. It's his heart you broke."

Abby nodded. She deserved this. She locked her hands together. "I know," she said. "But I can't fix that now. All I can do is go from here. That's why I wanted to talk to you."

Lindy folded her arms. Abby breathed in and out, once, twice. "I want to talk to Thaddeus," she finally said. "I don't know how to reach him, so I was hoping you'd tell me where he is, how to contact him."

Lindy stared at the ceiling.

"I know I have no right," Abby said. "But I am at a point where I have to ask."

Lindy glared at her. "My brother loved you. More than I've ever seen a man love a woman."

"I'm sorry I hurt him."

"You married the wrong man," she said, her hands in her lap. "And now you want a second chance, is that it? After all this time, you want another chance with Thaddeus?"

Abby nodded, not daring to admit it out loud.

Lindy kicked the floor. Then she stood, her eyes toward the pulpit. "I won't do it," she said.

Abby froze.

"I won't tell you," repeated Lindy.

"What?"

"I said it clear. You hurt him once, I won't give you another chance."

Abby jumped to her feet. "Lindy, please, you have to tell me!" Her voice bounced around in the sanctuary. "I need to see him."

Lindy shook her head. "No, I love him too. He's settled with his life, doing something good for the Lord. You'll just mess that up; you'll confuse him, make him question his work."

"Shouldn't you let him decide this? Let him say whether he wants to see me or not?"

"Sometimes men don't think right when it comes to a woman," said Lindy. "Thaddeus has no will when it comes to you. Whatever you say, he'll do. I can't let that happen."

Abby paused to think. Pushing Lindy harder wouldn't work. Fact is, it would no doubt backfire. But she couldn't just walk away with no answers to her questions. She gently laid a hand on Lindy's forearm. Somehow she had to get Lindy to understand, to see that she wouldn't hurt Thaddeus ever again. "I promise, Lindy, I won't contact him if you don't want me to. But for old times' sake, will you tell me this—is he where I can reach him?"

Lindy stared at her and Abby thought she saw a softening in her expression. They'd been such good friends before. Surely Lindy couldn't forget all that.

"He comes and goes," Lindy finally said, "in and out of the country."

"Will you tell me where he is now?"

Lindy hesitated but then shook her head. "I can't do that."

"Can't or won't?"

"It's the same either way."

Abby decided to ask her one more question, the one she most wanted answered. "Well, then, can you at least tell me, is Thaddeus—?"

"Is he married? Is that what you want to know?"

"Yes."

Lindy turned away. Abby wondered if she was going to walk away without saying anything more. But then Lindy faced her again. "No," she said. "He never married. Told me once he wouldn't make the same mistake you did. Wouldn't marry somebody not meant for him."

Abby's shoulders sagged. Instead of feeling thrilled as she expected, her heart suddenly sank. In one way this was worse than if Lindy had told her he *was* married. Then she would have no chance. She would have to accept it and move on with her life. But now? Now she knew he hadn't married because of her. Because of her, he'd taken on a solitary life. But Lindy wouldn't tell her where he lived, so she might go to him and try to make up for all the hurt she'd caused him. Now, even though Thaddeus wasn't married, she still had no way to give their love another chance, to see if it was as real as Thaddeus had always thought. To miss a chance at happiness with him because he was married was one thing. To miss it because she couldn't find him was even more horrible.

"Won't you please tell me where he is?" Abby cried.

"I . . . I can't," said Lindy. "It would kill him if you hurt him again. Me too."

"Will you ask him if he wants to see me?"

"That's the same as taking you to meet him. He wouldn't be able to do his work if he knew you wanted to see him."

Abby realized she'd pushed as far as she could. Now she had only one thing left to say, something she had decided today during her search for Lindy. "I'd still like to see you and Jubal more often. Figure it's time for us to put old hurts behind us."

Lindy studied her closely. "That might take me a while. I need to know you're not just visiting me in hopes I'll lead you to Thaddeus."

"I'm not that kind of person. I hope you know that."

"We all change," said Lindy. "Sometimes for the better, sometimes not."

Abby nodded. "Give me time and I will prove it to you."

"I hope so."

For several seconds neither of them said anything. Abby thought again about Thaddeus. So was this it, their last opportunity gone forever?

What did that mean for her? Was Thaddeus the one man the Lord had willed for her and now he was slipping away once more?

"What do you plan to do with yourself, Abby?" Lindy asked.

"What do you mean?"

"You know, what's your future? You're the smartest woman I ever met. Pa used to say you had a brain too big for your head. You can't just waste that, it would be a sin."

"I don't really know," Abby said. "I do some teaching for folks every now and again when I get asked. But I never quite finished my studies in Boone."

"You could marry again."

"I don't plan on doing that. Not unless it's with Thaddeus."

Lindy shook her head. "There's other men," she said.

"Not for me."

"You never know."

"I know."

"You sayin' you plan to live here the rest of your days, digging in your garden, wasting the smarts God gave you?"

Abby hung her head. She'd been wondering the same thing over the last year. "You got any bright ideas?" she asked Lindy.

"Maybe."

Abby looked her in the eye and saw that Lindy wore a sly grin. In spite of Lindy refusing to tell her how to find Thaddeus, Abby felt herself warming to her old friend again. "What are you thinkin'?"

"That you ought to reopen the school," said Lindy. "Lots of kids around here need educating, mine included. The county has no money to pay a teacher, but I don't expect they'd mind if somebody started up school again and did the teaching without pay."

Abby chuckled. "The government won't let just anybody walk into the school and start teaching."

"All the people around here know you. They all know how smart you are. If you show up in the fall as the new teacher and start class, it will probably take a year before anybody beyond Blue Springs even notices."

Abby could see that Lindy had thought some about this. But it was crazy talk, nothing more. She had no business opening the school.

"You think about it," said Lindy.

"Only if you think about telling me where your brother's living."

Lindy shook her head. "I'm trying to help you do something with your life," she said. "Not ruin his."

Abby moved to Lindy. "I'm not sure I understand," she said. "You won't take me to Thaddeus but you give me advice to help me out."

"Truth is, my kids need you. All the kids up here need you. And—" she paused briefly—"I think you need them."

Stepping back, Abby said, "I don't know."

"Think about it," Lindy repeated. "And pray about it."

Abby walked away then, walked home to wait for a telephone call from Raleigh, walked away to start her life over, knowing she would probably never again see the one man she'd hoped might give her a second chance at love.

CHAPTER TWENTY-FIVE

Sol left the hospital about ten weeks later, though not on his own two legs. The nurse who had met him when he was first admitted in March wheeled him out into a beautiful morning on the next to last day of May and helped Daniel load him into the truck.

"You just keep striving," the nurse said after she had him in the passenger seat. "You'll make it, I know you will."

Sol smiled but without much conviction. "I'm thanking you for your nursing," he said. "It ain't your fault that I ain't—"

"These things take time," she said, cutting him off. "I know a man who didn't walk till a year past his operation. You got a ways to go before that."

Daniel started the truck and the nurse stepped back. "Come see me after you get on your legs," she said and waved.

"I would enjoy that," said Sol.

Daniel backed up, changed gears, and they pulled away. A few minutes later Daniel turned the truck onto the main highway leading out of Raleigh. Sol leaned back, his elbow on the edge of the open window. They had a long trip ahead of them and he had little strength. The sun warmed his head and shoulders. His legs tingled a little. He thought of all the sweat he'd poured out in the last few weeks in the effort to take a step. *Like a baby,* he thought, *trying to walk again.*

He stared out the window. The scenery moved by fast now. Daniel stayed quiet as the truck rumbled down the road. Sol left him alone. About two hours into the journey they pulled over alongside a grove of scrub trees, and Daniel pulled out two glass jars filled with coffee and two brown paper sacks. He handed a jar and a sack to Sol. A light breeze ran through the truck. Sol opened the sack and checked the sandwich. Bologna and onion.

"How's everybody at your place?" asked Sol before taking a big bite of sandwich.

Daniel drank from his coffee, swallowed hard and said, "Passable. Deidre's mama took sick about a month ago, her heart is poundin' some funny. Deidre is staying in Asheville from time to time to help out with her."

"Marla doing the cookin' for you and your boys?"

"Most of it."

"I thought you had fallen off your weight some."

Daniel smiled and bit into his sandwich. A fly buzzed around in the truck. "You got any feeling in your legs yet?" he asked Sol.

"Some tinglin' is all, after I work them hard. Doc says that's a good sign."

Annoyed by the fly, Daniel pushed open his door. "What you think about your ma and Preacher Tuttle?"

"I think it's about time he asked her."

"I hear the wedding's set for June. Wonder if a man can be the groom and lead his own vows at the same time?"

"I expect Tuttle will try."

"They plan to live at Elsa's place?"

"I reckon so."

"What will happen to Abby and her boys?"

After a gulp of coffee, Sol said, "Ain't heard nobody say. Mama won't ask them to leave, that's for sure."

"But knowin' Abby, she ain't planning on staying there once Elsa marries."

"Probably true," said Sol. "Jewel told me she heard that Abby might try to open the school back up, do the teaching."

"I heard that too. She needs to do something. Too sharp to just sit in the house or work her garden the rest of her days."

"My kids sure need the schoolin'," added Sol.

"Raymond too," said Daniel.

"Jewel says Marla is about to marry."

"About a month after your mama and Tuttle."

"You like the boy okay?"

"He's passable. Comes from good stock over near Oak Grove. He got on at a cotton mill down in Greenville. He should make a decent living from it."

"Inside work?"

"I think with working in a mill, it's all inside."

"Don't reckon I could do that."

"Shoot me if I ever even study on it."

The fly landed on the steering wheel. Daniel shooed it away.

"You reckon Abby will marry again?" asked Sol.

"Hard to say. Not many men in Blue Springs up to her standards."

"Wonder what become of Thaddeus Holston?" Sol took another bite of his sandwich.

"Jubal told me Thaddeus left the country a while back. Doing some kind of mission work for a while. They last saw him down in Asheville a year ago. If you ask me, Abby should've married him a long time ago."

"Maybe it ain't too late."

"He's got to be married by now. Even if he ain't, it'd be pretty hard to find him."

Sol wiped his hands on his britches. "Maybe I can ask around," he said. "See what I can find out. Nothing much else to do until my legs get better."

"You gone to matchmaking?"

"Maybe. Abby helped raise me. I want her to be happy, that's all."

"I reckon we all do."

Daniel screwed the lid on his coffee jar and closed the truck door. Then for a couple of seconds he sat there not moving a muscle. Sol could see he had something he wanted to say. Daniel cleared his throat. "I ain't been able to help your missus much," he said. "Work has been hard to find and I don't have many dollars."

Sol shook his head in disbelief. "You beat all, Daniel Porter. You go with me to the Lolleyville jail 'cause I needed you, and you end up in jail yourself, lose your job because of it, then tell me now that you're sorry you can't help my wife. You take on too much, Daniel, way too much."

Daniel looked out the windshield. "I just want . . ."

"What do you want? You figured that out yet?"

Rubbing his hands on his overalls, Daniel said, "I reckon I want too much. I want my family's land back, want you to walk again, want Abby to find some happiness. Want my kids to grow up strong, turn out all right. I want to stop my drinkin', want things . . . to go back to the way they used to be, back when I was a boy, before Laban . . ."

"You want the Garden of Eden," Sol said. "The good Lord never promised us that."

"I don't want to talk anymore about the Lord," said Daniel. "We already done that."

"I reckon we have."

Daniel started the truck but didn't put it into gear. Sol put the food sack on the floorboard and rested his elbow on the edge of the window.

Daniel took a deep, shaky breath. Sol put his hand on Daniel's shoulder. "I know you're tryin' to be the pa," said Sol. "Tryin' to take care of all of us. But that's just too much for one man to do."

Daniel closed his eyes.

"You hearin' me?" Sol said. "This life is too heavy a thing for one man to handle all by himself, even you. Let us help you. Don't take everything on your own shoulders, no matter how strong you think they are."

Daniel nodded but didn't speak.

Sol wanted to say more, to make Daniel see he was running from Jesus, that part of his miseries had come because of just this fact. But he didn't want to push too hard.

"You done?" asked Daniel.

Sol sighed. "I am for now."

Daniel nodded, then steered the truck back onto the road. Not sure what else to say, Sol shut his eyes and said a prayer for his brother. Only the Lord could help Daniel now. Only the Lord.

CHAPTER TWENTY-SIX

In the middle of September 1939, Abby Waterbury took her spot in front of a class of twenty-one boys and girls between the ages of seven and sixteen, including her own boys, Sol's Nathan and Katy Ruth, and Daniel's Raymond. Also present were Lindy and Jubal's two youngest, the Cooledge kids, and a variety of others from out and about the town. Most hadn't attended school in over a year, and a couple of them had never seen the inside of a schoolhouse till this day.

Dressed in a plain gray skirt and blue blouse, her hair pinned back, Abby felt self-conscious and wondered if the kids could see the fear on her face. It wasn't that she feared the authorities finding out about what she was doing and making her stop. Most government people had more important matters than her to worry about. No, what scared her was the notion that she might fail as a teacher. What if none of the kids liked her? What if she found she didn't know how to lead a class? What if much of what she'd learned at the Appalachian Training School now deserted her?

She wiped her hands on her skirt and then clapped them together. "Okay, boys and girls," she said in the strongest voice she could muster. "Time for us to start. Raymond Porter?"

"Yes, ma'am."

"Would you stand and lead us in the Pledge of Allegiance?"

Raymond stood and put his hand over his heart. The other kids did the same, everybody facing the United States flag that hung from a pole in the corner to Abby's left. "I pledge allegiance . . ."

The school day had officially begun. Abby recited the familiar words with her hand over her heart and hoped the kids couldn't see her trembling. It had taken a long time to reach this place but now she was here; she was a teacher. Maybe it would only last a few months, maybe a year—however long it took for the state authorities to discover what she was doing and take action—yet until then, she'd give her life to the task of instructing highland children.

Following the Pledge of Allegiance, Abby turned to her Steve. "Steve, will you now lead us in prayer?"

Everybody closed their eyes. Steve licked his lips and prayed, "Lord Jesus, we thank you that we got us a school again. We thank you that folks in town pitched in to give us wood for the stove, that Mr. Cooledge bought us some chalk and erasers and books, and that the post office handed us a flag. Bless this day and please help us all with our learning. Thank you, amen."

Abby's heart pounded with pride. True, there had been more than a few setbacks for her family over the last few months. Sol still had to use a wheelchair. Deidre's mama in Asheville had turned sicker, which meant Deidre was hardly ever home now. Daniel hadn't yet found steady work, and Judge Wilson still refused to drop the charges against him and close the case. Jim had insisted on keeping his logging job so he could give her the money he made, and he couldn't work and come to school too. And she'd lost all hope of ever finding Thaddeus.

At the same time, some good had happened too.

Elsa had married Preacher Tuttle and the two of them seemed mighty happy. Marla and Billy had hitched up in marriage and moved to Greenville where he had work. Lindy and Jubal were Abby's friends again. Daniel seemed to have shut off most of his drinking. When he did partake of the bottle, he kept to himself. The county paid Sol enough to provide for him and his family. Abby, Jim and Steve had left Elsa's place and taken a couple of rooms in Mr. and Mrs. Cooledge's house in exchange for Abby's reopening the school.

Besides giving her the idea to teach, Lindy had also pitched in to help

Abby with the preparations. The whole town had caught on to the notion, and folks from all over volunteered to do some labor. The men painted, fixed the stove, and replaced the rotted front steps, while the women scrubbed away the spider webs, mopped the wood floors until they shined, and hung blue curtains over the windows. Although they had very little writing paper for the kids and no money to repair the two broken windowpanes on the back wall, the schoolhouse looked presentable.

Following Steve's amen, Abby walked to the blackboard and wrote *Anybody can learn* in large letters across the top. She turned back to the class. "Everyone, repeat this after me," she said, pointing to the words with her piece of chalk. "Anybody can learn."

The class recited the phrase. As Abby started to teach, pleasure ran through her bones, a sense of rightness about what she was doing. The classroom felt as comfortable as a good pair of shoes. *I was born for this,* she thought.

An inner peace settled on her. If God wanted her to stay in Blue Springs and teach for the rest of her days, that would be fine by her.

Abby almost lost her voice as she accepted that truth. She would stay right here, she realized. She would live in Blue Springs and finish raising her boys and teach the children. Although she would never again live beyond the highlands, she would help others get enough education so they'd have a choice as to whether they wanted to stay here or go somewhere else. She had crossed a river in her head and it felt good on the other side.

She paused in her speaking, stepped over to a book lying open on her desk. She closed the book and held it up for all the students to see. "Everyone listen. The person who can read can go anywhere," Abby said. "Anywhere in the whole world."

Outside, the sun rose higher. The children in Abby's class followed along as their teacher read out loud the first page of their textbooks. Her voice quivered. Words had such power; she'd always known that. Had known it since her aunt Francis first started reading the Bible to her when she was a young girl. Abby had always loved words, the sound of them rolling around in her head as she took them off a page and gave them life in her mind. Now she would teach others to read words. What better work could she do?

The first week of her teaching soon became the first month, the first month soon became December, and Abby shut down the school for the holidays. The weather turned real bad in January, leaving most of the kids unable to get to school, so Abby decided to keep the school closed until the first of February, when the weather finally improved some.

On the Saturday morning of the second week of that month, the first weekend after Abby had started teaching school again, she found herself sitting at Elsa's kitchen table with a cup of coffee in front of her. Elsa had just finished telling how her husband, Preacher Robert Tuttle, had got his Chevy stuck in the mud up past Edgar's Knob while visiting a man who swore he'd shoot the next preacher who came up trying to convert him to Jesus. The man had taken a shotgun and peppered Tuttle's Chevy with buckshot as Tuttle worked on getting the thing unstuck.

"If that man's wife hadn't wrestled his gun from him, Robert might have holes in his backside right now," said Elsa. "I never knew being a preacher could be so dangerous."

Abby laughed. Elsa sure did brighten her life. She and Tuttle seemed as happy as young newlyweds.

Envy cut through Abby but she pushed it away. Not decent on her part to covet Elsa's happiness. The woman deserved every bit of it. As kind as she had been, Abby could never resent her enjoyment over a new husband.

Abby sipped her coffee and heard a knock at the front door. "You expecting company?" she asked Elsa.

"Reckon not," she said.

"Maybe somebody from the church."

Both women got up to answer the door. To Abby's surprise, Jewel stood on the porch, her threadbare black coat hunched around her shoulders.

"Come on in," said Elsa.

Jewel shook her head. "It's Sol."

"Sol okay?" Abby asked, knowing not to trust unexpected visitors.

"He made me promise not to say anything," said Jewel. "He wants you both to come over."

"I'll get our coats," said Elsa.

Abby hoped that Jewel had brought them good news. But she had learned not to expect it.

It wasn't long before they reached Sol's place, a white-board house built against the bottom side of a hill that seemed to run straight up to the sky. The county truck was parked out front. Scraggly brown weeds had filled in around the steps of the front porch. Seeing them, Abby slumped a little. When Sol had been able to walk, a weed wouldn't have dared show its head so close to his house.

The three women entered the house silently. Jewel hadn't said more than ten words during the fifteen-minute walk from Elsa's. Abby's heart beat heavier and a sense of dread swept over her. Had Sol taken a turn for the worse?

They found him sitting in his wheelchair by the fireplace in the front room, with a blanket draped over his legs. He wore a brown flannel shirt, which was tucked into a pair of overalls. His hair lay flat, slicked back with hair tonic. A bruised lump about the size of a small egg cropped out of his right cheekbone. Abby inhaled sharply. What happened? Had he fallen? Or had somebody hit him? She started to question Sol but then stopped. Obviously he wanted to tell her and Elsa something. No doubt that would explain the injury.

She tried to read his eyes, but they revealed nothing. Both Elsa and Abby hugged Sol around the shoulders.

"Have a seat, Ma," offered Sol. Elsa eased into a rocker near her son. Abby sat on the edge of the sofa as Jewel disappeared into the kitchen.

"The school doing okay?" Sol asked Abby.

"Real fine. The children seem to like it. Better than working all day, they figure."

"I hear you're a good teacher," Sol said. "Doesn't surprise me."

"She's the best," said Elsa. "I go by sometimes, sit in to listen during reading time."

"Nobody bothered you any?"

"Not at all. Seems all the government people are too busy with other things to worry much about what's going on in a tiny school in Blue Springs."

Jewel reappeared with a trayful of cups filled with coffee and served everyone.

Abby's stomach stayed tight. What was all this about? Did Sol and Jewel plan to keep them in suspense forever? "Where are the kids?" she asked.

"Out playing somewheres," Jewel replied.

Sol sipped his coffee. "I have some news to share," he said calmly. "Fact is, I have a lot of news."

Abby rested her cup on her lap. Elsa moved to the edge of the rocker.

"Shut your eyes," said Jewel.

"They don't need to do that," said Sol.

"Yeah, they do. Go on now, close 'em up tight."

Abby looked at Elsa. Elsa shrugged and did as she was told. Abby did too. Several seconds ticked by, and Abby heard movement like the rustle of clothing. The heat from the fire warmed her face.

"You can look now," said Jewel.

Abby opened her eyes. Her mouth fell open. She glanced at Elsa and saw tears rolling down Elsa's cheeks. Sol's blanket lay on the floor.

"You're standing!" Elsa cried as she jumped up and wrapped her arms around him.

Jewel beamed. "That's not even the best part," she said. "Sol, go on and show your ma."

Sol held up his hand. "I need some space for this."

Elsa backed up a couple of steps.

"No, Ma, go over there." He pointed to the other side of the room. Elsa scurried over and faced Sol.

Sol placed both hands around his right thigh and moved the leg. The foot slid over the floor about eight inches. Abby went to Elsa, put an arm around her waist. Sol repeated the motion with his left leg. He did it again with the right, then the left once more.

Weeping now, Elsa shook in Abby's arms. Sol took another step, another and another. A few more and he reached his ma. Elsa released Abby and threw open her arms to receive her son. They were soon joined by Jewel and Abby, and the four of them held one another for what seemed a long while. It occurred to Abby in that moment that hurting and rejoicing felt a lot alike, both of them creating a flood of crying and an ache in the heart. The difference was that the ache caused by hurting seemed all empty somehow, whereas the ache from rejoicing felt full and overflowing, so much so she wanted to hold on to the feeling forever.

Abby heard the back door slam, and then Nathan ran into the front room. He had a bleeding scrape on his elbow. Jewel left their embrace to see to him.

"I fell playin' tag," Nathan explained. "It ain't too bad but I best clean it out."

Jewel led Nathan from the room. Sol nodded to his wheelchair. "Mind rolling that over to me?" he asked Elsa. "I'm some tired now."

Elsa maneuvered the chair to him.

"I'm not so good at getting back into it as I am leavin'," said Sol.

Elsa helped him sit down. Then she picked up the blanket and laid it over his legs and wheeled him back near the fireplace.

"When did this happen?" Elsa asked, returning to her spot in the rocker.

"Last night," said Sol. "You know how hard I been trying. Every day working my legs, pushin' myself up, building up my arms."

Jewel returned and pulled up a straight-backed chair by Abby, who was sitting on the sofa again.

Sol continued. "Last night I tried pushing up from my chair, was able to stand for a couple of seconds. The first time I thought I'd pass out. I wobbled mostly. But after restin' for a while, I gave it another try and stood a mite longer, and was less wobbly. Third time I pulled the leg up, took a step, and fell flat on my face." He pointed to the bruise on his cheek.

"It's a miracle," said Jewel. "Plain and simple."

"I do give the Lord credit for this blessing," agreed Sol, "though I might could've asked for a little less sweat than it took."

"Either way you been handed a gift," Elsa told him. "Walking is walking, no matter the sweat."

"Reckon the Lord sometimes asks us to help Him make our miracles," Abby said.

"Suppose so," said Sol.

Quiet fell on the room. Sol lifted his coffee cup again, drank from it. His face had a curious look to it, and Abby got the feeling he was holding back from them. She remembered that he'd said he had *a lot* of news.

She asked straight out, "What else is on your mind, Sol? Seems something more is going on here."

Sol grinned and said, "Well, it's Daniel. I got news for him."

"Shouldn't he hear it first?"

"I'm not yet in shape enough to go to his house, and Jewel here has the kids to tend. I thought you might take the word to him."

"What word?" asked Elsa.

"It's all over—the charges have been dropped," said Sol. "Daniel is cleared over in Lolleyville."

Abby clapped her hands. "How?"

"Beat all you ever saw. Conroy, you remember, the lawman over there who was killed?"

"We met his wife and kids."

"Turns out he was a right careful man. Kept all these records about everybody that came in and out of his jailhouse."

"I remember you told about that once, how Conroy had a ledger he wrote in. You said maybe it could back up your word that Clack had visited with Stephen."

Sol nodded. "But Judge Wilson didn't believe me because no one could find Conroy's book."

"Right."

"Well, that ledger turned up."

"But where?"

"Conroy's wife had it the whole time. Had taken her husband's things home a couple of days after the killings. The ledger wasn't an official document or anything, just Conroy's noting of things."

"So how did this latest word come out?"

"Mrs. Conroy went through her husband's things. Hadn't had the heart up till now. You know how that is. But she finally started cleaning out his belongings and found the book with the other stuff from his office. She saw the records, knew what it meant."

"So she went to the judge?"

"About a week or so ago. Sure enough, the ledger told how Topper came to see Stephen before the shooting. Backed up Daniel's story about the Clacks knowing Stephen. Plus, Conroy had made a note that Topper and Stephen had shared some hard words. He heard them arguin' in the cell the time Topper visited."

"Daniel is clear!"

"Clear as a breeze. Folks over there called our jail, and they brought word to me. Wilson threw out the whole thing, lock, stock, and barrel."

"This is going to please Daniel real fine," said Abby.

"I expect so."

"Wilson going after Ben Clack now?" asked Elsa.

"Reckon not," Sol said. "Nobody can prove for certain that Ben did any killin'. And there ain't any record of him ever visiting Stephen."

"He goes free, then?" said Abby.

"Seems so."

Abby stared into the fire. Somebody needed to pay for Stephen's death, Conroy's too. Not to mention the hurt all this had caused Sol. But maybe justice didn't always come in this world. Some evil got to wait to meet Jesus face-to-face to receive its punishment. She took a breath and reminded herself of all the good she'd heard today. No point in dwelling on this one bad thing. "I look forward to carrying this news to Daniel," she said.

Sol smiled at her. "Wish I could see his face when he hears."

"We can maybe get him to come here," Abby suggested.

Sol thought a second. "No," he decided. "No reason for that. Go on and tell him soon as you can."

"I reckon I ought to go right away," said Abby. "He's not home much during the week. If I tell him today, he can have the weekend to enjoy the news with Deidre." She stood to leave.

"Hold on there just one more minute," said Jewel. "Sol has got another morsel to tell you."

Abby arched an eyebrow. What else could Sol have to say? She checked Jewel's face but saw nothing to hint at what it might be. She faced Sol, and he looked like a hound dog with a fresh rabbit in his mouth.

"Have a seat," said Sol, pointing to the sofa. "You'll want to be sitting down when you hear what I'm about to say next."

Abby obeyed. She got the distinct notion she was the only one not told this particular secret.

"I just heard this too," he said. "Yesterday, in fact. I been askin' around some, making a call now and again. When you can't walk, you got lots of time for talking. Anyway, here's what I found." He grinned, winked at Elsa, then wheeled over closer to Abby and whispered in her ear. Her eyes widened. What Sol told her was just about the best news she had ever heard in her life.

CHAPTER TWENTY-SEVEN

It took her the rest of the day but Abby took the message to Daniel as soon as she could. Preacher Tuttle drove her up the mountain, walked with her the last mile up the trail, and waited on the porch soaking in the sun while she went inside to talk to Daniel. He didn't react with as much thrill as she had expected.

"I thank you for comin' to tell me," he said as they sat together at his kitchen table. "But I don't reckon it matters a whole lot either way."

"But you're free of it!" she said, wanting to cheer him some. "No more chance of going back to jail."

He nodded yet didn't seem very moved. "They've started logging the land," he said, leaving the subject of the trial. "I go by there every now and again. Sit up on the mountain, watch them cutting down the trees."

Abby couldn't understand why he wasn't jumping for joy. And what land was he talking about? Then it dawned on her. Mr. Cooledge's crew had started cutting timber on the property her family had once owned. But that was old news; they hadn't owned that land for over thirty years.

"All that is past," she told him. "No reason to fret over it now."

Daniel stood up. He seemed so distant to Abby. She felt like she hardly knew him anymore. Although he had good reason to take his rifle and go shoot it in the air in celebration, Daniel seemed bent on finding the bad in everything. His wife loved him, together they'd raised up good kids, he had enough work to hold body and soul together, and he still had his health. Such things brought at least some joy for most folks. But not Daniel. Nobody she knew had been spared from the hard times. If a man drew breath at all, he was bound to meet up with some rough spots. Still, he couldn't let that ruin everything.

Maybe that's where she and her brother differed, Abby figured. How they faced the scrapes that life brought. Not that she thought herself any better than him. After all, she hadn't watched Laban and Stephen die. She hadn't made promises she couldn't keep, least not to anybody but herself. But he shouldn't just throw up his hands and give in; he had to try to see the good in things, the flower growing among the weeds, the one streak of sun in a day filled with clouds.

Daniel had a hard time doing that. So far—except for when things got so difficult with Stephen that she had to move back to Blue Springs—Abby had managed to keep her head up.

Maybe Daniel was right about one thing: She didn't tend to blame the rough spots on the Lord, didn't let them cause her to turn her back on what she'd always believed. Despite her not having a notion as to the *why* of it all, she kept her heart set on Jesus. Perhaps she had more of their pa in her that way than Daniel did.

Daniel turned and stared out the window. "You say Mrs. Conroy found that ledger?"

"When she was going through her husband's things."

"I guess she dropped the notion I shot her husband."

"I would expect so."

"And her kids?"

"I reckon them too."

Daniel rubbed his beard. "I am glad for that," he said.

"Now you can put this behind you, get on with your life."

Daniel took his seat again. He patted her hand and said, "Abby, they're loggin' the land." His tone said he couldn't move on while that continued, that the axes and saws that cut the trees cut into him too, cut him and made him bleed like sap running to the ground.

"I know," said Abby. She wanted to shout at him, tell him to let the past rest. Tell him that if he kept playing with all those ghosts that it would surely kill him, pull him down until he couldn't rise up anymore. But she didn't know how to say that and could tell from his face that he wouldn't hear it anyway. "I pray for you," she said.

He gave her a weak smile.

"You'll tell Deidre this news?" she asked.

"Soon as she comes back home from Asheville."

"She with her ma again?"

He nodded. "Her pa needs her help real bad these days."

"You're alone a lot, brother."

"A body does what he's got to," he said. "Her folks need her."

Abby hugged him and left, her heart low that his spirits hadn't been more lifted by the good news. Tuttle drove her back to Blue Springs.

Now, as the sun disappeared on the horizon, Abby stepped to the front door of a small white house and took a breath. She had one more message to deliver today, one more word of news. She wondered if telling it would make things better or worse. She knocked on the door. Some seconds later Lindy opened it. An apron hung loosely on Lindy's hips and she had flour on her chin. Abby said hello and asked if she might come in for a few minutes. Lindy led her into the parlor and they sat down.

"Have you been baking pies?" Abby asked. She smelled cooked apples.

"Always knew you had a good nose on you. Yeah, you know how Jubal loves pie."

Abby rubbed her hands together. She felt much more nervous than she thought she would. Lindy might not like what she'd come to say. Should she even say it? But if she didn't and then acted on what she knew, Lindy would eventually find out anyway. Better to come from her lips than someone else's. Better to speak it straight out and deal with the result woman to woman.

"I got news," Abby said. "From Sol."

"Hope he's been gettin' better."

"He's walking some now. We're all so pleased and thankful."

"That Sol is a strong man," Lindy said with a big smile. "I knew he wouldn't stop till he could get out of that chair."

"And the judge in Lolleyville has dropped the charges against Daniel. Conroy's widow came upon some evidence that ended up clearing him."

Lindy clapped her hands. "You're full of pleasant tidings today!"

"Well . . . there *is* one more thing, and a harder one for me to say."

Lindy perched on the edge of her seat.

Abby stared at her hands. "Lindy, I know where Thaddeus is."

Her friend rocked back.

"Before you say anything, please hear what happened, how I found out. Sol made some phone calls over the last few months. I didn't ask him to do it. He said it wasn't really that hard once he knew where to go looking. He said he remembered your brother's visit over a year ago when you and Jubal went to Asheville to see him. Sol figured that Thaddeus must have left on the Asheville train, so he called some folks down there who checked the train records for him. They found out that when Thaddeus left Asheville, he headed to San Antonio, Texas. From there he took another train to Laredo. Knowing what he did about Thaddeus and his wanting to teach poor children, Sol guessed he had hooked up with a school, maybe one in Mexico. Sol asked Preacher Tuttle to find out about any missions down there, places where churches worked with kids around the border."

"Sol has been a busy man," said Lindy.

"Guess that's true. It took him a while but with the preacher's help they came across a mission in Laredo. A number of groups work there. Thaddeus lives with them, teaches in their school."

Abby stopped to let Lindy respond. Silence. Abby smelled the pies, wondered if they might burn if Lindy didn't check them.

Lindy wiped her hands on her apron. She stood and walked over to the window. "You think you're smart, don't you?"

"I didn't ask Sol to do this," Abby reminded her.

"He must have known you wanted it, though, so you bear the blame. Or the credit, I guess you might say. Whether you knew what Sol was up to or not, you're to blame."

Abby waited to hear what else she'd say.

"What you plan to do about this?" Lindy asked.

Abby placed her hands in her lap, tried to stay calm. Since first learning of Thaddeus's whereabouts, she hadn't stopped thinking about the question Lindy now raised. How would she go about contacting Thaddeus? Write him a letter? But would he write her back if she did? She thought about calling him on the telephone but that seemed too distant, disconnected. Also, she couldn't say the things she wanted to say to him over the telephone. Would she dare go see him? Just show up, walk into the school and announce herself?

She had never traveled anywhere except Boone and Asheville. Her world was so limited. How could she even consider hopping on a train and taking it so far away? It was pure craziness.

"I don't rightly know what I'll do next," Abby admitted.

"But you do plan to do something."

"Why wouldn't I?"

"You ever think of him?"

"Of course I think of him, all the time."

"What I meant was, have you thought about what might be best for his life?"

Abby weighed the question. Wasn't it best for Thaddeus to know she wanted to see him? For the two of them to test their love, see if it was the lasting kind? "I don't understand," she said.

Lindy knelt in front of Abby and held her hands. "Thaddeus is happy," she said. "I get letters from him. He says God has blessed his work, that he's doing what he always wanted to do, helping children, serving Jesus. Don't you see, you showing back up in his life could ruin all that."

"I won't hurt him," said Abby. "I promise."

"I know you want to do what's right," said Lindy, her voice softening. "I believe that. But you best think this over real good. It's serious business to take a man away from his calling—one who's serving the Lord, I mean."

Abby's heart sank. She hadn't thought of these things. Was Lindy right? If she and Thaddeus ever married, would that mean he was deserting God's purpose for his life? But wasn't it the Lord's will that she find him, that they marry and share their lives together? How could she know for sure? Had it not been the Lord's will for her to marry Stephen? To have Jim and Steve? She took a heavy breath. "I'm confused," she confessed.

Lindy chuckled. "I can see why."

Abby searched her friend's eyes. "What will happen to us, you and me, if I contact Thaddeus?"

Lindy squeezed her hands. "I wish I knew," she said. "I want what's best for my brother, that's all. If you two wind up getting married and he's happy, then I'll be happy. But if you find him and something awful happens . . . well, I don't think we could ever be friends after that."

Abby closed her eyes. Could she take a chance on losing Lindy again? Maybe she didn't know God's will, didn't know it at all. Could it be that her desire to find Thaddeus was just some kind of immature attempt to recapture her youth, to go back to the days when she'd felt the most content? If that was all this was, then she would surely hurt Thaddeus again if she went to him. Where would that leave her? Her head full of questions with no clear answers, Abby tried to figure what she should do next, if anything, to bring peace to her confused soul.

After Abby left him, Daniel sat by the fireplace and tried to figure what he should do. It made no sense to him, the way Conroy's wife had come up with the ledger that freed him from the arm of the law. But what difference did it make? He was the same man he had been before he heard the news, the same man who couldn't sleep much at night, who took on a headache about halfway through every day, the same who craved the drink so bad it made his mouth hurt if he didn't sneak off and have a snort every week or so. Guilt still tore at him when he lay down at night, alone a lot these days since Deidre had taken to looking after her ma in Asheville. Anger still rose up like a snake about to bite when he thought of the loggers cutting on what used to be his pa's land. So what difference did it make that Judge Wilson had finally lifted all the charges off his shoulders?

Rising from his rocker, Daniel picked up his rifle and coat and headed out to the porch. A couple of his dogs raised up and stared at him but then settled back down again when he didn't offer a hand to lick. He thought of Raymond and Ed, how they'd be coming home in a couple of hours and needing something to eat. With Deidre gone and Marla now married, he usually fixed their supper. Most of the time they ate what Deidre had put up in jars or what he'd purchased at the general store. Today they'd have to scrounge around for themselves.

Daniel laid the rifle across his shoulders and left the porch. A cold rain began falling and soon started dripping off his hat. Mud squished under his boots. He slipped now and again as he made his way down the road and then up the trail that led toward his old place. The trail was barren, most of the foliage brown and soggy from winter. Not a thing bloomed. The sound of water dripping surrounded him, and the air smelled of wet leaves and drenched soil. It took him close to an hour and a half to reach the bald that looked down over where the old cabin had been back before Hal Clack and his boys burned it down.

He walked carefully to the far edge of the bald and peered down over the side. From there he had an open view of a logging camp several hundred feet below. With no leaves on the trees, the camp was clearly visible. Smoke curled out of a couple of rough-looking tents the loggers had set up. Today, though, nobody worked outside. Other than the smoke, nothing moved. Daniel breathed in and the smell of the smoke touched his nostrils, reminded him of the smoky smell the day the Clacks set fire to his pa's cabin long ago.

He sat down on the wet rock, his rifle resting on his lap. Was that the way it was with the past? Once it happened, it never let go of you? Daniel figured it true. The past hung on like blackberry brambles, least the hard parts did. They hooked into a man's flesh and dug at his skin until he bled and bled, until he thought he might bleed to death.

Daniel hung his head. The past had cut him up a lot. Abby said he ought to let it go. Truth was, he wanted to do just that, to heed her advice and drop all the things that had plagued him for so long. He wanted to leave behind his hatred of the Clacks, his guilt over losing Laban and Stephen, his sorrow over not getting the land back for his pa. But how? Seemed to him that he had no power to make that happen regardless of how hard he tried. His past had hooked into him like it had a mind of its own, as if it would never let go.

Water dripped into Daniel's eyes and he wiped them. What if he could never shed his past? What if he was doomed to live with it all his days? What kind of life was that? Not much of one, that was for sure. A life of sadness, with no hope, no nothing.

Daniel fingered the barrel of his rifle. A man emerged from one of the tents and walked toward the woods, to the privy there. Daniel's anger boiled. The man had no right to be there; no right to come in from the flatlands and haul away the trees that nature had taken a hundred years or more to grow. He leveled the rifle at the man as if to take a shot at him, then after a few seconds lowered the gun back to his knees. What good would it do to shoot the man? Another would just take his place, and Daniel would end up getting hanged or spending the rest of his life in a jail cell.

Daniel wiped his face. How could he think of shaming his family that way? Of taking the life of a man who was only trying to make a living? He'd fallen about as far as a man could fall.

He held his rifle up and examined it from barrel to stock. One good shot and he could end all his miseries. One quick pull of the trigger would rid himself of his headaches and sleepless nights, the nightmares that wouldn't leave him alone.

He studied the thought for a minute. What did the Good Book say of such a thing? He couldn't recall. But what did that matter? He no longer believed what the Book had to say. Or did he?

The rain fell heavier. Daniel sat and watched as the man returned to his tent. The rain drenched Daniel's hat, ran down along his coat collar and onto his neck, shoulders. But he barely noticed. He had other things on his mind, dark and heavy things that only a man who had just about come to the end of his reason ever dared to think.

CHAPTER TWENTY-EIGHT

Abby struggled for more than a year with what to do. She didn't have the money nor the time to travel to find Thaddeus, and Lindy's words about pulling him away from his calling made her have second thoughts about writing him a letter. Every time she took out paper to write him, she imagined what he might think when he received it. Would he drop everything and return to Blue Springs? If he did, was that the right thing? What about the children he taught? How many lives would she upset if she caused Thaddeus to return home? Was her happiness worth all that? Unable to decide what to do, Abby did nothing. She felt paralyzed.

As much as she agonized about Thaddeus, Abby loved her work at the school. The children seemed to like her, their mamas and papas too, who thanked her almost every day for her teaching. She told herself that she had finally found her purpose in life—what more did she need? What right did she have to take Thaddeus from his?

Even while her heart ached as she lay down alone in bed to sleep at night, she had no stomach for possibly bringing harm and confusion to

Thaddeus's life. Lindy was right; her brother was content, doing what he loved.

It surprised her some that she was able to leave Thaddeus alone. She'd always figured she would go right after him once she discovered where he was. Now that she knew, however, she couldn't make herself act, couldn't trust herself to do the right thing. She'd made so many mistakes in the past that now she needed a way to guarantee she wasn't making yet another if she went to see him.

The weather turned real cold just as December rolled in. Snow followed the cold, so much so that many of the kids couldn't make it down to the school. Abby shut classes down for a few days. On Sunday she and Jim and Steve made their way to Jesus Holiness for service. Due to the cold and the snow, church didn't start till almost noon to give the congregation time to arrive. To Abby's surprise a number of folks she'd not seen in church before were sitting in the sanctuary, a couple of them in the pew where she and her boys always sat. Abby steered Jim and Steve to a pew some rows toward the back. The service began and she settled into it as she always did, the music and praying acting as a balm to her troubled soul.

Following the hymn singing, Preacher Tuttle announced they had a quartet visiting from Hickory who had come to sing for them and so everybody should just relax and let the Spirit move them because they might be there for a while.

The quartet moved to the platform and took off into their singing, not finishing until forty-five minutes later. The congregation then stood to do some more singing all together. Jim and Steve sang out strong. Abby smiled at Jim's off-key singing. He had a lot of wonderful traits, but carrying a tune wasn't one of them. Steve, on the other hand, had a firm baritone and sometimes sang solos before the preaching.

Abby's heart swelled with pride. Although both of them had their faults—Jim too stubborn sometimes and Steve too proud—her boys were fine individuals, hard laborers and steady churchgoers. Tuttle had baptized them both in Slick Rock Creek three years ago. She was glad to see they'd kept their distance from the drink, brought her almost all the money they made at their jobs, and treated the girls they liked with respect and gentleness. No matter what else had happened, she had raised two good boys. She and Stephen had at least done that right. The deacons passed the offering plates after they finished singing.

Abby glanced around the church. Deidre, Raymond, and Ed sat to the left and a couple rows back of her. A young woman sat by Ed, the daughter of a farmer who had a place about three miles out of town. Abby nodded at them. Deidre smiled at her, and Abby could tell she was happy to be home for a while. She wondered if her mama was any better. Abby also wondered about Daniel. He didn't come to services much these days. She'd been praying for him, but so far there had been no change that she could see. In fact, he seemed worse off than ever.

The offering ended, and Tuttle now approached the pulpit and started off fast in his preaching.

"Jesus is the light!" shouted Tuttle. "A light brighter than any electrical bulb hanging from your ceiling, brighter than the fire burning in your stove. He's the light, yes He is. Brighter even than the sun that shines down and warms your head when you step out on the porch in the morning. Brighter than the moon and stars with all their twinkling. He's the light, oh yes He is."

Abby looked over at Elsa. She seemed so content these days, a woman favored twice in her life with men she loved. So why couldn't Abby find favor at least once? If not by Stephen, why not then by somebody else? She thought of Thaddeus. He had never married. Why hadn't God favored him with a wife?

"Jesus will show you the way!" called Tuttle. "Like a lantern in the night. Yes, He'll help you down the right path. Like the headlights on an automobile, Jesus will guide you around the next turn in the road. Yes He will."

Abby bowed her head, closed her eyes. At the moment Jesus didn't seem much like a light to her. She felt she was walking in darkness all right, and didn't know which way to turn, which path to take. She pressed her hands together. *I need a light,* she prayed. *Something to show me the way. So does Daniel. Give him a light too, Lord. Please, give one to us both.*

Tuttle preached on for another half hour. His voice grew raspy, his face perspiring from the preaching and the heat of the stove. Abby tried to listen but part of her mind kept wandering.

All around her the world was changing. She knew from listening to the radio at Elsa's house that trouble was brewing across the Atlantic. Some said the United States had to pitch in and help England sooner or later. Abby wondered what that meant for her boys. Would Jim and Steve have to go fight in a war? She prayed that wouldn't happen. She thought of Daniel and how his experience as a soldier had affected him—the limp in his gait, the headaches and nightmares he still suffered.

Tuttle shouted, "Sometimes we go off on our own way, oh yes we do! We leave the light of Jesus and step into the darkness of our sins. But I got to tell you today, you leave the light of Jesus and you will hurt yourself in the dark, yes you will."

Abby prayed the problems beyond Blue Springs wouldn't drift close to home, that another war wouldn't come along and pull her boys into the dark.

A lot had changed around them, yet Blue Springs had stayed pretty much the same. Men and women still dressed mostly like they always had. True, the town had electric lights now, and autos outnumbered horses and buggies. But about half the folks still had outdoor privies and most were without a telephone. Abby sort of liked the way things had remained the same; it felt safe. A safe place for her and her boys, their future families, to live out their lives. As long as a war didn't take them away.

Tuttle started winding down the sermon, almost whispering now: "But if we turn back from our darkness and turn to Him, the Lord's light will rescue us. So turn to the light today. Turn to Jesus and let Him light up your life, your days and your nights."

Abby opened her eyes and studied the back of the pew in front of her, the hymnbook rack. Lindy and Thaddeus and their pa, Mr. Holston, used to sit together as a family in this very pew where she now sat, back when they were all kids. Thaddeus used to listen to the preacher on this very spot—five rows from the front, left side, he and his sister to the left of their pa, who sat on the end. Abby reached to touch the varnished wood of the pew's back.

"Let's all stand and sing the closing hymn," said Tuttle. "And if you need to come to Jesus and let Him light up your life, I'm right here at the front of the altar. Come and pray for Jesus to give you His light."

Abby stood with the rest of the congregation. It caught her eye when she slid the hymnal from the rack. She brought a hand to her lips, and tears suddenly stood in her eyes. For there on the pew in front of her, just above the hymnbook rack, a little heart had been scratched into the wood. Inside the heart: T.H. LOVES A.P.

She felt a dizziness come over her when she realized the meaning.

T. H. Thaddeus Holston! Loves A. P. Abigail Porter! Thaddeus Holston loves Abby Porter!

She'd never seen this before! When did Thaddeus write it? When they were kids, that was certain. Back when he sat here with Lindy and his pa. But she'd barely known him then. Had he had feelings for her from the beginning, even before she and Lindy became best friends?

She touched the heart cut into the pew, ran her fingers over it. All around her the people sang out, *"See the light, the blessed gospel light, let it shine from shore to . . ."*

The tears now streamed down Abby's face. Was God giving her a message, a light, letting her know that Thaddeus did indeed love her? That He wanted her to write him, go to him? That had to be it. It couldn't just be a coincidence that the singers from out of town would come to Jesus Holiness today, fill up the pew where she usually sat so that she'd be forced to move back to sit in this pew where the Holstons used to sit. If all that hadn't happened, she would never have seen the heart and its message.

She trembled, and Jim turned to her with a questioning look. She shook her head and strode out of the church. On the front steps she took a deep breath with her face tilted up toward the gray sky. Jim and Steve had hurried out behind her. Abby stood between her two sons. Jim put an arm around her to hold her steady.

"What is it, Mama? You okay?" Jim asked.

Abby smiled. "I think it's the Lord," she said. "So don't worry, I'll be fine. Better than in a long time." She put an arm around them both.

"I'm hungry," said Steve.

"Me too," said Jim. "Must be past two."

Abby heard the church's front door swing open behind her, and the congregation started filing out. At the same time she noticed a brown truck racing down the street and heading toward them. The truck skidded to a stop, and Mr. Cooledge jumped out with a frantic look on his face. Abby wondered why he hadn't been in church. Preacher Tuttle exited the church just as Mr. Cooledge raised his arms and stopped everybody in their tracks. Tuttle went to Mr. Cooledge and the two men whispered together for a few seconds. Then Tuttle turned around with fearful eyes and called for his congregation to quiet down and listen.

"The Japs have bombed us!" declared the preacher. "Over in the Pacific Ocean, at Pearl Harbor."

Everybody gulped. Tuttle continued, "We got us a war. No two ways about it."

Abby sagged back into Jim's arms. After a moment of stunned silence, everybody started talking at once. Tuttle dropped to his knees on the church steps and started to pray. Elsa ran to his side and joined him. Others did the same. Abby started to pray too but then thought of her boys and felt an overwhelming panic set in. She knew what war meant, had seen it once already in her life. It meant young men took up guns and left their homes and traveled off to fight for their country. It meant that some lived and some did not, and sometimes those who lived came home wishing they had died.

She held on to Jim with one hand and Steve with the other and prayed with all her heart that the war would begin and end long before her sons ever reached the age to fight in it.

Daniel spent the afternoon of December seventh in the yard cutting wood. By dusk he'd already cut a sizable stack, just finishing up the last of what he hauled earlier from the forest. He wiped the sweat off his face with a rag and lifted the ax to resume his chopping when he heard somebody yelling at him. He peered down the trail that led away from his cabin toward the road. Ed and Raymond appeared on the trail, their mama close behind them.

"Pa!" Ed shouted. "We been attacked! We at war now!"

Daniel held the ax steady. Ed and Raymond ran to him, both of their faces glistening with sweat, their eyes wide. Deidre followed a few seconds later, her breath coming in short gasps.

"What's that you're yellin'?" asked Daniel.

"War, Pa! Our Navy ships been bombed by the Japs at a place called Pearl Harbor."

Daniel let the ax fall to the ground. "Where's that?"

"Preacher Tuttle said it was over in the Pacific Ocean," replied Ed. "It just happened."

Daniel looked confused. Deidre moved to his side. "What's this nonsense the boys are talking?" he asked her.

"They're telling it true," she said. "Word reached everyone at the church right after services ended. Lots of men been killed over there."

Daniel studied his boots. "I know there's been trouble," he said. "But thought it might stay away from us."

"We headin' to war!" repeated Ed, his eyes wild with excitement. "I'm gone join soon as I can."

Daniel looked hard at his boy. "You ain't got no idea what you're sayin'," he said. "How bad it can get, how . . . awful and all."

"They come after us, Pa," argued Ed. "Snuck up on our boys like bushwhackers. That's all I need to know for now. Reckon I'll find out the rest soon enough."

"Lots of folks get killed in wars," said Daniel.

Ed shifted from one foot to the other. "I know that. But you did your fighting for our country. Reckon you can't expect me to do any less. I'm a grown man now. What kind of feller with any pride won't sign up to do his duty?"

Daniel sat down on a tree stump. "I just don't know what I'd do if anything happened to you. Don't know if I could stand up to it, if I could . . ." His voice trailed away, and he picked up the ax again and studied the blade as if searching for a way to protect his son from what lay ahead.

Ed stepped over to him. Deidre and Raymond too. Ed laid a hand on his pa's shoulder. "You don't have to worry, Pa. I'll take care of myself," he promised. "You taught me how to shoot, how to use my wits. All that will hold me in good stead."

Daniel ran his fingers over the ax blade. "None of that matters," he said quietly. "No matter how strong you are, no matter how careful or smart—war don't measure any of that. It's all chance whether a soldier lives or dies, comes home in a box or on his own two feet." He looked up at Ed. "I know you got to go. I ain't arguin' that. Seems every man has his own war to fight, least so long as I've known anything 'bout livin'. But I don't want you to go with the false notion you can do much about it if your time comes, that's all. That way you won't expect too much from yourself, won't take on the responsibility for anything bad that might happen."

Ed and his ma exchanged glances. "Daniel, you're talkin' nonsense," said Deidre. "Of course he can do something about protecting himself. The strongest men survive wars, the smartest too. Men with guile and a steady eye. Ed will come home from this . . . I just know he will."

"You sayin' you want him to go?" asked Daniel.

"Not saying that," she said. "But he's a man now, and on his own. We can't stop him if he wants to go."

Daniel understood. Deidre wanted to give Ed some confidence. That's why she'd said the silly things about what a man could do.

"Besides, the Lord will be going with him," said Deidre.

Daniel leaned the ax against the stump and took his wife's hand. He stood and looked her in the eyes. "I don't want to hear that," he whispered. "No reason to put such foolish hopes in the boy's head."

"It's what I believe," she said. "I won't throw it over just 'cause you decided to turn from it."

Daniel faced Ed. "You believe what your ma says?"

"Sure, Pa. You taught me that a long time ago. I'm a Jesus man just like you, like your pa before you."

Daniel caught Raymond's eye as he quickly thought over what Ed just told him. No reason to trample on the boy's beliefs. What would he say now? He couldn't just speak out plain against Jesus. "Long time ago your uncle Laban asked for evidence," Daniel said to Ed. "The night before he died. Said he wanted God to show him that He was truly there."

Both Deidre and Raymond stared at the ground. Ed turned to his pa and asked, "Did Uncle Laban ever get his evidence?"

"He thought he did," said Daniel. "And it gave him some comfort, me too at the time."

"But now?"

Daniel chuckled. "Now I need some evidence for myself. Been needin' it for a long time."

"Seems to me we got that evidence all around us," said Ed. "The way corn grows from a seed, the way people pitch in when somebody is suffering. The words of the Good Book—lots of signs of the Lord if you look for 'em."

"You believe that?" Daniel asked him.

Ed thought about it for a second. "I believe a man has to have faith."

"He can live without it."

"Not me, Pa. Some things I just believe. Like you and Mama lookin' after me and Raymond. Like the truth the roosters will crow when the sun comes up. I know those things, deep in my bones I know 'em."

Daniel wrapped his arm around Ed's shoulder. "I envy you, boy," he said.

"I wish I could help so you believed again, make it so the hurt you been through would go away," said Ed.

Daniel patted his son's shoulder. "I wish you could too, son, I really do."

CHAPTER TWENTY-NINE

The months between December 1941 and June of 1942 flew by fast. Jim told Abby almost every night that he couldn't wait till he turned seventeen so he could enlist in the war. Abby warned him she didn't know whether she would sign for him or not, and since a boy who hadn't turned eighteen couldn't go fight without his ma or pa's permission, he shouldn't get so set on wearing a uniform just yet.

Every time she said that, however, Jim set his jaw and said he'd hate to have to run off and lie about his age so he could defend his country, but if he had to do that, well, then he surely would. Abby wanted to argue with him and make him feel guilty for even thinking about disobeying her yet found she didn't have the heart for it. She came from patriotic stock so when somebody took to shooting at Americans with no good cause, she knew a man had to do his duty and fight back. Both her brothers had fought in the Great War and one had died in it, and as much as she didn't want her son involved in the war, she couldn't dishonor her brother's memory by trying to stop him from taking his spot in the ranks.

In addition to duty, Jim had another reason for wanting to fight: His cousin Ed had already joined up and that fact bothered him. "He got in the Air Force," he said almost daily, his envy obvious. "Told the military boys he wanted to fly."

Abby kept quiet whenever Jim brought up the subject, as if her silence might cause her son to drop the whole matter. But she knew the story from Deidre. Ed had informed the recruiters that he thought he could do his best for his country by dropping bombs on the enemy while seated behind the stick of an airplane. The recruiter told him that he didn't have enough education and training to be a pilot so he should just forget that notion. Ed then asked what else he could do to hurt the Japanese from the sky, and the recruiter told him the military had need for more gunners and if he passed the required eye and coordination tests, he might have a chance at becoming one.

Ed insisted they give him the tests right away, and since the head of the Air Force recruiting station down in Asheville had known Daniel back when he did brickwork there, he obliged Ed and signed him up for the tests. To Ed's pleasure, he turned up with excellent depth perception and also possessed the necessary quick hands and strong muscles in his arms and upper body. So the Air Force got him started on gunnery training for big bombers, and before anybody knew what to say, they shipped him out to Texas to begin training in B–24s.

Jim groused at Ed's good luck so much that Abby feared he might actually run away and join the service if she refused to sign the papers that would enlist him. She prayed every day that some miracle would happen and the war would end. But it didn't. Then, on the tenth of June, 1942, Jim celebrated his seventeenth birthday. Abby made him his favorite meal of fried chicken, mashed potatoes, and banana pudding, and he ate like he might never see that kind of food again. Abby sat by and watched, hoping she wouldn't start crying like her body told her it wanted to do.

She felt like crying a lot in those days. Not just for Jim either, hard as that was. She wanted to cry for herself too. Because she'd seen the heart on the pew at Jesus Holiness and taken it as a sign from the Lord that she should contact Thaddeus, she'd thought a lot about leaving Blue Springs to go find him, just show up at his door one morning and say hello as simple as that. But she had no money for the travel. Plus, with all of Jim's talk about enlisting, she knew she couldn't leave him right then, couldn't miss even one day of seeing him before he headed off to fight.

Unable to go to Thaddeus, Abby thought she ought to at least write him a letter, tell him how much she wanted to see him. To her dismay, Sol told her that he never got the exact address where Thaddeus was, so she couldn't know for sure if her letter would ever reach him. Sol promised he'd do more checking and see if he could come up with an address for her.

Abby considered going to Lindy and begging her for the address. If she insisted, Lindy might give in and tell her. But Abby didn't feel right about taking advantage of her friend that way. She and Lindy were gradually becoming close again, and if she pressed her on this it might push her away again, make her think she only spent time with her in order to reach her brother.

Abby felt trapped again, powerless to choose her course. She couldn't stop Jim from joining the war and she couldn't write to Thaddeus and explain her feelings to him. She was at the mercy of the situation, helpless to change anything.

Jim met her in the kitchen early in the morning the day after his birthday. She saw instantly that he had something important on his mind. Abby tied her apron around her waist and set the coffeepot on the stove to heat. Jim sat at the table. She took a plate of biscuits from the previous night's supper and placed them where he could reach them.

"Sleep good?" she asked.

"Yeah, like a babe."

Abby felt the urge to hug him, to hold him so he could never leave her. He looked so innocent, so young. She moved to a cabinet over the sink, pulled out a jar of jam, and put it by the biscuits. Jim opened the jar and dipped into it with a knife.

"I plan on going to the post office today," he said, covering a biscuit with the jam.

Abby wiped her hands on her apron. The military recruiters were set up at the post office. She checked the coffee. He'd said the words so easily, that today he would go and alter the course of his entire life, made the simple statement while smearing jam on his biscuit.

"You hearin' me, Mama?"

Abby fiddled with the coffeepot. What should she say? How could she make him see how foolish it was to head off to war with such eagerness? Men died in wars, good and godly men too. The Lord hadn't made man's flesh like steel. The bullets and bombs cut into his body regardless of the soldier's faith, of whether or not he put his trust in God.

"You can't ignore me all day," said Jim. "I plan on doing this, with or without your blessing."

Abby lifted the coffeepot and turned to him and poured him a cup.

Jim took the coffeepot from her hand, placed it on the table. "Sit down here, Mama," he said, pulling out the chair beside him.

Weak in the knees, Abby sat and buried her head in her arms on the tabletop.

Jim patted her on the back. "You know I have to do this," he said. "I believe in this country, in the cause that's brought us into this fracas."

"I'm not against that," she sobbed. "But I don't know if I can . . can bear to lose you. Not with everything else that's happened. If you go . . . if something . . ."

"Nothing will happen, Mama," he soothed. "I will see to that."

She sighed. Something always happened. But he was young yet; he hadn't lived long enough to understand what she knew.

"Mama, Steve will be here to take care of you. He promised me he would."

Abby smiled at the thought. The two of them had talked about her, the two strong sons providing for their mama.

"I'm a man now," Jim continued. "Old enough to decide this for myself."

Abby straightened and wiped at her eyes. "I have no doubt that you're a man now," she said. "But . . . I am so afraid."

"The Lord said we should fear not. I'm joinin' the war trusting that word."

"You're a brave man, Jim."

Jim kissed her hand. "I learned it from you. You're the bravest person I know, man or woman." Abby shook her head, but Jim held on to her hand and added, "You made me what I am. So blame yourself if I take this war as my duty. It's what you've done all your life, stood up to the trials that have come to you. I'm just standing up to the one that's come to me."

"You give me too much credit," she said.

"Fact is, I don't give you enough. It was always that way, from the time I was born. You held our family together. Pa, God rest his soul, he never knew how to deal with life's hard knocks. But you took them all on your shoulders and held up as firm as a mountain."

Abby's face reddened. "I think you are trying to butter me up," she said, lightening the conversation. "Reckon you figure that way you can get me to sign that paper for you."

"That idea's a good one," said Jim. "Wish I had the smarts to have thought of it."

"Oh, you got the smarts all right."

"I'm only smart enough to know that my words carry truth. But it don't take a real sharp brain to know that."

Abby stared at him. As before, she wanted to keep him close and never let him leave. But she knew she couldn't. Easier to hold back a waterfall than to keep a young man from following his convictions. She felt herself starting to cry again. "You and Steve are all I got," she said. "If—"

Someone knocked on the back door. Abby shot a glance at the door but didn't move. She had so much left to say, more words she wanted Jim to hear. A second knock. She wiped her eyes again.

"They'll go away," said Jim.

"Abby! You there?"

She recognized the voice. Her face wrinkled in confusion. "I better get it. Sounds like it's Lindy."

Jim let go of her hand, and she stood and hurried to the door. When she opened it she saw Lindy on her stoop. Her eyes were all red, and the color was drained from her face.

"Come in," said Abby, stepping back. "What's the matter?"

Lindy brushed past her and walked over to the table. Jim sprang up to pour her a cup of coffee as Abby tried to comfort her. The two women sat down together, Abby putting a hand on her back.

"You look all worked up," Abby said. Jim handed Lindy the coffee. She took it and drank down a full gulp. Knowing that Lindy's oldest son had gone off to the war a couple of months earlier, Abby wondered if something maybe had happened to him. Or was it Jubal? Had Jubal come up sick or something?

Lindy sat the cup on the table and wiped her mouth. "No reason to hold it in any longer. I've come to tell you about Thaddeus."

Abby's hands moved to her mouth.

"He's fallen ill," said Lindy. "Gravely so."

Abby's mind reeled. How could this happen? Another tragedy, so soon after the last! Was this all her life would be, one heartache after another? She forced herself to ask the next question that rose up in her head. "Are you saying he might not make it?"

Lindy bit her lip. "I don't know."

"What's wrong with him?"

"He's come down with a fever of some kind. I just got a letter from a priest in Nuevo Laredo who works some with Thaddeus. He's not sure what's caused the sickness, only that Thaddeus is in poor shape and needs the best care possible."

Abby considered the matter for a second, then said, "We must bring him home."

Lindy shook her head. "Not sure we've got time for that."

"What should we do then?"

Lindy hung her head. Abby's heart raced as she thought about how sick Thaddeus was, and how far away. She felt helpless. They couldn't just leave him there, separated from his home and his family, maybe to die without them by his side.

"He's asking for you," whispered Lindy. "The priest wanted to know who you were."

Abby glanced at Jim. She knew what she had to do. "I'll go to him," she said. "If he can't come to us, I'll go to him, try to bring him home."

Lindy stared at her. "Other than for Daniel's trial, you've never been out of the state. Mexico is a long ways off."

Lindy was right. She didn't know the first thing about how to go about getting to Thaddeus. But that didn't matter. If Thaddeus was sick and was asking for her, she would cross a desert with no water to see him. "Doesn't matter," Abby said. "I'm going to Mexico. Got no choice."

Jim put a hand on her shoulder. She looked up at him, and he smiled as he spoke to Lindy. "I expect she plans to go," he said. "Looks to me like wild horses couldn't hold her back."

Lindy nodded.

"I'll bring your brother home," Abby promised Lindy. "You'll see."

CHAPTER THIRTY

It took Abby almost three days to make things ready for her trip. Everybody helped. Sol decided to go with her. Preacher Tuttle would take the two of them to Asheville where they'd board a train to San Antonio, and from there they'd catch a bus to Laredo, Texas, just across the border from Nuevo Laredo, Mexico. Lindy wrote to the priest in Nuevo Laredo, a Father Shauley, asking him to meet Abby and Sol when they arrived.

"I only hope he receives the letter before you show up," Lindy said on the day of their departure.

"If not, then Sol and I will just have to find him," Abby said, the determination visible on her face.

Everybody but Daniel—who was working in Hickory at the time—gathered on her porch to say good-bye to her and Sol. Lindy cried the whole time. Abby hugged her close and whispered, "We'll bring him back."

"I just hope you reach him in time," sobbed Lindy.

Abby gave her one last hug and then climbed into the backseat of Tuttle's brown Chevy. Everybody waved and Tuttle pulled away, both

Abby and Sol waving back as they left Blue Springs behind them.

The journey passed in a blur—the drive to Asheville, the train ride which seemed to stop at every crossroads. Abby was too preoccupied with all that was happening to do much talking with Sol. But he'd brought along a book to read, and the first day passed smoothly into the night and the night into the next day. They switched trains in Atlanta, Georgia, and then again in Jackson, Mississippi. Each new one seemed to be more noisy and crowded than the last. Abby desperately wanted to bathe and freshen up, but she and Sol hadn't the money to get private compartments to do such things. She reminded herself that she'd most likely see Thaddeus in the next day or so and therefore could withstand any hardship for his sake. The day whirled by and became night again. Sometime in the wee hours of that night they finally reached San Antonio. Abby and Sol had breakfast at a small restaurant near the train depot and afterward they walked to the bus station to wait for their bus. About an hour later the bus pulled up and soon they were headed south toward Laredo.

Abby tried to sleep yet found it impossible. The closer they got to Laredo, the more alert she became. If everything went right, she might actually see Thaddeus by the end of the day. Her heart beat faster when she thought about it. How would he look? But what if he'd passed away already? She couldn't even consider the notion. God wouldn't put her through all this and then let Thaddeus die before she reached him. The heart etched into the church pew had been her sign that the Lord wanted them together. Could it be she'd mistaken the meaning, that in fact it meant nothing at all? She closed her eyes and forced herself to think of something else. She recalled the last time she'd seen Thaddeus, way back at Hal Clack's funeral. Thaddeus had looked so handsome then, so sure of his direction.

But now he needed her, had asked for her.

The bus pulled into Laredo and came to a halt. Abby and Sol climbed out, each holding a small canvas bag containing a change of clothes. A wave of heat smacked her in the face, and she squinted at the sun. Her face felt slick, like someone had poured oil over her head. She brushed back her hair and searched around the plain brick building that was the bus depot.

"You ever seen a priest before?" Sol asked as he stretched his back.

Abby shook her head. "Wonder if he's here?"

"Sure hope he got Lindy's letter in time."

They walked inside the building. Four large fans twirled overhead. Abby saw a sign for a rest room and told Sol she'd see him in a little bit. About fifteen minutes later—after washing up, brushing her teeth, and changing her clothes—she returned to the lobby and found Sol sitting on a bench, his hair neater, his eyes clearer.

"A little water and soap can make a big difference," he said.

"Not as good as a full bath but better than nothing," agreed Abby, taking a seat next to Sol.

"You reckon the priest will be wearin' one of them frock things?" asked Sol.

"Maybe. A collar for sure. If he even comes."

"Lindy says he wrote her a few times. Seems he liked Thaddeus a lot."

"What's not to like?"

The front door opened then, and a man walked in whom Abby figured must be Father Shauley. He was bald and had a square red face. He wore simple brown pants and a black shirt that had a tear in the right sleeve near the elbow. A white collar wrapped around his neck. Sol and Abby hurried his way and asked if he was Father Shauley.

"Indeed I am, and you must be Mr. Porter and Mrs. Waterbury," he said, shaking hands with both of them.

Fear suddenly gripped Abby. What if Shauley told her Thaddeus had died? What would she do then?

"I'm so glad you made it," said Shauley, his accent that of an Irishman who hadn't traveled home in many a year. "You never know with travel what it is these days."

Abby nodded but had little patience for small talk. "How long will it take to reach Mr. Holston?" she asked.

"He is in a hotel nearby. He was in Mexico up until a few days ago when I brought him across the border. Thought it'd be easier to get him the proper help this way."

Abby felt her heart leap. Thaddeus was alive!

"He's okay?" asked Sol.

"I'm no doctor," said Shauley. "But I do believe he's past the worst of it. His fever broke two days ago. Come, I'll take you to him."

Within fifteen minutes Abby found herself following Father Shauley up the stairs of a white two-story building that had a rickety walkway running along the entire front exterior. A few scraggly trees stuck up from the ground near the stairs but there wasn't much other vegetation. The sun beat down on her back; sweat dripped from her face. She knew she must look awful and wished she could fix herself up before Thaddeus saw her.

Shauley stopped in front of the second door from the end. "I'll go in first," he said, "to make sure that he's decent."

Shauley knocked on the door, then opened it and walked into the room before anyone responded, closing the door behind him. Abby combed her hair with her fingers, wiped her face, and smoothed down her dress. Her heart pounded like a young girl meeting a boy for the first time. Sol stood by her and sweated through his clothes. Abby tried to calm her nerves. What if she'd made too much of all this? Thaddeus might not have the same intentions that she did. Unless something happened to change her mind, she planned to tell him she loved him, that she wanted to see if they could make a life together. She'd made her peace with her origins and now wanted to live out her remaining days in Blue Springs. She hoped to marry Thaddeus, keep teaching in the school. But what would Thaddeus want to do?

What was taking Father Shauley so long? She thought again about how she looked. She now had some wrinkles around her eyes, a touch of gray in her hair at the temples. But her figure had stayed slim and her skin hadn't lost its luster. Elsa told her that she had the look of a woman ten years her junior. Thaddeus might still think her handsome enough.

The door swung open and Shauley appeared. "Come in," he said. "Thaddeus will see you now."

"I reckon I'll stay out here for now," Sol said to Abby. "Figure you might want a little time alone with Thaddeus afore I see him."

Abby hugged Sol and then entered the room. To her relief, Father Shauley stayed outside too. She closed the door, took a deep breath, and turned around. The room was spare: a single iron bed on the far wall, a table with an old lamp on one side of the bed, a door to a bathroom on the other. A fan turned slowly overhead, making little difference in the heat. A brown cloth chair waited by the bed.

Abby's inspection moved to Thaddeus and stopped. Her eyes filled with tears even as her face lit up with joy. Thaddeus lay on the bed, his head propped up on pillows. Although thin as a reed, his eyes burned with life. Abby stepped to the bed, and he held out his hand for her. His palm felt hot as she took it.

"Sit," he whispered, patting the bed by his side. "I promise I will remain a gentleman."

Glad he had enough strength to joke, Abby smiled and sat gently down on the bed. He stared at her. Up close now Abby could see how the fever had sapped his body. His hair appeared limp on his head, his lips dry and chapped.

"Abby, you're a pleasurable sight," he said, his voice weak but steady. "Thank you for coming all the way down here to see me."

Abby wanted to kiss his hand, take him in her arms and hold him, but she held back. "I was so scared," she said, "when Lindy told me the news, that you were so . . . so sick."

"Any sicker, I wouldn't want to get," he said.

"But you're getting better now," she said.

He raised up a little. "I believe I'll make it, thanks be to the good Lord."

"Thaddeus, I've been prayin' for you every day," she said. "Long before I knew of your illness."

Thaddeus took her hand and placed it on his chest. His eyes found hers and they gazed at each other in silence. Abby felt prompted to tell him right then that she loved him, that she'd always loved him, even when she didn't know it, even when time and circumstances had pulled her away from him and kept her from knowing her own heart. But she had no assurance that Thaddeus felt the same way about her so she said nothing.

Another notion came to Abby, a frightening one. Perhaps Thaddeus did love her yet felt he should stay where he was because he believed God had called him here to help teach the children. What if he said he couldn't just return to Blue Springs, marry her, and leave his work behind? What would she do then? What if he said he loved her and wanted her to move to southern Texas with him? Could she leave Steve in North Carolina and take her place by Thaddeus down here? Leave the children in the school without a teacher? Could she give all that up to be with the man she loved? Choices. Life seemed fraught with them, like apples on a tree. And a person had to pick them when they became ripe or they'd drop to the ground and spoil.

Thaddeus touched her mouth with his index finger. "You look like an angel," he whispered.

Abby shook her head. "A man who's been as close to death as you ought not to lie like that."

"You've never known how beautiful you are. Which always made you even more so."

"Time has made you better with your words."

"I've been away from the highlands for a while. Men there were always tight with their talking."

Thaddeus smiled and seemed to gain strength in it. His finger moved to her chin. Abby's skin tingled. She closed her eyes for a couple of seconds, then opened them again.

"I told you a long time ago I wanted to marry you," he said.

"I would like to hold you to that," said Abby. "But I have no right anymore. Too much water has flowed down the creek."

"Real love looks past all that's come and gone."

Abby held her breath.

Thaddeus raised up more. His fingers touched her neck. "I love you just like I did then. Only deeper now."

She closed her eyes again.

"I still love you, Abigail Faith," he whispered. "And as the Lord is my witness, I always will."

Abby felt him move in close, his breath touch her face. Tears edged to the corners of her eyes.

"Shhh," whispered Thaddeus. "No reason to cry."

The tears trickled down her cheeks. She felt Thaddeus closer, and his lips touched her cheekbones, the right one first, then the left at the spots where the tears had fallen. Her skin became alive, more sensitive, and her breath caught in her throat.

"Will you marry me, Abby?" he asked. "Will you let me live out the rest of my days at your side in Blue Springs? I can live out my calling right there. Me and you together, that's what I've always believed the Lord wanted. Will you, will you marry me?"

Abby cried openly now. "Yes, Thaddeus," she said. "I will marry you."

Thaddeus started to laugh. "I can die happy now," he said.

"You better not."

He kissed her then—a long, soft kiss that made Abby's heart pound and her head light. For the first time in her life she understood what love felt like. It felt like Thaddeus.

CHAPTER THIRTY-ONE

On the last Saturday of April 1943, Abby and Thaddeus stood up in front of Preacher Tuttle at Jesus Holiness Church and pledged their vows to each other. Abby wore a dress the green of the shuck of a ripe ear of corn, and the color made her auburn hair stand out bright as it fell onto her shoulders.

A lot of folks were surprised to see how Thaddeus filled out his gray suit. Hard to believe a man so thin less than a year ago could look so healthy today. But because of the steady care of his sister and Abby, he had gradually gained back his strength and weight in the months since Abby and Sol brought him home.

Sitting in the second pew to the right of Tuttle, Daniel listened as the vows were exchanged and truly felt glad for Abby. She deserved something good to happen to her. Of all the people he'd ever known she had a spirit stronger than anybody's but his pa. In spite of all her tough times, she had kept her head up, her faith hale and hardy. He admired that even if he couldn't do the same.

Tuttle asked Abby and Thaddeus to kneel at the altar. He then placed his hands on their heads and prayed, "Almighty Lord, we do ask you to bless these two precious people. Give them the power of the Holy Ghost on this here marriage of theirs. Give them . . ."

Daniel sneaked a look around as Tuttle continued to pray. Steve sat in the pew in front of him, a handsome boy of fifteen with a headful of hair. Although not big, Steve carried a presence in his body, a touch of confidence not usually seen in mountain boys his age. Their heads bowed, Lindy and Jubal and their kids filled up the front pew on the other side of the aisle. Daniel knew they were almost as happy as the bride and groom. Abby was getting the man she probably should have gotten a long time ago and, with Jubal and Lindy as best friends again, they could return to being the gang they'd been before as kids.

The kids from Abby's school squirmed behind Lindy and Jubal. They had asked Preacher Tuttle to reserve the section for them so they could see their teacher marry up. Behind the children, the rest of the town had squeezed into every inch of the church's pews, with some having to stand at the back to witness the big day.

Daniel looked at his hands, picked at the calluses on his palms. Loneliness settled on his shoulders, and he suddenly wished he could see Deidre, that he could have her and his kids beside him today. But Deidre had moved to Asheville for a while to care for her mama, and she'd taken Raymond along with her. It wasn't that he begrudged her going to Asheville. He surely didn't. Any child worth his or her salt would provide for his ma or pa when sickness rose up. Still, his Marla had moved to Charleston to live near her husband who had joined the Navy, and the Air Force had shipped Ed out to Texas to train him on operating a gun on a bomber. So, Daniel had nobody sitting by him as his only sister married up.

The preacher finished his praying and asked the couple to stand. He produced a simple ring from his pocket, then declared for all those in the church, "Thaddeus bought this here ring a long time ago. Bought it long afore Miss Abby ever consented to betroth him. He had confidence the Lord would find a way to make it happen." Tuttle smiled.

Daniel wanted to smile but found it hard. He remembered the last time he'd seen Deidre. It was about six weeks ago; she'd come to him on the porch after supper with a letter in her hand. She'd sat down in the rocker next to his, laid the letter in her lap.

"Picked this up this morning," Deidre had said, indicating the letter.

"Pa wrote it. Looks like Mama has turned for the worse. Her heart's just plain worn out."

Daniel nodded as he struck a match and lit his pipe. Mrs. Shaller had stayed sick almost since the day her husband lost his bank. "You need to go see her," said Daniel.

Deidre lifted the letter and quietly said, "Pa says he can't do for her anymore. Says he needs me there."

"Reckon you should go this weekend then, help out your pa."

"He wants me to stay," said Deidre. "I mean, until . . ."

Daniel stopped rocking and looked his wife in the eyes. Her worry over her ma had kept her up a lot lately. Like him, she'd spent many hours out here on the porch, staring into the late-night darkness.

"I want you to do what you believe is best," he'd said. "I ain't gone fake it to say I won't miss you. Especially if you stay away for more than a week or so. But I'm not gone keep you from goin' to your ma and stayin' as long as there's a need. Wouldn't be right for me to do that. I'm able-bodied. I can fend for myself."

Deidre put down the letter. "I don't want to leave you, Daniel. You need me too."

He removed the pipe from his mouth. "I admit I'm pretty lonesome when you're gone," he said. "But your ma and pa got troubles, so you do what you can to help them." Daniel puffed his pipe again.

The dusk gathered around them. Deidre suggested, "Why don't you go with me? Plenty of room in the house."

"You know I got to turn down that offer. I lived in Asheville once. Didn't turn out too good. I ain't planning on doin' it again. I don't take to the city."

"But you might find good work there. With the war and all, things are picking up. Pa said a man like you could do well there again, could—"

Daniel held up his pipe to stop her. "I ain't goin' with you. No reason to waste your breath trying to convince me. I made myself a promise when we come back home in twenty-nine. No more pretending what I'm not. It's the quiet of these mountains for me for the rest of my days. No two ways about it."

Deidre opened her mouth and he saw she wanted to argue. But he shook his head and stood and walked into the yard.

About a week later she loaded up a sackful of clothes for her and another one for Raymond and hauled them to the porch. Daniel hugged them both real hard and told her to write him a letter every now and again.

"I will," said Deidre.

"I'll come see you every month or so," he said.

Deidre was crying when Daniel turned from her to Raymond. "Take care of your mama," he said to his son.

"I will, Pa," promised Raymond.

Daniel shook Raymond's hand, hugged Deidre again, and let them go. They disappeared from the clearing into the woods for the long walk down the holler to the road. Preacher Tuttle picked them up there and drove them to the train station for the trip to Asheville.

Now Daniel sat alone in the church as Tuttle finished up the wedding.

"So, by the power vested in me by the Lord Jesus and this here state of North Carolina, I do pronounce you two as husband and wife. What the good Lord has matched together, let nothing on this old earth tear apart. Amen and amen." Tuttle beamed. "Thaddeus, you may kiss the bride."

Thaddeus leaned to kiss Abby. Watching them, Daniel couldn't help but smile. What should have happened a long time ago had finally taken place. Abby had found and married her man.

CHAPTER THIRTY-TWO

For a long time after Abby and Thaddeus's wedding, it seemed that things settled some on Blue Springs Mountain, or at least as much as they could settle what with the nation at war and everything. Thaddeus moved in with Abby and Steve, Abby kept on teaching at the school, and her life took on a rhythm that she'd long desired but never found till now. From time to time Thaddeus showed up in her classroom and lent a hand teaching math—a subject Abby taught but never with much comfort. When not busy at the school or in their garden, Thaddeus took to doing chores down at Jesus Holiness. He painted the outside, fixed up the pulpit, put a new pipe on the coal stove. Whatever Preacher Tuttle asked, he tried to do.

Abby felt happier than she could ever remember. She and Thaddeus spent long hours together reading books and talking about them, listening to the radio and discussing world events, serving at the church and pondering matters of the faith. For the first time she had someone she could discuss things with head on, one mind and soul open to another mind and soul. It wasn't that she and Thaddeus agreed on everything. They didn't. For instance, she thought Roosevelt hadn't done as much as he could have for the poor. Thaddeus said, "Nonsense. If anything, maybe the man went too far, spending a lot of government money on make-work jobs." She hated all the autos that had been showing up on the mountain, whereas Thaddeus thought this showed that Blue Springs had finally made some progress. She liked it that the church spent most of its dollars on caring for people right at home. Thaddeus thought they should send more of it away to pay for missionaries to preach Jesus where people had never heard of Him.

All in all they didn't argue that much. But when they did, Thaddeus challenged her in ways no man had ever challenged her before. And Abby loved him for it.

Months peeled off the calendar and 1943 turned into '44 with winter slamming into Blue Springs. The snow piled up and blanketed everything with a hard crust of cold. One morning toward the end of February Abby left Thaddeus sleeping at her side and climbed out of bed about an hour after sunrise. She slipped on her robe, made her way to the kitchen and got a fire going in the stove. She set a pot of coffee on the burner and set the table for breakfast. She was taking a plate of biscuits from the cabinet when she suddenly felt light-headed. She paused, waited for the sensation to pass. She leaned on the table as her stomach fluttered with nausea. After a couple of minutes everything returned to normal. She washed her face in the sink, then headed back to the bedroom to wake Thaddeus. "You plan to waste the whole day?" she said, kissing him on the forehead.

Thaddeus smiled and sat up. "You're worse than a rooster. Won't let a man take his rest even on a Saturday."

Abby sat down beside him. "Porter folks never had a lazy bone in their bodies. I reckon you got enough for the both of us."

Thaddeus grabbed her and threw her down beside him and started tickling her feet. She was laughing before his fingers touched her skin. She fought him off as best she could, but since his health had returned he had more strength than she could counter, and he held her arms down with one hand and tickled her with the other.

"I'll . . . never . . . kiss . . . you . . . again!" she cried. "If . . . you . . . don't stop . . . right . . . now!"

"I'll take your kisses when I want," he said, still tickling her. "And there's nothing you can do to stop me."

Abby howled with laughter. Thaddeus rolled her over and stopped his tickling. Instead, he began caressing her chin, lips, and neck.

Her laughter subsiding, Abby kissed his fingers and closed her eyes. Thaddeus softly kissed her. She felt her face warm.

"I love you, Abigail Faith," he whispered.

"I love you, Thaddeus."

They lay side by side, Abby snuggled into the crook of his arm. She loved the warmth of his body, so steady and secure. The sun drifted in through the bedroom window. Finally, at forty-three years of age, she'd come to experience real contentment and peace.

True, there were still some things that made her anxious. Jim at war stood at the top of that list. He sent her a letter every month. She wrote him at least once a week, sometimes more often. The Army had given him some tests, determined he had a good head for electronics, and so trained him as a radioman. After several months in Charleston, South Carolina, they shipped him over to Italy. He couldn't say anything more in the letters, just that he ate regular, liked the buddies in his platoon, read his Bible most every day, and missed her and Steve something awful.

Abby prayed for him daily. She believed her prayers made a difference and she wanted to cover Jim as best she could with the presence of the Almighty.

She thought of Daniel. She checked in on him from time to time, wished she could help him more but didn't know how. He didn't come around much. Since Deidre had moved to Asheville, he'd become more and more withdrawn, hardly ever showing up at Jesus Holiness. The times she did run into him and tried to talk, he just mumbled a little before making some excuse and walking away. She wondered if he'd taken to drinking some again.

Other than Jim and Daniel, her other worries seemed trivial. Yes, Steve wanted to join the war like his brother had, but he wouldn't turn seventeen until May, so she'd decided not to worry much yet about what might happen. Besides, he'd recently had to start wearing thick glasses and maybe his poor eyesight would keep him from serving. "Let that matter rest," she told him every time he brought it up. "We got enough to handle today."

Indeed they did. Teaching at the school, tending the garden, keeping up the house, serving in the church—all of it made her days full. Abby snuggled closer to Thaddeus. The Lord had blessed her. What more could she ask?

Peace between the Clacks and her kin, that was the only other thing.

Every now and again she saw Eugenia Clack and her family in town, and Abby always tried to say a friendly word. Mrs. Clack would say hello but nothing much more than that. Abby didn't try to push the conversation any deeper. Abby wondered sometimes why the Lord had given her that word at Stephen's place. Nothing had come of it, and try as she might, she didn't know of anything she could do to make things better. Ben Clack kept everybody in his family under his meanness.

The fluttering sensation rolled through her stomach again. She waited for the nausea to leave but it didn't. The fluttering moved higher and caused her body to tingle. Then came the light-headedness like what she'd felt in the kitchen. She took a deep breath and told herself to relax, but the nausea grew worse and she knew she had to get to the privy in case she couldn't hold it down. She rolled away from Thaddeus and stood. She threw a hand out to the dresser to steady herself.

"Where you going?" asked Thaddeus.

"I'm not . . . feelin' well."

Thaddeus sat up. "I'll get you some water," he said.

The telephone rang. Abby's brow furrowed. People didn't usually make phone calls this early on a Saturday morning. Her nausea suddenly eased, her head cleared. She pointed toward the living room. "You get the telephone," she said. "I'm okay. Just need to wash my face, rest a few minutes."

Thaddeus headed to the phone as Abby moved to the bathroom. Standing at the sink, she looked into the mirror and suddenly realized what was happening. She had felt like this three other times in her life. With Jim and Steve. Then with Rose Francis. The last time had almost killed her.

For what seemed like a long time she stared at herself and struggled to figure what she ought to be feeling. At her age she knew she shouldn't have any more babies. She'd taken precautions against it but that had obviously not worked. Sometimes, no matter what a body did, the precautions failed. Did God make it that way? Did God want her in this condition again?

Abby closed her eyes. She was pregnant for sure; her heart tore over the idea. Yes, she loved the notion of giving Thaddeus a baby, of raising a child born from their love. Maybe she would have the girl she'd always wanted—a sweet little doll she could clothe in frilly dresses and take to church and raise into a young woman.

But she knew another baby might threaten her health. After Rose Francis, the doctor in Boone had said she ought not to have any more babies. Was she strong enough to bring a baby into the world? Or was it her destiny to die as her mama had died, her child born at the cost of her own life?

Abby gritted her teeth and made the only choice she knew how to make. If she died giving birth, so be it. Her mama had traded her life for her child's; Abby could do the same for hers.

Another notion crossed Abby's mind. What if another baby died before she could birth it? Could she survive the grief that such a loss would bring?

Abby wiped her eyes. It didn't matter. She had a baby growing inside her, and one way or the other, she'd carry it so long as God allowed. If the baby lived, praise be to the good Lord. If it didn't, well, then she'd deal with that when the time came. With Thaddeus beside her, she could face anything, even something as horrible as the death of a child.

She took a washrag from the side of the sink and ran water over it. She squeezed out the rag and wiped her face. The water cooled her skin and made her feel stronger. She put the rag down and turned to leave the bathroom. Thaddeus stood at the door, his face drained of color. Her heart leaped to her throat.

"That was the Army who called," he said. "Abby, Jim's been hurt."

Abby rushed to him. "What do you mean he's been hurt?"

Thaddeus took her hands. "He's in a hospital, wounded in action over in Italy."

"He's okay then?" she asked, crying now.

"They said he was injured bad but didn't know exactly how bad. Said they would get back in touch soon with more details."

Abby prayed with Thaddeus. With her eyes squeezed shut and holding Thaddeus's hands, she prayed her Jim would be all right, would sense the Lord there with him.

When they finished praying, she let go of Thaddeus and headed to the kitchen. "Who was it called?" she asked.

"Jensen," said Thaddeus. "From the post office."

Will Jensen worked for the military as a cross between a recruiter and a messenger. When news from the front came to Blue Springs, Will Jensen passed it on to the folks in the area.

"Did Will say when we'd find out more about what happened to Jim?"

"Only that he'd call us back just as soon as he got more word."

Abby poured two cups of coffee, set them on the table, and took a chair by Thaddeus. She tried to stay calm. "Least he's alive," she said.

Thaddeus took a drink of coffee. "If he's in a hospital, he'll probably do fine. It's the ones that don't make it to the hospital who don't usually live."

"The Army has got good hospitals," said Abby. "Better than anybody else."

"They'll take good care of him."

"He's strong too."

"He'll be fine."

Abby sipped her coffee and told herself it was true. Jim was strong and the hospitals were good and she'd been praying for him ever since he left to go fight. She took another gulp of coffee, her mind busy trying to convince herself that everything would turn out fine. As the sun rose higher, however, she admitted to herself that she had no control over anything. If Jim lived or died, she could do nothing about it either way.

CHAPTER THIRTY-THREE

When Jim Waterbury woke up, his head felt as though somebody had slugged him with a tree branch when he wasn't looking. He tried opening his eyes but found he couldn't. His fingers moved instantly to his face, and he realized he had bandages wrapped around his head from the chin up. A hole at the nose gave him breathing space.

He touched the bandages over his eyes and wondered if everything was black because his eyes were covered or because he couldn't see anymore. He couldn't figure where he was and why. He rolled over. The smell of the place was unlike that of the battlefield. That's when he realized he was in a hospital. All at once the whole scene rushed back to him: A cold morning. He and his platoon, part of the Fifteenth Infantry Division in the action at Anzio, were scouting out the perimeter to make sure no German boys snuck up on the American positions. They'd run into some enemy. Before he knew it, the quiet of the frosty morning had turned into a noisy, confusing, deadly struggle to stay alive. From out of nowhere another bunch of Germans had joined up with the first group and the enemy had the high ground. Jim and his buddies ended up pinned down next to an old stone well outside a farmhouse.

For nearly an hour the Germans had poured machine gun and mortar fire down on them. Three of Jim's buddies had taken hits; two had died and a third one, the medic in the group, was moaning something awful. They weren't able to call for reinforcements because when Jim left his radio gear to tend to the medic, a German mortar shell landed square on the radio and destroyed it.

His head down behind the well, Jim looked at Spence Tolar, his best friend in the platoon. "We got to do something!" Jim shouted over the guns. "We stay here much longer, they'll kill us all for sure."

Spence, short in stature and redheaded, pulled his helmet down tighter on his head and pointed to a stand of trees about fifty yards away. "Maybe you and me can make a run for them trees," he said. "Then Slick"—he nodded to his right toward a skinny soldier with three days of whiskers on his face—"can run to the barn there." He gestured to the dilapidated wood building to the left. "If we split up their fire, maybe we can keep 'em occupied till help comes."

Jim gave him the A-Okay sign. He figured anything was better than staying where they were, with mortar shells raining down on their heads, bullets zinging by. He slid over to Slick and relayed to him the plan. Slick nodded his agreement and turned to the man at his side and filled him in. Jim rolled back to Spence, checked his rifle, and set his helmet on straight.

"Okay," he said to Spence.

"On three?" yelled Spence. Slick tapped his gun.

"One . . . two . . . three!"

The men rushed from behind the well, their boots kicking up dust. Jim made it halfway across the yard before it happened. The shell exploded not far from him, and a piece of shrapnel the size of a fingernail blasted out and cut into the back of Jim's head at the base. The percussion from the mortar filled Jim's eyes with smoke and dirt and he fell to the ground and cracked his head against a rock. A knot rose up on his skull in the front. He lay on the ground gritting his teeth against the pain.

He heard the sound of an engine rushing at him, becoming ever louder. For a second he thought the Germans had surrounded them with a tank and that he wouldn't live to see another day. He thought of his family and started to pray Psalm Twenty-three. "The Lord is my shepherd; I shall not want."

The tank rumbled toward him. He saw the words *Pride of Philly* written on the tank's side, and he realized he might not die after all. Still, he kept going with the psalm. "He maketh me to lie down in green pastures: he leadeth me beside the still waters. . . ."

His voice faltered, his head throbbed. The tank drove on past him and then he blacked out and couldn't remember anything else. Until now.

He raised up on the hospital bed but a jabbing pain in his head caused him to fall back. He touched his eyes once more. He couldn't see; it wasn't just the bandages! He was blind! Jim jerked up and threw his feet over the bedside, ignoring his protesting head. He needed to talk to somebody, a doctor, to tell him his condition wasn't serious, that he'd see again soon. The mortar blast must have sent so much dust into his eyes that he was temporarily blinded, that's all. He struggled to find the floor with his feet.

"Whoa there!" said a woman's voice. "Lay back down there, soldier. No need to rush off anywhere."

"Where am I?" Jim asked. He remained seated on the edge of the bed.

"In an Army surgical hospital, near Naples." He smelled a pleasant perfume, like honeysuckle but slightly more feminine.

"How long have I been here?"

"They brought you in about two weeks ago. Here, lie back down now."

Jim couldn't believe it. Two weeks! He hadn't seen anything in two weeks? The idea of it made him angry, so much so that he decided he wouldn't lie down, no sir. To do so would mean he'd accepted what had happened, that he'd be lying down and resigning himself to his condition.

Against all reason he got the idea that if he could just get up and walk out of the hospital, his eyesight would return. Just make it outside, he figured. Outside where he could take off the bandages, open his eyes and look up at the sky.

His feet touched the floor and he stood before the nurse could respond. His body swayed, his knees nearly buckled, and his head burned with pain. He felt a hand on his back and another on his right forearm. The hands felt strong yet soft too.

"Easy, soldier," said the woman. "Where do you think you're going?"

Jim tried pushing away from her, but his arms lacked strength. The woman put steady pressure on his shoulders so that he fell back onto the bed. She pulled the sheet and blanket over his legs and smoothed them down around him. Jim fought to steady his head. He got the feeling that if he blacked out again, he might never wake up. He decided he'd better think of something to say, something to make his mind stay busy and conscious.

"What's your name?" he asked the nurse. His voice sounded far away.

"I'm Nurse Rebecca Stowe."

"You takin' care of me, then?"

"Best I can," she said.

"Thank you."

"You're welcome, soldier."

Jim liked her voice. It sounded familiar, reminded him of home. He was about to ask her where she was from when he heard footsteps approaching so he held off. A second or two later he felt a finger under his chin.

"You finally come to," a scratchy voice said. "For a while there we wondered if maybe you'd just keep sleeping until we put you on a ship home." A set of fingers turned Jim's head from side to side. "I'm Doctor Leaver. I've been checking on you and everything seems to be on the mend."

"How long afore I can see again?" Jim asked, a touch of panic in his voice.

Leaver chuckled. "Right to the point, eh? I like that." He felt the bandages over Jim's eyes. "I wish I could pin down the answer to your question, but an injury like yours doesn't lend itself to the kind of clear outcome a doctor can predict. Things can go a lot of different ways. Sometimes it all comes back at once—blind one day, seeing the next. Other times . . . well"—his fingers left Jim's face—"other times the vision never does return."

Jim's mind went blank for a second. How could Leaver even suggest he might never see again? Of course he would!

"You got a fine nurse watching out for you," said Leaver. "You let her know if you need anything."

Jim wanted to ask some more questions, but the doctor left before he could.

"You need to rest now," said Nurse Stowe, fluffing his pillow. "But it's good you're back with us."

Jim inhaled deeply of her perfume, then his mind drifted off, the sweet aroma the last thing he remembered before falling back to sleep.

Over the next six weeks it seemed to Jim that every time he woke up he found Rebecca Stowe close by. After he had most of the bandages removed she helped him eat; she shaved his face in the morning and tucked him in at night. Lots of days she read to him from the Army newspapers, told him about the war's progress.

"I hope this will all end soon," he kept saying.

Rebecca agreed. "We can all go home then," she said. "That will be a happy day."

Jim wasn't so sure about that. There was nothing happy about going home blind.

Despite his misgivings, he didn't argue with her. What man would? She smelled like honeysuckle, had a voice like an angel and hands as smooth as a silk pillowcase.

Jim found out that she, like him, hailed from North Carolina. To his surprise, though, she refused to pin it down more than that.

"You've spent some time in the highlands," he told her one morning in late March as she led him out of the hospital tent into the compound for a walk. "You can't hide the mountains from your voice, no matter how much education you slap on it."

Rebecca laughed but didn't tell him anything else. He wondered why she kept such a mystery about her. From time to time he pressed her further, asking about her family, her upbringing, how she ended up in the Army. She told him some about the last thing.

"I've been wanting to nurse since I was about twelve," she said one morning while spooning scrambled eggs into his mouth. "I lost a baby sister to the fever that spring. When she fell sick nobody knew what to do. Tried some old hillbilly cures on her, called in a doctor at the end. But the doc showed up too late. I watched her die. Figured right then and there that such a thing shouldn't happen, that maybe I should do what I could to stop it the next time. Figured what better thing could a person do than tend to the sickness of others? Like having the power of life and death in the palms of your hands."

"You talk nice," said Jim. She laughed. His face flushed, and his stomach felt all jittery. "Are you as pretty as you are kind?" he asked.

"Maybe you ought not ask that kind of question."

Jim reached out, felt the air in an effort to find and touch her face. "I know I'm young," he said. "But I want to see you, see what you look like."

"I could be fifty years old with a face like a pig for all you know."

"Maybe so," said Jim. "But I got a guess that ain't the case."

"Well, you're right about the age at least. I'm twenty-one."

"I bet you're pretty too. Sure smell pretty."

"You're talking like a soldier now," she said. "A young man a long way from home, a long way from his girl."

"I ain't got a girl back home."

"A boy as handsome as you with no girl? That's hard to believe."

"I'm glad you think I'm handsome." He heard her breathing, slow and steady. He searched the air again for her face and found her chin. It dawned on him that he now knew what a man felt like when he stood in danger of losing his heart to a woman. He quickly pulled his hand away. No woman would want to fall in love with a blind man.

"I've had enough eggs," he said gruffly, his mood suddenly sour. "You best go on to some of your other patients."

He felt Rebecca's hands on his face. "You okay?" she asked.

"I spoke out of turn," he said.

"That crack about a pig got you to thinking, didn't it?"

Jim lay back, his head shaking. "No, that ain't it."

"Then what?"

Jim refused to answer and, after a few seconds, Rebecca got up and left. He told himself to let it drop. No reason to fret over something that would never happen. No matter how good she smelled, no matter that she had some highland in her, he had no reason to pin any hopes on her. A blind man didn't deserve a woman like Rebecca Stowe.

April rolled in fresh and clean. Nurse Stowe still looked after him, though they didn't come close to any flirtatious talk again. That didn't mean he didn't find out a whole lot more about her. She'd done her schooling in Raleigh, plus her nurse's training. It was true she'd spent some time in the mountains, yet she still wouldn't tell him exactly where. A Baptist preacher in Raleigh had plunged her real deep in a river the year she turned twelve, and she had no doubts that the Lord had saved her. She had a good mama named Elizabeth but refused to talk much about her pa. "Let's just say he had a few rough edges," she'd said when he asked about him. "Not worth much more talk than that."

Jim pried no more about him. People needed their quiet about some things. He figured he probably wouldn't tell everything about his pa either, not to a stranger at least.

Of course, Nurse Stowe wasn't a stranger. Not anymore. Although they avoided flirting now, Jim had no doubt that she spent more time with him than she did with her other patients. When she had time off she visited with him, took him on walks, read to him from the Bible.

The days warmed, the spring rains fell less often. Jim's body took on more and more strength. Except for his eyes, he started to feel like his old self. Doctor Leaver checked on him most every day, told him that his head injury had healed up well and that maybe he could go home by the end of May. Jim pressed him on whether or not he could expect his vision to return.

"I already told you all I know," said Leaver. "Anything more and it's just a guess."

So Jim let it go. If the doctor had anything more to say, he would have said it.

One day near the end of April, he and Rebecca headed out of the hospital just before lunchtime.

"I'm done working for the day," she said, her hand at his elbow. "So I thought I'd take you for a long walk."

"You bring anything to eat? I'm hungry as a newborn pup."

"Sure did. I brought us a picnic lunch. Hope you like ham from a can."

He smiled and said, "Well, it'll have to do till I can go home and eat the real thing."

She laughed, which made Jim's heart race. Whether he liked it or not, he had fallen in love, and her being pretty or not didn't matter to him. He felt it wasn't just the war either, a battlefield romance. From what he could tell Rebecca had everything a man might want in a woman—a kind heart, a willingness to do hard work, good humor, and a belief in Jesus. But did she have feelings like that for him? Would she have spent her afternoon off to take him on a picnic if she didn't?

The strong smell of oil told Jim they'd walked past the motor pool. A few minutes later Rebecca stopped him. He sniffed the air; everything smelled clean, like laundry drying in the sun. A breeze brushed through his hair as the sun warmed his back. The war seemed a long way off. He had a hard time remembering the fighting. Maybe his head injury had done that, made him forget the bombs falling, the guns firing, the men dying. He felt Rebecca at his side and heard something flap.

"Sit," she said. "I put a blanket down and there's a tree for you to lean on."

Jim took a spot on the ground. He heard her arranging things. Soon she sat down beside him.

"You ready to eat?" she asked.

"My hunger is eatin' away my stomach."

"Try this." She took his hand, placed a ham sandwich on his palm. He bit into it immediately. "You any good as a cook?" he asked between bites.

"Don't you like the sandwich?"

He laughed. "You know what I mean. Real cookin'—fried chicken, sausage and gravy, biscuits, fried okra, banana pudding—home food."

"I know my way around a stove."

Jim took another bite. She handed him a canteen of water. After taking a drink, he wiped his mouth and turned toward her. He had something he needed to say. His heart ached to see her face. "I'm eighteen," he said. "But nineteen in June."

"A regular old man," said Rebecca.

"War can make you that in a hurry."

A bird chirped overhead. Jim wondered if he would ever see a bird again. He raised his sandwich to take another bite, but Rebecca held his wrist and kept him from it.

"Jim," she started, "I need to tell you something."

"That makes two of us. You go first."

He heard her voice catch, then realized she was crying. He extended his hand in search of her face. She guided the hand to her cheeks, wet with tears. "What's wrong?" he asked.

"I've . . . kept something from you," she said. "I shouldn't have done it but I did."

Jim's mind reeled. What did this mean? Did she know something about his eyes that he didn't? Would he never see again? Or was it some other secret, like the fact that she was married? He decided that had to be it so he pulled his hand away. "I reckon you already got a husband," he said.

Rebecca chuckled. "I wish it was that simple."

"Then what?"

"I don't know how to put it into words."

"Just say it straight out. That's the best way."

"Okay." She paused to gather herself. Jim held his breath. "I didn't see any need to tell you this at first. But . . . I'm finding myself drawn to you . . . falling in love with you."

"How is that bad?" Jim asked, his heart glad at the thought. "I feel the same way but didn't think I should tell you 'cause I can't see. Figured you deserve more than I can give."

"You don't understand."

"Then tell me. Tell me what I don't understand."

Rebecca moved, and he felt her standing up. When she spoke her voice came from above. "You know I've got the highlands in my blood," she said. "You recognized it in my voice."

"Sure. That's good, means I won't have to teach you how to make corn bread."

He hoped she would laugh at that. She didn't.

"Truth is, I've known you for a long time," she said.

Jim leaned back against the tree. What was she talking about?

"I saw your name on the list when you were brought here. I asked to be assigned to you, to be your nurse. Wanted the chance to see if what I'd always heard was true."

"So we met somewhere before—is that what you're sayin'?"

"You still don't understand, do you?"

She knelt beside him, and her perfume touched his nose. He wanted to pull her into his arms. Other than a quick kiss or two out behind Jesus Holiness with a couple of Blue Springs girls, he hadn't had much experience with women. He had a feeling that with Rebecca it would come easy, natural like. When he was with her, he felt as if he could do anything. "No, I don't understand," he said.

"I grew up real close to Blue Springs," she said. "Saw you in town from time to time."

Jim tried to figure it all out. Who was Rebecca Stowe? Did he know her? Had they gone to school together when they were kids? He thought of her voice. No doubt it had the highland accent, yet her speech was cleaner, different somehow from the way most of the women spoke from around Blue Springs. The voice had education in it, learning that covered over a lot of the twang of her mountain origins.

"I told you my last name's Stowe," Rebecca said. "But there's one name I left off. Left it off because my pa never claimed me, least not in any public way."

A crazy notion dawned on Jim. He shook his head against the idea.

"I told you my mama is Elizabeth Stowe."

Fear gripped him. "So then who's your pa?"

"My pa is . . . Topper Clack."

Jim couldn't believe his ears. His stomach lurched. Although halfway across the world, he had fallen in love with a woman from the one family in all the earth that he and his folks couldn't abide, the family of the man who had shot and killed his own pa. He started to stand but Rebecca pulled him back down.

"Say something!" she pleaded.

"I got nothin' to say."

"I guess this means the end for us."

Jim hung his head. She put a hand on his knee. "My mama said your folks were the salt of the earth," she said. "Said everybody in the highlands knew they could trust the Porters. I never had any respectability, grew up without a pa, an illegitimate child. When the war started, I joined up. Wanted to leave my past behind me. The Army put me here. When I saw your name on the hospital list, I just had to talk to you, see what kind of man you were. Then, I don't know, the more we talked, the more, well, I fell in love with you. I didn't mean to, but it just happened."

Jim's heart soared again. *She loves me!* But wait . . . he couldn't let himself get too happy about that. They had no future together. It just wasn't possible. Jim turned the talk in another direction. "So Clack never claimed you?"

"Nope, he had a wife, remember? My mama loved him on the side."

"Not easy on you, I reckon."

Rebecca laughed yet it had no joy in it. "A highland woman with a child and no husband lives a hard life," she said. "The child too. I got out of there soon as I got old enough. Had an aunt that lived in Raleigh. Mama sent me there, made Topper pay for it."

"How'd she manage that?"

"Women got their ways. My mama is a looker. She told Topper she wouldn't see him anymore if he didn't provide the money for me to move, go to school and all. That's where I got my nurse training."

Jim slumped, his head busting with confusion. He loved Rebecca Stowe, he couldn't deny it. But bad things would surely happen if he showed up in Blue Springs with a Clack woman at his side. What would his mama say? A Clack had shot her husband. "You know your pa killed mine, don't you?"

"I'm aware of the troubles between our families. I met your uncle Sol once. He came looking for my pa, back before the troubles got so bad, a few months before I left Blue Springs for good."

"But you still wanted to take care of me?"

"Like I said, I've long admired your folks. When I saw it was you, it just seemed right—a connection with someone from back home." He nodded. Rebecca continued, "I never knew my pa that well. He only showed up once every couple of weeks, stayed a day or so, and then disappeared again. Guess I'm far enough removed from the Clacks that I didn't hold it against you that your family all hates them."

Jim gave her a half smile and said, "Mighty nice of you. Still, that don't solve all the problems we got."

She laid a hand on his shoulder. "Jim, I'm sorry about your pa, all that happened between him and mine. But I had no part in that. I hope it won't keep us from each other, from what we might have together."

Jim weighed the situation. Topper Clack had shot his pa. Yet Rebecca was right, she had no connection to what Topper had done. Why should he blame her? "My pa wasn't the finest of men either," he said, admitting something he'd never voiced, not even to himself.

"He sure didn't deserve what he got, though."

"That's true. But none of it is your fault." He thought again of his mama. Would she be able to look past Rebecca's connection to Topper? "I'm afraid of what my mama will say about all this."

"From what I hear, your mama is a good woman," Rebecca said. "Surely she won't shut me out just because I got Clack blood in me."

What would his mama do? His shoulders relaxed some as he came to the realization that Abby would love whomever he did. Sure, it might take her some time to get used to the idea. When push came to shove, however, his ma would give him and Rebecca her blessing. As a Jesus woman she had to accept everybody, didn't she? How could she claim to follow the Lord if she held Rebecca's blood against her?

Jim thought of Daniel and Sol. What would they think? And Elsa—how would she feel? Not too happy, he knew that for sure. But he couldn't let that stop him, not if he truly loved Rebecca. He smiled as he made his decision.

"You as good-lookin' as you say your mama is?" he asked.

"Well, I don't look like a pig, I'll say that much."

He reached for her hand. "This won't be easy," he said. "I still can't see, you know."

"I know that."

"Some of my folks might not take too kindly to you."

"That won't surprise me."

"You sure about this?"

She kissed his hand. "As sure as anything in my whole life."

"Then I reckon I'm asking you to marry me."

"And I reckon I'm saying yes."

Jim's hands moved to her face. "I reckon I want to kiss you now."

"Go on and do it then."

"I haven't kissed many girls."

"I thought the Porter men weren't given to a lot of talk."

"You wantin' me to shut up?"

"Yes, if that's what it takes for you to kiss me."

"I love you," he said.

"And I love you."

He kissed her then and, for the moment at least, all his worries disappeared.

CHAPTER THIRTY-FOUR

On the first of June Abby received a letter from Jim. She carried it unopened from the post office to her house, sitting down to read it on the sofa across from the fireplace. She enjoyed his letters so much and lately they had contained good news. He'd started seeing shapes and shadowy images, and the doctor said this meant he might soon regain his vision in full. Maybe even better, he'd met a woman and fallen in love. The news thrilled Abby. Maybe even in war God could bring about good things. Abby opened the letter and started to read. Halfway down the first page, the words she read caused her to feel light-headed. She finished the letter and then read it through a second time.

I'm now a married man, Jim wrote. *To Rebecca Stowe, the nurse I told you about. As I've said, she comes from our part of the world, a highlander woman. I know you will love her.*

Abby stood and walked to the window, hoping she might see Thaddeus in the yard. She needed somebody to talk to about this. Thaddeus wasn't anywhere to be seen. She glanced at the letter again. How could Jim have done this?

She went out to the porch and into the hot day. Birds chirped in the trees. Lazy clouds drifted across the sky. She read the last part of the letter again, the part that shook her up the most: *Ma, I need to tell you, Rebecca is Elizabeth Stowe's daughter. Do you remember Elizabeth? She comes down to Blue Springs sometimes.*

Yes, she knew who Elizabeth and Rebecca Stowe were. Didn't know them well, of course, but around Blue Springs Mountain everybody knew everybody, at least a little. Elizabeth Stowe had been one of Topper Clack's women. Abby looked at Jim's letter once more. Topper Clack was Rebecca's pa, Jim had written.

Abby sat in a rocker and looked out into the yard. How could this have happened? Jim knew better. After all that had happened between these two families, how could he have done such a thing? Topper had fired the gun that killed his own pa! No self-respecting highland man would have anything to do with anybody from that clan.

Her jaw set, Abby got up to head back inside. But then a cramp ran through her stomach, and she stopped to wait for it to ease. She rubbed her hands over the apron that covered her stomach. The baby. The doctor had told her she was about six months along. It hadn't been going too well. She'd spotted some blood more than once. She held off telling Thaddeus about this and asked the doctor to do the same, just keep to himself the fact that she was having trouble. Abby prayed every day that she could bring her baby to birth and that they would both live through it.

Feeling better, she made her way to the kitchen, splashed water on her face, and took a chair at the table. She spread out the letter before her as she tried to sort through her thoughts. Her stomach cramped again and she wondered if maybe her labor pains were starting early. But she couldn't deliver the baby this early! It was too dangerous! She heard a knock on the door. "Back here, in the kitchen!" she yelled.

The front door creaked open, and a few seconds later Elsa stuck her head into the kitchen. Abby rose to greet her but her legs buckled and she had to sit again.

"You okay?" Elsa asked, at her side now.

"I think so," said Abby. She covered her pain as best she could. "Just a couple of cramps, you remember how carrying a baby can be."

"Let's get you to bed," said Elsa, taking her by the elbow and helping her stand. "You got to rest more, that's all there is to it."

Abby started to protest but then thought better of it. Maybe she did need more time off her feet. Maybe that would help her baby.

In the bedroom she stretched out on the covers while Elsa brought her a glass of water. Placing the glass on the nightstand, Elsa sat down on the bed's corner. Abby looked at her friend, gratitude in her eyes. Elsa held up the letter from Jim.

"You left this on the table," she said. "You want me to put it somewhere?"

Abby shook her head. "Read it," she said. "What that letter says affects you too."

Elsa looked at her for a second, then dropped her eyes to read. A couple of times she paused to glance at Abby, then went right back to Jim's words. She laid the letter on the bed. Neither woman said anything for a while.

"I don't like what Jim has gone and done," Abby finally said. "Marrying up so quick like he did."

"And with a Clack to boot," added Elsa.

Abby took her hand. "You're a Clack," she said.

"Half of me is."

Abby thought about that. While it was true Elsa had as much Clack in her as Jim's new wife, she'd still turned out good as gold. Maybe Rebecca Stowe would too. After all, she'd made herself a nurse and had left home to help out in the war, help tend to the men wounded on the battlefield. What right did she have to judge Jim's wife so fast?

From out of nowhere she suddenly remembered how the Lord had spoken to her, the pledge she'd made during Daniel's trial to bring peace between the Clacks and Porters. How could she resist what her son had done in light of that? If she showed her disapproval of the union between Jim and Rebecca Stowe, wouldn't she just be stirring things up again?

"You're as good a woman as ever breathed air," she said to Elsa. "Somehow my pa saw that in you when nobody else did."

"Maybe Jim sees the same in this Rebecca," said Elsa.

Abby pondered the possibility. The marriage between her pa and Elsa had brought happiness to them both. Maybe it'd work out that way with Jim and Rebecca. "It could be Clacks and Porters do better together than they do apart," she said.

Elsa smiled.

Abby raised up on her pillow and stared out the window. "You remember Daniel's trial?"

"A hard time for everybody."

"Well . . . I believe the Lord gave me a chore to do when all that was going on. It came to me almost like a vision, a whispering voice." She told Elsa about the experience at the boardinghouse in Knoxville. "The Lord works in mysterious ways," Elsa said when she had finished.

"You figure that was truly Him speaking?"

"Not for me to say. You were the one there. I got no reason not to trust your word if you think it so."

"I never knew what to do about it. After the trial ended, things settled some between our two families, have been quiet a good while. I figure maybe the Lord is making things better without my help."

"Ben seems to have disappeared to the hills," said Elsa.

Abby's brow furrowed. "Well, this marriage is sure to bring him back down again."

"He won't take kindly to a Clack and a Porter getting themselves married," agreed Elsa.

Abby sipped from her water, studied the letter once more. "I figure it's time we declared the feud over for good," she said. "Don't want it visited on the next generation, Jim and Rebecca, any kids they might have."

"It'd be good to see it finally end, that's for sure. But how you plan on doing that?"

Abby carefully got to her feet and eased over to the window. She touched the lace curtain. "There is an ancient way," she said. "Hasn't been done in a long time, not that I know of anyway."

"What old way?"

"Pa told me about it years ago. The old highland way to declare a feud at an end."

"You talking about the Mingling?" whispered Elsa.

"Maybe the only thing Ben will respect."

"The Mingling is a hard thing, harder than most can get themselves to do."

Abby ran her hands over her stomach. Elsa was right. The Mingling would call for more sacrifice than she'd ever imagined making. But she knew of no other way to fulfill her promise to the Lord.

"Could be that Ben will fight it," said Elsa. "Maybe it's best not to stir the water, just let things lie where they are."

"But this marriage will stir the water," said Abby. "The Mingling may be the only way to cut Ben out. One man can't stop it, not if everyone else goes along."

"So you reckon the rest of the Clacks will go along with your idea?"

"I got no way to know. But I see Eugenia Clack from time to time. She seems a reasonable woman."

"Now that Topper's gone."

"Maybe she's like your mama, God rest her soul."

Elsa smiled and said, "Mama did good in spite of my pa."

"You'll need to talk to Eugenia," Abby said. "She's the key."

"And we'll need a Clack baby," said Elsa. "You got to bring yours to term. Anything goes wrong with your pregnancy, and the Mingling—"

"I know," interrupted Abby. "Without this baby we don't have a Mingling." Abby rubbed her stomach and said a silent prayer. Then she opened the window. A light breeze played through her hair. She stared outside and tears came to her eyes. "I'll need your prayers to do this," she said, turning to Elsa.

"It's a sacrifice few can manage," said Elsa.

Abby wiped her eyes. "I believe the Lord spoke to me," she said. "Plain as day. I got to do it, no matter how hard."

"I reckon so."

Elsa moved to her and took her hands. "You're a brave woman, Abby. Braver than any I know."

Abby shook her head. "I made this vow a long time ago. Now the Lord expects me to keep it."

Elsa hugged her.

"Talk to Eugenia as quick as you can," Abby said. "Before I change my mind."

Elsa let her go and left the room. Abby sat back on the bed and wondered about the Mingling. Just the thought of what it called her to do made her hair stand on end.

Daniel got word about Jim's marriage to Rebecca about a week later. Sol told him as the two of them made their way home from fishing at a pond close to Slick Rock Creek. Daniel stopped in midstep, his fish string dangling in the air as he shook his head.

"What kind of craziness is that?" Daniel said to Sol. "Of all the women in the world, he has to find one from a family like the Clacks!"

"I reckon we got no choice about it," said Sol. "It's already done."

"But Topper is the one killed his pa!" Daniel shouted. "Don't that mean anything to him?"

"Abby says he didn't know who she was when he fell in love with her."

"That ain't no excuse. A man don't mix mongrel pups with good stock."

"You sayin' we're the good stock?"

"Least we're not Clacks. Nothin' lower than a Clack, you know that. One of them shot you. Don't this rile you none?"

Sol sat on a rock. Daniel threw a leg over a fallen tree.

"Back a few years ago when I couldn't walk I did me some thinking," Sol said. "Got myself straight on a few things."

"Sounds like you have gone soft on me too," said Daniel.

"No, it ain't that. Just that life is mighty short. If you spend it mad all the time, no matter the reasons—somebody cheated you, got a last name you don't like, something awful happened—you end up hurtin' yourself as much as the other man. So I decided I ought to let some things pass on, let bygones stay bygones. I decided to try and live for right now, not let what's behind rule what might still be ahead."

"So you're willing to forget everything the Clacks have done, how they shot you and killed Stephen, stole our family's land, kept me in jail for so long . . . you just washin' your hands of all that."

"I don't reckon I'll forget it. But I ain't gone let it rule my life either. Figure that's what forgiveness is. Puttin' something to the side so you can go on living without the burn in your gut over it."

Daniel stared at the sky. "I wish I could do that."

"Any man can forgive," said Sol. "If he sets his heart to it."

Daniel grunted. "I don't plan on doin' that. Not for the Clacks."

Two days later Daniel visited Abby at her house. He'd gotten even more upset in those two days. He decided he couldn't count on Sol anymore, the one man who before had always seen things eye to eye with him. If Sol and Abby turned on him, he had nobody left.

He found Abby snapping beans on her porch, her hair pinned up, her apron stretching to cover her belly. Daniel took a rocker by hers. His mind was swirling. He didn't want to upset his sister during her expectancy, but how could he ignore what was on his mind? He pulled out his pipe and tapped it on the rocker's arm.

"I reckon you dropped by to talk about Jim," said Abby.

Daniel almost chuckled. "I see you still like to move fast to the point," he said.

"No time to waste. Least ways not on something like this."

"You plan to bless this coupling?"

Abby scratched her forehead. "Daniel, it's a finished thing. They got married over in Europe. What God has joined, I don't plan on tearing apart."

"You sayin' God had something to do with this?"

Abby rocked, her hands busy snapping beans. "I got no reason not to give God some credit," she said. "Two people fall in love, that love is of God. They marry up. That's the way I see it."

"I don't like it that she's a Clack."

"Neither do I. But I can't hate somebody just because of their family name."

"She doesn't even have his name. Just his blood."

"Is that worse or better?"

"Don't know."

They fell quiet for a few minutes. Daniel took a handful of beans and started snapping them.

"You see Deidre much lately?" asked Abby.

"Every couple of months is all. She's still helpin' out with her ma."

"You ought not to stay alone."

"Not my choice," said Daniel. "Sometimes a body don't get any choices."

"I know how that is. Who a son decides to marry ain't a choice a mama gets to make."

"I'm not sayin' this is your fault. I just wish you'd be stronger against it."

Abby stopped her bean snapping and faced Daniel. He stopped too, his hands in his lap. Abby pushed back her hair. "I am going to call for a Mingling," she said.

Daniel jerked back.

"It's our only chance," Abby continued. "Time to end all this meanness between the Porters and Clacks."

"But the Clacks started the whole thing."

"That don't matter. It was a long time ago. I plan to end it, right here and now."

Daniel ground his teeth. "I'm not sure I can abide this," he said.

"I figured it wouldn't sit well with you. But if all the others agree, then you can't hold it up. You know the way of the ceremony—one man can't stop it."

"You think you can bring the Clacks into doing a Mingling?"

"Elsa is working now to see what can be done."

"I won't agree to it," Daniel said. "Maybe Sol won't either."

"Elsa thinks he'll go along."

"What's Thaddeus saying?"

"He's still praying about it."

"If he goes along, I'm all alone then."

"Sorry if that be the case. But I believe the Lord wants me to help make this happen."

"Even if it cuts you off from your only livin' brother?"

"That's a choice my brother will have to make. I'd prefer otherwise, though. Daniel, the Lord never promised everything would be easy."

"I expect I know about that."

"I expect you do."

"You really believe you can do this with your baby?"

"I pray every day for the strength."

"It'll be a miracle if you can."

"Guess I believe in miracles then. If God could give up His only son for us, I reckon I can try to do this for Him."

Daniel stood. "I will always love you," he said, leaning closer to her. "But if you do this, I don't know that I can sit on your porch again."

"It breaks my heart to hear that," Abby said, fighting back tears. "But I have to do this, for my children and yours too. We can't let this feud go on. It hurts all of us, keeps bitterness boiling in our blood. The Lord don't want that, I know it. Now's the time to stop it. I know that as sure as I know I pray for you every day I breathe."

Daniel kissed her on the head. "I love you, Abby. Always have, always will." Then he turned and headed toward the yard. Abby got up and followed him down the steps.

"The Lord waits on you," she called. "Like the father with the wayward son."

Daniel spun around and said, "I know I'm wayward. But I'm not sure I believe the Lord is waiting."

With that he left her yard, his shoulders shaking with the effort to keep from busting out into tears.

Jim's ship landed in Charleston, South Carolina, in early July. He stepped off with his eyes covered by a pair of sunglasses, a blind man's cane in his hand to give him assistance. Though he couldn't see much in the way of certain colors and shapes, he could make out larger objects, at least enough to keep from bumping into them. From Charleston the Army sent him by train to Greenville and from there to Asheville. His mama met him at the depot in Asheville, Thaddeus at her side. Abby hugged him so tight he could hardly breathe. When she'd finished Jim stuck out a hand and Thaddeus shook it hard.

"I reckon you're mighty tired," said Thaddeus.

"It's been a long trip," said Jim. "When I get to my own bed I might sleep for a week."

They all laughed. "We ought to head on home right away then," Thaddeus said.

"I brought some food along," said Abby. "We can eat on the way."

"You got fried chicken?" asked Jim.

"Your favorite," said Abby. "You knew I'd bring it."

"Where's Steve?" Jim asked.

Abby glanced at Thaddeus. "He didn't want to come," she said. "He's still upset the Army wouldn't take him. His eyes, you know."

Jim nodded. Then Abby took his hand and led him to Preacher Tuttle's Chevy, which they had borrowed. Thaddeus threw Jim's two bags in the back, and they all climbed in and started heading back to Blue Springs. Jim removed his uniform jacket and dug into the food like he'd not eaten anything so good in all his life. "This sure beats Army chow," he said between bites. "I near forgot how good you cooked, Ma."

"Glad to know I haven't lost my touch," she said.

After he'd finished, Jim lay his head against the seat back.

"You got a lot of medals on your jacket," said Thaddeus, looking at him through the rearview mirror. "Must have done some real fighting to get those."

Jim smoothed down the front of his shirt. "I did what all the boys did," he said. "Defended my country, that's all."

"You're all so brave," said Abby. "And it looks like we're finally making some progress in the war. Maybe it'll all end soon."

"Not soon enough," Thaddeus said. "Ed's still over there, in the Pacific."

"You get any word from him?" asked Jim.

"Not much," said Abby. "Least not that Daniel tells me about."

"It's been rough taking back all those islands," said Thaddeus. "The Japanese won't hardly give up. Lots of our men dyin' on the beaches over there."

"Maybe we ought to talk about something else for a while," Jim suggested.

Thaddeus turned off the highway and drove up an incline. For several minutes nobody spoke. The wind whipped through the Chevy as the sun—high in the sky now—heated up the inside of the car.

Jim took off his hat. "You get my letters?" he asked his ma.

"Every one. Wrote you back, you know that."

Jim grinned. "You okay with Rebecca?"

Abby said, "I have to admit it did shake me some when I first read about you gettin' married."

"Thought it might. But Rebecca is the best thing that ever happened to me. She's sweet as you, Ma, and from what I hear, pretty too."

"She's a pretty one all right. I've seen her a few times, though it's been a while."

"She told me she's got dark hair and brown eyes. I know for a fact that her skin is as soft as a baby's. She's got a nice figure too. Sorry, Ma, maybe you don't need to hear that."

Abby laughed. "I'm aware of a young man's appreciation for a fine figure on a woman," she said.

"Your mama's got one of the best," said Thaddeus.

"Well, you might've seen the last of it," said Abby. "As heavy as I am with this baby."

Jim laughed too. It felt good to come home, even if he did have to leave Rebecca behind. His mind shot back to the time he'd shared with his new wife since their wedding day. The Army had given Rebecca ten days' leave and they'd spent it in Naples, Italy. Even in the midst of war, the couple had found pleasure there. He'd never felt so happy, had never laughed so much or talked so much or loved so much. But the days sped by and soon it was time to return to their base. Some weeks after Rebecca had gone back to work, Jim received his discharge to go home.

Now he was an ocean away from the woman who had made him so happy it sometimes hurt. He cleared his throat and decided not to dwell on how much he missed her. "When are you due to have your baby?" he asked Abby.

"End of August, first part of September maybe."

"She's doing well," Thaddeus said. "Eating like a lumberjack."

Abby poked him in the ribs.

"I reckon you're wantin' a girl?"

"I expect so."

"I want me a boy," said Jim. "Least the first couple. Then a girl I reckon."

"It'll be good when Rebecca can come home," Abby said. "You can start your family."

Jim leaned forward, found his mama's shoulder and patted her. She turned around and took his hand. To Jim his ma's face was but a shadowy image. "Rebecca is expecting too," he announced.

"What?"

Jim beamed. "She's due sometime in March. You and her will be raisin' babies at the same time."

"I don't understand."

"Maybe you're not hearin' me," he said. "Rebecca, she's going to have a baby. The Army is sending her home in less than a month. It won't be long and we'll be calling you Grandma."

He heard his mama sigh. "You are full of news," she said.

"I hope that's good," he said.

"I hope so too."

They drove on up the mountain. Jim rested in the back. Maybe by the time his baby came he'd be able to see again, he told himself.

CHAPTER THIRTY-FIVE

To everybody's relief, Abby bore a baby girl on September third, a child so perfect everybody forgot they had worried a lot about her safe delivery. Abby gave her the name Rose Francis. Rebecca had arrived home by this time, and she and Jim moved in with Abby and Thaddeus. Since Rebecca was still early in her expectancy, she was able to help Abby with the chores around the house and with taking care of the new baby. And even though the house was somewhat crowded, they were all getting along fine.

By the time the first snow fell, Jim's vision had almost completely returned and he and Rebecca were much content. Christmas came and went, winter rolled on, and then before anybody could hardly look up it was March. At the end of that month Rebecca birthed a boy and they named him Porter James Waterbury. Now two squalling babies made the house jump with life.

With Elsa helping them, Abby and Rebecca nursed their babies, washed diapers, and kept the house clean and everyone fed. When they got a few minutes of quiet during the rare times the babies napped together, they liked to sit out on the porch, rock and talk. Abby fell in love with Rebecca real quick. The young woman had such a generous heart and was full of laughter. She did more than her share around the house and had a real knack for baking pies and cakes.

"How does the daughter of a Clack turn out so good?" Abby couldn't help asking her once.

"Like Elsa," said Rebecca. "Clack men stay gone a lot, and a good mama goes a long way."

Abby nodded. Elsa's mama had proven her mettle many a time before she died. "You make me almost glad Jim had to go to war," she said.

"If it took a war to make it so we'd fall in love, that's fine by me."

The two women fast became friends. Abby told Rebecca about her hopes for the Mingling. Rebecca had heard of the ancient way yet wasn't sure how a woman could ever go through with it.

"I am hoping I'll be able to do it," said Abby. "Pray for me." Rebecca agreed that she would.

Abby and Rebecca talked with Elsa about the Mingling as well. Elsa told them she'd spoken with Eugenia Clack who, upon hearing about trying the Mingling to end the feud, had hesitated. "She needs some time to study on it," Elsa said.

"Least she didn't say no," said Abby.

"I'll talk to her," said Rebecca. "Mama too. They're friends."

"They are?"

Rebecca nodded. "Eugenia knew about my mama all along. Said it kept Topper out of her bed, and that pleased her."

"Not exactly the way a Jesus woman would look at it. But I expect she had a point about Topper."

"You believe she'll agree with this?"

Rebecca shrugged. "She'll do what she feels is best for her kin."

Spring ended, and the heat of summer beat down on everything. Abby saw Daniel in town every once in a while, and although he kept his reserve around her, she made it a point to ask about Ed.

"He's busy fightin' the Japs," Daniel always said. "Don't hear much from him, a letter ever now and again. He's a grown man now."

"The war's supposed to come to an end pretty soon," she told him. "We already won against the Germans."

"The Japs don't give up so easy. I hear tell we might have to invade the place, take 'em on right in their own front yard."

"I sure pray it won't come to that."

"So do I. But if we got to go in there, Ed will lead the way."

Abby could hear the pride in her brother's voice. She knew how he felt. Only thing was, her boy had already come home, and his eyesight had returned. He was home safe and in one piece. On top of that, he'd brought home a wife and they now had a healthy baby. In April Jim had taken a job with a road crew working about ten miles away. He drove out and back to the job every morning and night. Abby felt guilty every time she saw Daniel. While it was true she'd suffered her share of hardships, for her everything had turned out for the good now. Why was she enjoying such blessing when her poor brother still had so many rocks stacked on his back?

The times she saw him, Daniel asked if she still planned to go through with the Mingling. She told him it depended on Eugenia Clack. He ground his teeth at that but didn't argue with her. Abby always told him she loved him before they parted ways again. He seemed distant, though, and she feared she'd lost him forever. She wanted to tell him to move to Asheville to be with Deidre and Raymond. He could find work there, stay with his family. But she knew he would never leave Blue Springs. He'd made a promise that he would stay put in the highlands, not leave ever again. All Abby could do was keep praying for him.

Starting in July, Jim took on work fixing cars at the general store where a new owner named Lester had added a gasoline pump and garage for filling up and repairing autos. Midafternoon on the seventh of that month Abby and Rebecca found themselves sitting on the front porch, both Rose and Porter napping inside. Abby waved a fan to cool her face, while Rebecca rested her head on the back of her rocking chair. Abby smiled when she spotted Sol heading their way. He looked so handsome in his sheriff's uniform. He and Jewel seemed steady and strong. Their three kids had grown up and were doing well. Sol stopped by Abby's fairly often for a glass of cold water and to check on everybody. Feeling weary today, she waited on him to step up to the porch before she stood.

"Afternoon, Sol," greeted Abby.

He tipped his hat to her and Rebecca.

"You thirsty?" she asked.

He shook his head and said, "Not a social call today. I need you to come with me."

Abby stopped fanning and thought of Thaddeus and Steve.

"It ain't nothin' with Thaddeus," said Sol, reading correctly the fright in her eyes. "Nothin' with any of your family."

She started breathing again.

"I got Mrs. Eugenia Clack down in my office," he said. "She wants to talk to you."

"You know the reason for her wanting me?"

"I reckon you can guess that."

Abby turned to Rebecca. "You mind watching Rose while I'm gone?"

"Not at all, you go on now. Don't you worry about things here."

Abby followed Sol off the porch and down the street. A few minutes later they reached his office and stepped inside. Abby saw Eugenia sitting across the room, her large girth barely fitting into the chair. As she walked closer their eyes met, and Abby's hands flew to her mouth. She ran to Eugenia and kneeled beside her. The poor woman's face looked like somebody had slugged her with a shovel. Black, blue, and yellowish bruises covered her cheeks and forehead. A cut the shape of a crescent moon hung over her left eye. The right sleeve of her blouse had been torn away. Abby didn't need to ask what had happened. Ben Clack.

"I'm so sorry!" Abby cried. "What kind of man could do this to a woman?"

Eugenia shook her head almost as if what Ben had done to her didn't matter. She looked firm as a boulder. Sol brought Eugenia a glass of water. She took it and drank deeply. When she'd finished, she handed the glass back to Sol, wiped her eyes and took a full breath. "He saw me with Elsa," said Eugenia. "Saw me talkin' with her."

"He beat you for talking with her?"

"He's mighty stirred up about your Jim and our Rebecca. Says he'll take his revenge on anybody who don't fight this marriage."

"So he beat you just for talkin' to Elsa?" repeated Abby in disbelief.

Eugenia shrugged. "He caught me right at nightfall, out behind the barn. Snuck up on me with a huge stick, knew he couldn't take me in any fair fight in full sunlight."

"He know all of what you and Elsa were discussing?"

"Not sure."

"So you came to Sol."

Eugenia glanced at Sol. "He's helped me a couple times before when Ben . . . when he took out after somebody in the family."

Sol stared at the floor.

"I'm done with him," Eugenia declared. "He's scared my clan for the last time, the women especially. I'm moving his wife over to Knoxville; she's got a sister there. He can't get to me through her anymore. I ain't dumb, you know."

Abby gripped her hand tighter. "I'm sure you're not."

Eugenia stared at Abby. "I'm ready for that Mingling," she said. "All the kin are, except Ben of course. We're all tired of the bad blood, want it off our kids, theirs to follow. We know that if Ben hurts your Jim, then Sol will have to go after him. Your brother Daniel too. That'll start everything up again. None of us want that."

"You got a baby less than a year?"

"Got one on my side of the family. A grandbaby by my second boy, you may know of him, William. His wife's name is Daisy. They got a boy, seven months. We call him Sam."

"And they're both willing?"

"They'll do it if I say so. William has served in the Navy, down in Charleston. He knows the feuding days are past. If this'll bring peace, he'll want it, no matter how hard."

"This will make Ben even madder," said Abby.

"Let him be mad. I won't let him sneak up on me again."

Abby faced Sol. "Can you make sure she stays safe?" she asked.

"I won't let her out of my sight," he said. "When you reckon on doing the Mingling?"

Abby thought for a minute. She needed to see Preacher Tuttle, take care of a couple of other things. "Let's try for the last Saturday night of the month," she said. "At Jesus Holiness. At midnight."

"We got to keep this to ourselves," said Sol. "No need givin' Ben a written invitation to come make a mess of things."

Eugenia looked at Sol, then Abby. "Ben's most likely to be drunk at midnight," she said.

Abby nodded. "That's reason enough to do it that late."

"What about Daniel?" said Sol.

"I hate to leave him out," Abby said, "but I don't see him agreeing to it."

"I expect not," said Sol. "Best he don't know about it either."

"Agreed," said Abby.

"I'll put out the word to my kin," said Eugenia.

Abby squeezed her hand. Maybe after all these years all the anger and bad blood would cease. Even if Ben and Daniel held out against it, the time had come. After the Mingling, the feud between the Porters and the Clacks would come to an end.

CHAPTER THIRTY-SIX

Daniel spent most of that July like he had many of the other months since Deidre left for Asheville—alone for the most part. He tended his corn crop, milked his cow, cooked his meals, and kept the cabin respectable. Every couple of weeks he traveled down to Blue Springs early on Friday afternoon and visited a little while with Sol. At Sol's office he always placed a telephone call to Deidre. Every time he talked to her she told him she and Raymond missed him and wanted him to come see them. He promised he would before August ended. He would then ask about her mama, and Deidre always gave him the same response: Her mama lay in bed all day and hung on between life and death. Daniel wanted to tell her that her mama had done this for a long time now and maybe Deidre should come on home because it didn't seem to help any that she was there. But, not wanting to pull Deidre between her love for him and her care for her ma, he held his tongue. He would tell Deidre that he loved her and Raymond; she said the same back to him. He always hung up at that point in the conversation because he didn't want to start tearing up.

After thanking Sol for the use of the telephone, he always left and headed straight to a run-down house a half mile out of town. A torn-up bench seat from a car sat on the man's front porch and a big stone well sat off to the side of the house. Daniel waited by the car seat while the man who lived there brought him a bottle from a room in the back. His head down, Daniel always took the bottle, paid the man, and hurried off the porch.

He waited until he reached the bald before opening the bottle. Once there, he'd twist off the cap as quick as he could and take a long drink. The liquid burned his throat as it slid down, settled into his stomach. Once he'd taken that first swig, though, he would nip at the bottle slowly, his eyes busy watching the logging crew as the men cut away on the land his pa used to own. From what he could tell they never saw him. But he was there all the same, holding a pair of binoculars he had picked up at the general store in one hand, the bottle in the other.

Daniel didn't exactly know why he kept returning to the bald. In one way it was torture to sit there and watch a bunch of strangers chop and saw and haul out his trees. In another way the bald called to him, drew him like a salt lick drew deer. Sometimes being there on the bald that overlooked his land made him feel less alone. His mama was buried on that land, his pa's folks too.

As each Friday ended and the night fell, Daniel kept on drinking. Before the night was over, he would finish off the bottle of liquor and fall into a deep sleep, so deep he usually didn't even dream.

On the last Friday of July 1945, Daniel labored in his garden till early in the afternoon, then had some dinner and cleaned up and headed for town. After walking the mile and a half to where he kept the old Ford parked, he found it wouldn't start. At first he figured he'd just go on back home and skip the trip to Blue Springs. But since this was the only time in the week that he talked with Deidre and Raymond, he didn't want to miss going. So he waited on the roadside until a man he knew drove by in a truck and stopped to help him. They worked on the car's starter for close to an hour before getting the Ford to run again. A couple of minutes later the two of them drove off, the man and his truck headed in one direction, Daniel the opposite way in the Ford.

He made it into Blue Springs by midafternoon. After stopping off at the barber's to get a haircut, he drove over to Sol's office and asked if he could use the telephone. Sol said yes and left the room so he could have some privacy. The operator connected Daniel to Deidre's number. To Daniel's surprise no one answered on the Asheville end. He thanked the operator for trying, then hung up and called Sol in from the other room.

"So how's Deidre and Raymond?" asked Sol, back at his desk.

"Fine," said Daniel, deciding not to say he hadn't talked to them. "Raymond is almost grown. I sure hope this war ends soon so he won't have to go."

Sol put his feet on his desk and leaned back in his chair. "What you hear from Ed?"

"He's still in the Pacific. Navigating now in one of those B–29 bombers. That's a big plane, you know, newest thing in the war. Ed says it's got a tail about twice taller than any building in Blue Springs."

"I can see you're proud of him," said Sol.

"That's right," Daniel said.

"He been writing you?"

"Every now and again. I'm going over to the post office when I leave here to see if any mail has come in."

Sol nodded. Daniel left Sol's office and drove over to Lester's Store and Gas Station. He saw Jim standing out by the gasoline pump. He pulled the Ford up to the pump.

"You takin' to this work?" Daniel asked as Jim filled it up.

"Pretty good," said Jim. "Don't know that I'd want to do it forever, but I like the mechanical part a lot. Maybe open up my own garage someday."

"A man needs a trade," said Daniel.

Jim finished with the gas, and Daniel paid him for it. The two of them walked inside the store. The place smelled like bread. Jim stuck the money in the cash register and faced Daniel. "Mama says you ought to come by more often," said Jim. "No reason for you to stay by yourself so much."

"How's that baby of yours?" Daniel asked, hoping to change the subject.

"Getting big," said Jim. "Eats night and day."

"They sure grow up quick."

Jim took a rag from his back pocket and wiped his hands.

"I hear you're seein' all better now," said Daniel.

"So far as I can tell."

"Wish my limp went away like that."

"You got that in the first big war, didn't you?"

Daniel nodded and instantly thought of the night Laban died, the night he got shot. Though the injury had happened a long time ago, the memory still seemed fresh in his head. He heard footsteps approaching from behind and turned around to see Will Jensen walking toward him. Jensen held out an envelope.

"I was just about to come see you," Jensen said. "This come into the post office about midday. Government man brought it and asked where you lived. I told him he'd never find your place. I promised him I would make the delivery myself after I closed up."

Jensen handed him the envelope, and Daniel's hands shook a little as he took it. He'd heard of folks receiving official mail like this, the words printed in block letters on the stationery of the United States Government. Such letters usually carried messages the receiver dreaded to hear.

Daniel saw Jim and Jensen glance at each other.

"I need to get back to the post office," said Jensen.

"I got work too," said Jim.

After the two men disappeared, Daniel walked to his car and held the envelope up to the sun. A hot wind blew over his face as sweat broke out on his brow. He leaned against the car. His eyes blurred as he studied the envelope. "Let it say he's coming home," he muttered, almost as if praying. "Let it say the Air Force has let him go."

He heard thunder in the distance. He tore open the envelope. The message was short: *It is our duty to inform you that Lieutenant Laban Edsel Porter is missing in action in the Pacific theater. The government of the United States and all its military authorities are doing their utmost to find your loved one and bring him safely home.*

Daniel instantly figured the worst. The enemy had no doubt shot down Ed's plane.

Maybe Ed managed to get out, Daniel hoped. Maybe he popped his parachute and landed safely.

He shook his head and told himself not to count on such an outcome. Even if Ed did make it to the ground all right, the Japanese would shoot him the second he touched earth. Either way, his son was most likely dead. He knew things like this never came out for the good.

As calmly as he could Daniel folded the envelope, stuck it in his overalls, and climbed into his car. Ten minutes later he made it to the house with the car seat on the porch and knocked. Before long he was stepping off the porch, this time with three bottles in his hands.

Back in the Ford, he reached for the key and turned it. The starter hesitated for a second or two but then turned over. Daniel pointed the car toward the bald. His stomach ached for a drink but he made himself wait. No use getting drunk and getting in a car wreck. That wouldn't help things one bit.

A terrible loneliness settled on his shoulders. The worst thing he could imagine had happened. His eldest son was dead. Honorably so, that was sure. But this brought little solace. Daniel choked back the tears and suddenly pulled the Ford over to the edge of the road.

Not caring anymore, he pulled a bottle from his pocket, twisted off the top and poured the liquid down his throat. Another drink quickly followed that one and before he knew it he'd finished one bottle and had started on another. Rain began to fall, and he felt the car quiver in the wind. Daniel sucked down another drink. Lightning struck. He felt like screaming. Nobody was safe! Nobody! Not his ma or pa, not his brothers, Laban and Luke, not his son Ed. Nobody! Not Marla, not Raymond, not Deidre. Daniel banged his head on the wheel.

It dawned on him that Deidre hadn't yet heard about Ed. The government didn't know she lived in Asheville. Her son was probably dead and she didn't know it. He raised his head. The rain battered his car. He felt as if it might get washed away any second. The idea attracted him—the notion that the rain would wash him and the Ford right off the mountain, down into Blue Springs Creek and send him under. He'd disappear to the creek's bottom, never to surface again.

A tree branch broke off and flew against the car. Daniel rolled down his window and stuck his head out to see where the branch had hit. The rain washed over his face. As he rolled up the window, he thought again of Deidre and what he had to do. He wished the government could deliver the news to his wife, that some man in a uniform could show up on Deidre's folks' doorstep and spare him the awful task. But that wasn't going to happen. This was his duty. Deidre would hear this news from him, nobody else. No matter how much it hurt, a man had to do his duty as a husband.

Daniel stuck the whiskey bottle back in his pocket and drove off. The road swayed on him from the effects of the liquor, but he kept driving anyway. Deidre needed to know about Ed, and it was up to Daniel to tell her.

The sun rose hot the next morning. Dressed in a long skirt and wrinkled gray blouse, Deidre Porter rubbed her eyes as she escorted a tall man in a black suit and hat to the front door of her pa's house. At the door he placed his hand on Deidre's elbow. "I'm truly sorry about your mama," he said. "She lived a good life." Deidre followed him onto the porch and down the steps. In the yard, he stopped and stared back at the house. "You think your pa will be okay?" he asked.

"He's expected this for some time," said Deidre. "After he grieves some, he'll see that her passing is a blessing."

"She went peaceful."

Deidre wrapped her arms around her waist. "Thank you for all you did to make my ma comfortable in her final days."

"I treated her for almost ten years," the man said. "Figured I'd see her through to the very end."

Deidre grasped both of the man's hands in her own. "Please," she said, "tell your Eva I said thank you for letting you stay out all night. You two have been such good friends to Ma and Pa."

"Eva will come check on you in a few hours. Meantime I'll call the funeral parlor. You need anything else you let us know." With that the man turned and headed toward his car, leaving Deidre standing on the porch.

Deidre watched him drive away. She then smoothed down her skirt and trudged back into the house to sit by her pa in his grief.

Not far from Woodrow Shaller's house Daniel watched with confusion as Deidre walked the stranger toward his car. His head ached from too much whiskey and a long night. He vaguely remembered the evening. The drive from Blue Springs had taken several hours as he navigated the rain-slicked roads. At one point he'd come to a tree that had been blown down over the pavement. Unable to move it by himself, he waited for someone to come along to help. Afterward his car didn't want to start for a couple of hours. Finally it caught and he drove on.

Arriving in Asheville at four A.M., he had decided to wait until sunup before waking Deidre. No reason to scare her in the middle of the night. Besides, he wanted to make sure the liquor had lost its effect on him. Nothing would make matters worse than for him to show up with whiskey on his breath.

Parking under a massive oak a couple of houses down from the Shallers', Daniel had fallen asleep. The first peek of sun had awakened him. Soon after he'd opened his eyes he saw his wife and the tall man walk out together. Who was this man? What was he doing with Deidre this early in the morning?

What's all this about? Daniel wondered.

Daniel's breath stopped when he realized what he'd just seen. The man had spent the night with Deidre! He banged his fists on the steering wheel. Deidre had taken up with another man!

He could hardly believe it—Deidre with another man? Wasn't she a fine, God-fearing woman? His shoulders slumped when he thought about what kind of husband he'd been lately. Why shouldn't Deidre find somebody else? He hadn't taken good care of her in their marriage. She'd grown up in Asheville the daughter of a successful banker. She'd married below her station, and he'd failed to provide her the comforts she had known. Add that failure to his love for the drink and she had every reason to fall for a city man like the one in the black suit.

Daniel rested his head on the steering wheel. He stared at Mr. Shaller's house and tried to figure what to do. Should he barge inside, tell Deidre what he'd just seen, demand that she explain how she could've done such a thing? Should he go and yell at her and call her names?

He lifted his head, rubbed his eyes. No, he wouldn't holler at Deidre. If he'd been a better man, she wouldn't have taken this path. It was his fault, not hers.

He took the government telegram from his pocket, unfolded it, and read the words one more time. No matter what he saw this morning, Deidre needed to know about what the telegram said. He folded the paper, climbed out of his car, and walked quietly to Mr. Shaller's house. He crept onto the porch. After sliding the telegram under the front door, he turned and rushed away.

Back in his auto, he started it up and shifted into gear. After taking one final look at the house, he drove off. The way he saw it he had no other choice about what to do next.

CHAPTER THIRTY-SEVEN

Daniel made it back to Blue Springs a little after ten that morning, his eyes bloodshot and his head hurting so bad he told himself that only more liquor would make it stop pounding. So, on his way home, he picked up four more bottles of whiskey. When he got home he decided he should write Deidre a note. He found paper and a pencil in Raymond's room, sat down at the kitchen table, and scratched off a short message.

Deidre, Marla and Raymond. I got word about Ed. He was shot down, dead I'm sure. It was me who put the telegram under Mr. Shaller's door. I'm going now. I'm sorry. Your husband and pa.

He signed the note, carried it to the bedroom and laid it on Deidre's pillow. For a few seconds he stood still and looked around the room. A lot had happened in here. Long talks with Deidre, three children born, a man and woman sharing each other's lives, loving each other. He wiped his eyes. All that was past, as dead and gone as Ed.

Daniel pulled his pistol from under the bed and left the room. Without looking back he headed out of the house. In the yard, he blinked against the bright sun and tried to figure what to do next. He thought of

Abby and realized he wanted to see her one more time. He hitched up his overalls and headed to the Ford and an hour later reached Blue Springs again. He stepped onto Abby's porch and knocked. Nobody answered. He knocked a second time. Again no response. He peeked in the window. Everything was quiet.

Daniel pulled out a bottle and took a drink. How could everything stay so regular on a day like today? Deidre had taken up with another man. Ed had been shot down. He glanced through Abby's window again, saw his pa's old walking stick standing by the mantel in the living room. His eyes locked on the cane. For some reason he couldn't figure, he suddenly wanted to hold it one last time, to feel the smooth wood and take in the finely carved figures.

He tried the front door and found it open. He walked into the house and picked up the cane. It felt familiar, good and solid. He studied the figures etched into the wood. They made him feel better. Figuring Abby wouldn't mind, he took the cane and left, steering the Ford toward the bald above his family's old property.

It took him until nearly three to reach the top. By then the sun was so hot the rock seemed on fire. Daniel sat down in the shade of an oak about twenty feet from the edge of the bald. He laid the walking stick by his side, then pulled a bottle from one pocket, his pistol from the other. Setting the pistol next to the cane, he opened the bottle and took a long pull. Then he lifted the binoculars that hung from around his neck and peered down into the valley. Around him nothing stirred—no breeze, no animals, nothing.

Daniel wiped his face and gazed down at the loggers across the way. An hour passed, then two. Daniel finished the first bottle and started on another. His face flushed from the heat. His mind wandered as he looked out over the land where he'd been born. He thought about his ma—the way she'd held him, the way she used to sing to him at night as he closed his eyes to sleep. He thought of Solomon too, the feel of his pa's calloused hands when he hoisted him up on the mule, the way he smelled after he washed up with lye soap after a day of labor. He saw Laban again and the last seconds before he died over in France, the way his eyes rolled back in his head and his mouth sagged in final slumber. Luke's face followed Laban's, his sweet voice singing as he dropped off in death. Now Ed, his oldest boy, his face stretched in pain, his body broken.

Sobbing, Daniel shook his head against the pictures in his head. He picked up his pa's cane and held it up. His knuckles turned white from squeezing it so hard. He saw the image of the bald his pa had carved long ago. He saw how Solomon had made the intricate features, how the rocks seemed to mark out a face. What his pa had called "the face of God."

"If you ever get lost, look for the bald and walk toward it," Solomon used to say. "Your home is always toward the bald where you see God's face."

He rolled the cane in his hand. "I'm on the bald, Pa," he whispered. "But I don't see God nowhere about." Silence answered him. Daniel twirled the cane, his fingers searching the wood as if looking for some sign, some message. Nothing offered itself.

Then, hearing a motor, Daniel looked down again. A black truck he had never seen before pulled into the logging camp. Daniel put down the cane, lifted the binoculars and studied the truck. A man wearing denims, a flannel shirt, and logger's cap stepped out of the truck and shut the door. Daniel saw the words *Gant's Land and Lumber* written on the door. The name on the truck sounded familiar to him, yet he couldn't place it.

He looked again. Several men gathered around the driver of the truck. Daniel figured him to be Mr. Gant, the boss.

Daniel rubbed his beard. Had Gant bought the land? His mind felt all fuzzy from the whiskey. Again he trained the binoculars on Gant. The man appeared clean-shaven, his clothes fresh. Daniel inspected him head to toe. He had wavy red hair and a flat nose. All seemed strangely recognizable to him. He focused again on the man's face. No, he'd never seen him before.

Gant walked over to a tent. Daniel lowered the binoculars, figuring it didn't really matter if somebody new owned the property; the land was gone forever. Anyway, he'd come here to the bald to end his worries about such things.

He took the third flask from a paper sack and stood to stretch himself. He opened it and drank. The sun boiled down on him. Daniel caught sight of his shadow stretching across the huge rock. His shoulders pushed out wide. He almost smiled. After he was gone, his shadow would disappear, gone like a leaf falling from a tree.

He drank again from the bottle. His body felt numb. He tried thinking of Deidre but found he couldn't focus too well anymore. She would understand, he decided. Since she already had another man, it wouldn't take her long to get over him. She might feel some guilt for a little while, but then she'd see that all the blame lay on him.

Moving back to the shade of the tree, Daniel sat down and scolded himself. He'd sure messed up bad. It was time to settle things once and for all. No reason to wait any longer, no reason to put it off.

He studied the whiskey bottle through bloodshot eyes. It looked harmless, just a brownish liquid surrounded by glass. How could it control a body so much? How could such a simple thing hurt a man so much?

Daniel had no answers to his troublesome questions. He licked his lips. Sweat dripped from his chin to the rock where he sat. He took off his hat and threw it to the ground, opened the bottle and held it to his lips. A breeze stirred. Daniel paused and, from somewhere deep inside, felt himself sober up just a mite. Enough for something to take hold in him.

Daniel shook his head. Would taking a drink be his final deed on earth? No. No matter all the bad he'd done up to now and how much a failure he was, he wouldn't let that be his last act! Using the cane, he struggled to his feet, then edged himself to the side of the bald. Then he flung the bottle over the cliff. It dropped toward the creek, shattering into a thousand pieces when it landed. Strangely pleased, Daniel grunted and stepped back from the ledge.

He pulled the pistol from his overalls. The sun glinted off the barrel as Daniel fingered the trigger. Abruptly, as with the whiskey bottle, he sensed this wasn't the way. No reason to make it so obvious. It would hurt Deidre too much if someone found him up here, done in by his own hand. He pocketed the pistol.

Only one way to do this. Make it seem like an accident. Simple enough. Like what happened to old Hal Clack when he went over the side of Edgar's Knob. Nobody knew if he'd actually fallen or been pushed. Make it a mystery, ease Deidre's mind at least that much. Daniel took several steps back, the cane in his hand to steady himself. He needed a good start to make sure he made it out far enough to drop all the way down.

Standing in the middle of the bald, Daniel took a big breath. He lifted the cane toward the sky, studied it one last time. His eyes landed on one of the carvings—the image of Jesus on the cross, His arms stretched from side to side on the tree.

"I been tryin' to find you for a long time," he said to the image of Jesus. "Reckon you ain't to be found."

Silence answered him.

"My brother Laban wanted some evidence," he said to the carving. "Thought he found some. I reckon I could use some too. I know it's kinda late. So, if there's a sign to be had, I suppose it's now or forget it."

Nothing happened.

"All right then." He laid the cane horizontally across the top of his shoulders, his hands near the edge on opposite ends. He started moving toward the edge of the bald, his feet moving quicker as he got closer. Somebody watching at a distance might've thought him crazy, trying to fly off the cliff like some prehistoric bird, the cane acting as his wings.

Daniel lost all sense of feeling. His body seemed to move of its own accord. He kept his eyes on the rock at his feet, at the shadow his body made as he rushed to the edge, to the end of all his troubles. His shadow loomed large on the rock, moving swiftly forward in time with his steps. The shadow seemed to call to him, to beckon for his attention. He kept his eyes down. The shadow rose up off the rock, rose up as though a living thing, something moving and alive and real! He saw it then.

The shadow.

It sobered him. He halted in his tracks less than ten feet from the edge. The shadow captivated him. With his fingers wrapped around near the ends of the cane, his arms extended along the stick, the shadow reminded him of a . . .

A man on a cross.

Daniel closed his eyes and shook his head. When he opened his eyes again, the shadow remained. The image of a man hanging on a cross. He puzzled over it and wondered if he could believe the meaning or not. Without a doubt the cane over his shoulders formed the likeness of a crucifixion, much like the carving of Jesus his pa had cut into the stick so many years ago.

Unsure what to do, Daniel took a shaky breath. He'd asked for a sign—was this it? Something this simple? His pa always said a man could see God's face on the mountain if he looked for it. "That what you tellin' me now, Pa?" said Daniel.

Was this God's face? His way of showing up when Daniel least figured to see Him? Daniel studied the shadow again. Jesus. He lifted the cane from his shoulders, turned it to see the carving of the cross, of Jesus sacrificing himself. "What you tryin' to tell me?" he asked.

Abby had told him once that his pa had given the cane to him for a reason, that it would mean something important someday. Had his pa given him this cane for just such a day as this? Daniel ran his finger over the image of Jesus. Was this the hand of the Lord touching him in a way he couldn't understand in the short space of his head?

Tears welled up in his eyes. "I'm a sorry man," he said. "I know you said you'd forgive us all our sorriness. But it's hard for me to forgive my own mistakes. Well, I am sorry. I know I grieved your heart. Please forgive me for all I done—all my drinkin', all my messin' up, all I done to Deidre and the kids."

Daniel sensed a quiet settle over him there on the mountain, a stillness in the air as though everything waited to hear what would happen next. His body began to quake. He knew either he accepted what the Good Book said and believed in the mercy of Jesus or he might as well go on and pitch his body over the cliff, be done with what he'd started.

He placed the cane over his shoulders to see the shadow one more time, but the sun had dropped too low for it to appear again. Daniel took the cane back in his hands and looked through wet eyes at the face of Jesus once more. "I reckon I got to choose," he whispered.

Jesus seemed to nod.

"I got to end it or come on home."

Jesus watched.

Daniel thought of Deidre. Of Raymond and Marla. Yes, Ed might be dead. But Deidre still needed him, the others too. He made his choice.

"I ask for your mercy," Daniel said. "And for your forgiveness. I . . . I want to come home."

Peace rolled through him then, and his sobs became sobs of joy. Great heaves of body and soul pouring out the hurt of years past. As the tears fell they washed out Daniel's heartache, washed it out and left room for something new to enter, something new and alive.

After a while Daniel quieted. He wiped his eyes and the wet from his beard and breathed a good full breath. From down below he heard a door slam, followed by a truck's engine coming to life. He stepped over to the edge of the cliff and saw the black truck pulling away, the redheaded man behind the wheel. *Gant's Land and Lumber.*

He watched the truck disappear. The name Gant stuck in his head though he didn't know from where. "What is it?" he asked out loud. He looked at the cane, the carving of Jesus. "Somethin' else you trying to speak to me?"

Silence.

Daniel picked up his hat. His notion of finishing his days had ended. He couldn't run from his troubles in such a cowardly way. Whether God had handed him a sign with the shadow or not, he couldn't say for sure. Nevertheless, the shadow had stopped him from doing an awful thing.

The cane in hand, he headed off the rock. As he was walking down the path that led back to the road, it hit him out of nowhere and he halted. Back in the war! A man named Oscar Gant, a red-faced man who had died the same night as Laban. Daniel had been there beside him as he breathed his last. Gant had asked a favor of him: to take his wedding ring back to his wife in Raleigh. The dying soldier had pulled off the ring and handed it to Daniel.

Daniel promised he would find the man's wife, give her the ring. And, after Daniel returned from the war, he'd kept that promise. The widow, a woman by the name of Lydia Gant, had been most grateful.

Daniel recalled that Gant's wife had been carrying a boy on her hip when he met her. No doubt that boy was a man by now, about the age of the man driving the truck. Had Gant bought the land his family used to own? Did the Gant family now possess the one thing he wanted more than anything else? But what difference would it make if they did? So what if he'd brought back a soldier's wedding ring to his wife and now that same family owned the old property? Why would they do him any favors? They didn't owe him a thing.

He held up the cane. *All the same, it's all mighty curious.* His head swirling but his heart settled, Daniel started again down the trail toward home. He had a lot to tell Deidre, oh yes he did.

CHAPTER THIRTY-EIGHT

A little before midnight Abby stood with Daisy Clack at the altar of Jesus Holiness Church. Daisy, a thin woman of less than twenty years, looked scared. Abby's heart went out to her. The Mingling called for a sacrifice from her that not many women could make.

A kerosene lamp burned on a table in each corner of the sanctuary. About thirty or so people, every relative of the Clacks and Porters who lived in or near Blue Springs—with the exception of Daniel and Ben—sat in the wood pews. Abby held Rose Francis in her arms; Daisy held Sam. The babies were unclothed, wrapped in homespun blankets. Abby wore a simple black dress. The ceremony of the Mingling called for it to happen this way, at the stroke of midnight just as the Sabbath began.

Abby glanced at Preacher Tuttle as he moved to the pulpit. The Mingling didn't always have a preacher involved; in times past it had even taken place outside under the stars. But nothing said it couldn't happen in a church.

Abby looked out at the crowd. Thaddeus and Elsa sat in the front row on the right, with Steve beside them. Jim, Rebecca, and Porter sat in the next pew, along with Sol and his family. None of Daniel's family had come. On the left side was the Clack kin. To Abby's relief, Eugenia had brought them all into agreement. They wanted no more feuding with the Porters nor with their offspring or in-laws.

"My folks see the need to cease the bad blood," Mrs. Clack had told her more than once over the last few days as they worked at putting together the Mingling. "Most have got some education now, know that a man's people don't have to stay as mean as the man who sired them."

Abby had come to admire Eugenia. She had stayed true to her word. Like most highlander women, she had a fierce loyalty to her family. But since Topper had died, she'd found her own strength.

"We're all gathered," announced Tuttle, "and the midnight hour has come."

Everyone nodded. They knew the stories of old, of how the Mingling allowed for the ending of a feud, how it provided the only way to guarantee someone wouldn't later break the peace.

"I'm new to this," said Tuttle. "But I have become a highlander." Having been around long enough to show his mettle, the preacher had earned the right to speak out the ceremony to them. "The women are here with their babies. They shall turn to me now."

Abby and Daisy faced Tuttle.

"Now is the hour for peace to come," Tuttle said, repeating the words always said at a Mingling. "Time for bad blood to end. Time for the laying down of guns and knives. Time for men to stop fighting and taking revenge on other men."

The crowd held its breath. The kerosene lights flickered, casting their shadows on the walls.

"Time for families to come into union with each other."

Abby shivered. Could this really be happening? Could she make the sacrifice necessary for peace to come? Would these two families that had warred against each other for over half a century finally give up their anger and their grudges, the awful things that had come between them?

Tuttle waved a hand over the two women. "Are all those gathered here in agreement that the time has come?" he asked.

The people agreed. "We are in agreement that such a time has come."

Tuttle looked at Abby, then at Daisy. "Unwrap the babies," he said.

Abby felt a lump in her throat. The moment had come. She took the blanket off Rose Francis and hung it over her shoulder. Daisy did the same. Now little Rose and Sam were completely uncovered, nestled in their mothers' arms.

"Is this your natural born child?" Tuttle asked Abby.

"This is my natural born child," she answered.

Tuttle asked Daisy the same question. "This is my natural born child," she said.

"It is time then for the Mingling," said Tuttle.

Holding Rose with her left hand, Abby reached for the buttons on her dress with her right. She pulled down the top left side of her dress, laying the blanket over her breast.

Tuttle looked at those in the pews. "They come bare before us and God," he said.

"Bare before us and God," they all repeated.

"To share in the Mingling," said Tuttle.

"To share in the Mingling."

Abby held Rose to her breast and the baby suckled. Abby closed her eyes. Tears crept to the edges. Rose pulled at her, and Abby felt as if her baby were tugging the very life from her, a life she'd willingly have given so her baby could live. But now she had to hand over her baby's life, hand her over for—

Abby heard a thumping on the back door of the church, then the snarl of a man filled with rage. She tried to ignore the sound, but the crowd behind her groaned, and she somehow knew that Ben Clack had found them. She turned and saw Ben staggering down the center aisle.

"I won't abide this!" he shouted, moving toward the altar. "No, I won't!" He held a rifle in his hands, its barrel pointed at Tuttle one second, Abby and Daisy the next. He reached the altar, his eyes wild in the light of the lamps. His breath was strong with the smell of whiskey. Grabbing Daisy by the hair, he dragged her away from the altar. "You ain't no Clack!" he growled. "Performin' the Mingling with a Porter!" He threw her off to the side and turned on Abby. "Git over there," he shouted, pointing to the sidewall, "afore I shoot you dead on the spot!"

Abby quickly buttoned her dress and did as she was told.

"And you!" Ben shouted at Tuttle. "Stand back from that pulpit!"

His fists clenched, Tuttle moved away.

Ben faced Abby. Abby glanced at Thaddeus, saw him on the edge of his seat. She caught his eye and shook her head, trying to tell him to stay put.

"You always thought yourself better than me," said Ben. "A high-and-mighty Porter girl."

He stepped closer and Abby thought she might get sick. She held her ground and stayed still. Ben reached for Rose, but Abby pulled the baby away from his hand. He grinned and stepped even closer. Abby wanted to smack him across the face. She sensed movement behind Ben and realized that Thaddeus had risen from his seat. Ben noted it at the same time, swung his rifle around, and aimed the gun right at Thaddeus. The gun roared before Abby could do anything to stop it.

After leaving the bald, Daniel drove straight down to Asheville. No matter that Deidre had taken up with another man, he wanted to see her and Raymond and talk to them about Ed.

He reached Asheville early in the evening and, to his surprise, saw a large group of people milling about outside Mr. Shaller's house. He soon found out they were there because Mrs. Shaller had passed on in the early hours of the morning. To his shame he also learned that the man he had seen with Deidre was Mrs. Shaller's doctor, who had come in the middle of the night to take care of her. He found that out when Deidre introduced him to the man within minutes of his arrival.

Deciding to keep his previous suspicions quiet, he hugged Deidre and told her he loved her and wanted to talk to her alone. She led him to a bedroom on the second floor where Daniel shared with her what had happened to him up on the bald. Telling it out made it seem even more real to him, and his voice gained strength as he explained the shadow of the cross, how it had come as a sign from the Lord himself, a sign that he had no doubt about now.

As Deidre listened her eyes turned brighter. She squeezed Daniel's hand.

"I'm a changed man," Daniel said after he'd finished. "I know I got some hard times still ahead, but somethin' happened to me up there and I can't deny it." He held Deidre close and dabbed at her eyes. For a long while he just held her. Then he knew he had one more thing to say, the hardest of all. "Did you see the government telegram I stuck under your pa's door? About Ed and his plane gettin' shot down?"

"Yes, but he's just missing," she said. "That don't mean he's . . ."

She couldn't finish the thought, and Daniel didn't try either. Despite his own notions about Ed's chances of still being alive, he didn't see any point in dashing her hopes.

"This war will end soon," said Deidre. "They'll find him then, just you wait and see."

Daniel stayed quiet. They held each other for another few minutes, until Daniel said she should rejoin the crowd downstairs. But before heading downstairs Daniel kissed her on the lips and she responded warmly. His heart rose up in his chest. Maybe he could change things around, he decided, and do the right thing from now on, in spite of what he feared for Ed. Even if they never found his boy, he still had a daughter and another son and a wife, and they deserved the best from him, the absolute best he could muster.

They walked back downstairs where Daniel saw Raymond and pulled him aside. Deidre had already told him about the telegram.

"My big brother is tough," said Raymond. "Ed will make it through this, I know he will."

Daniel patted Raymond on the back and told him he would see him again in a day or so.

"Where you going?" Raymond asked.

"Got to go back to Blue Springs, need to talk to your aunt Abby."

"You going tonight?"

"After a while. I got something I need to tell her, something that can't wait till tomorrow."

Daniel found Deidre in the kitchen. "I'll come back tomorrow," he promised her. "Soon as I can do a couple of things."

Deidre kissed him, and he left the house. He made it back to Blue Springs around eleven that night, his body weary but his mind and heart more at peace than in a long time. He drove straight to Abby's house to tell her what had happened on the mountain. But the place was empty. Confused, he drove over to Sol's. Again he found the house quiet and dark.

Although disappointed, he climbed back into the Ford and decided to go home, figuring he could visit Abby in the morning, Sol too. Driving through Blue Springs toward home, he saw a flickering light in the window of Jesus Holiness. He thought it curious and so slowed down a bit. He wondered what could be going on inside the church at such a late hour. He turned off the main road, swung around a side street, and was taken aback to see several vehicles parked behind the church. He recognized Sol's brown-and-white sheriff's car.

Daniel stopped and killed the engine. Something big was happening here and he planned to find out what it was. Leaving his cane in the car, he got out and walked to the front of the church and leaned in close to the door. Somebody inside shouted, "Stand back from that pulpit!"

Ben Clack! But what was he doing here?

Without thinking, Daniel pulled his pistol from his overalls and tiptoed through the door into the front room of the church. Another door separated him from the sanctuary. He pushed gently on the door and peeked in. That's when he saw Thaddeus stepping toward the front. Daniel's eyes moved from Thaddeus to Ben Clack, who was standing by Abby with a rifle in his hand.

Daniel slipped into the sanctuary just as the gun exploded, his body shifting into a gear he hadn't felt since his time in the war. Thaddeus fell to the floor. Daniel heard a scream and knew it was Abby. Ducking low, he started moving toward Ben from behind the rows of pews, his finger itching on the pistol's trigger. Everybody in the place began shouting.

Ben aimed his rifle at Sol now. Daniel stayed down and out of sight, frantically trying to figure what to do. Ben yelled above the panicked crowd, "Sol, you try anything and you'll be followin' him!" His head twitched in the direction of Thaddeus. "Anybody who moves will suffer the same!"

The crowd grew quiet again. Creeping to the front of the church, Daniel inched his way into the shadows along the wall. Ben faced the opposite direction, toward Sol and the rest of the Porter kin. Abby was crying, kneeling on the floor by Thaddeus. A baby started wailing. The baby drowned out the sound of Daniel's movements as he drew closer to Ben. Ben paid the baby no attention but walked over to Sol, the rifle pointed at Sol's middle.

Daniel crawled onto the platform behind the pulpit.

"I'm tired of all this," Ben said.

"So are we," replied Sol. "That's why we're all here for the Mingling."

Ben laughed. "You think you can end a feud in such a way as this?" He waved his hand over the crowd. "It's a bunch of foolishness, dreamed up by some old witchy woman a thousand years ago!"

"It's our way. Yours too, you know that. If all agree but one, the Mingling takes hold."

"Not if that one's got *this*," said Ben raising his gun, "and the guts to use it."

Daniel slid slowly across the platform. He wanted to shoot but in such poor light and with Sol so close to Clack he couldn't be sure of his aim. Another couple of feet and he could take a shot at Ben.

"I got another way to end the feud," said Clack. "Just finish off you and the boys right here." Ben nodded at Jim and Steve. "Then that sorry Daniel. That'll do it as I figure, all the Porter men. Already got that chicken Stephen Waterbury. Time to finish the job. Show once and for all that I ain't no quitter to my clan."

"You're crazy!" said Sol. "Everybody here will know what you did. The law ain't like the old days. You can't fool the judge like you did the last time."

Ben shrugged. "Don't matter to me. So long as I know I took you with me."

Daniel rose to his knees. Ben was no more than fifteen feet away now. One good shot and he could drop him where he stood. His finger edged to the trigger. Daniel wanted to shoot him as bad as he'd ever wanted anything. Dead in the back, end this man's mean life. His fingers twitched, but he couldn't pull the trigger. Couldn't shoot a man this way, without warning.

"Hold it right there, Clack!" Daniel said.

Ben froze. "That you, Daniel?"

"I got the drop on you," continued Daniel. "You move so much as a muscle and I'll plug you dead. Now drop that rifle."

"You wouldn't shoot me in the back," said Ben. "Not honorable. Everybody knows the Porter men live by their honor."

"Don't forget I'm the black sheep of the Porter clan," bluffed Daniel. "I do the doublings, you know that." Daniel could see that his bad reputation caused Ben to hesitate.

"How's Thaddeus?" Daniel called to Abby.

"He's shot in the side," she said. "But it looks tolerable if he can soon see a doctor."

Daniel glanced toward Abby, and when he did, Ben shifted suddenly, his gun swinging toward Daniel. Daniel rushed at him, his head down. Ben fired off a round but the shot missed. Daniel slammed into his knees and knocked him down. The rifle sounded again and somebody screamed. Daniel jerked the gun from Ben's grasp and it hit the floor;

then he grabbed Ben by the neck and started choking him.

Behind him he felt someone else pressing in. He ignored it, though, and kept on squeezing Ben's throat. His fingers dug into Clack's skin, his fury rising. He wanted to choke the life out of this man who had done so much to hurt him and his family.

"Daniel! Stop!"

He heard the voice as if from the bottom of a pond. But he couldn't let go that easy. Ben needed to pay for all he'd done, needed to suffer!

"We got him, Daniel!"

Daniel recognized Sol's voice, and he thought about releasing his grip yet something told him to keep choking, keep choking until Clack stopped struggling. Daniel bore down one more time. Just a few more seconds . . .

"Daniel!"

From somewhere deep inside it came to Daniel, and his heart ached. If he killed Ben, he had become like him, full of revenge and hate. If he killed Ben, he hadn't truly trusted Jesus back on the bald when he saw the cross.

Suddenly weary, Daniel let go of Ben, and Ben sagged to the floor. He sucked in gulps of air, his fingers on his own throat as he regained his breath. Daniel stood there, looking at his hands as they trembled in the dim light of the kerosene lamps.

Sol snapped handcuffs on Ben and then moved to Daniel. "It's over," whispered Sol. "It's over. I'll take him to the jail. He'll be charged for killing Stephen and for trying to kill Thaddeus. He confessed tonight and we all heard it."

With Rose in her arms, Abby stood up from tending Thaddeus and joined Daniel and Sol. Daniel hugged his sister. "I've come home," he said. "I'll go along with the Mingling now."

Abby stepped back and stared at him though she didn't say anything.

Sol checked Thaddeus. "He needs a doctor," he said.

"No, it can wait," said Thaddeus, his hand pressing a white handkerchief to the wound. "It's not all that bad." Thaddeus looked up at Preacher Tuttle, then to his wife. "Go on with the Mingling," he urged.

"We can do it later," said Abby.

Thaddeus gritted his teeth and shook his head. "Now. Do it now."

Abby nodded. Daniel went to Thaddeus and held him up, while Abby returned to the altar with Rose. Daisy did too, her baby in her arms.

Tuttle stood back at the pulpit, his hands gripping the sides as if to hold himself up. The two families returned to their seats, and Abby and Daisy held their babies to their breasts again.

Tuttle declared, "It's time, then, for the Mingling."

"Time for the Mingling," repeated everybody.

Once more Abby held Rose to her body to suckle. So also did Daisy. The crowd settled.

As Abby nursed her baby, she started to shake. So much had happened. Could she still go through with this? But how could she back away now? She couldn't. God had brought her to this point, she knew that for sure.

Her mind made up, Abby moved her hands to Rose's lips and pulled the baby from her breast. The tiny hands reached for her mama's face. Abby kissed her daughter's fingers, then gave her to Daisy. Daisy handed Sam to her.

Abby looked into the baby boy's face, so quiet and peaceful. She caressed his face. "I forgive you all your transgressions," she said. "Yours and those of your kin."

Daisy said the same to Rose. Abby held Sam up to the crowd. "I accept this baby," she proclaimed, "by the mercy of our Lord." She moved Sam to her breast, and he grabbed for her and began to suckle. His little face wrinkled for a second as if scared but then he relaxed and swallowed the milk flowing from her body.

Beside her, Daisy nursed Rose. After a minute, Abby pulled Sam from her breast as did Daisy with Rose, and they gave back each other's babies. With Daniel's help, Thaddeus eased over to Abby. William Clack joined his wife at the altar as well.

"Now it is time," said Preacher Tuttle, "for the Mingling to go forward."

Everyone nodded in agreement.

"From child to family, the mercy is offered," Tuttle said. "Mercy to forgive and forget, mercy to leave the dead in the ground so the living might find peace." The Porters and Clacks sitting in the pews nodded again. Tuttle turned his focus to Abby and Daisy.

Abby sighed and kissed Rose on the forehead and cheeks. "I love you, my baby," she said. "I always will."

She looked over at Thaddeus and saw tears flowing down his face.

Only a man who loved her completely would let her do what she now had to do. "It's all right," Thaddeus whispered. Abby handed Rose to him. He held his daughter with one arm and kissed her, then released the baby back to Abby.

Abby turned to Daisy. Both women wept as they exchanged babies—Rose to Daisy, Sam to Abby.

"For the first three years," said Tuttle, "child of Porter shall be child of Clack, and child of Clack shall be child of Porter. By the mercy of God. Amen."

Abby clasped hands with Thaddeus. Daniel supported him on his other side, with Elsa and the rest of the family close by, everyone standing now and holding hands and hugging. The Clack clan, too, had moved forward and joined hands with one another.

Then Jim and Rebecca stepped into the center near the altar between the two families. Rebecca had little Porter in her arms. Jim held his hand out to Abby. She took it. Rebecca held her hand out to Daisy. She took it.

Now, with everyone in the church holding hands, the Mingling was complete. The kin of one joined to the kin of the other by a ceremony as ancient and sacred as the mountains that looked down on them. Tuttle stood above them all, his tall figure acting as middle ground from which to give the benediction.

"The blood is now mixed," he announced. "It is mixed in the life of Porter Waterbury, the child of Clack and Porter. And so the families are now mixed, one child for each. For three years let it be so. Let peace reign between these families from this day forward. Amen and amen."

"Amen," agreed the crowd.

"Amen," said Abby and Thaddeus.

"Amen," said Daisy and William.

The crowd murmured and embraced each other.

Abby turned to Thaddeus, and he took her into his arms. Her tears wet the front of his shirt. "I did what the Lord wanted," she whispered.

"I believe it," he said.

Abby held him tightly. A Mingling hadn't happened in a long time. But now that it had, peace could come. *By the mercy of God,* she prayed. *Let it be so. Amen.*

EPILOGUE

"You mean you gave your baby to William and Daisy Clack?" I said.

Granny Abby shook her head, her chin tilted low. "I took her baby to my house. It's the way of the Mingling, the only way to keep the quiet between the families. Anybody in your family hurts anybody in theirs, you then forfeit the child. Same on the other side."

I stood and walked over to the window. I'd never known any of this. Outside, a light rain had begun to fall. We'd moved inside from the front porch earlier when it had started to cloud up, the breeze turning to gusts of wind. The afternoon had about disappeared. I faced Granny Abby and saw that her eyes were closed. She looked worn out. Her breath came in short gasps.

"Was that the end of the feud, then?" I asked.

Granny Abby slowly raised her head. "I reckon I have talked enough for one day. I'm right tired if you want to know the truth of it."

I heard a wheeze in her voice and stepped closer to her chair. "But what about Daniel? Did he stay sober? And that Gant man, the logger—was he from the family Daniel visited after the war?"

Granny Abby waved me off. "I'm sorry, Lisa. We can start in again tomorrow. I'll feel stronger then."

I thought of poor Ed. What happened to him?

I paced back to the window, stared out. Granny Abby had shared nearly half a century of my family's story, but I still had half a century to go. Of course I knew some of the more recent years, the years I'd lived through. Even so, much of my kin's history remained a mystery to me. I ran my fingers through my hair and realized I'd have to wait at least a few more days to hear the rest.

I turned again to Granny. Her chin rested on her chest. Sprigs of wispy hair dropped down around her face. Her hands hung by the sides of the chair, which had stopped rocking. She looked like she'd fallen asleep. I almost smiled, but then something about the way she sat made me uneasy.

"Granny Abby?"

She didn't move, so I called again. She didn't respond.

My breath caught in my throat as I rushed to her. "Granny Abby!"

I squatted by the chair and gathered her hands into her lap. Her hands were cold and her eyes remained closed.

"Granny Abby!"

Quickly I searched for signs of life. I checked the pulse in her right wrist and felt something faint but erratic.

"Granny Abby!"

She didn't awaken.

I grabbed the phone on the table by her rocker and dialed 9–1–1. Then, taking a blanket from the bedroom, I used it to cover her legs and upper body. I started to pray for the first time in years. If anything happened to her now, I didn't know if I could stand it. I had so much more I wanted to learn from her. More importantly, I desperately wanted to express my gratitude to her.

The clock in the hallway ticked. Still praying, I held Granny Abby's hand and wondered if she would ever talk again.

NOTE TO THE READER

The experience described in this work of fiction as the Mingling arises from a practice that did actually occur on rare occasions in the highlands of Appalachia. On such occasions, when two families sought to terminate a feud, those women with nursing children passed their children from one mother to the next so the child could nurse from the breast of the other family. This act signified that the feud had indeed ended, that the people of both sides drew life from the same source and therefore should no longer hold bad feelings toward one another.

Whether or not the families actually exchanged children for a number of years is a matter of continued speculation. Some ancient stories from my kin say it may have happened that way, though no one seems to remember exactly how many years the babies remained separate from their mothers. The term *Mingling* is a fictitious description of the experience.

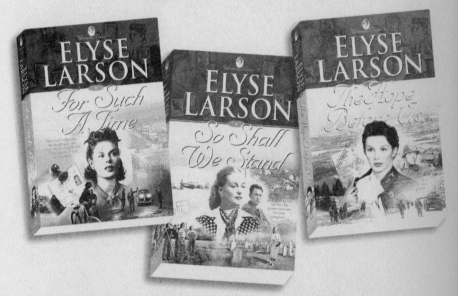

DATE			

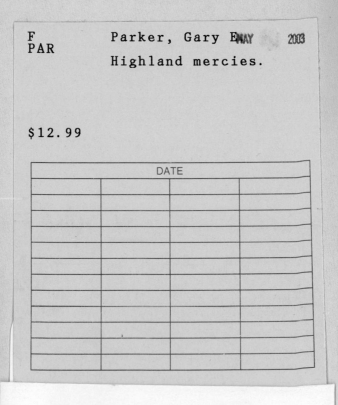